PENGUIN BOOKS

THE PENGUIN BOOK OF
JEWISH SHORT STORIES

The Penguin Book of
Jewish Short Stories

EDITED BY
EMANUEL LITVINOFF

PENGUIN BOOKS

PENGUIN BOOKS

Published by the Penguin Group
Penguin Books Ltd, 27 Wrights Lane, London W8 5TZ, England
Penguin Putnam Inc., 375 Hudson Street, New York, New York 10014, USA
Penguin Books Australia Ltd, Ringwood, Victoria, Australia
Penguin Books Canada Ltd, 10 Alcorn Avenue, Toronto, Ontario, Canada M4V 3B2
Penguin Books (NZ) Ltd, 182–190 Wairau Road, Auckland 10, New Zealand

Penguin Books Ltd, Registered Offices: Harmondsworth, Middlesex, England

First published 1979
10

Printed in England by Clays Ltd, St Ives plc
Set in Monotype Garamond

The Acknowledgements on pages 11–12 constitute
an extension of this copyright page.

CONTENTS

INTRODUCTION

THE problem of deciding what makes a story Jewish touches
on the ambiguity of Jews as a people. It is difficult, perhaps
impossible, to reach an agreed definition of a Jew in racial,
religious or social terms and the same goes for Jewish writing.
Language alone is an inadequate guide. Yiddish stories in the
Moscow journal *Sovietish Heimland* are usually mass-production
propaganda moralities and the Hebrew book on display in
Tel Aviv is likely to be the current international best-seller.
Besides, the majority of Jews do not speak or have forgotten
Yiddish and at best can recite some liturgical Hebrew without
understanding it. They have become multilingual; they contribute to the literature of many nations. Is Kafka, composing
parables of alienation in German in the Czech city of Prague,
a Jewish writer? Yes, but . . . Or Boris Pasternak, who turned
to Christianity in Communist Russia, or Anatole France, or
Rilke who had a Jewish mother? Or, to turn from author to
subject, is *The Rabbi Slept on Sunday*, about a fictional detective,
a Jewish story? Do we include the Hyman Kaplan comedies
of mispronunciation? And what of stories about Jews by non-
Jews, a recent example being John Updike's series featuring
Henry Bech, 'the moderately well-known American author'
who is a bit like a character of Bernard Malamud's?

Because of their long dispersion Jews have constantly been
subject to the haemorrhage of assimilation. A century before
the birth of Christ a third of the population of Alexandria
was Jewish. The splendour and sophistication of Greek
culture proved overwhelmingly attractive and except in
religion they were indistinguishable from other Alexandrians.
Jewish communities elsewhere in the Near East absorbed
Persian and Arabic influences, and Jews were no more immune
than other subject nations to the conquering civilization of
Rome. Cultural symbiosis can of course be fertilizing, as in
Moorish Spain which produced the golden age of post-
biblical Hebrew poetry, mysticism and art, but Jewish assimi-

lation is often a kind of secular apostasy. The convert recoils from what he sees as the ignorance and parochialism of Jewishness. He may also fear identification with the anti-Christ of European mythology, the traditional scapegoat. The assimilated Jew is inclined to be flattered when told he doesn't look Jewish and to regard his native tradition, of which he has only rudimentary knowledge, as being anachronistic and somehow hook-nosed, unprepossessing. Heinrich Heine, who reluctantly became a Christian ('baptized but not converted'), considered Judaism an inherited misfortune, a 'family evil'. But in a more positive sense, like other minority groups, the assimilated Jew has preferred to be part of the mainstream. Only recently have we begun to realize that the world is being impoverished by uniformity – that Welshness, Gaelicness, Jewishness, the fast-disappearing French of New Orleans, should, like real bread and unprocessed food, be defended from extinction.

Traditional Jewish culture is religious, its literature written in Hebrew and except for moral tales eschewing fiction. The great secular period is coincident with the emancipation of Jews in Western Europe after the French Revolution, a period known as the Enlightenment. The most phenomenal upsurge of Jewish creativity in modern times, however, occurred in the Russian empire scarcely more than 100 years ago when Jewish writers changed from Hebrew to Yiddish. It was a yeasty language, alive with experience of sorrow, exile, the knock-about humour of the market place; the language of Jewish peasants, artisans and the emerging industrial proletariat dwelling in semi-feudal poverty in the vast territorial ghetto known as the Pale of Settlement to which Jews were by law confined. Yiddish literature delivered them from the dark ages. Not only were they provided with poetry, stories and plays about their own lives, they also read translations of Tolstoy and Shakespeare, Plato and Marx, history, science, economics and theories of art. The pale students burning like tapers with the flame of Talmud in ghetto seminaries were hungry for such intellectual sustenance. It released a turbulence of ideas, a hitherto untapped source of creative energy that overflowed into the neighbouring Gentile society and, after 1881 when Russian pogroms stimulated mass-emigration to America, Western Europe and other places, began to have important impact on an international scale.

Until the 1920s this vital and exuberant Yiddish culture continued to produce a Jewish civilization as brilliant as that of Judaic Spain during the heyday of Islam. There was no inkling that a terrifying disaster was imminent. The Bolshevik Revolution seemed at first eager to encourage the development of Jewish national expression, at least within the then flexible boundaries of socialism, although the Hebrew language was outlawed as reactionary. Yiddish writers in Russia appeared in great numbers, books poured off the presses, magazines were filled with stories and poems influenced by the iconoclastic sensibility in early revolutionary Russian literature. By 1926 the party was over, not only for Jews and not only for writers. Bureaucracy imposed the dead hand of conformity on individual self-expression and the situation grew steadily more ominous as internal terror spread the bacillus of fear that paralysed creative initiative.

Then came war: the Holocaust. The Yiddish-speaking inhabitants of Poland, Hungary, Czechoslovakia, Lithuania, the Baltic States, Western Russia and the Ukraine were immolated. Their towns and villages were turned into graveyards, their civilization brought to the point of total destruction. And in 1948 Stalin ferociously turned on the survivors. Anti-semitism was officially resurrected in the guise of a struggle against 'rootless cosmopolitans'. Overnight, the security organs closed down every Jewish publication, school, theatre and communal institution, leaving only a handful of synagogues and dereliction. Books were destroyed, Yiddish type was melted down, the prison camps filled with Jews. On 12 August 1952, twenty-six of the leading Yiddish writers and intellectuals were shot and Jewish culture died before the firing squad.

Stalinism was officially buried four years later (although its ghost persists) but not anti-semitism. A museum of Yiddish literature was re-installed, sufficient for propaganda purposes yet effectively fossilized: otherwise Jewish culture is not permitted in the U.S.S.R., neither in the Russian language which most Soviet Jews speak, nor in their officially designated mother-tongue, nor in the Hebrew of traditional scholarship and learning. For this reason a sixty-year gap exists in the literary contribution of Russian Jews and the most gifted of all Jewish communities, those of Eastern Europe, are silenced or non-existent. Grief is not too extreme a term to express the sense of bereavement left by this tragedy. No collection of Jewish stories can be made that does not contain desolate echoes of torture, imprisonment and mass-murder. Nor can one be brought together that does not show how the human spirit transcends despair with fortitude, humour and fellowship.

EMANUEL LITVINOFF

ACKNOWLEDGEMENTS

For permission to reprint the stories specified we are indebted to:

André Deutsch Ltd and Viking Penguin, Inc., for I. L. Peretz's 'The Golem' and 'Bontsha the Silent' from *A Treasury of Yiddish Literature*, edited by Irving Howe and Eliezer Greenberg, copyright © The Viking Press, Inc., 1954.

Crown Publishers, Inc., for Sholom Aleichem's 'Hodel' from *The Old Country*, copyright © Crown Publishers, Inc., 1946, 1974.

André Deutsch Ltd and Viking Penguin, Inc., for Lamed Shapiro's 'White Chalah' and 'Smoke' from *A Treasury of Yiddish Stories*, edited by Irving Howe and Eliezer Greenberg, copyright © The Viking Press, Inc., 1954.

André Deutsch Ltd and Viking Penguin, Inc., for Abraham Reisen's 'The Recluse' from *A Treasury of Yiddish Stories*, edited by Irving Howe and Eliezer Greenberg, copyright © The Viking Press, Inc., 1954.

Schocken Books, Inc., for S. Y. Agnon's 'Friendship' and 'First Kiss' from *Twenty-One Stories*, copyright © Schocken Books, Inc., 1970.

Methuen & Co., Ltd, and S. G. Phillips, Inc., for Isaac Babel's 'The Story of My Dovecot' from *Collected Stories*, copyright © Isaac Babel, 1957.

Partisan Review for Isaac Babel's 'The Journey' from *Partisan Review*, Vol. 3-4, 1961, copyright © Isaac Babel, 1961.

Jonathan Cape Ltd and Farrar, Straus & Giroux, Inc., for Isaac Bashevis Singer's 'A Friend of Kafka' from *A Friend of Kafka and Other Stories*, copyright © Isaac Bashevis Singer, 1968, 1970.

David Higham Associates Ltd for Emanuel Litvinoff's 'Fanya' from *Journey through a Small Planet*, published by Michael Joseph Ltd, copyright © Emanuel Litvinoff, 1972.

Ariel and the author for Aharon Appelfeld's 'Badenheim 1939' from *Ariel*, No. 35, 1974, copyright © Aharon Appelfeld, 1974.

Weidenfeld & Nicolson Ltd and Russell & Volkening, Inc., for

Dan Jacobson's 'The Zulu and the Zeide' from *A Long Way to London*, copyright © Dan Jacobson, 1958.

André Deutsch Ltd and Houghton Mifflin Company for Philip Roth's 'The Conversion of the Jews' from *Goodbye, Columbus*, copyright © Philip Roth, 1959.

Weidenfeld & Nicolson Ltd and Viking Penguin, Inc., for Saul Bellow's 'The Old System' from *Mosby's Memoirs and Other Stories*, copyright © Saul Bellow, 1968.

Alfred A. Knopf, Inc., and the author for Cynthia Ozick's 'The Pagan Rabbi' from *The Pagan Rabbi and Other Stories*, © Cynthia Ozick, 1966.

Deborah Owen and *Ariel* for Amos Oz's 'Setting the World to Rights' from *Ariel*, No. 41, 1976, copyright © Amos Oz, 1976.

Eyre Methuen Ltd and Farrar, Straus & Giroux, Inc., for Bernard Malamud's 'Man in the Drawer' from *Rembrandt's Hat*, copyright © Bernard Malamud, 1968.

Harold Ober Associates, Inc., for Muriel Spark's 'The Gentile Jewesses' from the *New Yorker*, June 1963, copyright © Muriel Spark, 1963.

I. L. Peretz

THE GOLEM

Translated by Irving Howe

BONTSHA THE SILENT

Translated by Hilde Abel

I. L. Peretz

ISAAC LEIB PERETZ (1851-1915) was the founder of modern Yiddish literature. Born in Poland, he became a lawyer and published his first book, a volume of Hebrew poems, at the age of twenty-seven. During most of his literary career he lived in Warsaw and was an official of the Jewish community.

THE GOLEM

GREAT men were once capable of great miracles.

When the ghetto of Prague was being attacked, and they were about to rape the women, roast the children, and slaughter the rest; when it seemed that the end had finally come, the great Rabbi Loeb put aside his *Gemarah*, went into the street, stopped before a heap of clay in front of the teacher's house, and molded a clay image. He blew into the nose of the *golem* – and it began to stir; then he whispered the Name into its ear, and our *golem* left the ghetto. The rabbi returned to the House of Prayer, and the *golem* fell upon our enemies, threshing them as with flails. Men fell on all sides.

Prague was filled with corpses. It lasted, so they say, through Wednesday and Thursday. Now it is already Friday, the clock strikes twelve, and the *golem* is still busy at its work.

'Rabbi,' cries the head of the ghetto, 'the *golem* is slaughtering all of Prague! There will not be a Gentile left to light the Sabbath fires or take down the Sabbath lamps.'

Once again the rabbi left his study. He went to the altar and began singing the psalm 'A song of the Sabbath'.

The *golem* ceased its slaughter. It returned to the ghetto, entered the House of Prayer, and waited before the rabbi. And again the rabbi whispered into its ear. The eyes of the *golem* closed, the soul that had dwelt in it flew out, and it was once more a *golem* of clay.

To this day the *golem* lies hidden in the attic of the Prague synagogue, covered with cobwebs that extend from wall to wall. No living creature may look at it, particularly women in pregnancy. No one may touch the cobwebs, for whoever touches them dies. Even the oldest people no longer remember the *golem*, though the wise man Zvi, the grandson of the great Rabbi Loeb, ponders the problem: may such a *golem* be included in a congregation of worshipers or not?

The *golem*, you see, has not been forgotten. It is still here!

But the Name by which it could be called to life in a day of need, the Name has disappeared. And the cobwebs grow and grow, and no one may touch them.

What are we to do?

BONTSHA THE SILENT

HERE on earth the death of Bontsha the Silent made no impression at all. Ask anyone: Who was Bontsha, how did he live, and how did he die? Did his strength slowly fade, did his heart slowly give out – or did the very marrow of his bones melt under the weight of his burdens? Who knows? Perhaps he just died from not eating – starvation, it's called.

If a horse, dragging a cart through the streets, should fall, people would run from blocks around to stare, newspapers would write about this fascinating event, a monument would be put up to mark the very spot where the horse had fallen. Had the horse belonged to a race as numerous as that of human beings, he wouldn't have been paid this honor. How many horses are there, after all? But human beings – there must be a thousand million of them!

Bontsha was a human being; he lived unknown, in silence, and in silence he died. He passed through our world like a shadow. When Bontsha was born no one took a drink of wine; there was no sound of glasses clinking. When he was confirmed he made no speech of celebration. He existed like a grain of sand at the rim of a vast ocean, amid millions of other grains of sand exactly similar, and when the wind at last lifted him up and carried him across to the other shore of that ocean, no one noticed, no one at all.

During his lifetime his feet left no mark upon the dust of the streets; after his death the wind blew away the board that marked his grave. The wife of the gravedigger came upon that bit of wood, lying far off from the grave, and she picked it up and used it to make a fire under the potatoes she was cooking; it was just right. Three days after Bontsha's death no one knew where he lay, neither the gravedigger nor anyone else. If Bontsha had had a headstone, someone, even after a hundred years, might have come across it, might still have been able to read the carved words, and his name, Bontsha the Silent, might not have vanished from this earth.

His likeness remained in no one's memory, in no one's heart. A shadow! Nothing! Finished!

In loneliness he lived, and in loneliness he died. Had it not been for the infernal human racket someone or other might have heard the sound of Bontsha's bones cracking under the weight of his burdens; someone might have glanced around and seen that Bontsha was also a human being, that he had two frightened eyes and a silent trembling mouth; someone might have noticed how, even when he bore no actual load upon his back, he still walked with his head bowed down to earth, as though while living he was already searching for his grave.

When Bontsha was brought to the hospital ten people were waiting for him to die and leave them his narrow little cot; when he was brought from the hospital to the morgue twenty were waiting to occupy his pall; when he was taken out of the morgue forty were waiting to lie where he would lie forever. Who knows how many are now waiting to snatch from him that bit of earth?

In silence he was born, in silence he lived, in silence he died – and in an even vaster silence he was put into the ground.

Ah, but in the other world it was not so! No! In Paradise the death of Bontsha was an overwhelming event. The great trumpet of the Messiah announced through the seven heavens: Bontsha the Silent is dead! The most exalted angels, with the most imposing wings, hurried, flew, to tell one another, 'Do you know who has died? Bontsha! Bontsha the Silent!'

And the new, the young little angels with brilliant eyes, with golden wings and silver shoes, ran to greet Bontsha, laughing in their joy. The sound of their wings, the sound of their silver shoes, as they ran to meet him, and the bubbling of their laughter, filled all Paradise with jubilation, and God Himself knew that Bontsha the Silent was at last here.

In the great gateway to heaven Abraham, our father, stretched out his arms in welcome and benediction. 'Peace be with you!' And on his old face a deep sweet smile appeared.

What, exactly, was going on up there in Paradise?

There, in Paradise, two angels came bearing a golden throne for Bontsha to sit upon, and for his head a golden crown with glittering jewels.

'But why the throne, the crown, already?' two important saints asked. 'He hasn't even been tried before the heavenly court of justice to which each new arrival must submit.' Their voices were touched with envy. 'What's going on here, anyway?'

And the angels answered the two important saints that, yes, Bontsha's trial hadn't started yet, but it would only be a formality, even the prosecutor wouldn't dare open his mouth. Why, the whole thing wouldn't take five minutes!

'What's the matter with you?' the angels asked. 'Don't you know whom you're dealing with? You're dealing with Bontsha, Bontsha the Silent!'

When the young, the singing angels encircled Bontsha in love, when Abraham, our father, embraced him again and again, as a very old friend, when Bontsha heard that a throne waited for him, and for his head a crown, and that when he would stand trial in the court of heaven no one would say a word against him – when he heard all this, Bontsha, exactly as in the other world, was silent. He was silent with fear. His heart shook, in his veins ran ice, and he knew this must all be a dream or simply a mistake.

He was used to both, to dreams and mistakes. How often, in that other world, had he not dreamed that he was wildly shoveling up money from the street, that whole fortunes lay there on the street beneath his hands – and then he would wake and find himself a beggar again, more miserable than before the dream.

How often in that other world had someone smiled at him, said a pleasant word – and then, passing and turning back for another look, had seen his mistake and spat at Bontsha.

Wouldn't that be just my luck, he thought now, and he was afraid to lift his eyes, lest the dream end, lest he awake and find himself again on earth, lying somewhere in a pit of snakes and loathesome vipers, and he was afraid to make the smallest sound, to move so much as an eyelash; he trembled and he could not hear the paeans of the angels; he could not see them as they danced in stately celebration about him; he could not answer the loving greeting of Abraham, our father, 'Peace be with you!' And when at last he was led into the great court of justice in Paradise he couldn't even say 'Good morning.' He was paralyzed with fear.

And when his shrinking eyes beheld the floor of the courtroom of justice, his fear, if possible, increased. The floor was of purest alabaster, embedded with glittering diamonds. On such a floor stand my feet, thought Bontsha. My feet! He was beside himself with fear. Who knows, he thought, for what very rich man, or great learned rabbi, or even saint, this whole thing's meant? The rich man will arrive, and then it will all be over. He lowered his eyes; he closed them.

In his fear he did not hear when his name was called out in the pure angelic voice: 'Bontsha the Silent!' Through the ringing in his ears he could make out no words, only the sound of that voice like the sound of music, of a violin.

Yet did he, perhaps, after all, catch the sound of his own name, 'Bontsha the Silent'? And then the voice added, 'To him that name is as becoming as a frock coat to a rich man.'

What's that? What's he saying? Bontsha wondered, and then he heard an impatient voice interrupting the speech of his defending angel. 'Rich man! Frock coat! No metaphors, please! And no sarcasm!'

'He never,' began the defending angel again, 'complained, not against God, not against man; his eye never grew red with hatred, he never raised a protest against heaven.'

Bontsha couldn't understand a word, and the harsh voice of the prosecuting angel broke in once more. 'Never mind the rhetoric, please!'

'His sufferings were unspeakable. Here, look upon a man who was more tormented than Job!'

Who? Bontsha wondered. Who is this man?

'Facts! Facts! Never mind the flowery business and stick to the facts, please!' the judge called out.

'When he was eight days old he was circumcised –'

'Such realistic details are unnecessary – '

'The knife slipped, and he did not even try to staunch the flow of blood – '

' – are distasteful. Simply give us the important facts.'

'Even then, an infant, he was silent, he did not cry out his pain,' Bontsha's defender continued. 'He kept his silence, even when his mother died, and he was handed over, a boy of thirteen, to a snake, a viper – a stepmother!'

Hm, Bontsha thought, could they mean me?

'She begrudged him every bite of food, even the moldy rotten bread and the gristle of meat that she threw at him, while she herself drank coffee with cream.'

'Irrelevant and immaterial,' said the judge.

'For all that, she didn't begrudge him her pointed nails in his flesh – flesh that showed black and blue through the rags he wore. In winter, in the bitterest cold, she made him chop wood in the yard, barefoot! More than once were his feet frozen, and his hands, that were too young, too tender, to lift the heavy logs and chop them. But he was always silent, he never complained, not even to his father – '

'Complain! To that drunkard!' The voice of the prosecuting angel rose derisively, and Bontsha's body grew cold with the memory of fear.

'He never complained,' the defender continued, 'and he was always lonely. He never had a friend, never was sent to school, never was given a new suit of clothes, never knew one moment of freedom.'

'Objection! Objection!' the prosecutor cried out angrily. 'He's only trying to appeal to the emotions with these flights of rhetoric!'

'He was silent even when his father, raving drunk, dragged him out of the house by the hair and flung him into the winter night, into the snowy, frozen night. He picked himself up quietly from the snow and wandered into the distance where his eyes led him.

'During his wanderings he was always silent; during his agony of hunger he begged only with his eyes. And at last, on a damp spring night, he drifted to a great city, drifted there like a leaf before the wind, and on his very first night, scarcely seen, scarcely heard, he was thrown into jail. He remained silent, he never protested, he never asked, Why, what for? The doors of the jail were opened again, and, free, he looked for the most lowly filthy work, and still he remained silent.

'More terrible even than the work itself was the search for work. Tormented and ground down by pain, by the cramp of pain in an empty stomach, he never protested, he always kept silent.

'Soiled by the filth of a strange city, spat upon by unknown mouths, driven from the streets into the roadway, where, a human beast of burden, he pursued his work, a porter, carrying the heaviest loads upon his back, scurrying between carriages, carts, and horses, staring death in the eyes every moment, he still kept silent.

'He never reckoned up how many pounds he must haul to earn a penny; how many times, with each step, he stumbled and fell for that penny. He never reckoned up how many times he almost vomited out his very soul, begging for his earnings. He never reckoned up his bad luck, the other's good luck. No, never. He remained silent. He never even demanded his own earnings; like a beggar, he waited at the door for what was rightfully his, and only in the depths of his eyes was there an unspoken longing. "Come back later!" they'd order him; and, like a shadow, he would vanish, and then, like a shadow, would return and stand waiting, his eyes begging, imploring, for what was his. He remained silent even when they cheated him, keeping back, with one excuse or another, most of his earnings, or giving him bad money. Yes, he never protested, he always remained silent.

'Once,' the defending angel went on, 'Bontsha crossed the roadway to the fountain for a drink, and in that moment his whole life was miraculously changed. What miracle happened to change his whole life? A splendid coach, with tires of rubber, plunged past, dragged by runaway horses; the coachman, fallen, lay in the street, his head split open. From the mouths of the frightened horses spilled foam, and in their wild eyes sparks struck like fire in a dark night, and inside the carriage sat a man, half alive, half dead, and Bontsha caught at the reins and held the horses. The man who sat inside and whose life was saved, a Jew, a philanthropist, never forgot what Bontsha had done for him. He handed him the whip of the dead driver, and Bontsha, then and there, became a coachman – no longer a common porter! And what's more, his great benefactor married him off, and what's still more, this great philanthropist himself provided a child for Bontsha to look after.

'And still Bontsha never said a word, never protested.'

They mean me, I really do believe they mean me, Bontsha encouraged himself, but still he didn't have the gall to open his eyes, to look up at his judge.

'He never protested. He remained silent even when that great philanthropist shortly thereafter went into bankruptcy without ever having paid Bontsha one cent of his wages.

'He was silent even when his wife ran off and left him with her helpless infant. He was silent when, fifteen years later, that same helpless infant had grown up and become strong enough to throw Bontsha out of the house.'

They mean me, Bontsha rejoiced, they really mean me.

'He even remained silent,' continued the defending angel, 'when that same benefactor and philanthropist went out of bankruptcy, as suddenly as he'd gone into it, and still didn't pay Bontsha one cent of what he owed him. No, more than that. This person, as befits a fine gentleman who has gone through bankruptcy, again went driving the great coach with the tires of rubber, and now, now he had a new coachman, and Bontsha, again a porter in the roadway, was run over by coachman, carriage, horses. And still, in his agony, Bontsha did not cry out; he remained silent. He did not even tell the police who had done this to him. Even in the hospital, where everyone is allowed to scream, he remained silent. He lay in utter loneliness on his cot, abandoned by the doctor, by the nurse; he had not the few pennies to pay them – and he made no murmur. He was silent in that awful moment just before he was about to die, and he was silent in that very moment when he did die. And never one murmur of protest against man, never one murmur of protest against God!'

Now Bontsha begins to tremble again. He senses that after his defender has finished, his prosecutor will rise to state the case against him. Who knows of what he will be accused? Bontsha, in that other world on earth, forgot each present moment as it slipped behind him to become the past. Now the defending angel has brought everything back to his mind again – but who knows what forgotten sins the prosecutor will bring to mind?

The prosecutor rises. 'Gentlemen!' he begins in a harsh and bitter voice, and then he stops. 'Gentlemen – ' he begins again, and now his voice is less harsh, and again he stops. And finally, in a very soft voice, that same prosecutor says, 'Gentlemen, he was always silent – and now I too will be silent.'

The great court of justice grows very still, and at last from the judge's chair a new voice rises, loving, tender. 'Bontsha my child, Bontsha' – the voice swells like a great harp – 'my heart's child . . .'

Within Bontsha his very soul begins to weep. He would like to open his eyes, to raise them, but they are darkened with tears. It is so sweet to cry. Never until now has it been sweet to cry.

'My child, my Bontsha . . .'

Not since his mother died has he heard such words, and spoken in such a voice.

'My child,' the judge begins again, 'you have always suffered, and you have always kept silent. There isn't one secret place in your body without its bleeding wound; there isn't one secret place in your soul without its wound and blood. And you never protested. You always were silent.

'There, in that other world, no one understood you. You never understood yourself. You never understood that you need not have been silent, that you could have cried out and that your outcries would have brought down the world itself and ended it. You never understood your sleeping strength. There in that other world, that world of lies, your silence was never rewarded, but here in Paradise is the world of truth, here in Paradise you will be rewarded. You, the judge can neither condemn nor pass sentence upon. For you there is not only one little portion of Paradise, one little share. No, for you there is everything! Whatever you want! Everything is yours!'

Now for the first time Bontsha lifts his eyes. He is blinded by light. The splendor of light lies everywhere, upon the walls, upon the vast ceiling, the angels blaze with light, the judge. He drops his weary eyes.

'Really?' he asks, doubtful, and a little embarrassed.

'Really!' the judge answers. 'Really! I tell you, everything is yours. Everything in Paradise is yours. Choose! Take! Whatever you want! You will only take what is yours!'

'Really?' Bontsha asks again, and now his voice is stronger, more assured.

And the judge and all the heavenly host answer, 'Really! Really! Really!'

'Well then' – and Bontsha smiles for the first time – 'well then, what I would like, Your Excellency, is to have, every morning for breakfast, a hot roll with fresh butter.'

A silence falls upon the great hall, and it is more terrible than Bontsha's has ever been, and slowly the judge and the angels bend their heads in shame at this unending meekness they have created on earth.

Then the silence is shattered. The prosecutor laughs aloud, a bitter laugh.

Sholom Aleichem

HODEL

Translated by Julius and Frances Butwin

Sholom Aleichem

SHOLOM ALEICHEM (1859-1916). Born in Russia, his real name was Sholom Rabinowitz and he chose as his pen-name the Hebrew greeting 'Peace unto you'. Like Peretz, he began by writing in Hebrew and altogether produced about forty volumes of novels, short stories and plays. The greatest of all Yiddish writers and a creative genius of world stature, Sholom Aleichem distilled the comedy, pathos and tragic irony of Jewish life in Eastern Europe.

HODEL

You look, Mr Sholom Aleichem, as though you were surprised that you hadn't seen me for such a long time. You're thinking that Tevye has aged all at once, his hair has turned gray.

Ah, well, if you only knew the troubles and heartaches he has endured of late! How is it written in our Holy Books? 'Man comes from dust, and to dust he returns.' Man is weaker than a fly, and stronger than iron. Whatever plague there is, whatever trouble, whatever misfortune – it never misses me. Why does it happen that way? Maybe because I am a simple soul who believes everything that everyone says. Tevye forgets that our wise men have told us a thousand times: 'Beware of dogs...'

But I ask you, what can I do if that's my nature? I am, as you know, a trusting person, and I never question God's ways. Whatever He ordains is good. Besides, if you do complain, will it do you any good? That's what I always tell my wife. 'Golde,' I say, 'you're sinning. We have a *midrash* –'

'What do I care about a *midrash*?' she says. 'We have a daughter to marry off. And after her two more are almost ready. And after these two, three more – may the evil eye spare them!'

'Tut,' I say. 'What's that? Don't you know, Golde, that our sages have thought of that also? There is a *midrash* for that too –'

But she doesn't let me finish. 'Daughters to be married off,' she says, 'are a stiff *midrash* in themselves.'

Try to explain something to a woman!

Where does that leave us? Oh yes, with a houseful of daughters, bless the Lord, each one prettier than the next. It may not be proper for me to praise my own children, but I can't help hearing what the whole world calls them, can I? Beauties, every one of them! And especially Hodel, the one that comes after Tzietl, who, you remember, fell in love with the tailor. And Hodel – how can I describe her to you? Like Esther in the Bible, 'of beautiful form and fair to look upon'. And as if that weren't bad enough, she has to have brains too. She can write and she can read – Yiddish and Russian both. And books she swallows like dumplings. You may be wondering how a daughter of Tevye happens to be reading books when her father deals in butter and cheese? That's what I'd like to know myself.

But that's the way it is these days. Look at these lads who haven't got a pair of pants to their name, and still they want to study! Ask them, 'What are you studying? Why are you studying?' They can't tell you. It's their nature, just as it's a goat's nature to jump into gardens. Especially since they aren't even allowed in the schools. 'Keep off the grass!' read all the signs as far as they're concerned. And yet you ought to see how they go after it! And who are they? Workers' children. Tailors' and cobblers', so help me God! They go away to Yehupetz or to Odessa, sleep in garrets, eat what Pharaoh ate during the plagues – frogs and vermin – and for months on end do not see a piece of meat before their eyes. Six of them can make a banquet on a loaf of bread and a herring. Eat, drink, and be merry! That's the life!

Well, one of that band had to lose himself in our corner of the world. I used to know his father – he was a cigarette-maker and as poor as a man could be. But that is nothing against the young fellow. For if Rabbi Jochanan wasn't too proud to mend boots, what is wrong with having a father who makes cigarettes? There is only one thing I can't understand: why should a pauper like that be so anxious to study? True, to give the devil his due, the boy has a good head on his shoulders, an excellent head. Pertschik, his name was, but we called him Feferel – Peppercorn. And he looked like a peppercorn, little, dark, dried up, and homely, but full of confidence and with a quick, sharp tongue.

Well, one day I was driving home from Boiberik, where I had got rid of my load of milk and butter and cheese, and as usual I sat lost in thought, dreaming of many things, of this and that, and of the rich people of Yehupetz who had everything their own way while Tevye, the *shlimazel*, and his wretched little horse slaved and hungered all their days. It was summer, the sun was hot, the flies were biting, on all sides the world stretched endlessly. I felt like spreading out my arms and flying!

I lift up my eyes, and there on the road ahead of me I see a young man trudging along with a package under his arm, sweating and panting. 'Rise, O Yokel the son of Flekel, as we say in the synagogue,' I called out to him. 'Climb into my wagon and I'll give you a ride. I have plenty of room. How is it written? "If you see the ass of him that hateth thee lying under its burden, thou shalt forbear to pass it by." Then how about a human being?'

At this the *shlimazel* laughs and climbs into the wagon.

'Where might the young gentleman be coming from?' I ask.

'From Yehupetz.'

'And what might a young gentleman like you be doing in Yehupetz?' I ask.

'A young gentleman like me is getting ready for his examinations.'

'And what might a young gentleman like you be studying?'

'I only wish I knew!'

'Then why does a young gentleman like you bother his head for nothing?'

'Don't worry, Reb Tevye. A young gentleman like me knows what he's doing.'

'So, if you know who *I* am, tell me who *you* are!'

'Who am I? I'm a man.'

'I can see that you're not a horse. I mean, as we Jews say, *whose* are you?'

'Whose should I be but God's?'

'I know that you're God's. It is written, "All living things are His." I mean, whom are you descended from? Are you from around here or from Lithuania?'

'I am descended,' he says, 'from Adam, our father. I *come* from right around here. You know who we are.'

'Well then, who is your father? Come, tell me.'

'My father,' he says, 'was called Pertschik.'

I spat with disgust. 'Did you have to torture me like this all that time? Then you must be Pertschik the cigarette-maker's son!'

'Yes, that's who I am. Pertschik the cigarette-maker's son.'

'And you go to the university?'

'Yes, the university.'

'Well,' I said, 'I'm glad to hear it. Man and fish and fowl – you're all trying to better yourselves! But tell me, my lad, what do you live on, for instance?'

'I live on what I eat.'

'That's good,' I say. 'And what do you eat?'

'I eat anything I can get.'

'I understand,' I say. 'You're not particular. If there is something to eat, you eat. If not, you bite your lip and go to bed hungry. But it's all worth while as long as you can attend the university. You're comparing yourself to those rich people of Yehupetz –'

At these words Pertschik bursts out, 'Don't you dare compare me to them! They can go to hell as far as I care!'

'You seem to be somewhat prejudiced against the rich,' I say. 'Did they divide your father's inheritance among themselves?'

'Let me tell you,' says he, 'it may well be that you and I and all the rest of us have no small share in *their* inheritance.'

'Listen to me,' I answer. 'Let your enemies talk like that. But one thing I can see: you're not a bashful lad. You know what a tongue is for. If you have the time, stop at my house tonight and we'll talk a little more. And if you come early, you can have supper with us too.'

Our young friend didn't have to be asked twice. He arrived at the right moment – when the borscht was on the table and the knishes were baking in the oven. 'Just in time!' I said. 'Sit down. You can say grace or not, just as you please. I'm not God's watchman; I won't be punished for your sins.' And as I talk to him I feel myself drawn to the fellow somehow; I don't know why. Maybe it's because I like a person one can talk to, a person who can understand a quotation and follow an argument about philosophy or this or that or something else. That's the kind of person I am.

And from that evening on our young friend began coming to our house almost every day. He had a few private students, and when he was through giving his lessons he'd come to our house to rest up and visit for a while. What the poor fellow got for his lessons you can imagine for yourself, if I tell you that the very richest people used to pay their tutors three roubles a month; and besides their regular duties they were expected to read telegrams for them, write out addresses, and even run errands at times. Why not? As the passage says, 'If you eat bread you have to earn it.' It was lucky for him that most of the time he ate with us. For this he used to give my daughters lessons too. One good turn deserves another. And in this way he almost became a member of the family. The girls saw to it that he had enough to eat and my wife kept his shirts clean and his socks mended. And it was at this time that we changed his Russian name of Pertschik to Feferel. And it can truthfully be said that we all came to love him as though he were one of us, for by nature he was a likeable young man, simple, straightforward, generous. Whatever he had he shared with us.

There was only one thing I didn't like about him, and that was the way he had of suddenly disappearing. Without warning he would get up and go off; we would look around: no Feferel. When he came back I would ask, 'Where were you, my fine-feathered friend?' And he wouldn't say a word. I don't know how you are, but as for me, I dislike a person with secrets. I like a person to be willing to tell what he's been up to. But you can say this for him: when he did start talking, you couldn't stop him. He poured out everything. What a tongue he had! 'Against the Lord and against His anointed; let us break their bands asunder.' And the main thing was to break the bands. He had the wildest notions, the most peculiar ideas. Everything was upside down, topsy-turvy. For instance, according to his way of thinking, a poor man was far more important than a rich one, and if he happened to be a worker too, then he was really the brightest jewel in the diadem! He who toiled with his hands stood first in his estimation.

'That's good,' I say, 'but will that get you any money?'

At this he becomes very angry and tries to tell me that money is the root of all evil. Money, he says, is the source of all falsehood, and as long as money amounts to something, nothing will ever be done in this world in the spirit of justice. And he gives me thousands of examples and illustrations that make no sense whatever.

'According to your crazy notions,' I tell him, 'there is no justice in the fact that my cow gives milk and my horse draws a load.' I didn't let him get away with anything. That's the kind of man Tevye is. But my Feferel can argue too. And how he can argue! If there is something on his mind he comes right out with it.

One evening we were sitting on my stoop talking things over, discussing philosophic matters, when he suddenly says, 'Do you know, Reb Tevye, you have very fine daughters.'

'Is that so?' say I. 'Thanks for telling me. After all, they have someone to take after.'

'The oldest one especially is a very bright girl. She's all there!'

'I know without your telling me,' say I. 'The apple never falls very far from the tree.'

I glowed with pride. What father isn't happy when his children are praised? How should I have known that from such an innocent remark would grow such fiery love?

Well, one summer twilight I was driving through Boiberik, going from villa to villa with my goods, when someone stopped me. I looked up and saw that it was Ephraim the matchmaker. And Ephraim, like all matchmakers, was concerned with only one thing – arranging marriages. So when he saw me here in Boiberik he stopped me.

'Excuse me, Reb Tevye,' he says, 'I'd like to tell you something.'

'Go ahead,' I say, stopping my horse, 'as long as it's good news.'

'You have,' says he, 'a daughter.'

'I have,' I answer, 'seven daughters.'

'I know,' says he. 'I have seven too.'

'Then together,' I tell him, 'we have fourteen.'

'But joking aside,' he says, 'here is what I have to tell you. As you know, I am a matchmaker; and I have a young man for you to consider, the very best there is, a regular prince. There's not another like him anywhere.'

'Well,' I say, 'that sounds good enough to me. But what do you consider a prince? If he's a tailor or a shoemaker or a teacher, you can keep him. I'll find my equal or I won't have anything. As the *midrash* says – '

'Ah, Reb Tevye,' says he, 'you're beginning with your quotations already! If a person wants to talk to you he has to study up first. But better listen to the sort of match Ephraim has to offer you. Just listen and be quiet.'

And then he begins to rattle off all his client's virtues. And it really sounds like something. First of all, he comes from a very fine family. And that is very important to me, for I am not just a nobody either. In our family you will find all sorts of people – spotted, striped, and speckled, as the Bible says. There are plain, ordinary people, there are workers, and there are property owners. Secondly, he is a learned man who can read small print as well as large; he knows all the commentaries by heart. And that is certainly not a small thing either, for an ignorant man I hate even worse than pork itself. To me an unlettered man is worse, a thousand times worse, than a hoodlum. You can go around bareheaded, you can even walk on your head if you like, but if you know what Rashi and the others have said, you are a man after my own heart. And on top of everything, Ephraim tells me, this man of his is as rich as can be. He has his own carriage drawn by two horses so spirited that you can see a vapor rising from them. And that I don't object to either. Better a rich man than a poor one! God Himself must hate a poor man, for if He did not, would He have made him poor?

'Well,' I ask, 'what more do you have to say?'

'What more can I say? He wants me to arrange a match

with you. He is dying, he's so eager. Not for you, naturally, but for your daughter. He wants a pretty girl.'

'He is dying? Then let him go on dying. And who is this treasure of yours? What is he? A bachelor? A widower? Is he divorced? What's wrong with him?'

'He is a bachelor,' said Ephraim. 'Not so young any more but he's never been married.'

'And what is his name, may I ask?'

But this he wouldn't tell me. 'Bring the girl to Boiberik, and then I'll tell you.'

'Bring her? That's the way one talks about a horse or a cow that's being brought to market. Not a girl!'

Well, you know what these matchmakers are. They can talk a stone wall into moving. So we agreed that early next week I would bring my daughter to Boiberik. And, driving home, all sorts of wonderful thoughts came to me, and I imagined my Hodel riding in a carriage drawn by spirited horses. The whole world envied me, not so much for the carriage and horses as for the good deeds I accomplished through my wealthy daughter. I helped the needy with money – let this one have twenty-five roubles, that one fifty, another a hundred. How do we say it? 'Other people have to live too.' That's what I think to myself as I ride home in the evening, and I whip my horse and talk to him in his own language.

'Hurry, my little horse,' I say, 'move your legs a little faster and you'll get your oats that much sooner. As the Bible says, "If you don't work, you don't eat."'

Suddenly I see two people coming out of the woods – a man and a woman. Their heads are close together and they are whispering to each other. Who could they be? I wonder, and I look at them through the dazzling rays of the setting sun. I could swear the man was Feferel. But whom was he walking with so late in the day? I put up my hand and shield my eyes and look closely. Who was the damsel? Could it be Hodel? Yes, that's who it was! Hodel! So? So that's how they'd been studying their grammar and reading their books together? Oh, Tevye, what a fool you are!

I stop the horse and call out, 'Good evening! And what's

the latest news of the war? How do you happen to be out here this time of the day? What are you looking for, the day before yesterday?'

At this they stop, not knowing what to do or say. They stand there, awkward and blushing, with their eyes lowered. Then they look up at me, I look at them, and they look at each other.

'Well,' I say, 'you look as if you hadn't seen me in a long time. I am the same Tevye as ever; I haven't changed by a hair.'

I speak to them half angrily, half jokingly. Then my daughter, blushing harder than ever, speaks up.

'Father, you can congratulate us.'

'Congratulate you?' I say. 'What's happened? Did you find a treasure buried in the woods? Or were you just saved from some terrible danger?'

'Congratulate us,' says Feferel this time. 'We're engaged.'

'What do you mean, engaged?'

'Don't you know what engaged means?' says Feferel, looking me straight in the eyes. 'It means that I'm going to marry her and she's going to marry me.'

I look him back in the eyes and say, 'When was the contract signed? And why didn't you invite me to the ceremony? Don't you think I have a slight interest in the matter?' I joke with them and yet my heart is breaking. But Tevye is not a weakling. He wants to hear everything out. 'Getting married,' I say, 'without matchmakers, without an engagement feast?'

'What do we need matchmakers for?' says Feferel. 'We arranged it between ourselves.'

'So?' I say. 'That's one of God's wonders! But why were you so silent about it?'

'What was there to shout about?' says he. 'We wouldn't have told you now either, but since we have to part soon, we decided to have the wedding first.'

This really hurt. How do they say it? It hurt to the quick. Becoming engaged without my knowledge – that was bad enough, but I could stand it. He loves her, she loves him – that I'm glad to hear. But getting married? That was too much for me.

The young man seemed to realize that I wasn't too well
pleased with the news. 'You see, Reb Tevye,' he offered,
'this is the reason: I am about to go away.'

'When are you going?'

'Very soon.'

'And where are you going?'

'That I can't tell you. It's a secret.'

What do you think of that? A secret! A young man named
Feferel comes into our lives – small, dark, homely, disguises
himself as a bridegroom, wants to marry my daughter and
then leave her – and he won't even say where he's going!
Isn't that enough to drive you crazy?

'All right,' I say. 'A secret is a secret. But explain this to me,
my friend. You are a man of such – what do you call it? –
integrity; you wallow in justice. So tell me, how does it
happen that you suddenly marry Tevye's daughter and then
leave her? Is that integrity? Is that justice? It's lucky that you
didn't decide to rob me or burn my house down!'

'Father,' says Hodel, 'you don't know how happy we are
now that we've told you our secret. It's like a weight off our
chests. Come, Father, kiss me.'

And they both grab hold of me, she on one side, he on the
other, and they begin to kiss and embrace me, and I to kiss
them in return. And in their great excitement they begin to
kiss each other. It was like going to a play. 'Well,' I say at
last, 'maybe you've done enough kissing already? It's time to
talk about practical things.'

'What, for instance?' they ask.

'For instance,' I say, 'the dowry, clothes, wedding expenses,
this, that, and the other –'

'We don't need a thing,' they tell me. 'We don't need anything. No this, no that, no other.'

'Well then, what do you need?' I ask.

'Only the wedding ceremony,' they tell me.

What do you think of that! Well, to make a long story
short, nothing I said did any good. They went ahead and had
their wedding, if you want to call it a wedding. Naturally it
wasn't the sort that I would have liked. A quiet little wedding

– no fun at all. And besides, there was a wife I had to do something about. She kept plaguing me: what were they in such a hurry about? Go try to explain their haste to a woman. But don't worry. I invented a story – 'great, powerful, and marvelous', as the Bible says, about a rich aunt in Yehupetz, an inheritance, all sorts of foolishness.

And a couple of hours after this wonderful wedding I hitched up my horse and wagon and the three of us got in, that is, my daughter, my son-in-law, and I, and off we went to the station at Boiberik. Sitting in the wagon, I steal a look at the young couple, and I think to myself, What a great and powerful Lord we have and how cleverly He rules the world. What strange and fantastic beings He has created. Here you have a new young couple, just hatched; he is going off, the Good Lord alone knows where, and is leaving her behind – and do you see either one of them shed a tear, even for appearance's sake? But never mind – Tevye is not a curious old woman. He can wait. He can watch and see.

At the station I see a couple of young fellows, shabbily dressed, down at the heels, coming to see my happy bridegroom off. One of them is dressed like a peasant and wears his blouse like a smock over his trousers. The two whisper together mysteriously for several minutes. Look out, Tevye, I say to myself. You have fallen among a band of horse thieves, pickpockets, housebreakers, or counterfeiters.

Coming home from Boiberik, I can't keep still any longer and tell Hodel what I suspect. She bursts out laughing and tries to assure me that they are very honest young men, honorable men, who were devoting their lives to the welfare of humanity; their own private welfare meant nothing to them. For instance, the one with his blouse over his trousers was a rich man's son. He had left his parents in Yehupetz and wouldn't take a penny from them.

'Oh,' said I, 'that's just wonderful. An excellent young man! All he needs, now that he has his blouse over his trousers and wears his hair long, is a harmonica, or a dog to follow him, and then he would really be a beautiful sight!' I thought I was getting even with her for the pain she and this new

husband of hers had caused me. But did she care? Not at all!
She pretended not to understand what I was saying. I talked
to her about Feferel and she answered me with 'the cause of
humanity' and 'workers' and other such talk.

'What good is your humanity and your workers,' I say,
'if it's all a secret? There is a proverb: "Where there are
secrets, there is knavery." But tell me the truth now. Where
did he go, and why?'

'I'll tell you anything,' she says, 'but not that. Better don't
ask. Believe me, you'll find out yourself in good time. You'll
hear the news – and maybe very soon – and good news at
that.'

'Amen,' I say. 'From your mouth into God's ears! But may
our enemies understand as little about it as I do.'

'That,' says she, 'is the whole trouble. You'll never understand.'

'Why not?' say I. 'Is it so complicated? It seems to me that
I can understand even more difficult things.'

'These things you can't understand with your brain alone,'
she says. 'You have to feel them, you have to feel them in
your heart.'

And when she said this to me, you should have seen how
her face shone and her eyes burned. Ah, those daughters of
mine! They don't do anything halfway. When they become
involved in anything it's with their hearts and minds, their
bodies and souls.

Well, a week passed, then two weeks – five – six – seven –
and we heard nothing. There was no letter, no news of any
kind. 'Feferel is gone for good,' I said and glanced over at
Hodel. There wasn't a trace of color in her face. And at the
same time she didn't rest at all; she found something to do
every minute of the day, as though trying to forget her
troubles. And she never once mentioned his name, as if there
never had been a Feferel in the world.

But one day when I came home from work I found Hodel
going about with her eyes swollen from weeping. I made a
few inquiries and found out that someone had been to see
her, a long-haired young man who had taken her aside and

talked to her for some time. Ah! That must have been the young fellow who had disowned his rich parents and pulled his blouse down over his trousers.

Without further delay I called Hodel out into the yard and bluntly asked her, 'Tell me, daughter, have you heard from him?'

'Yes.'

'Where is he, your predestined one?'

'He is far away.'

'What is he doing there?'

'He is serving time.'

'Serving time?'

'Yes.'

'Why? What did he do?'

She doesn't answer me. She looks me straight in the eyes and doesn't say a word.

'Tell me, dear daughter,' I say, 'according to what I can understand, he is not serving for a theft. So if he is neither a thief nor a swindler, why is he serving? For what good deeds?'

She doesn't answer. So I think to myself, If you don't want to, you don't have to. He is your headache, not mine. But my heart aches for her. No matter what you say, I'm still her father.

Well, it was the evening of *Hashono Rabo*. On a holiday I'm in the habit of resting, and my horse rests too. As it is written in the Bible: 'Thou shalt rest from thy labors and so shall thy wife and thine ass.' Besides, by that time of the year there is very little for me to do in Boiberik. As soon as the holidays come and the *shofar* sounds, all the summer villas close down and Boiberik becomes a desert. At that season I like to sit at home on my own stoop. To me it is the finest time of the year. Each day is a gift from heaven. The sun no longer bakes like an oven but caresses with a heavenly softness. The woods are still green, the pines give out a pungent smell. In my yard stands the *succah* – the booth I have built for the holiday, covered with branches, and around me the forest looks like a huge *succah* designed for God Himself. Here, I think, God celebrates His holiday, here and not in town, in the noise and tumult where people run this way and that, panting for breath as they chase after a small crust of bread, and all you hear is money, money, money.

As I said, it is the evening of *Hashono Rabo*. The sky is a deep blue and myriads of stars twinkle and shine and blink. From time to time a star falls through the sky, leaving behind it a long green band of light. This means that someone's luck has fallen. I hope it isn't my star that is falling, and somehow Hodel comes to mind. She has changed in the last few days, has come to life again. Someone, it seems, has brought her a letter from him, from over there. I wish I knew what he had written, but I won't ask. If she won't speak, I won't either. Tevye is not a curious old woman. Tevye can wait.

And as I sit thinking of Hodel, she comes out of the house and sits down near me on the stoop. She looks cautiously around and then whispers, 'I have something to tell you, Father. I have to say good-by to you, and I think it's for always.'

She spoke so softly that I could barely hear her, and she looked at me in a way that I shall never forget.

'What do you mean, good-by for always?' I say to her and turn my face aside.

'I mean I am going away early tomorrow morning, and possibly we shall never see each other again.'

'Where are you going, if I may be so bold as to ask?'

'I am going to him.'

'To him? And where is he?'

'He is still serving, but soon they'll be sending him away.'

'And you're going there to say good-by to him?' I ask, pretending not to understand.

'No. I am going to follow him,' she says. 'Over there.'

'There? Where is that? What do they call the place?'

'We don't know the exact name of the place, but we know that it's far – terribly, terribly far.'

And she speaks, it seems to me, with great joy and pride, as though he had done something for which he deserved a medal. What can I say to her? Most fathers would scold a child for such talk, punish her, even beat her maybe. But Tevye is not a fool. To my way of thinking, anger doesn't get you anywhere. So I tell her a story.

'I see, my daughter, as the Bible says, "Therefore shalt thou leave thy father and mother" – for a Feferel you are ready to forsake your parents and go off to a strange land, to some desert across the frozen wastes, where Alexander of Macedon, as I once read in a storybook, once found himself stranded among savages . . .'

I speak to her half in fun and half in anger, and all the time my heart weeps. But Tevye is no weakling; I control myself. And Hodel doesn't lose her dignity either; she answers me word for word, speaking quietly and thoughtfully. And Tevye's daughters can talk.

And though my head is lowered and my eyes are shut, still I seem to see her – her face is pale and lifeless like the moon, but her voice trembles. Shall I fall on her neck and plead with her not to go? I know it won't help. Those daughters of mine – when they fall in love with somebody, it is with their heads and hearts, their bodies and souls.

Well, we sat on the doorstep a long time – maybe all night. Most of the time we were silent, and when we did speak it was in snatches, a word here, a word there. I said to her, 'I want to ask you only one thing: did you ever hear of a girl marrying a man so that she could follow him to the ends of the earth?' And she answered, 'With him I'd go anywhere.' I pointed out how foolish that was. And she said, 'Father, you will never understand.' So I told her a little fable, about a hen that hatched some ducklings. As soon as the ducklings could move they took to the water and swam, and the poor hen stood on shore, clucking and clucking.

'What do you say to that, my daughter?'

'What can I say?' she answered. 'I am sorry for the poor hen; but just because she stood there clucking, should the ducklings have stopped swimming?'

There is an answer for you. She's not stupid, that daughter of mine.

But time does not stand still. It was beginning to get light already, and within the house my old woman was muttering.

More than once she had called out that it was time to go to bed, but, seeing that it didn't help, she stuck her head out of the window and said to me, with her usual benediction, 'Tevye, what's keeping you?'

'Be quiet, Golde,' I answered. 'Remember what the Psalm says: "Why are the nations in an uproar, and why do the peoples mutter in vain?" Have you forgotten that it's *Hashono Rabo* tonight? Tonight all our fates are decided and the verdict is sealed. We stay up tonight. Listen to me, Golde, you light the samovar and make some tea while I get the horse and wagon ready. I am taking Hodel to the station in the morning.' And once more I make up a story about how she has to go to Yehupetz, and from there farther on, because of the same old inheritance. It is possible, I say, that she may have to stay there through the winter and maybe the summer too, and maybe even another winter; and so we ought to give her something to take along – some linen, a dress, a couple of pillows, some pillow slips, and things like that.

And as I give these orders I tell her not to cry. 'It's *Hashono Rabo*, and on *Hashono Rabo* one mustn't weep. It's a law.' But naturally they don't pay any attention to me, and when the time comes to say good-by they all start weeping – their mother, the children, and even Hodel herself. And when she came to say good-by to her older sister Tzeitl (Tzeitl and her husband spend their holidays with us), they fell on each other's necks and you could hardly tear them apart.

I was the only one who did not break down. I was firm as steel – though inside I was more like a boiling samovar. All the way to Boiberik we were silent, and when we came near the station I asked her for the last time to tell me what it was that Feferel had really done. If they were sending him away there must have been a reason. At this she became angry and swore by all that was holy that he was innocent. He was a man, she insisted, who cared nothing about himself. Everything he did was for humanity at large, especially for those who toiled with their hands – that is, the workers.

That made no sense to me. 'So he worries about the world,'

I told her. 'Why doesn't the world worry a little about him? Nevertheless, give him my regards, that Alexander of Macedon of yours, and tell him I rely on his honor – for he is a man of honor, isn't he? – to treat my daughter well. And write to your old father sometimes.'

When I finish talking she falls on my neck and begins to weep. 'Good-by, Father,' she cries. 'Good-by! God alone knows when we shall see each other again.'

Well, that was too much for me. I remembered this Hodel when she was still a baby and I carried her in my arms, I carried her in my arms. . . . Forgive me, Mr Sholom Aleichem, for acting like an old woman. If you only knew what a daughter she is! If you could only see the letters she writes! Oh, what a daughter . . .

And now let's talk about more cheerful things. Tell me, what news is there about the cholera in Odessa?

Lamed Shapiro

WHITE CHALAH

Translated by Norbert Guterman

SMOKE

Translated by Irving Howe and Eliezer Greenberg

Lamed Shapiro

LAMED SHAPIRO (1878–1948) was born in the Ukraine and emigrated to the United States in 1906 after living for a while in London. A notable stylist, he is said to have been influenced by Chekhov and Flaubert.

WHITE CHALAH

I

ONE day a neighbor broke the leg of a stray dog with a heavy stone, and when Vasil saw the sharp edge of the bone piercing the skin he cried. The tears streamed from his eyes, his mouth, and his nose; the towhead on his short neck shrank deeper between his shoulders; his entire face became distorted and shriveled, and he did not utter a sound. He was then about seven years old.

Soon he learned not to cry. His family drank, fought with neighbors, with one another, beat the women, the horse, the cow, and sometimes, in special rages, their own heads against the wall. They were a large family with a tiny piece of land, they toiled hard and clumsily, and all of them lived in one hut – men, women, and children slept pell-mell on the floor. The village was small and poor, at some distance from a town; and the town to which they occasionally went for the fair seemed big and rich to Vasil.

In the town there were Jews – people who wore strange clothes, sat in stores, ate white *chalah,* and had sold Christ. The last point was not quite clear: who was Christ, why did the Jews sell him, who bought him, and for what purpose? – it was all as though in a fog. White *chalah*, that was something else again: Vasil saw it a few times with his own eyes, and more than that – he once stole a piece and ate it, whereupon he stood for a time in a daze, an expression of wonder on his face. He did not understand it all, but respect for white *chalah* stayed with him.

He was half an inch too short, but he was drafted, owing to his broad, slightly hunched shoulders and thick short neck. Here in the army beatings were again the order of the day: the corporal, the sergeant, and the officers beat the privates, and the privates beat one another, all of them. He could not learn the service regulations: he did not understand and did not think. Nor was he a good talker; when hard pressed he usually could not utter a sound, but his face grew tense, and his low forehead was covered with wrinkles. *Kasha* and borscht, however, were plentiful. There were a few Jews in his regiment – Jews who had sold Christ – but in their army uniforms and without white *chalah* they looked almost like everybody else.

2

They traveled in trains, they marched, they rode again, and then again moved on foot; they camped in the open or were quartered in houses; and this went on so long that Vasil became completely confused. He no longer remembered when it had begun, where he had been before, or who he had been; it was as though all his life had been spent moving from town to town, with tens or hundreds of thousands of other soldiers, through foreign places inhabited by strange people who spoke an incomprehensible language and looked frightened or angry. Nothing particularly new had happened, but fighting had become the very essence of life; everyone was fighting now, and this time it was no longer just beating, but fighting in earnest: they fired at people, cut them to pieces, bayoneted them, and sometimes even bit them with their teeth. He too fought, more and more savagely, and with greater relish. Now food did not come regularly, they slept little, they marched and fought a great deal, and all this made him restless. He kept missing something, longing for something, and at moments of great strain he howled like a tormented dog because he could not say what he wanted.

They advanced over steadily higher ground; chains of giant mountains seamed the country in all directions, and winter ruled over them harshly and without respite. They inched their way through valleys, knee-deep in dry powdery snow, and icy winds raked their faces and hands like grating irons, but the officers were cheerful and kindlier than before, and spoke of victory; and food, though not always served on time, was plentiful. At night they were sometimes permitted to build fires on the snow; then monstrous shadows moved noiselessly between the mountains, and the soldiers sang.

Vasil too tried to sing, but he could only howl. They slept like the dead, without dreams or nightmares, and time and again during the day the mountains reverberated with the thunder of cannon, and men again climbed up and down the slopes.

3

A mounted messenger galloped madly through the camp; an advance cavalry unit returned suddenly and occupied positions on the flank; two batteries were moved from the left to the right. The surrounding mountains split open like freshly erupting volcanoes, and a deluge of fire, lead, and iron came down upon the world.

The barrage kept up for a long time. Piotr Kudlo was torn to pieces; the handsome Kruvenko, the best singer of the company, lay with his face in a puddle of blood; Lieutenant Somov, the one with girlish features, lost a leg, and the giant Neumann, the blond Estonian, had his whole face torn off. The pock-marked Gavrilov was dead; a single shell killed the two Bulgach brothers; killed, too, were Chaim Ostrovsky, Jan Zatyka, Staszek Pieprz, and the little Latvian whose name Vasil could not pronounce. Now whole ranks were mowed down, and it was impossible to hold on. Then Nahum Rachek, a tall slender young man who had always been silent, jumped up and without any order ran forward. This gave new spirit to the dazed men, who rushed the jagged hill to the left and practically with their bare hands conquered the batteries that led the enemy artillery, strangling the defenders like cats, down to the last man. Later it was found that of the entire company only Vasil and Nahum Rachek remained. After the battle Rachek lay on the ground vomiting green gall, and next to him lay his rifle with its butt smeared with blood and brains. He was not wounded, and when Vasil asked what was the matter he did not answer.

After sunset the conquered position was abandoned, and the army fell back. How and why this happened Vasil did not know; but from that moment the army began to roll down the mountains like an avalanche of stones. The farther they went, the hastier and less orderly was the retreat, and in the end they ran – ran without stopping, day and night. Vasil did not recognize the country, each place was new to him, and he knew only from hearsay that they were moving back. Mountains and winter had long been left behind; around them stretched a broad, endless plain; spring was in full bloom; but the army ran and ran. The officers became savage, they beat the soldiers without reason and without pity. A few times they stopped for a while; the cannon roared, a rain of fire whipped the earth, and men fell like flies – and then they ran again.

4

Someone said that all this was the fault of the Jews. Again the Jews! They sold Christ, they eat white *chalah*, and on top of it all they are to blame for everything. What was 'everything'? Vasil wrinkled his forehead and was angry at the Jews and at someone else. Leaflets appeared, printed leaflets that a man distributed among the troops, and in the camps groups gathered around those who could read. They stood listening in silence – they were silent in a strange way, unlike people who just do not talk. Someone handed a leaflet to Vasil too; he examined it, fingered it, put it in his pocket, and joined a group to hear what was being read. He did not understand a word, except that it was about Jews. So the Jews must know, he thought, and he turned to Nahum Rachek.

'Here, read it,' he said.

Rachek cast a glance at the leaflet, then another curious glance at Vasil; but he said nothing and seemed about to throw the leaflet away.

'Don't! It's not yours!' Vasil said. He took back the leaflet, stuck it in his pocket, and paced back and forth in agitation. Then he turned to Rachek. 'What does it say? It's about you, isn't it?'

At this point Nahum flared up. 'Yes, about me. It says I'm a traitor, see? That I've betrayed us – that I'm a spy. Like that German who was caught and shot. See?'

Vasil was scared. His forehead began to sweat. He left

Nahum, fingering his leaflet in bewilderment. This Nahum, he thought, must be a wicked man – so angry, and a spy besides, he said so himself, but something doesn't fit here, it's puzzling, it doesn't fit, my head is splitting.

After a long forced march they stopped somewhere. They had not seen the enemy for several days and had not heard any firing. They dug trenches and made ready. A week later it all began anew. It turned out that the enemy was somewhere near by; he too was in trenches, and these trenches were moving closer and closer each day, and occasionally one could see a head showing above the parapet. They ate very little, they slept even less, they fired in the direction the bullets came from, bullets that kept hitting the earth wall, humming overhead, and occasionally boring into human bodies. Next to Vasil, at his left, always lay Nahum Rachek. He never spoke, only kept loading his rifle and firing, mechanically, unhurriedly. Vasil could not bear the sight of him and occasionally was seized with a desire to stab him with his bayonet.

One day, when the firing was particularly violent, Vasil suddenly felt strangely restless. He cast a glance sidewise at Rachek and saw him lying in the same posture as before, on his stomach, with his rifle in his hand; but there was a hole in his head. Something broke in Vasil; in blind anger he kicked the dead body, pushing it aside, and then began to fire wildly, exposing his head to the dense shower of lead that was pouring all around him.

That night he could not sleep for a long time; he tossed and turned, muttering curses. At one point he jumped up angrily and began to run straight ahead, but then he recalled that Rachek was dead and dejectedly returned to his pallet. The Jews … traitors … sold Christ … traded him away for a song!

He ground his teeth and clawed at himself in his sleep.

5

At daybreak Vasil suddenly sat up on his hard pallet. His body was covered with cold sweat, his teeth were chattering, and his eyes, round and wide open, tried greedily to pierce the darkness. Who has been here? Who has been here?

It was pitch-dark and fearfully quiet, but he still could hear the rustle of the giant wings and feel the cold hem of the black cloak that had grazed his face. Someone had passed over the camp like an icy wind, and the camp was silent and frozen – an open grave with thousands of bodies, struck while asleep, and pierced in the heart. Who has been here? Who has been here?

During the day Lieutenant Muratov of the fourth battalion of the Yeniesey regiment was found dead – Muratov, a violent, cruel man with a face the color of parchment. The bullet that pierced him between the eyes had been fired by someone from his own battalion. When the men were questioned no one betrayed the culprit. Threatened with punishment, they still refused to answer, and they remained silent when they were ordered to surrender their arms. The other regimental units were drawn up against the battalion, but when they were ordered to fire, all of them to a man lowered their rifles to the ground. Another regiment was summoned, and in ten minutes not a man of the mutinous battalion remained alive.

Next day two officers were hacked to pieces. Three days later, following a dispute between two cavalrymen, the entire regiment split into two camps. They fought each other until only a few were left unscathed.

Then men in mufti appeared and, encouraged by the officers, began to distribute leaflets among the troops. This time they did not make long speeches, but kept repeating one thing: the Jews have betrayed us, everything is their fault.

Once again someone handed a leaflet to Vasil, but he did not take it. He drew out of his pocket, with love and respect, as though it were a precious medallion, a crumpled piece of paper frayed at the edges and stained with blood, and showed it – he had it, and remembered it. The man with the leaflets, a slim little fellow with a sand-colored beard, half closed one of his little eyes and took stock of the squat broad-shouldered private with the short thick neck and bulging gray watery eyes. He gave Vasil a friendly pat on the back and left with a strange smile on his lips.

The Jewish privates had vanished: they had been quietly gathered together and sent away, no one knew where. Everyone felt freer and more comfortable, and although there were several nationalities represented among them, they were all of one mind about it: the alien was no longer in their midst.

And then someone launched a new slogan – 'The Jewish government'.

6

This was their last stand, and when they were again defeated they no longer stopped anywhere but ran like stampeding animals fleeing a steppe fire, in groups or individually, without commanders and without order, in deadly fear, rushing through every passage left open by the enemy. Not all of them had weapons, no one had his full outfit of clothing, and their shirts were like second skins on their unwashed bodies. The summer sun beat down on them mercilessly, and they ate only what they could forage. Now their native tongue was spoken in the towns, and their native fields lay around them, but the fields were unrecognizable, for last year's crops were rotting, trampled into the earth, and the land lay dry and gray and riddled, like the carcass of an ox disemboweled by wolves.

And while the armies crawled over the earth like swarms of gray worms, flocks of ravens soared overhead, calling with a dry rattling sound – the sound of tearing canvas – and swooped and slanted in intricate spirals, waiting for what would be theirs.

Between Kolov and Zhaditsa the starved and crazed legions caught up with large groups of Jews who had been ordered out of border towns, with their women, children, invalids, and bundles. A voice said, 'Get them!' The words sounded like the distant boom of a gun. At first Vasil held back, but the loud screams of the women and children and the repulsive, terrified faces of the men with their long earlocks and caftans blowing in the wind drove him to a frenzy, and he cut into the Jews like a maddened bull. They were destroyed with merciful speed: the army trampled over them like a herd of galloping horses.

Then, once again, someone said in a shrill little voice, 'The Jewish government!'

The words suddenly soared high and like a peal of thunder rolled over the wild legions, spreading to villages and cities and reaching the remotest corners of the land. The retreating troops struck out at the region with fire and sword. By night burning cities lighted their path, and by day the smoke obscured the sun and the sky and rolled in cottony masses over the earth, and suffocated ravens occasionally fell to the ground. They burned the towns of Zykov, Potapno, Kholodno, Stary Yug, Sheliuba; Ostrogorie, Sava, Rika, Beloye Krilo, and Stupnik were wiped from the face of the earth; the Jewish weaving town of Belopriazha went up in smoke, and the Vinokur Forest, where 30,000 Jews had sought refuge, blazed like a bonfire, and for three days in succession agonized cries, like poisonous gases, rose from the woods and spread over the land. The swift, narrow Sinevodka River was entirely choked with human bodies a little below Lutsin and overflowed into the fields.

The hosts grew larger. The peasant left his village and the city dweller his city; priests with icons and crosses in their hands led processions through villages, devoutly and enthusiastically blessing the people, and the slogan was, 'The Jewish government'. The Jews themselves realized that their last hour had struck – the very last; and those who remained alive set out to die among Jews in Maliassy, the oldest and largest Jewish center in the land, a seat of learning since the fourteenth century, a city of ancient synagogues and great yeshivas, with rabbis and modern scholars, with an aristocracy of learning and of trade. Here, in Maliassy, the Jews fasted and prayed, confessing their sins to God, begging forgiveness of friend and enemy. Aged men recited Psalms and Lamentations, younger men burned stocks of grain and clothing, demolished furniture, broke and destroyed everything that might be of use to the approaching army. And this army came, it came from all directions, and set fire to the city from all sides, and poured into the streets. Young men tried to resist and went out with revolvers in their hands. The revolvers sounded like pop guns. The soldiers answered with thundering laughter, and drew out the young men's veins one by one, and broke their bones into little pieces. Then they went from house to house, slaying the men wherever they were found and dragging the women to the market place.

7

One short blow with his fist smashed the lock, and the door opened.

For two days now Vasil had not eaten or slept. His skin smarted in the dry heat, his bones seemed disjointed, his eyes were bloodshot, and his face and neck were covered with blond stubble.

'Food!' he said hoarsely.

No one answered him. At the table stood a tall Jew in a black caftan, with a black beard and earlocks and gloomy eyes. He tightened his lips and remained stubbornly silent. Vasil stepped forward angrily and said again, 'Food!'

But this time he spoke less harshly. Near the window he had caught sight of another figure – a young woman in white, with a head of black hair. Two large eyes – he had never before seen such large eyes – were looking at him and through him, and the look of these eyes was such that Vasil lifted his arm to cover his own eyes. His knees were trembling, he felt as if he were melting. What kind of woman is that? What kind of people? God! Why, why, did they have to sell Christ? And on top of it all, responsible for everything! Even Rachek admitted it. And they just kept quiet, looking through you. Goddam it, what are they after? He took his head in his hands.

He felt something and looked about him. The Jew stood there, deathly pale, hatred in his eyes. For a moment Vasil stared dully. Suddenly he grabbed the black beard and pulled at it savagely.

A white figure stepped between them. Rage made Vasil

dizzy and scalded his throat. He tugged at the white figure with one hand. A long strip tore from the dress and hung at the hem. His eyes were dazzled, almost blinded. Half a breast, a beautiful shoulder, a full, rounded hip – everything dazzling white and soft, like white *chalah*. Damn it – these Jews are *made* of white *chalah*! A searing flame leaped through his body, his arm flew up like a spring and shot into the gaping dress.

A hand gripped his neck. He turned his head slowly and looked at the Jew for a moment with narrowed eyes and bared teeth, without shaking free of the weak fingers that were clutching at his flesh. Then he raised his shoulders, bent forward, took the Jew by the ankles, lifted him in the air, and smashed him against the table. He flung him down like a broken stick.

The man groaned weakly; the woman screamed. But he was already on top of her. He pressed her to the floor and tore her dress together with her flesh. Now she was repulsive, her face blotchy, the tip of her nose red, her hair disheveled and falling over her eyes. 'Witch,' he said through his teeth. He twisted her nose like a screw. She uttered a shrill cry – short, mechanical, unnaturally high, like the whistle of an engine. The cry penetrating his brain maddened him completely. He seized her neck and strangled her.

A white shoulder was quivering before his eyes; a full, round drop of fresh blood lay glistening on it. His nostrils fluttered like wings. His teeth were grinding; suddenly they opened and bit into the white flesh.

White *chalah* has the taste of a firm juicy orange. Warm and hot, and the more one sucks it the more burning the thirst. Sharp and thick, and strangely spiced.

Like rushing down a steep hill in a sled. Like drowning in sharp, burning spirits.

In a circle, in a circle, the juices of life went from body to body, from the first to the second, from the second to the first – in a circle.

Pillars of smoke and pillars of flame rose to the sky from the entire city. Beautiful was the fire on the great altar. The cries of the victims – long-drawn-out, endless cries – were sweet in the ears of a god as eternal as the Eternal God. And the tender parts, the thighs and the breasts, were the portion of the priest.

SMOKE

1

At the first puff his face turned deep red, as if he were straining to lift a heavy load. He broke into a violent cough. Still, there must be something to it: the grown-ups smoked. He grew stubborn – and got used to it.

His father was a poverty-stricken teacher, and besides boys aren't supposed to smoke – so he picked up butts.

Later, studying in the synagogue, he would occasionally have a pack of tobacco. He never denied anyone a cigarette when he had it; he was never ashamed to ask for one when he didn't.

His name was Menasha.

From the synagogue he went as son-in-law to Reb Shoel Marawaner. Reb Shoel himself came to the synagogue with the matchmaker. The imposing Jew with the drooping eyes examined Menasha for a few minutes: a tall youth, broad and sturdy; the half-length frock coat of the Hasidic merchant will fit him perfectly. Reb Shoel peered into the book Menasha was studying, asked a few questions, began a casual conversation, and while glancing sideways listened with pricked-up ears to the youth's modest, somewhat cryptic replies. Rising suddenly from the bench, Reb Shoel ended the conversation with, 'Bring your phylacteries.'

2

In one of their most intimate moments his young wife asked, 'Tell me, what sort of taste do you get from your cigarette? Give me a puff – let me try it.'

He took the rolled-up burning cigarette from his mouth and moved it to her lips. Etta's lips closed like two pillows over the cigarette.

'Phew!' she coughed. 'It's only smoke.'

Menasha smiled. 'Smoke – but it's good.'

'What's so good about it? It's bitter and gets in your eyes.'

He laughed. 'But it's good,' he repeated, as a whirlwind of shame and shamelessness wrapped the two young people in its folds.

3

He accepted the wealth of his father-in-law's household without betraying any of the pauper's greed. In only one thing did he indulge himself: he used the best tobacco that could be had. Knowing this, the younger people in the synagogue would frequently dip into his tobacco tin.

Once Reb Shoel's older son-in-law, Nehemiah, called Menasha aside. 'Why do you let them smoke up your tobacco, those pigs? They themselves buy *mahorka*.'

Menasha looked at him quietly. 'How can you refuse anyone a cigarette?'

Nehemiah turned and glanced cautiously around the synagogue. One eye closed, the other lit up with wisdom. 'Fool, don't you understand? Do as I do – two kinds,' he burbled with a little laugh.

Menasha said nothing. But he did not introduce two kinds of tobacco.

He frequented the synagogue, studied at home, strolled about with a stick in his hand. Often he would sit quietly, listening to the business conversations Reb Shoel held with Jewish merchants. Those were the years of journeying to Danzig or Leipzig or Königsberg. Reb Shoel was one of the travelers to Danzig. For his older son-in-law Nehemiah he opened a dry-goods store: 'Sit and measure linens.' Nehemiah would have preferred to talk about Danzig, but Reb Shoel dismissed him with a wave of the hand. To Menasha he never said a word about business. And Menasha too was silent – until Etta was brought to bed and gave birth to twins, boys.

The evening after the double circumcision the father-in-law called Menasha into his room, handed him a packet of money, and said, 'Go.'

Menasha was a little frightened. 'I don't even know where or what –'

'You'll learn. When you're rid of the money you'll know.'

This took place during *Chanukah*. By Passover, Menasha was back. They celebrated the first two days of the holiday, and Danzig was never mentioned. Only on the evening of the second day did Reb Shoel invite Menasha to his room.

'What's new?'

'I've learned something,' said Menasha, blushing.

Reb Shoel nodded.

After Passover, Menasha received another roll of bills and left for Danzig. From then on he would travel regularly for two or three months each year, and often twice a year.

4

With the passage of the years children sprang up in every corner of the house. Some were getting older, others crawled around, new ones were born. Reb Menasha – in time he became 'Reb' Menasha – looked on and laughed quietly. Reb Shoel was no more; his business had been taken over by Reb Menasha, as had the old house with the spacious rooms.

During the months Reb Menasha stayed home in Marawan he lived as before: visited the synagogue twice a day, studied in the afternoon, talked business in the evening. The outer world made one change in his habits: he smoked cigars.

'A cigarette is for a youngster,' he explained, smiling. 'A Jew with a beard, a father of children, has to smoke cigars. The Germans are no fools.'

Cigars were not the only thing that the outer world had brought, but of this only Etta knew. That is, she did not know: she sensed. How did he live there, in that outer world? What was it really like? She did not think about this, but it seemed to her that her husband grew steadily broader and taller, and she wondered why the measure of his clothes did not change. He had a habit of smiling with his eyes alone, and this smiling glance wrapped her into itself, carrying her along in a flow that was peaceful, deep, and unceasing, as the river that passed by the town flowed, year in and year out, into the distant world. She was not frightened; on the contrary, she felt secure in this wide stream. And many times she curled up against her husband and even tried to take a puff from his cigar. But this only brought tears to her eyes and spasms of coughing. He would slap her lightly on the back and laugh.

5

There were already a few sizable boys in the house, and a whole flock of half-grown ones and small fry were pushing after them.

Danzig was no longer the Danzig of old. Etta skimped – except for Reb Menasha's cigars, and in this one regard he did not oppose her. It went so far that the family had to leave the old house with its spacious rooms and rent another. At that time Reb Menasha sat down by himself in his room and became engrossed in the problem: what is wrong with Danzig? He sat there, looking through the window, smoking cigars, reflecting. The next day he left for the Don.

For several weeks he wandered about in the tumultuous region between the lower Don and the Caspian Sea, observing, considering, counting, measuring – and at the end he bent a finger of his right hand with his left and said, 'Caviare.' And he began to connect the Don with Danzig.

He was away for two years, and these were the hardest for the family at home. But after these two years, when he came home to rest for several months, people began to figure according to a new calendar: this or the other incident occurred 'at the time Reb Menasha first went to the Don'. And when he came home he bought back Reb Shoel's house and life continued as in earlier times.

He would now go to Danzig only once every two or three years, but for that very reason he spent two thirds of his time on the Don. After caviare, he began to trade in smoked *wobla* – a local kind of sardine he had himself discovered. He earned much and spent much: one child after the other grew up, lived, and studied. In the end the father put each of them on his feet. For the wedding of the youngest he called together all his children. They celebrated in the old style, and at the end of the wedding meal Reb Menasha rose at the head of the table.

'Children, I shall no longer go to the Don. I have enough for myself and the old lady to live out our few years. The rest is for you. Go in good health, and may the Almighty let you live your years no worse than I have mine. You need not worry about us – we will not burden you.'

6

Life flowed like a river nearing its mouth: the wider and deeper, the more peacefully and quietly. Menasha's high smooth forehead showed only one narrow crease from temple to temple, his black hair had grayed in only a few places. In the early summer evenings, against the orange glow of the sinking sun, he would stroll, as always, with his stick in hand; and his step remained certain and measured, his back strong and erect. Only his eyes were absorbed, deeply absorbed.

In his middle years he had studied mainly with his eyes. But now, in the quiet afternoon, his voice would rise more frequently through the old synagogue, taking up the mild and sad melody of his youth, taking it quietly, still more quietly, until it sank into the surrounding stillness, like the reverberation of a string – and then rising again until it reached its full strength, sweet and bitter, like the tears of childhood.

He enjoyed spending his time in the synagogue with the younger students, discussing Torah and justice. About the outer world and his life away from home he said little.

'People live and die there just as they do here,' he would answer shortly, smiling with his eyes. 'A Talmud made in Slawite or in Danzig – what's the difference? Only the printing and the covers. The content on the other hand –' And he would stare at the thread of smoke, taking care that the white ash, which sat like a Cossack's hat on the head of his cigar, should not fall but remain there as long as possible.

Coming home one morning from the synagogue with his prayer shawl and phylacteries under his arm, he found Ziessel, his youngest son. 'Ah! I knew you'd come.'

The young man's face changed color.

'Now, now,' his father soothed him. 'I did not mean to shame you. Things don't go well, eh? But first wash, and then we'll eat.'

Listening to his son's story, Reb Menasha nodded his head: a fine plan ... who could have expected that ...

'I knew you'd come. You're rash and a little hasty, but you'll learn. I put away a small sum for you. Not much, but you'll be able to start again; and keep your eyes open. Here, take it – and don't come for more: there isn't any. We are old, and if I die first your mother must not be left in want. She won't go to you children.

'And another thing –' He called back his son from the door. 'Now it's not like the old days. In my time, when a Jew came to Danzig with a thick beard and a high forehead, it was enough; if the corn and wheat were good one sold them at a profit, if not, one had a loss. We didn't run our business, it ran itself. That the world is now different I needn't tell you – you're younger than I. Danzig is no longer Danzig, the beard and the forehead no longer assets. Nowadays business has to be conducted, you understand? Well, go in good health and may good fortune be with you.'

7

A summer and a winter passed, and then another summer. Again the winter came, early and bitter, with snows and frosts and wild angry winds. In December, Reb Menasha caught cold, coughed, and spat blood: it was the return of an old inflammation from the early days in Danzig, which was supposed to have left no scars. It spread quickly, and one gray morning, when the thin snowflakes melted in people's eyes and for no reason at all the air smelled different, his children came running from the outer world to stand by their father's bed. A few old friends and the rabbi had remained through the night.

For several hours the cough had not troubled the sick man and his temperature had fallen, but the young doctor did not leave. He sat not far away, at a table, and silently twisted his pencil between his nervous fingers.

Reb Menasha opened his eyes. It was hard to recognize him, but the eyes with their hidden smile had remained the same. He asked for a smoke.

'But Papa –'

The doctor's shrug cut short Ziessel's protest. He turned pale and handed his father a cigar.

'Not that,' said the sick man. 'Hasn't anyone a cigarette?' And his eyes smiled.

He took a puff from the thin little cigarette and called, 'Etta ...'

She lowered her hands from her eyes and dragged herself out of the corner. In recent years she had become rather fat and short of breath. Now her small round face was drawn together like a child's fist, and her glance seemed helpless and lost: the river, close to its end, threw her upon an unknown shore.

'Menasha, Menasha,' she whispered.

'Want a puff?' He laughed. 'Smoke ... but it's good.'

A whirlwind seized the old woman. She let out a cry, a laugh, a cough, all at the same time, as if smoke were choking her. Reb Menasha put aside the cigarette and winked to the rabbi, who went over to the bed and began reciting the last prayer with him. After the first few words Reb Menasha lost himself in coughing. The cough never ceased: it froze in the air, and there it remained.

Abraham Reisen

THE RECLUSE

Translated by Sarah Zweig Betsky

Abraham Reisen

ABRAHAM REISEN (1876-1953), Russian born, was a member of the Jewish Socialist movement who subsequently settled in America where he was a leading figure in New York Yiddish literary circles.

THE RECLUSE

IN the synagogue the evening prayers are over. The miserly assistant sexton, a scrawny Jew with a pointed black beard, has darkened all the lights but one, which is turned very low. 'Oil is expensive,' he growls as he turns out lamp after lamp.

The few who have remained in the synagogue are squatters, and while they resent the despotic assistant sexton who has left them in almost total darkness, they do not dare to protest. Besides, they are too lazy to study. And how can they blame the assistant? His orders to economize come from the chief sexton, whose orders, in turn, come from the treasurer himself.

The dim light suits their mood. It is a few weeks after *Succoth*. Outside the cold rain strikes monotonously on the window-panes. The faces of Moses and Aaron, carved in wood on the altar, stare, sterile and morose. Even the leopard placed between them, which the village woodcarver had hoped would blaze with life and brightness, droops wearily, dreaming perhaps of the forests of Lebanon from which it came.

The black curtain over the Holy Ark, donated by the rich woman of the village and made from one of her left-over dress lengths, breathes upon the old synagogue with sadness and yearning. On the wall the shadows cast by the few remaining people resemble corpses returned from the grave.

Five people are usually left in the synagogue each night, besides the assistant sexton. Two of them are yeshiva students who have been studying here for the last few years and are planning to move to a richer town if they ever find the energy. One of them – called the Zelver after his birthplace – is about twenty years old, with a long thin neck and a large Adam's apple that hops in time to every word that comes out of his wide mouth. The other is the Dohlinever, a year younger. He looks older than the Zelver because he doesn't believe very

strongly in washing his face, which is also covered with a
thick beard. But despite these differences in appearance, the
two live peaceably together. They lend each other lumps of
sugar. They share their cigarettes, even though the Zelver
happens to smoke more. They disagree violently, however,
about definitions of heaven. The Zelver says heaven is
really here on earth, but not in the way it is usually imagined,
in grossly material terms: the Messianic bull and Leviathan,
he says, are merely symbols. Paradise, to quote Maimonides,
is only for the spirit, and the spirit raises itself to the Seventh
Heaven. But the Dohlinever, who is rather more practical,
thinks that Paradise is for the body as well, and that the wild
bull and whale are not symbols but solid facts. When their
quarrel flames to real intensity, they smoke a cigarette
together and thus come to some accord.

The third resident of the synagogue is the Recluse. He is a
little over forty, and there are silver hairs twining through his
thick beard. He became a recluse not through piety but from a
desire for freedom. Or so he once told the Dohlinever.

'A man,' he explained, 'should not wear a yoke. He should
be able to feel that he is always alive, and he can feel this only
when he is free from the burden of labor. I realized as much
when I was thirty. Now my only regret is for the years I lost
keeping a store. Not only my clothes, but my spirit as well,
stank of herring and oil in those days.'

The Dohlinever was not too pleased with this explanation.
'Suppose all men wanted to live as freely as you, what would
the world come to?'

'Little fool,' said the Recluse, laughing. 'Who told you the
world must come to something?'

Now the Dohlinever was truly distressed. 'What do you
mean – after all – the world! It's such a beautiful world.'
But he had no chance to argue it through with the Recluse,
who was skilled in dialectic and could quote pages of Aristotle
and Plato, of whom the Dohlinever knew almost nothing.

These profound discussions would always cost the
Dohlinever a cigarette, for the Recluse, though not a regular
smoker, had to have one after a sharp exchange. The Dohlin-

ever would call over the Zelver, who acted as the communal tobacco pouch, and say, 'Treat the Recluse to a cigarette.'

Rolling the tobacco in a piece of paper, the Recluse would philosophize good-naturedly. 'You say the world would not come to anything. True, true. But what of it? You think, children, that this is the first world that ever existed? There have been thousands of worlds already – read the books they've written. And they knew something too. Even more than our rabbi.'

His free-thinking stabbed the two yeshiva students to the heart, but they never betrayed him. Somehow they felt pity for the Recluse and from time to time would give him a baked potato, a glass of tea, a cigarette.

The fourth inhabitant of the synagogue is called Yankel the Dog. A boy of eighteen, he wandered into town several years ago, and no one knows who his parents are or where he comes from. Terribly lazy, he idles about day after day and has finally taken the bench near the door as his bed.

At night other people appear. First, Chaim the teacher, a man who has lost his job and looks it. Despair itself. He stands near the pulpit, musing for a while, rouses himself, approaches the assistant sexton and asks for a pinch of snuff. The assistant glares at him but complies. Chaim the teacher sniffs, sneezes, and, his strength renewed, continues to the corner where the Zelver, the Dohlinever, and the Recluse are talking.

About seven o'clock Chieneh the widow appears with her apple basket. She is the only woman who is permitted to sell in the synagogue. Standing near the entrance, she eyes the emptiness of the place, thinking wryly, the luck I'll find here! She goes over to the oven and, feeling the cold of the white tiles, retreats in disappointment.

She smiles again. 'Imagine, not to be able to warm up a bit even in the synagogue!' As the assistant sexton comes over she asks him familiarly, 'What's the story, why is the oven so cold?'

'After all,' he jokes, 'why shouldn't you donate a wagonload of wood? They say you have plenty of money.'

'Of course, I'm rich. Why not?'

The assistant sexton, a widower, scratches the back of his neck lustily. 'The devil only knows – if I were sure you had money I'd court you myself.'

'Well, are you going to buy something?'

'It's too expensive.'

'Take some. For you I'll sell it cheaper.'

He selects three spoiled apples from the basket. 'And what, for example, would you charge for these?'

'You've picked the biggest apples, but since it's you – a kopeck.'

'You're as expensive as a druggist,' he complains. 'Three tiny apples for a kopeck? And a groschen wouldn't do?'

The widow swears she can't.

'Just as you say,' and he begins to put back the apples.

She thrusts another little one into his hand. 'Here, now you have four.'

He smiles. 'In that case, make it five.'

The widow hunts for a fifth little apple and hands it to him. 'You've picked my bones bare,' she says, groaning.

The Zelver points out Chieneh to the Dohlinever. 'Look, the apples have come.'

'They cost so much!'

'What's the difference?' says the Zelver stubbornly. 'After all, we're no more than human.'

'All right, buy some, I'll pay half.'

The Recluse sighs quietly and walks over to the woman. His large eyes look straight at her. Their eyes meet. Abashed, she lowers hers.

The Zelver bargains for ten apples for two kopecks and returns with them to the Dohlinever. The Recluse remains alone, face to face, with the widow. 'It's so late, he murmurs.

'What can one do?' she answers quietly. 'One wants to sell.'

'Yes,' the Recluse says and looks at her more tenderly. 'Selling ... I understand.' Instinctively he raises his eyes to the balcony where the women sit during services. 'It's dark up there,' he says as if to himself.

'What did you say?'

'I mean,' he stammers, 'it's completely dark up there, in the women's section.'

'Why do you mention it?' the widow wonders.

'I only mean ... they skimp so. A lamp should be burning there too. It's always so dark there at night.' He looks about him. The assistant sexton is sitting in a dark, remote corner, chewing on his apple. The Zelver and the Dohlinever have also withdrawn to a corner and are sharing their apples. Chaim the teacher, his head propped on a bookrest, is snoring loudly. Yankel the Dog has left. The Recluse stands rooted to the spot, gazing at the window, and thinks, And why not?

The widow senses something. Shyly she tugs her kerchief tighter over her head and turns to leave.

'You're going already?' he stammers.

'What can one do? One must go.'

'Far?'

'Yes, almost to the cemetery.'

'A pity.' He sighs. 'Such a long way to go.' Again he looks up at the women's section, where the little windows beckon with their dark eyes.

'Good night,' calls the widow and leaves with her basket.

The Recluse stares after her for a long time and then returns with a sigh to the students. 'What do you think that woman wants here anyway?' he asks.

'She wants to sell apples,' answers the Dohlinever.

'And I' – the Recluse smiles oddly – 'suspect it's for something else.'

'You mean she comes to steal?' asks the Dohlinever hesitantly.

'Who knows –' replies the Recluse, stopping in the middle of his sentence. He walks away, over to the window, where his eyes follow the road to the cemetery.

The two young men bring him an apple. 'Eat.'

As if shaken from a dream he turns from the window. 'Thanks.'

Eating the apple calms him. He speaks quietly. 'Once we were talking about the way of the world,' he begins, wiping the moisture of the frozen apple from his mustache. 'The way of the world is a deep secret, and not only the way of the world but of each man. Every man is a universe and his way a secret.' He looks at them and laughs cheerfully.

Chaim the teacher snores heavily behind the bookrest. 'Some snoring,' remarks the Zelver.

'Let him be,' says the Recluse amiably. 'Happy is he who sleeps. In fact, I think I'll rest a bit. Somehow I feel very tired.'

As he speaks he goes over to a corner bench, takes off his coat, makes a pillow out of it, and stretches out lengthwise.

In a few minutes he is asleep. In his dream he sees the apple woman. He reaches out his arms and grasps a bookrest that stands near his head.

At first the bookrest sways back and forth, but soon it settles into balance and stands quietly, clasped by the sleeping man.

S. Y. Agnon

FRIENDSHIP

Translated by Misha Louvish

FIRST KISS

Translated by Neal Kozodoy

S. Y. Agnon

S. Y. AGNON (1888–1970), Israel's great Hebrew writer, was a joint winner of the 1966 Nobel Prize for Literature. He was born in the Polish province of Galicia but settled in Palestine at the age of eighteen. His collected works have been published in many volumes and he has profoundly influenced renaissant modern Hebrew literature.

FRIENDSHIP

My wife had returned from a journey, and I was very happy. But a tinge of sadness mingled with my joy, for the neighbours might come and bother us. 'Let us go and visit Mr So-and-So, or Mrs Such-and-Such,' I said to my wife, 'for if they come to us we shall not get rid of them in a hurry, but if we go to them we can get up and be rid of them whenever we like.'

So we lost no time and went to visit Mrs Klingel. Because Mrs Klingel was in the habit of coming to us, we went to her first.

Mrs Klingel was a famous woman and had been principal of a school before the war. When the world went topsy-turvy, she fell from her high estate and became an ordinary teacher. But she was still very conscious of her own importance and talked to people in her characteristic patronizing tone. If anyone acquired a reputation, she would seek his acquaintance and become a frequent visitor in his house. My wife had known her when she was a principal, and she clung to my wife as she clung to anyone who had seen her in her prime. She was extremely friendly to my wife and used to call her by her first name. I too had known Mrs Klingel in her prime, but I doubt whether I had talked to her. Before the war, when people were not yet hostile to each other, a man could meet his neighbour and regard him as his friend even if he did not talk to him.

Mrs Klingel was lying in bed. Not far away, on a velvet-covered couch, sat three of her woman friends whom I did not know.

When I came in I greeted each of them, but I did not tell them my name or trouble myself to listen to theirs.

Mrs Klingel smiled at us affectionately and went on chattering as usual. I held my tongue and said to myself: I have really nothing against her, but she is a nuisance. I shall be walking in the street one day, not wanting anyone to notice me, when suddenly this woman will come up to me and I will ask her how she is and be distracted from my thoughts. Because I knew her several years ago, does that mean that I belong to her all my life? I was smouldering with anger, and I did not tell myself: If you come across someone and you do not know what connection there is between you, you should realize that you have not done your duty to him previously and you have both been brought back into the world to put right the wrong you did to your neighbour in a previous life.

As I sat nursing my anger, Mrs Klingel said to my wife, 'You were away, my dear, and in the meantime your husband amused himself.' As she spoke, she shook her finger at me and said, laughingly, 'I am not telling your wife that pretty girls came to visit you.'

Nothing had been further from my thoughts in those days than pleasure. Even in my dreams there was nothing to give me pleasure, and now this woman tells my wife, 'Your husband had visits from pretty girls, your husband took his pleasure with them.' I was so furious that my very bones trembled. I jumped up and showered her with abuse. Every opprobrious word I knew I threw in her face. My wife and she looked at me in wonderment. And I wondered at myself too, for after all Mrs Klingel had only been joking, and why should I flare up and insult her in this way? But I was boiling with anger, and every word I uttered was either a curse or an insult. Finally I took my wife by the arm and left without a farewell.

On my way out I brushed past Mrs Klingel's three friends, and I believe I heard one saying to the other, 'That was a strange joke of Mrs Klingel's.'

My wife trailed along behind me. From her silence it was obvious that she was distressed, not so much because I had shamed Mrs Klingel but because I had fallen into a rage. But she was silent out of love, and said nothing at all.

So we walked on without uttering a word. We ran into three men. I knew one of them, but not the other two. The one I knew had been a Hebrew teacher, who had gone abroad and come back rich; now he spent his time stuffing the periodicals with his verbiage. These teachers who never cease to be school masters, forever repeating their trivial lessons. But in one of his articles I had found a good thing, and now we met I paid him a compliment. His face lit up and he presented me to his companions, one of whom had been a senator in Poland, while the other was the brother of one of Mrs Klingel's three friends – or perhaps I am mistaken and she has no brother.

I should have asked the distinguished visitors if they liked the city, and so forth, but my wife was tired from the journey and still distressed. So I cut conversation short and took my leave.

My wife had already gone off, without waiting for me. I was not angry at her for not waiting. It is hard for a young woman to stand and show herself to people when she is sad and weary.

While I was walking, I put my hand in my pocket and took out an envelope or a letter, and stopped to read: 'The main trials of the Book of Job were not those of Job, but of the Holy One, blessed be He, as it were, because He had placed His servant Job in the power of Satan. That is, God's trial was greater than Job's. He had a perfect and upright man, and He placed him in the power of Satan.' After reading what I had written, I tore up the envelope and the letter, and scattered the pieces to the wind, as I usually do to every letter, sometimes before I read it and sometimes at the time of reading.

After I had done this, I said to myself: I must find my wife. My thoughts had distracted me and I had strayed from the road; I now found myself suddenly standing in a street where I had never been before. It was no different from all the other streets in the city, but I knew I had strayed to a place I did not know. By this time all the shops were locked up, and little lamps shone in the windows showing all kinds of commodities. I saw that I had strayed far from home, and I knew I must go by a different road, but I did not know which. I looked at a stairway bounded on both sides by an iron fence and went up until I reached a flower shop. There I found a small group of men standing with their backs to the flowers, and Dr Rischel standing among them, offering them his new ideas on grammar and language.

I greeted him and asked: 'Which way to . . .' but before I could say the name of the street I started to stammer. I had not forgotten the name of the street, but I could not utter the words.

It is not easy to understand the feelings of a man, who is looking for the place he lives, and then as he is about to ask, cannot pronounce the name of the street. However, I took heart and pretended I was joking. Suddenly I was bathed in a cold sweat. What I wanted to conceal I was compelled to reveal. When I tried again to ask where the street was, the same thing happened.

Dr Rischel stood there amazed: he was in the midst of expounding his new ideas, and I had come along and interrupted him. Meanwhile, his companions had gone away, looking at me mockingly as they left. I looked this way and that. I tried to remember the name of my street, but could not. Sometimes I thought the name of the street was Humboldt and sometimes that it was West Street. But as soon as I opened my mouth to ask, I knew that its name was neither Humboldt nor West. I put my hand in my pocket, hoping to find a letter on which I would see my address. I found two letters I had not yet torn up, but one had been sent to my old home, which I have left, and another was addressed 'poste restante'. I had received only one letter in this house where I was living, and I had torn it up a short time before. I started reciting aloud names of towns and villages, kings and nobles, sages and poets, trees and flowers, every kind of street name: perhaps I would remember the name of my street – but I could not recall it.

But Rischel's patience exhausted itself, and he started scraping the ground with his feet. 'I am in trouble and he wants to abandon me' I said to myself. We are friends, we are human beings, aren't we? How can you leave a man in such distress? Today my wife came back from a journey and I cannot reach her, for the trivial reason that I have forgotten where I live. 'Get into a street-car and come with me,' said Dr Rischel. I wondered at his inappropriate suggestion, but he took me by the arm and got in with me.

I rode on against my will, wondering why Rischel had seen fit to drag me into this tramcar. Not only was it not bringing me home, but it was taking me further away from my own street. I remembered that I had seen Rischel in a dream wrestling with me. I jumped off the tramcar and left him.

When I jumped off the car I found myself standing by the Post Office. An idea came into my head: to ask for my address there. But my head replied: Be careful, the clerk may think you are crazy, for a sane man usually knows where he lives. So I asked a man I found there to ask the clerk.

In came a stout, well-dressed man, an insurance agent, rubbing his hands in pleasure and satisfaction, who interrupted us with his talk. My blood seethed with indignation. 'Have you no manners,' I said to him. 'When two people are talking, what right have you to interrupt them?' I knew I was not behaving well, but I was in a temper and completely forgot my manners. The agent looked at me in surprise, as if saying: What have I done to you? Why should you insult me? I knew that if I was silent he would have the best of the argument, so I started shouting again, 'I've got to go home, I am looking for my house, I've forgotten the name of my street, and I don't know how to get to my wife!' He began to snigger, and so did the others who had gathered at the sound of my voice. Meanwhile, the clerk had closed his window and gone away, without my knowing my address.

Opposite the Post Office stood a coffeehouse. There I saw Mr Jacob Tzorev. Mr Jacob Tzorev had been a banker in another city; I had known him before the war. When I went abroad, and he heard I was in difficulties, he had sent me money. Since paying the debt I had never written to him. I used to say: Any day now I will return to the Land of Israel and make it up with him. Meanwhile, twenty years had passed and we had not met. Now that I saw him I rushed into the coffeehouse and gripped both his arms from behind, clinging to them joyfully and calling him by name. He turned his head towards me but said nothing. I wondered why he was silent and showed me no sign of friendship. Didn't he see how much I liked him, how much I loved him?

A young man whispered to me, 'Father is blind.' I looked and saw that he was blind. It was hard for me not to rejoice in my friend, and hard to rejoice in him, for when I had left him and gone abroad there had been light in his eyes, but now they were darkened.

I wanted to ask how he was, and how his wife was. But when I started to speak I spoke about my home. Two wrinkles appeared under his eyes, and it looked as if he were peeping out of them. Suddenly he groped with his hands, turned toward his son, and said, 'This gentleman was my friend.' I nodded and said, 'Yes, that's right, I was your friend and I am your friend.' But neither his father's words nor my own made any impression on the son, and he paid no attention to me. After a brief pause, Mr Tzorev said to his son, 'Go and help him find his home.'

The young man stood still for a while. It was obvious that he found it hard to leave his father alone. Finally he opened his eyes and gazed at me. His two beautiful eyes shone, and I saw myself standing beside my home.

FIRST KISS

FRIDAY afternoon; Sabbath eve. Father was out of town on business and had left me alone, like a kind of watchman, to take care of the store. Dusk. Time to lock up, I said to myself, time to go home and change my clothes. Time to go to synagogue.

I took down the keys from where we keep them hidden, but as I went outside to lock the door, three monks appeared. They were bareheaded and wore heavy dark robes and sandals on their feet. 'We want to talk with you,' they said.

I thought to myself, if they've come to do business, Friday afternoon close to sunset is no time to do business; and if they've come to have a talk I'm not the man for them. But they saw that I was hesitant to reply and they smiled.

'Don't be afraid,' one of them said, 'we're not about to delay you from your prayers.'

'Look to the heavens and see,' added the second. 'The sun has yet to go down, we still have time.'

The third one nodded his head, and in the same words, or in different words, repeated what the first two had already said. I locked the door and walked along with them. It so happened that we came out opposite my house. One of the monks raised his left hand.

'Isn't this your house?'

'This is his house,' answered the second.

'Of course it's his house,' added the third. 'This is his house.' And he pointed three fingers at Father's house.

'If you'd like, we can go in,' I said.

They nodded their heads: 'By your leave.'

We made a circuit of the entire street and walked down a short incline that took us below street level. I forgot to say that there are two entrances to Father's house, one onto the street, where his shop is, and another onto an alleyway, opposite his study-house. Both entrances are kept open on weekdays, but at dusk on Friday afternoon we close the door that gives onto the street and unlock the one to the study-house.

I pushed open the door and we went in. I brought them into the parlor. They sat on chairs that in preparation for the Sabbath meal had been arranged around a table set for the Sabbath. Their robes dragged beneath their sandals over the special rug which Mother lays out in honor of the Sabbath. The eldest of the three, who sat at the head of the table, was fat and fleshy. The others sat on either side of him: one was long and thin, with pale hair and a small wound that glowed red on the back of his head where the monks leave a round spot without hair. The others had no distinguishing marks except for a large Adam's apple. Myself – I didn't sit down, but remained standing, as is only reasonable for a man who is in a hurry but has had to receive guests.

They began to talk; I kept quiet. When they saw the two candlesticks on the table they said, 'There are three of you, aren't there? There's you, your father, and your mother. Why doesn't your mother light a third candle for her son?'

'Mother is simply continuing a custom she began on the first Sabbath after her marriage,' I told them, 'which is to light two candles only.'

They started discussing the various regulations that pertain to the ritual of candle-lighting, and what each one of them means.

'No,' I broke in, 'it's not for any of the reasons you've mentioned, it's just that one candle is for the Written Law and one is for the Oral Law. And the two are actually one, which is why we refer to the Sabbath candles in the singular. But anyway I see you're all quite expert in Jewish custom.'

They smiled, but the smile disappeared into the wrinkles in their faces.

'Well, and why shouldn't we be experts in Jewish custom,' said the one that I've been calling the third. 'After all, we belong to the order of . . .'

I thought he said they were Dominicans; but outside the monastery Dominicans don't usually wear their habits, and these three had their habits on. So he must have named a different order, but his Adam's apple got in the way and I didn't catch what he said.

The conversation was preventing me from keeping track of time, and I forgot that a man has to make himself ready to greet the Sabbath. I asked the maid to serve refreshments. She brought in the special delicacies that we prepare in honor of the Sabbath. I put a flask of whisky in front of them. They ate and drank and talked. Since I was agitated about the time, I didn't hear anything they said.

Two or three times it occurred to me that the hour had come to receive the Sabbath. But when I looked out the window, the sun was in the same place it had been when the monks first accosted me. Now you can't say there was some kind of black magic here, because I had mentioned the name of God any number of times during the conversation; and you can't say that I'd made a simple mistake in time, because the beadle had not yet called for prayers. The whole thing was quite astonishing: when the monks first came, the sun was close to setting, and all this time they'd been eating and drinking and talking, yet the sun was precisely where I'd last seen it before they ever appeared. And it's even harder, for that matter, to explain away the problem of our clock, because even if you claim that I was so preoccupied with my guests I didn't think to set it for the Sabbath, all the same I assure you it's a fine instrument, and would keep proper time even without a daily winding.

Mother came in to light the candles. The monks stood up, and in the selfsame movement walked out.

I got up to accompany them. In the street, one of them shoved me aside.

I was stunned. After all the honor I'd shown him, to be treated like that – while the other two, who saw him push me, didn't even bother to rebuke him.

I didn't want Mother to notice that something had happened

to me, so I decided not to return home. And I didn't go to
synagogue, because by the time I could have washed myself
from the touch of the monk's hand, they would have already
finished the prayers. I stood there like a man with nothing to
do, neither here nor there.

Two young novices came along.

'Where did the Fathers go,' they said.

I was dumbfounded by what I heard. Men like that they call
Father. Before I could rouse myself to answer, one of the
novices disappeared. Vanished, right before my eyes. He left
the other one behind.

I just stood there, shocked and speechless. For a while it
was as if no one else existed. Then I glanced at him and saw
that he was very young, about the height of a small youth,
with black eyes. If it hadn't been for the commandment which
tells us not to show them grace, which also means not to
impute grace to them, I would even have said that his eyes
were graceful, and sweet. His face was quite smooth, without
the slightest trace of a beard. He had the kind of beauty
you used to be able to see in every Jewish town, the
beauty of young Jewish boys who had never tasted the
taste of sin. And beyond that there was something else
about him, that imparted all the more grace to his graceful
features.

I began talking with him so that I could examine him more
closely. As I talked, I laid my hand on his shoulder and I said
to him, 'Listen my brother, aren't you a Jew?'

I felt his shoulders tremble beneath my hand; I felt his eyes
tremble; he lowered his head on his chest and I felt his heart
tremble.

'Tell me,' I repeated my question, 'aren't you a Jew?'

He raised his head from his heart: 'I am a Jew.'

I said to him, 'If you're a Jew, what are you doing with
them?'

He bowed his head.

'Who are you,' I said, 'and where are you from?'

He stood in silence before me.

I brought my face close to his, as if to transfer my sense of hearing to my mouth.

He lifted his head and I could see how his heart was shuddering, and my heart too began to shudder. I felt his black, sweet eyes upon me. He looked at me with such loving grace, with such tender faith, such glorious kindness, and above all with such grief – like a man trying to control himself before he finally reveals a long-kept secret.

I said to myself, what is all this?

As much time went by as went by, and still he said nothing.

'Is it so hard for you to tell me where you're from?'

He whispered the name of a city.

I said, 'If I heard you correctly you're from the town of Likovitz.'

He nodded his head.

'If you're from Likovitz,' I said, 'then you must certainly know the Tzaddik of Likovitz. I was in his prayer-house once on New Year's day, and the Tzaddik himself led the prayers. Let me tell you, when he came to the verse, "And all shall come to serve Thee", I imagined that I heard the approaching footsteps of all the nations of the world who fail to recognize the people of Israel or their Father in heaven. I say I heard them running to the prayer-house of the Tzaddik of Likovitz. And when he sang, "And the wayward shall learn understanding", I imagined they were all bowing down as one to worship the Lord of Hosts, the God of Israel ... My brother, are you in pain?'

He shook with sobs.

'What are you crying about?'

Tears flooded his eyes. He wiped them away. Still weeping, he said, 'I am his daughter. His youngest daughter. The daughter of his old age.'

My heart thundered and my mouth fastened to hers, and her mouth to mine. And the purest sweetness flowed from her mouth to mine and – it is possible – from my mouth to hers. We call this in Hebrew 'the kiss of the mouth', and it must be the same in other languages too. I should say here that this was the first time I ever kissed a young girl, and it seems almost certain to me that it was her first kiss as well: a kiss of innocence that carries with it no pain, but goodness and blessing, life, grace, and kindness, whereby a man and a woman live together till calm old age.

Isaac Babel

THE STORY OF MY DOVECOT

Translated by Walter Morison

THE JOURNEY

Translated by Mirra Ginsburg

Isaac Babel

ISAAC BABEL (1894-1941) was born in Odessa, the son of a Jewish tradesman. He is regarded by many as the greatest master of the short story in Russian literature since Chekhov. In the introduction to the Penguin edition of his *Collected Stories*, the American critic Lionel Trilling describes Babel as 'the author of the most remarkable work of fiction that had yet come out of revolutionary Russia, the only work, indeed, that I knew of as having upon it the mark of exceptional talent, even genius'. Babel was arrested in May 1939, and nothing more was heard of him. The official date of his death was given as 17 March 1941.

THE STORY OF MY DOVECOT

To M. GORKY

When I was a kid I longed for a dovecot. Never in all my life have I wanted a thing more. But not till I was nine did father promise the wherewithal to buy the wood to make one and three pairs of pigeons to stock it with. It was then 1904, and I was studying for the entrance exam to the preparatory class of the secondary school at Nikolayev in the Province of Kherson, where my people were at that time living. This province of course no longer exists, and our town has been incorporated in the Odessa Region.

I was only nine, and I was scared stiff of the exams. In both subjects, Russian language and arithmetic, I couldn't afford to get less than top marks. At our secondary school the *numerus clausus* was stiff: a mere five per cent. So that out of forty boys only two that were Jews could get into the preparatory class. The teachers used to put cunning questions to Jewish boys; no one else was asked such devilish questions. So when father promised to buy the pigeons he demanded top marks with distinction in both subjects. He absolutely tortured me to death. I fell into a state of permanent daydream, into an endless, despairing, childish reverie. I went to the exam deep in this dream, and nevertheless did better than everybody else.

I had a knack for book-learning. Even though they asked cunning questions, the teachers could not rob me of my intelligence and my avid memory. I was good at learning, and got top marks in both subjects. But then everything went wrong. Khariton Efrussi, the corn-dealer who exported wheat to Marseille, slipped someone a 500-rouble bribe. My mark was changed from A to A minus, and Efrussi Junior went to the secondary school instead of me. Father took it very badly. From the time I was six he had been cramming me with every scrap of learning he could, and that A minus drove him to despair. He wanted to beat Efrussi up, or at least bribe two longshoremen to beat Efrussi up, but mother talked him out of the idea, and I started studying for the second exam the following year, the one for the lowest class. Behind my back my people got the teacher to take me in one year through the preparatory and first-year course simultaneously, and conscious of the family's despair I got three whole books by heart. These were Smirnovsky's *Russian Grammar*, Yevtushevsky's *Problems*, and Putsykovich's *Manual of Early Russian History*. Children no longer cram from these books, but I learned them by heart line upon line, and the following year in the Russian exam Karavayev gave me an unrivalled A plus.

This Karavayev was a red-faced, irritable fellow, a graduate of Moscow University. He was hardly more than thirty. Crimson glowed in his manly cheeks as it does in the cheeks of peasant children. A wart sat perched on one cheek, and from it there sprouted a tuft of ash-coloured cat's whiskers. At the exam, besides Karavayev, there was the Assistant Curator Pyatnitsky, who was reckoned a big noise in the school and throughout the province. When the Assistant Curator asked me about Peter the Great, a feeling of complete oblivion came over me, an awareness that the end was near: an abyss seemed to yawn before me, an arid abyss lined with exultation and despair.

About Peter the Great I knew things by heart from Putsykovich's book and Pushkin's verses. Sobbing, I recited these verses, while the faces before me suddenly turned upside down, were shuffled as a pack of cards is shuffled. This cardshuffling went on, and meanwhile, shivering, jerking my back straight, galloping headlong, I was shouting Pushkin's stanzas at the top of my voice. On and on I yelled them, and no one broke into my crazy mouthings. Through a crimson blindness, through the sense of absolute freedom that had filled me, I was aware of nothing but Pyatnitsky's old face with its silver-touched beard bent toward me. He didn't interrupt me, and merely said to Karavayev, who was rejoicing for my sake and Pushkin's:

'What a people,' the old man whispered, 'those little Jews of yours! There's a devil in them!'

easy to stereotype

And when at last I could shout no more, he said:

'Very well, run along, my little friend.'

I went out from the classroom into the corridor, and there, leaning against a wall that needed a coat of whitewash, I began to awake from my trance. About me Russian boys were playing, the school bell hung not far away above the stairs, the caretaker was snoozing on a chair with a broken seat. I looked at the caretaker, and gradually woke up. Boys were creeping toward me from all sides. They wanted to give me a jab, or perhaps just have a game, but Pyatnitsky suddenly loomed up in the corridor. As he passed me he halted for a moment, the frock-coat flowing down his back in a slow heavy wave. I discerned embarrassment in that large, fleshy, upper-class back, and got closer to the old man.

'Children,' he said to the boys, 'don't touch this lad.' And he laid a fat hand tenderly on my shoulder.

'My little friend,' he went on, turning me toward him 'tell your father that you are admitted to the first class.'

On his chest a great star flashed, and decorations jingled in his lapel. His great black uniformed body started to move away on its stiff legs. Hemmed in by the shadowy walls, moving between them as a barge moves through a deep canal, it disappeared in the doorway of the headmaster's study. The little servingman took in a tray of tea, clinking solemnly, and I ran home to the shop.

In the shop a peasant customer, tortured by doubt, sat scratching himself. When he saw me my father stopped trying to help the peasant make up his mind, and without a moment's hesitation believed everything I had to say. Calling to the assistant to start shutting up shop, he dashed out into Cathedral Street to buy me a school cap with a badge on it. My poor mother had her work cut out getting me away from the crazy fellow. She was pale at that moment; she was experiencing destiny. She kept smoothing me, and pushing me away as though she hated me. She said there was always a notice in the paper about those who had been admitted to the school, and that God would punish us, and that folk would laugh at us if we bought a school cap too soon. My mother was pale; she was experiencing destiny through my eyes. She looked at me with bitter compassion as one might look at a little cripple boy, because she alone knew what a family ours was for misfortunes.

All the men in our family were trusting by nature, and quick to ill-considered actions. We were unlucky in everything we undertook. My grandfather had been a rabbi somewhere in the Belaya Tserkov region. He had been thrown out for blasphemy, and for another forty years he lived noisily and sparsely, teaching foreign languages. In his eightieth year he started going off his head. My Uncle Leo, my father's brother, had studied at the Talmudic Academy in Volozhin. In 1892 he ran away to avoid doing military service, eloping with the daughter of someone serving in the commissariat in the Kiev military district. Uncle Leo took this woman to California, to Los Angeles, and there he abandoned her, and died in a house of ill-fame among Negroes and Malays. After his death the American police sent us a heritage from Los Angeles, a large trunk bound with brown iron hoops. In this trunk there were dumbbells, locks of women's hair, uncle's talith, horsewhips with gilt handles, scented tea in boxes trimmed with imitation pearls. Of all the family there remained only crazy Uncle Simon-Wolf, who lived in Odessa, my father, and I. But my father had faith in people, and he used to put them off with the transports of first love. People could not forgive him for this, and used to play him false. So my father believed that his life was guided by an evil fate, an inexplicable being that pursued him, a being in every respect unlike him. And so I alone of all our family was left to my mother. Like all Jews I was short, weakly, and had headaches from studying. My mother saw all this. She had never been dazzled by her husband's pauper pride, by his incomprehensible belief that our family would one day be richer and more powerful than all others on earth. She desired no success for us, was scared of buying a school jacket too soon, and all she would consent to was that I should have my photo taken.

On 20 September 1905 a list of those admitted to the first

class was hung up at the school. In the list my name figured
too. All our kith and kin kept going to look at this paper, and
even Shoyl, my grand-uncle, went along. I loved that boastful
old man, for he sold fish at the market. His fat hands were
moist, covered with fish-scales, and smelt of worlds chill and
beautiful. Shoyl also differed from ordinary folk in the lying
stories he used to tell about the Polish Rising of 1861. Years
ago Shoyl had been a tavern-keeper at Skvira. He had seen
Nicholas I's soldiers shooting Count Godlevski and other
Polish insurgents. But perhaps he hadn't. Now I know that
Shoyl was just an old ignoramus and a simple-minded liar,
but his cock-and-bull stories I have never forgotten: they
were good stories. Well now, even silly old Shoyl went along
to the school to read the list with my name on it, and that
evening he danced and pranced at our pauper ball.

My father got up the ball to celebrate my success, and asked
all his pals – grain-dealers, real-estate brokers, and the travell-
ing salesmen who sold agricultural machinery in our parts.
These salesmen would sell a machine to anyone. Peasants and
land-owners went in fear of them: you couldn't break loose
without buying something or other. Of all Jews, salesmen are
the widest-awake and the jolliest. At our party they sang
Hasidic songs consisting of three words only but which took
an awful long time to sing, songs performed with endless
comical intonations. The beauty of these intonations may only
be recognized by those who have had the good fortune to
spend Passover with the Hasidim or who have visited their
noisy Volhynian synagogues. Besides the salesmen, old
Lieberman, who had taught me the Torah and ancient Hebrew
honoured us with his presence. In our circle he was known as
Monsieur Lieberman. He drank more Bessarabian wine than
he should have. The ends of the traditional silk tassels poked
out from beneath his waistcoat, and in ancient Hebrew he
proposed my health. In this toast the old man congratulated
my parents and said that I had vanquished all my foes in single
combat: I had vanquished the Russian boys with their fat
cheeks, and I had vanquished the sons of our own vulgar
parvenus. So too in ancient times David King of Judah had

overcome Goliath, and just as I had triumphed over Goliath, so too would our people by the strength of their intellect conquer the foes who had encircled us and were thirsting for our blood. Monsieur Lieberman started to weep as he said this, drank more wine as he wept, and shouted '*Vivat!*' The guests formed a circle and danced an old-fashioned quadrille with him in the middle, just as at a wedding in a little Jewish town. Everyone was happy at our ball. Even mother took a sip of vodka, though she neither liked the stuff nor understood how anyone else could – because of this she considered all Russians cracked, and just couldn't imagine how women managed with Russian husbands.

But our happy days came later. For mother they came when of a morning, before I set off for school, she would start making me sandwiches; when we went shopping to buy my school things – pencil-box, money-box, satchel, new books in cardboard bindings, and exercise-books in shiny covers. No one in the world has a keener feeling for new things than children have. Children shudder at the smell of newness as a dog does when it scents a hare, experiencing the madness which later, when we grow up, is called inspiration. And mother acquired this pure and childish sense of the ownership of new things. It took us a whole month to get used to the pencil-box, to the morning twilight as I drank my tea on the corner of the large, brightly-lit table and packed my books in my satchel. It took us a month to grow accustomed to our happiness, and it was only after the first half-term that I remembered about the pigeons.

I had everything ready for them: one rouble fifty and a dovecot made from a box by Grandfather Shoyl as we called him. The dovecot was painted brown. It had nests for twelve pairs of pigeons, carved strips on the roof, and a special grating that I had devised to facilitate the capture of strange birds. All was in readiness. On Sunday, 20 October, I set out for the bird market, but unexpected obstacles arose in my path.

The events I am relating, that is to say my admission to the first class at the secondary school, occurred in the autumn of

1905. The Emperor Nicholas was then bestowing a constitution on the Russian people. Orators in shabby overcoats were clambering on to tall kerbstones and haranguing the people. At night shots had been heard in the streets, and so mother didn't want me to go to the bird market. From early morning on 20 October the boys next door were flying a kite right by the police station, and our water-carrier, abandoning all his buckets, was walking about the streets with a red face and brilliantined hair. Then we saw baker Kalistov's sons drag a leather vaulting-horse out into the street and start doing gym in the middle of the roadway. No one tried to stop them: Semernikov the policeman even kept inciting them to jump higher. Semernikov was girt with a silk belt his wife had made him, and his boots had been polished that day as they had never been polished before. Out of his customary uniform, the policeman frightened my mother more than anything else. Because of him she didn't want me to go out, but I sneaked out by the back way and ran to the bird market, which in our town was behind the station.

At the bird market Ivan Nikodimych, the pigeon-fancier, sat in his customary place. Apart from pigeons, he had rabbits for sale too, and a peacock. The peacock, spreading its tail, sat on a perch moving a passionless head from side to side. To its paw was tied a twisted cord, and the other end of the cord was caught beneath one leg of Ivan Nikodimych's wicker-chair. The moment I got there I bought from the old man a pair of cherry-coloured pigeons with luscious tousled tails, and a pair of crowned pigeons, and put them away in a bag on my chest under my shirt. After these purchases I had only forty kopecks left, and for this price the old man was not prepared to let me have a male and female pigeon of the Kryukov breed. What I liked about Kryukov pigeons was their short, knobbly, good-natured beaks. Forty copecks was the proper price, but the fancier insisted on haggling, averting from me a yellow face scorched by the unsociable passions of bird-snarers. At the end of our bargaining, seeing that there were no other customers, Ivan Nikodimych beckoned me closer. All went as I wished, and all went badly.

Toward twelve o'clock, or perhaps a bit later, a man in felt
boots passed across the square. He was stepping lightly on
swollen feet, and in his worn-out face lively eyes glittered.

'Ivan Nikodimych,' he said as he walked past the bird-
fancier, 'pack up your gear. In town the Jerusalem aristocrats
are being granted a constitution. On Fish Street Grandfather
Babel has been constitutioned to death.'

He said this and walked lightly on between the cages like
a barefoot ploughman walking along the edge of a field.

'They shouldn't,' murmured Ivan Nikodimych in his wake.
'They shouldn't!' he cried more sternly. He started collecting
his rabbits and his peacock, and shoved the Kryukov pigeons
at me for forty kopecks. I hid them in my bosom and watched
the people running away from the bird market. The peacock
on Ivan Nikodimych's shoulder was last of all to depart. It
sat there like the sun in a raw autumnal sky; it sat as July sits
on a pink riverbank, a white-hot July in the long cool grass.
No one was left in the market, and not far off shots were
rattling. Then I ran to the station, cut across a square that had
gone topsy-turvy, and flew down an empty lane of trampled
yellow earth. At the end of the lane, in a little wheeled armchair, sat the legless Makarenko, who rode about town in his
wheel-chair selling cigarettes from a tray. The boys in our
street used to buy smokes from him, children loved him, I
dashed toward him down the lane.

'Makarenko,' I gasped, panting from my run, and I
stroked the legless one's shoulder, 'have you seen Shoyl?'

The cripple did not reply. A light seemed to be shining
through his coarse face built up of red fat, clenched fists,
chunks of iron. He was fidgeting on his chair in his excitement, while his wife Kate, presenting a wadded behind, was
sorting out some things scattered on the ground.

'How far have you counted?' asked the legless man, and
moved his whole bulk away from the woman, as though
aware in advance that her answer would be unbearable.

'Fourteen pairs of leggings,' said Kate, still bending over,
'six undersheets. Now I'm a-counting the bonnets.'

'Bonnets!' cried Makarenko, with a choking sound like

a sob; 'it's clear, Catherine, that God has picked on me, that I must answer for all. People are carting off whole rolls of cloth, people have everything they should, and we're stuck with bonnets.'

And indeed a woman with a beautiful burning face ran past us down the lane. She was clutching an armful of fezzes in one arm and a piece of cloth in the other, and in a voice of joyful despair she was yelling for her children, who had strayed. A silk dress and a blue blouse fluttered after her as she flew, and she paid no attention to Makarenko, who was rolling his chair in pursuit of her. The legless man couldn't catch up. His wheels clattered as he turned the handles for all he was worth.

'Little lady,' he cried in a deafening voice, 'where did you get that striped stuff?'

But the woman with the fluttering dress was gone. Round the corner to meet her leaped a rickety cart in which a peasant lad stood upright.

'Where've they all run to?' asked the lad, raising a red rein above the nags jerking in their collars.

'Everybody's on Cathedral Street,' said Makarenko pleadingly, 'everybody's there, sonny. Anything you happen to pick up, bring it along to me. I'll give you a good price.'

The lad bent down over the front of the cart and whipped up his piebald nags. Tossing their filthy croups like calves, the horses shot off at a gallop. The yellow lane was once more yellow and empty. Then the legless man turned his quenched eyes upon me.

'God's picked on me, I reckon,' he said lifelessly; 'I'm a son of man, I reckon.'

And he stretched a hand spotted with leprosy toward me.

'What's that you've got in your sack?' he demanded, and took the bag that had been warming my heart.

With his fat hand the cripple fumbled among the tumbler pigeons and dragged to light a cherry-coloured she-bird. Jerking back its feet, the bird lay still on his palm.

'Pigeons,' said Makarenko, and squeaking his wheels he rode right up to me. 'Damned pigeons,' he repeated, and struck me on the cheek.

He dealt me a flying blow with the hand that was clutching the bird. Kate's wadded back seemed to turn upside down, and I fell to the ground in my new overcoat.

'Their spawn must be wiped out,' said Kate, straightening up over the bonnets. 'I can't a-bear their spawn, nor their stinking menfolk.'

She said more things about our spawn, but I heard nothing of it. I lay on the ground, and the guts of the crushed bird trickled down from my temple. They flowed down my cheek, winding this way and that, splashing, blinding me. The tender pigeon-guts slid down over my forehead, and I closed my solitary unstopped-up eye so as not to see the world that spread out before me. This world was tiny, and it was awful. A stone lay just before my eyes, a little stone so chipped as to resemble the face of an old woman with a large jaw. A piece of string lay not far away, and a bunch of feathers that still breathed. My world was tiny, and it was awful. I closed my eyes so as not to see it, and pressed myself tight into the ground that lay beneath me in soothing dumbness. This trampled earth in no way resembled real life, waiting for exams in real life. Somewhere far away Woe rode across it on a great steed, but the noise of the hoofbeats grew weaker and died away, and silence, the bitter silence that sometimes overwhelms children in their sorrow, suddenly deleted the boundary between my body and the earth that was moving nowhither. The earth smelled of raw depths, of the tomb, of flowers. I smelled its smell and started crying, unafraid. I was walking along an unknown street set on either side with white boxes, walking in a get-up of bloodstained feathers, alone between the pavements swept clean as on Sunday, weeping bitterly, fully and happily as I never wept again in all my life. Wires that had grown white hummed above my head, a watchdog trotted on in front, in the lane on one side a young peasant in a waistcoat was smashing a window-frame in the house of Khariton Efrussi. He was smashing it with a wooden mallet, striking out with his whole body. Sighing, he smiled all around with the amiable grin of drunkenness, sweat, and spiritual power. The whole street was filled with

he knows,
he understands

a splitting, a snapping, the song of flying wood. The peasant's whole existence consisted in bending over, sweating, shouting queer words in some unknown, non-Russian language. He shouted the words and sang, shot out his blue eyes; till in the street there appeared a procession bearing the Cross and moving from the Municipal Building. Old men bore aloft the portrait of the neatly-combed Tsar, banners with grave-yard saints swayed above their heads, inflamed old women flew on in front. Seeing the procession, the peasant pressed his mallet to his chest and dashed off in pursuit of the banners, while I, waiting till the tail-end of the procession had passed, made my furtive way home. The house was empty. Its white doors were open, the grass by the dovecot had been trampled down. Only Kuzma was still in the yard. Kuzma the yardman was sitting in the shed laying out the dead Shoyl.

'The wind bears you about like an evil wood-chip,' said the old man when he saw me. 'You've been away ages. And now look what they've done to granddad.'

Kuzma wheezed, turned away from me, and started pulling a fish out of a rent in grandfather's trousers. Two pike perch had been stuck into grandfather: one into the rent in his trousers, the other into his mouth. And while grandfather was dead, one of the fish was still alive, and struggling.

'They've done grandfather in, but nobody else,' said Kuzma, tossing the fish to the cat. 'He cursed them all good and proper, a wonderful damning and blasting it was. You might fetch a couple of pennies to put on his eyes.'

But then, at ten years of age, I didn't know what need the dead had of pennies.

'Kuzma,' I whispered, 'save us.'

And I went over to the yardman, hugged his crooked old back with its one shoulder higher than the other, and over this back I saw grandfather. Shoyl lay in the sawdust, his chest squashed in, his beard twisted upwards, battered shoes on his bare feet. His feet, thrown wide apart, were dirty, lilac-coloured, dead. Kuzma was fussing over him. He tied the dead man's jaws and kept glancing over the body to see what else he could do. He fussed as though over a newly-purchased garment, and only cooled down when he had given the dead man's beard a good combing.

'He cursed the lot of 'em right and left,' he said, smiling, and cast a loving look over the corpse. 'If Tartars had crossed his path he'd have sent them packing, but Russians came, and their women with them, Rooski women. Russians just can't bring themselves to forgive, I know what Rooskis are.'

The yardman spread some more sawdust beneath the body, threw off his carpenter's apron, and took me by the hand.

'Let's go to father,' he mumbled, squeezing my hand tighter and tighter. 'Your father has been searching for you since morning, sure as fate you was dead.'

And so with Kuzma I went to the house of the tax-inspector, where my parents, escaping the pogrom, had sought refuge.

THE JOURNEY

THE front collapsed in 1917. I left it in November. At home
mother prepared a bundle of underwear and dry bread for me.
I got to Kiev the day before Muraviev began to bombard the
city. I was on my way to Petersburg. For twelve days we sat
it out in the cellar of Chaim the Barber's hotel in the Bes-
sarabka. I got a permit to leave the city from the Soviet
commandant of Kiev.

There is no drearier sight in the world than the Kiev railway
station. For many years its makeshift wooden barracks have
blighted the approaches to the city. Lice crackled on the wet
boards. Deserters, gypsies and black marketeers were lying all
over the place. Old Galician women urinated standing on the
platform. The lowering sky was furrowed with clouds,
suffused with rain and gloom.

Three days went by before the first train left. At first it
stopped at every verst, but then it gathered speed; the wheels
began to rumble with a will, singing a song of power. Everyone was happy in our freight car. In 1918, rapid travel made
people happy. During the night the train shuddered and came
to a stop. The doors of our car slid open and we saw the

1. This story is largely autobiographical. As a child in Odessa, Babel
had endured the pogroms of Tsarist Russia; as a young Bolshevik during
the Civil War he was witness to the White Army's acts of violence against
Jews, described here. During the Civil War and the war with Poland,
Babel was a political commissar in Budyonny's cavalry, and, for a brief
period, a clerical worker for the Cheka. In 'Red Cavalry' and other stories,
like 'The Journey', Babel described the savagery of war with scrupulous
objectivity, making no attempt to draw the moral which socialist realism
demands. As a result he was always under attack for 'naturalism'.
Publication of his work ceased altogether in 1937; he was arrested two
years later and died in a concentration camp in 1941.

'The Journey', written in the twenties, was first published in an obscure
literary magazine, 30 Days, in 1932. It reappeared in a censored version
in a collection of Babel stories published in Moscow in 1957, after his
posthumous rehabilitation. The censored passage, which is indicated in
this translation, was evidently omitted for reasons of prudery.

greenish gleam of snow. A railroad telegrapher entered the car, wearing a wide fur coat fastened with a leather belt, and soft Caucasian boots. He stretched out his hand and rapped his palm with one finger.

'Your papers. Put them here!'

Near the door, a quiet old woman lay huddled on some bales. She was going to her son, a railroad worker in Luban. Next to me, a teacher, Yehuda Weinberg, and his wife, sat dozing. The teacher had been married a few days earlier and was taking his young wife to Petersburg. All the way they had talked in whispers about new methods of teaching, and then had fallen asleep. Even in sleep their hands were linked, clinging to each other.

The telegrapher read their travel document, signed by Lunacharsky, took a Mauser with a slender, grimy muzzle from under his coat and shot the teacher in the face.

A large, stooping peasant wearing a fur cap with the ear-flaps undone shuffled behind the telegrapher. The telegrapher winked at the peasant who put his lamp on the floor, unbuttoned the trousers of the dead man, cut off his genitals with a knife and began stuffing them into his wife's mouth.

'*Treif* wasn't good enough for you,' said the telegrapher. 'So here's some kosher for you.'[1]

The woman's soft neck bulged. Not a sound came from her. The train had come to a halt in the steppe. The snow-drifts shimmered with an arctic glitter. Jews were being flung out of the cars on the roadbed. Shots rang out like exclamations. A peasant in a fur hat with dangling ear-flaps led me behind a frozen woodpile and began to search me. A cloud-dimmed moon shone down on us. The violet wall of forest was smoking. Stiff icy fingers like wooden stumps crept over my body. The telegrapher shouted from the open door of the car:

'Jew or Russian?'

'Russian,' the peasant muttered, feeling me over. 'Some Russian! He'd make a fine rabbi . . .'

He brought his crumpled worried face closer to mine, ripped

1. The two previous paragraphs were excised in the censored 1957 version.

out the four ten-rouble gold coins my mother had sewn into my underpants for the journey, took off my boots and coat, then turned me around, struck the back of my neck with the edge of his hand and said in Yiddish:

'*Ankloif*, Chaim . . . Get going, Chaim . . .'

I walked away, my bare feet sinking into the snow. My back lit up like a target, its bull's eye centered on my ribs. The peasant did not shoot. Between the columns of pines, in the subterranean shelter of the forest, a light swayed in a crown of blood-red smoke. I ran up to the hut. Its chimney smoked from dung fire. The forester groaned when I burst in. Swathed in strips of cloth cut out from overcoats, he sat in a little bamboo, velvet-cushioned armchair, shredding tobacco in his lap. His image was drawn out in the smoky air. He moaned. Then, rising from the chair, he bowed low before me:

'Go away, my good man . . . Go away, my good citizen . . .'

He led me out to a path and gave me rags to wrap my feet. By late morning I had dragged myself to a little town. There was no doctor at the hospital to amputate my frozen feet. A male nurse was in charge of the ward. Every day he raced up to the hospital on a short-legged black colt, tethered him to a post and came in blazing, with glittering eyes.

'Friedrich Engels,' he would say bending over my pillow, his pupils glowing like embers, 'teaches the likes of you that there mustn't be any nations, but we say: a nation must exist . . .'

Tearing the bandages from my feet, he would straighten up and, gritting his teeth, ask me in a low voice:

'Where are you headed? What devil drives you? Why is it always on the move, this tribe of yours? . . . Why are you making all this trouble, why all this turmoil? . . .'

One night the town Soviet had us taken away in a cart – patients who didn't get along with the male nurse, and old Jewish women in wigs, the mothers of local commissars.

My feet healed up. I set out further along the hunger-stricken road to Zhlobin, Orsha and Vitebsk.

From Novo-Sokolniki to Loknya, I found shelter under the

muzzle of a howitzer. We were riding on a flatcar. Fediukha, my chance companion who was on the great odyssey of a deserter, was a storyteller, punster and wit. We slept under the mighty, short, upturned muzzle of the gun, keeping each other warm in a canvas den, lined with hay like the lair of a beast. Past Loknya, Fediukha stole my traveling box and disappeared. The box had been given me by the town Soviet and contained two sets of army underwear, some dry bread and a little money. For two days – we were then approaching Petersburg – I had no food. At the Tsarskoye Selo station I had my last taste of shooting. A patrol fired into the air to greet the oncoming train.

The black marketeers were led out onto the platform and the soldiers began to strip off their clothes. The liquor-filled rubber bags in which they were encased flopped down on the asphalt next to the real men. At nine in the evening, the howling prison of the station disgorged me onto Zagorodny Prospect. Across the street, on the wall of a boarded-up pharmacy, the thermometer registered twenty-four degrees below zero. The wind roared through the tunnel of Gorokhovaya Street. A gas light flickered wildly over the canal. Our chilled, granite Venice stood motionless. I entered Gorokhovaya, an icy field hemmed in by cliffs.

The Cheka was housed in Number 2, in what had been the Governor's palace. Two machine guns, two iron dogs, stood in the vestibule with raised muzzles. I showed the commandant a letter from Vanya Kalugin, the N.C.O. under whom I had served in the Shuisky Regiment. Kalugin, who was now an interrogator in the Cheka, had written me to come.

'Go to the Anichkov Palace,' said the commandant. 'That's where he works now . . .'

'I'll never make it,' I smiled in reply.

Nevsky Prospect flowed into the distance like the Milky Way. Dead horses punctuated it like milestones. Their raised legs propped up a low-fallen sky. Their slit bellies gleamed white and clean. An old man who looked like a guardsman went by, pulling a carved toy sled. Straining forward, he dug his leather feet into the ice. A Tyrolean hat was perched on his head, and his beard, tied up with string, was tucked into his scarf.

'I'll never make it,' I said to the old man.

He stopped. His furrowed, leonine face was calm. He thought about his own troubles and went on with his sled.

'And so, there is no longer any need to conquer Petersburg,' I thought, and tried to recall the name of the man who was trampled to death by Arab horses at the very end of his journey. It was Yehuda Halevi.

Two Chinese in bowler hats, with loaves of bread under their arms, stood on the corner of the Sadovaya. With frozen nails they marked off tiny portions of the bread and showed them to approaching prostitutes. The women went past them in silent parade.

At the Anichkov Bridge I sat down on a ledge below one of Klodt's bronze horses. My arm slipped under my head, and I stretched out on the polished slab. But the granite stung me, struck me and catapulted me toward the palace.

The door of the cranberry-colored wing was open. A blue gas light gleamed over the doorman, who was sleeping in a chair. His lower lip drooped; his wrinkled face was inky and deathlike. Under his brilliantly lit, unbelted tunic, he wore court uniform trousers embroidered in gold braid. An arrow, raggedly drawn in ink, pointed the way to the commandant's office. I climbed the stairway and walked through empty low-ceilinged rooms. Women, painted in dark and gloomy colors, danced in endless rings over the walls and ceilings. Metal gratings covered the windows, forced bolts hung from the window frames. At the end of this suite of rooms, behind a table, sat Kalugin with his cap of straw-colored peasant hair, lit up as on a stage. On the table lay a pile of children's toys, bits of colored cloth, torn picture books.

'So here you are,' said Kalugin, raising his head. 'Hello ... We need you ...'

I brushed aside the toys littering the table, lay down on the gleaming top and woke – seconds or hours later – on a low sofa. The bright rays of a chandelier played over me in a cascade of glass. My rags had been cut from me and lay in a puddle on the floor.

'And now for a bath,' said Kalugin who stood over the sofa. He lifted me and carried me to a bathtub. The tub was the old-fashioned kind, with low sides. There was no water in the faucets; Kalugin poured water over me from a pail. Clothing was laid out for me on the pale yellow satin cushions of the backless wicker chairs: a dressing gown with clasps, a shirt and socks of heavy silk. I sank into the underpants up to my neck. The dressing gown was made for a giant; I stepped on the flapping ends of the sleeves.

'Don't joke with Alexander Alexandrovich,' said Kalugin, rolling up my sleeves. 'The fellow must have weighed 300 pounds.'

We managed to tuck up the dressing gown of Alexander the Third and returned to the first room. It was the library of Maria Fyodorovna – a perfumed box in which gilded bookcases with raspberry stripes were pushed against the walls.

I told Kalugin who had been killed in our Shuisky Regiment, who had been elected commissar, who had gone to join the Whites in the Kuban. We drank tea, and stars swam and dissolved in the cut glass walls of our tumblers. With the stars, we ate horsemeat sausage, black and moist. The dense fine silk of the curtains divided us from the world; the sun suspended from the ceiling splintered and shone, waves of stifling heat came from the radiators.

'Hell, we only live once,' said Kalugin when we had finished off the horsemeat. He went out and returned with two boxes – a present from Sultan Abdul-Hamid to the Russian sovereign. One was made of zinc, the other was a cigar box pasted over with ribbons and paper insignia. '*A sa majesté, l'Empereur de toutes les Russies,*' was engraved on the zinc lid, 'from your loving cousin . . .'

The aroma which Maria Fyodorovna had known so well a quarter of a century before drifted across the library. The cigarettes, twenty centimeters long and as thick as fingers, were wrapped in pink paper; I do not know whether anyone but the

Emperor of all the Russias ever smoked such cigarettes, but I chose a cigar. Kalugin smiled, looking at me.

'We'll chance it,' he said, 'maybe they weren't counted ... The servants told me Alexander the Third was a great smoker: he loved tobacco, *kvas* and champagne ... Yet look at those five-kopeck earthenware ashtrays on his table, and the patches on his trousers ...'

Indeed, the dressing gown I wore was greasy, shiny and had often been mended.

We spent the rest of the night sorting the toys of Nicholas the Second, his drums and locomotives, his christening shirts and copybooks covered with childish scrawls. There were photographs of grand dukes who had died in infancy, locks of their hair, diaries of the Danish Princess Dagmara, letters from her sister, the Queen of England, breathing perfume and decay, crumbling away in our fingers. On the fly-leaves of Bibles and of a volume of Lamartine, friends and ladies in waiting – daughters of burgomasters and state councillors – bid their farewells in slanting, diligent lines to the princess who was departing for Russia. Queen Louise, her mother, who ruled over a small kingdom, had taken care to place her children well: she married off one of her daughters to Edward VII, Emperor of India and King of England; another was married to a Romanov; her son George was made King of Greece. Princess Dagmara became Maria in Russia. Far away now were the canals of Copenhagen and King Christian's chocolate-brown sideburns. Bearing the last Tsars, this little woman raged like an angry vixen behind her guard of Preobrazhensky Grenadiers, but her blood flowed into an implacable vengeful granite earth ...

Till dawn we could not tear ourselves away from this mute, disastrous chronicle. Abdul-Hamid's cigar was smoked to the end. In the morning Kalugin took me to the Cheka at Number 2 Gorokhovaya Street. He spoke to Uritsky. I stood behind the draperies which flowed to the floor in waves of cloth. Snatches of the conversation reached me through them.

'He is one of ours,' said Kalugin. 'His father is a shop-

keeper, but he has broken with them... He knows languages
...'

The Commissar of Internal Affairs of the Northern Com-
munes walked out of the office with his swaying gait. Behind
his pince-nez bulged swollen flabby eyelids, scorched with
sleeplessness.

I was made a translator in the Foreign Department. I received a soldier's uniform and meal coupons. In a corner
assigned to me in the large hall of the former Governor's
palace, I went to work translating the testimony of diplomats,
incendiaries and spies.

Before the day was over, I had everything – clothes, food,
work and comrades, true in friendship and in death, such comrades as are found in no country in the world but ours.

Thus, thirteen years ago, began my splendid life, a life of
thought and merriment.

Isaac Bashevis Singer

A FRIEND OF KAFKA

Translated by the author and Elizabeth Shub

Isaac Bashevis Singer

ISAAC BASHEVIS SINGER (1904–91) was born in Poland into a rabbinical family and lived in New York from 1935 until his death. A prolific storyteller of genius, for a considerable part of his working life he wrote for newspapers, and much of his work was first published in the New York newspaper, the *Jewish Daily Forward*. His works include *The Family Moskat*, *The Slave*, *The Estate*, *Enemies: A Love Story* and *Shosha*. He won the US Book Award and, in 1978, the Nobel Prize for Literature for 'his impassioned narrative art which, with roots in Polish-Jewish tradition, brings universal human conditions to life'.

A FRIEND OF KAFKA

I HAD heard about Franz Kafka years before I read any of his books from his friend Jacques Kohn, a former actor in the Yiddish theatre. I say 'former' because by the time I knew him he was no longer on the stage. It was the early thirties, and the Yiddish theatre in Warsaw had already begun to lose its audience. Jacques Kohn himself was a sick and broken man. Although he still dressed in the style of a dandy, his clothes were shabby. He wore a monocle in his left eye, a high old-fashioned collar (known as 'father-murderer'), patent-leather shoes, and a derby. He had been nicknamed 'the lord' by the cynics in the Warsaw Yiddish writers' club that we both frequented. Although he stooped more and more, he worked stubbornly at keeping his shoulders back. What was left of his once yellow hair he combed to form a bridge over his bare skull. In the tradition of the old-time theatre, every now and then he would lapse into Germanized Yiddish – particularly when he spoke of his relationship with Kafka. Of late, he had begun writing newspaper articles, but the editors were unanimous in rejecting his manuscripts. He lived in an attic room somewhere on Leszno Street and was constantly ailing. A joke about him made the rounds of the club members: 'All day long he lies in an oxygen tent, and at night he emerges a Don Juan.'

We always met at the club in the evening. The door would open slowly to admit Jacques Kohn. He had the air of an important European celebrity who was deigning to visit the ghetto. He would look around and grimace, as if to indicate that the smells of herring, garlic, and cheap tobacco were not to his taste. He would glance disdainfully over the tables covered with tattered newspapers, broken chess pieces, and ashtrays filled with cigarette stubs, around which the club members sat endlessly discussing literature in their shrill voices. He would shake his head as if to say, 'What can you expect from such schlemiels?' The moment I saw him entering, I would put my hand in my pocket and prepare the zloty that he would inevitably borrow from me.

This particular evening, Jacques seemed to be in a better mood than usual. He smiled, displaying his porcelain teeth, which did not fit and moved slightly when he spoke, and swaggered over to me as if he were on-stage. He offered me his bony, long-fingered hand and said, 'How's the rising star doing tonight?'

'At it already?'

'I'm serious. Serious. I know talent when I see it, even though I lack it myself. When we played Prague in 1911, no one had ever heard of Kafka. He came backstage, and the moment I saw him I knew that I was in the presence of genius. I could smell it the way a cat smells a mouse. That was how our great friendship began.'

I had heard this story many times and in as many variations, but I knew that I would have to listen to it again. He sat down at my table, and Manya, the waitress, brought us glasses of tea and cookies. Jacques Kohn raised his eyebrows over his yellowish eyes, the whites of which were threaded with bloody little veins. His expression seemed to say, 'This is what the barbarians call tea?' He put five lumps of sugar into his glass and stirred, rotating the tin spoon outwards. With his thumb and index finger, the nail of which was unusually long, he broke off a small piece of cookie, put it into his mouth, and said, '*Nu ja,*' which meant, One cannot fill one's stomach on the past.

It was all play-acting. He himself came from a Hasidic family in one of the small Polish towns. His name was not Jacques but Jankel. However, he had lived for many years in Prague, Vienna, Berlin, Paris. He had not always been an actor in the Yiddish theatre but had played on the stage in both France and Germany. He had been friends with many celebrities. He had helped Chagall find a studio in Belleville. He had been a frequent guest at Israel Zangwill's. He had appeared in a Reinhardt production, and had eaten cold cuts with Piscator. He had shown me letters he had received not only from Kafka but from Jakob Wassermann, Stefan Zweig, Romain Rolland,

Ilya Ehrenburg, and Martin Buber. They all addressed him by his first name. As we got to know each other better, he had even let me see photographs and letters from famous actresses with whom he had had affairs.

For me, 'lending' Jacques Kohn a zloty meant coming into contact with Western Europe. The very way he carried his silver-handled cane seemed exotic to me. He even smoked his cigarettes differently from the way we did in Warsaw. His manners were courtly. On the rare occasion when he reproached me, he always managed to save my feelings with some elegant compliment. More than anything else, I admired Jacques Kohn's way with women. I was shy with girls – blushed, became embarrassed in their presence – but Jacques Kohn had the assurance of a count. He had something nice to say to the most unattractive woman. He flattered them all, but always in a tone of good-natured irony, affecting the blasé attitude of a hedonist who has already tasted everything.

He spoke frankly to me. 'My young friend, I'm as good as impotent. It always starts with the development of an over-refined taste – when one is hungry, ones does not need marzipan and caviare. I've reached the point where I consider no woman really attractive. No defect can be hidden from me. That is impotence. Dresses, corsets are transparent for me. I can no longer be fooled by paint and perfume. I have lost my own teeth, but a woman has only to open her mouth and I spot her fillings. That, by the way, was Kafka's problem when it came to writing: he saw all the defects – his own and everyone else's. Most of literature is produced by such plebeians and bunglers as Zola and D'Annunzio. In the theatre, I saw the same defects that Kafka found in literature, and that brought us together. But, oddly enough, when it came to judging the theatre Kafka was completely blind. He praised our cheap Yiddish plays to heaven. He fell madly in love with a ham actress – Madam Tschissik. When I think that Kafka loved this creature, dreamed about her, I am ashamed for man and his illusions. Well, immortality is not choosy. Anyone who happens to come in contact with a great man marches with him into immortality, often in clumsy boots.

'Didn't you once ask what makes me go on, or do I imagine that you did? What gives me the strength to bear poverty, sickness, and, worst of all, hopelessness? That's a good question, my young friend. I asked the same question when I first read the Book of Job. Why did Job continue to live and suffer? So that in the end he would have more daughters, more donkeys, more camels? No. The answer is that it was for the game itself. We all play chess with Fate as partner. He makes a move; we make a move. He tries to checkmate us in three moves; we try to prevent it. We know we can't win, but we're driven to give him a good fight. My opponent is a tough angel. He fights Jacques Kohn with every trick in his bag. It's winter now; it's cold even with the stove on, but my stove hasn't worked for months and the landlord refuses to fix it. Besides, I wouldn't have the money to buy coal. It's as cold inside my room as it is outdoors. If you haven't lived in an attic, you don't know the strength of the wind. My windowpanes rattle even in the summertime. Sometimes a tomcat climbs up on the roof near my window and wails all night like a woman in labour. I lie there freezing under my blankets and he yowls for a cat, though it may be he's merely hungry. I might give him a morsel of food to quiet him, or chase him away, but in order not to freeze to death I wrap myself in all the rags I possess, even old newspapers – the slightest move and the whole works comes apart.

'Still, if you play chess, my dear friend, it's better to play with a worthy adversary than with a botcher. I admire my opponent. Sometimes I'm enchanted with his ingenuity. He sits up there in an office in the third or seventh heaven, in that department of Providence that rules our little planet, and has just one job – to trap Jacques Kohn. His orders are "Break the keg, but don't let the wine run out." He's done exactly that. How he manages to keep me alive is a miracle. I'm ashamed to tell you how much medicine I take, how many pills I swallow. I have a friend who is a druggist, or I could never afford it. Before I go to bed, I gulp down one after another – dry. If I drink, I have to urinate. I have prostate trouble, and as it is I must get up several times during the night. In the dark, Kant's categories no longer apply. Time ceases to be time and space is no space. You hold something in your hand and suddenly it isn't there. To light my gas lamp is not a simple matter. My matches are always vanishing. My attic teems with demons. Occasionally, I address one of them: "Hey, you, Vinegar, son of Wine, how about stopping your nasty tricks!"

'Some time ago, in the middle of the night, I heard a pounding on my door and the sound of a woman's voice. I couldn't tell whether she was laughing or crying. "Who can it be?" I said to myself. "Lilith? Namah? Machlath, the daughter of Ketev M'riri?" Out loud, I called, "Madam, you are making a mistake." But she continued to bang on the door. Then I heard a groan and someone falling. I did not dare to open the door. I began to look for my matches, only to discover that I was holding them in my hand. Finally, I got out of bed, lit the gas lamp, and put on my dressing gown and slippers. I caught a glimpse of myself in the mirror, and my reflection scared me. My face was green and unshaven. I finally opened the door, and there stood a young woman in bare feet, wearing a sable coat over her nightgown. She was pale and her long blonde hair was dishevelled. "Madam, what's the matter?" I said.

' "Someone just tried to kill me. I beg you, please let me in. I only want to stay in your room until daylight."

'I wanted to ask who had tried to kill her, but I saw that she was half frozen. Most probably drunk, too. I let her in and noticed a bracelet with huge diamonds on her wrist. "My room is not heated," I told her.

' "It's better than to die in the street."

'So there we were both of us. But what was I to do with her? I only have one bed. I don't drink – I'm not allowed to – but a friend had given me a bottle of cognac as a gift, and I had some stale cookies. I gave her a drink and one of the cookies. The liquor seemed to revive her. "Madam, do you live in this building?" I asked.

' "No," she said. "I live on Ujazdowskie Boulevard."

'I could tell that she was an aristocrat. One word led to

another, and I discovered that she was a countess and a widow, and that her lover lived in the building – a wild man, who kept a lion cub as a pet. He, too, was a member of the nobility, but an outcast. He had already served a year in the Citadel, for attempted murder. He could not visit her, because she lived in her mother-in-law's house, so she came to see him. That night, in a jealous fit, he had beaten her and placed his revolver at her temple. To make a long story short, she had managed to grab her coat and run out of his apartment. She had knocked on the doors of the neighbours, but none of them would let her in, and so she had made her way to the attic.

' "Madam," I said to her, "your lover is probably still looking for you. Supposing he finds you? I am no longer what one might call a knight."

' "He won't dare make a disturbance," she said. "He's on parole. I'm through with him for good. Have pity – please don't put me out in the middle of the night."

' "How will you get home tomorrow?" I asked.

' "I don't know," she said. "I'm tired of life anyhow, but I don't want to be killed by him."

' "Well, I won't be able to sleep in any case," I said. "Take my bed and I will rest here in this chair."

' "No. I wouldn't do that. You are not young and you don't look very well. Please, go back to bed and I will sit here."

'We haggled so long we finally decided to lie down together. "You have nothing to fear from me," I assured her. "I am old and helpless with women." She seemed completely convinced.

'What was I saying? Yes, suddenly I find myself in bed with a countess whose lover might break down the door at any moment. I covered us both with the two blankets I have and didn't bother to build the usual cocoon of odds and ends. I was so wrought up I forgot about the cold. Besides, I felt her closeness. A strange warmth emanated from her body, different from any I had known – or perhaps I had forgotten it. Was my opponent trying a new gambit? In the past few years he had stopped playing with me in earnest. You know,

there is such a thing as humorous chess. I have been told that
Nimzowitsch often played jokes on his partners. In the old
days, Morphy was known as a chess prankster. "A fine move,"
I said to my adversary. "A masterpiece." With that I realized
that I knew who her lover was. I had met him on the stairs –
a giant of a man, with the face of a murderer. What a funny
end for Jacques Kohn – to be finished off by a Polish Othello.

'I began to laugh and she joined in. I embraced her and held
her close. She did not resist. Suddenly a miracle happened. I
was a man again! Once, on a Thursday evening, I stood near
a slaughterhouse in a small village and saw a bull and a cow
copulate before they were going to be slaughtered for the
Sabbath. Why she consented I will never know. Perhaps it
was a way of taking revenge on her lover. She kissed me and
whispered endearments. Then we heard heavy footsteps.
Someone pounded on the door with his fist. My girl rolled
off the bed and lay on the floor. I wanted to recite the prayer
for the dying, but I was ashamed before God – and not so
much before God as before my mocking opponent. Why grant
him this additional pleasure? Even melodrama has its limits.

'The brute behind the door continued beating it, and I was
astounded that it did not give way. He kicked it with his foot.
The door creaked but held. I was terrified, yet something in
me could not help laughing. Then the racket stopped. Othello
had left.

'Next morning, I took the countess's bracelet to a pawn-
shop. With the money I received, I bought my heroine a dress,
underwear, and shoes. The dress didn't fit, neither did the
shoes, but all she needed to do was get to a taxi – provided,
of course, that her lover did not waylay her on the steps.
Curious, but the man vanished that night and never reappeared.

'Before she left, she kissed me and urged me to call her,
but I'm not that much of a fool. As the Talmud says, "A
miracle doesn't happen every day."

'And you know, Kafka, young as he was, was possessed
by the same inhibitions that plague me in my old age. They
impeded him in everything he did – in sex as well as in his
writing. He craved love and fled from it. He wrote a sentence

and immediately crossed it out. Otto Weininger was like that, too – mad and a genius. I met him in Vienna – he spouted aphorisms and paradoxes. One of his sayings I will never forget: "God did not create the bedbug." You have to know Vienna to really understand these words. Yet who did create the bedbug?

'Ah, there's Bamberg! Look at the way he waddles along on his short legs, a corpse refusing to rest in its grave. It might be a good idea to start a club for insomniac corpses. Why does he prowl around all night? What good are the cabarets to him? The doctors gave him up years ago when we were still in Berlin. Not that it prevented him from sitting in the Romanisches Café until four o'clock in the morning, chatting with the prostitutes. Once, Granat, the actor, announced that he was giving a party – a real orgy – at his house, and among others he invited Bamberg. Granat instructed each man to bring a lady – either his wife or a friend. But Bamberg had neither wife nor mistress, and so he paid a harlot to accompany him. He had to buy her an evening dress for the occasion. The company consisted exclusively of writers, professors, philosophers, and the usual intellectual hangers-on. They all had the same idea as Bamberg – they hired prostitutes. I was there, too. I escorted an actress from Prague, whom I had known a long time. Do you know Granat? A savage. He drinks cognac like soda water, and can eat an omelette of ten eggs. As soon as the guests arrived, he stripped and began dancing madly around with the whores, just to impress his high-brow visitors. At first, the intellectuals sat on chairs and stared. After a while, they began to discuss sex. Schopenhauer said this . . . Nietzsche said that. Anyone who hadn't witnessed it would find it difficult to imagine how ridiculous such geniuses can be. In the midst of it all, Bamberg was taken ill. He turned as green as grass and broke out in a sweat. "Jacques," he said, "I'm finished. A good place to die." He was having a kidney or a gall-bladder attack. I half carried him out and got him to a hospital. By the way, can you lend me a zloty?'

'Two.'

'What! Have you robbed Bank Polski?'

'I sold a story.'

'Congratulations. Let's have supper together. You will be my guest.'

2

While we were eating, Bamberg came over to our table. He was a little man, emaciated as a consumptive, bent over and bow-legged. He was wearing patent-leather shoes, and spats. On his pointed skull lay a few grey hairs. One eye was larger than the other – red, bulging, frightened by its own vision. He leaned against our table on his bony little hands· and said in his cackling voice, 'Jacques, yesterday I read your Kafka's *Castle*. Interesting, very interesting, but what is he driving at? It's too long for a dream. Allegories should be short.'

Jacques Kohn quickly swallowed the food he was chewing. 'Sit down,' he said. 'A master does not have to follow the rules.'

'There are some rules even a master must follow. No novel should be longer than *War and Peace*. Even *War and Peace* is too long. If the Bible consisted of eighteen volumes, it would long since have been forgotten.'

'The Talmud has thirty-six volumes, and the Jews have not forgotten it.'

'Jews remember too much. That is our misfortune. It is two thousand years since we were driven out of the Holy Land, and now we are trying to get back in. Insane, isn't it? If our literature would only reflect this insanity, it would be great. But our literature is uncannily sane. Well, enough of that.'

Bamberg straightened himself, scowling with the effort. With his tiny steps, he shuffled away from the table. He went over to the gramophone and put on a dance record. It was known in the writers' club that he had not written a word in years. In his old age, he was learning to dance, influenced by the philosophy of his friend Dr Mitzkin, the author of *The Entropy of Reason*. In this book Dr Mitzkin attempted to prove that the human intellect is bankrupt and that true wisdom can only be reached through passion.

Jacques Kohn shook his head. 'Half-pint Hamlet. Kafka was afraid of becoming a Bamberg – that is why he destroyed himself.'

'Did the countess ever call you?' I asked.

Jacques Kohn took his monocle out of his pocket and put it in place. 'And what if she did? In my life, everything turns into words. All talk, talk. This is actually Dr Mitzkin's philosophy – man will end up as a word machine. He will eat words, drink words, marry words, poison himself with words. Come to think of it, Dr Mitzkin was also present at Granat's orgy. He came to practise what he preached, but he could just as well have written *The Entropy of Passion*. Yes, the countess does call me from time to time. She, too, is an intellectual, but without intellect. As a matter of fact, although women do their best to reveal the charms of their bodies, they know just as little about the meaning of sex as they do about the intellect.

'Take Madam Tschissik. What did she ever have, except a body? But just try asking her what a body really is. Now she's ugly. When she was an actress in the Prague days, she still had something. I was her leading man. She was a tiny little talent. We came to Prague to make some money and found a genius waiting for us – *Homo sapiens* in his highest degree of self-torture. Kafka wanted to be a Jew, but he didn't know how. He wanted to live, but he didn't know this, either. "Franz," I said to him once, "you are a young man. Do what we all do." There was a brothel I knew in Prague, and I persuaded him to go there with me. He was still a virgin. I'd rather not speak about the girl he was engaged to. He was sunk to the neck in the bourgeois swamp. The Jews of his circle had one ideal – to become Gentiles, and not Czech Gentiles but German Gentiles. To make it short, I talked him into the adventure. I took him to a dark alley in the former ghetto and there was the brothel. We went up the crooked steps. I opened the door and it looked like a stage set: the whores, the pimps, the guests, the madam. I will never forget that moment. Kafka began to shake, and pulled at my sleeve. Then he turned and ran down the steps so quickly I was afraid he would break a leg. Once on the street, he stopped and vomited like a schoolboy. On the way back, we passed an old synagogue, and Kafka began to speak about the *golem*. Kafka believed in the *golem*, and even that the future might well bring another one. There must be magic words that can turn a piece of clay into a living being. Did not God, according to the cabala, create the world by uttering holy words? In the beginning was the Logos.

'Yes, it's all one big chess game. All my life I have been afraid of death, but now that I'm on the threshold of the grave I've stopped being afraid. It's clear, my partner wants to play a slow game. He'll go on taking my pieces one by one. First he removed my appeal as an actor and turned me into a so-called writer. He'd no sooner done that than he provided me with writer's cramp. His next move was to deprive me of my potency. Yet I know he's far from checkmate, and this gives me strength. It's cold in my room – let it be cold. I have no supper – I won't die without it. He sabotages me and I sabotage him. Some time ago, I was returning home late at night. The frost burned outside, and suddenly I realized that I had lost my key. I woke up the janitor, but he had no spare key. He stank of vodka, and his dog bit my foot. In former years I would have been desperate, but this time I said to my opponent, "If you want me to catch pneumonia, it's all right with me." I left the house and decided to go to the Vienna station. The wind almost carried me away. I would have had to wait at least three-quarters of an hour for the streetcar at that time of night. I passed by the actors' union and saw a light in a window. I decided to go in. Perhaps I could spend the night there. On the steps I hit something with my shoe and heard a ringing sound. I bent down and picked up a key. It was mine! The chance of finding a key on the dark stairs of this building is one in a billion, but it seems that my opponent was afraid I might give up the ghost before he was ready. Fatalism? Call it fatalism if you like.'

Jacques Kohn rose and excused himself to make a phone call. I sat there and watched Bamberg dancing on his shaky legs with a literary lady. His eyes were closed, and he leaned his head on her bosom as if it were a pillow. He seemed to be

dancing and sleeping simultaneously. Jacques Kohn took a
long time – much longer than it normally takes to make a
phone call. When he returned, the monocle in his eye shone.
'Guess who is in the other room?' he said. 'Madam Tschissik!
Kafka's great love.'

'Really.'

'I told her about you. Come, I'd like to introduce you to
her.'

'No.'

'Why not? A woman that was loved by Kafka is worth
meeting.'

'I'm not interested.'

'You are shy, that's the truth. Kafka, too, was shy – as shy
as a yeshiva student. I was never shy, and that may be the
reason I have never amounted to anything. My dear friend,
I need another twenty groschen for the janitors – ten for the
one in this building, and ten for the one in mine. Without the
money I can't go home.'

I took some change out of my pocket and gave it to him.

'So much? You certainly must have robbed a bank today.
Forty-six groschen! Piff-paff! Well, if there is a God, He will
reward you. And if there isn't, who is playing all these games
with Jacques Kohn?'

Emanuel Litvinoff

FANYA

Emanuel Litvinoff

EMANUEL LITVINOFF, born in London's Whitechapel of Russian Jewish parents, has published poems, novels and short stories and has had several television plays produced. His most recent books are the autobiographical *Journey through a Small Planet* and the Russian Revolution trilogy of novels, *A Death Out of Season*, *Blood on the Snow* and *The Face of Terror*.

FANYA

WHEN I was growing up you could spend three hours in the gallery of a picture palace for fourpence and see two terrific all-star features. The living theatre couldn't compete: no wonder everyone said it was dying. Then Herschel Rosenheim broke Fanya Ziegelbaum's heart when the New York Yiddish troupe played a season at the Whitechapel Pavilion, and because I tasted a drop of that bitterness Rosenheim's Hamlet remained with me long after I'd forgotten *The Four Horsemen of the Apocalypse* or who played Al Jolson's sonny boy in *The Jazz Singer*.

Fanya first came to work for us when she was fourteen, a scraggy brown-faced orphan whose stockings wrinkled on her matchstick legs. She smelled of dirty knickers and aroused all my nine-year-old mistrust of girls. My mother took her as an apprentice because it was a *mitzvah*. She lived with a stingy aunt in a tall barrack-like building in one of the worst streets off Commercial Road. The aunt economized on Fanya's food to stuff the mouths of her own four fat children. She and her husband made a living out of watching corpses, a ritual requirement, augmenting their income by selling the deceased's clothes to a second-hand dealer with whom they had an arrangement. Such an environment could have a dreadful effect on a young girl, but Fanya had the remedy in her own hands. Quick to pick up the essentials of dressmaking, after a year or so she went up West with my mother's blessing to earn good money in the high-class trade. Still, she was always ready to help out with a big wedding order or in other emergencies, and so never became a stranger.

Every time she returned skinny Fanya seemed to grow plumper, particularly in the tender region of the chest and behind, where the flesh curved like twin full moons. She'd left her aunt to lodge with a young widow, a saleslady in the cosmetics trade who knew a lot about being smart. As a result, the change in Fanya became startling. She walked around in West End dresses copied from ladies' magazines and stitched by her own hand. Her mouth pouted kissprufe lipstick the colour of raspberry jam. She scented her breath with cachous and did something to her eyes to make them large and brilliant. In short, she'd suddenly turned into a beauty, and although not everybody approved – some of the women said she'd made herself look common – most people agreed that such a picture as Fanya was sure to find a marvellous boy, maybe even with his own business. I hoped so too because she was one of the first girls I really loved.

The summer my mother was pregnant with David, Uncle Solly's third child, Fanya came over to help out most evenings. She was a stimulating influence. Abie, nearly fifteen and rather cocky because his wages were a pound a week, hung around her speaking in a gruff voice and blowing smoke from Player's Weights through his nostrils. Uncle Solly practically stopped going to boxing or the dog-track. He talked restlessly of old times in South Africa before he was married, or even farther back in the trenches, pulling up his trouser-leg to show us his shrapnel wounds and letting Fanya feel the metal under the skin. As for my mother, for whom things were going well at the time, she sang as she treadled the sewing machine, remembered Odessa, spoke seriously with Fanya about love, and occasionally turned towards Solly with the eyes of a young girl.

Late one night, about eleven o'clock, I was detailed to walk Fanya home. Her route led under the railway arch where *goyim* were supposed to lurk madd̄ened with drink and lust. My mother wouldn't let her go alone, nor with my stepfather, nor with Abie, for that matter. Not that she didn't trust them exactly, but she was inclined to believe the *dybbuk* of temptation haunted certain dark and evil places and I suppose it seemed less likely that the fiend would seize a sexually unready boy of thirteen. For my part I was flattered to play the protector of so lovely a girl and felt older every minute as we walked side by side.

There were no unusual signs of debauchery when we came to the railway arch although couples grappled against the drip-

ping walls and tramps lay around parcelled in old newspaper.
The evil of the place was in its gloom, its putrid stench, in the
industrial grime of half a century with which it was impreg-
nated. The sinister possibilities excited me: I was not immune
to the *dybbuk*, after all.

'We're walking past the scene of Jack the Ripper's most
famous murder,' I announced. 'It was a foggy night. The
woman came out of a pub when she saw this figure in a black
coat. He dragged her under the railway arch and slashed her
so much, the blood ran down the gutter.'

'You're trying to frighten me.' Her eyes were black and
enormous. 'I'll tell your mum.'

I hadn't realized that scaring girls was so thrilling. 'God's
honour, Fanya. He was a famous doctor who got a disease and
became a sex maniac. That's why he cut up women. You can
read all about it in the library.'

'They haven't got things like that in the library,' Fanya
said, beginning to go faster. 'It wouldn't be allowed.'

'But, Fanya – '

'I don't want to hear any more!' She spoke in a severe,
grownup voice, so I shrugged and let her walk on alone.
She'd only gone a few yards, glancing back at me nervously,
when two men lurched round the corner, roaring drunk.

They staggered along the narrow pavement towards us singing a dirty song. We clung together for mutual protection,
pressing close to the wall. The softness of her was a shock of
illicit delight: my pressure became urgent. As our bellies
touched my boy's cock strained towards a premature maturity
and even when the men had gone, we did not immediately
separate. We were about the same height. She had a rich dark
smell like a pungent animal. Our mouths came together
clumsily and I tasted the sophistication of cachous on her
breath. A sinful, corrupt, oriental flavour.

She wrenched herself away. The night throbbed with darkness and shame. We walked along in silence, interminably. At
last we reached the lights of Whitechapel and exchanged a
sideways glance. Electric music came out of pin-table saloons.
Young men with heavily padded shoulders swaggered by

whistling aimlessly. Fanya was obviously anxious to get rid of me as quickly as possible. I understood her embarrassment. She didn't want to be seen promenading with a boy in short trousers, especially after what had happened. As she hurried away a youth with brilliantined hair called out in an American drawl: 'Hey, sugar, what's your hurry?'

I went home very slowly, remembering the shape of that softness and confused by it. Undressing for bed, I looked at the hair that had started to grow below my thin belly. It reminded me that I must inevitably inherit the hairiness of men, their grotesque, depressing lusts. And all night long I burned with a shameful fever.

The New York Yiddish Theatre opened its London season that autumn with what the drama critic of our building, a watchmaker named Shmulik, described as a daring translation of Gotthold Ephraim Lessing's *Nathan the Wise*. I heard him discussing it with old Mrs Rosen, the grocer, while she was at her daily task of weighing sugar into blue paper bags. Lessing was an assimilationist of the worst kind, according to Shmulik, and consequently he made his heroine, Recha, fall in love with a *goy* of exceptional vulgarity, a *sheigetz*. Mrs Rosen shook her head with disapproving vigour, her ritual wig almost slipping into the sugar. Even at the best of times *Nathan the Wise* wasn't Shmulik's favourite play, but on top of everything he had the bad luck to sit next to a woman who didn't stop eating fried fish the whole performance. She must also have been a critic, he remarked sourly.

The failure of *Nathan the Wise* was redressed by the next production, a Goldfaden comedy, the title of which I have forgotten. It succeeded because it made people laugh and cry and remember the past, all at the same time. And even though one always heard how bitter everything was in the past, the old people were still crazy to relive it. After the triumphant first night, there was a stampede for the box-office by every class of Jew from master tailor to under-presser. The moneyed rolled up in taxis all the way from Park Lane and Stamford Hill but mingled on equal terms with class-conscious proletarians. Toothless crones who could barely hobble to the market place, raced along Whitechapel as if rejuvenated and used their stick-like elbows to reach the front of the uproarious queue. Trampled peanut shells and discarded sweet papers made the pavement look like Victoria Park on a Bank Holiday. There were vendors selling hot beigels, baked potatoes, fruit, chestnuts, fizzy drinks. Down-at-heel rabbinical types with matted beards solicited alms for *yeshivot* in Vilna or Jerusalem. Street musicians who hadn't played the fiddle for years scratched out their rusty tunes. Everybody said it was like the old days at the Pavilion and elderly intellectuals in Goide's restaurant, squeezing the last drop of lemon juice into their tea, predicted a miraculous revival of Yiddish culture.

All this, of course, hardly affected the younger generation and Fanya Ziegelbaum might never even have met Rosenheim if the American troupe's costumes had not needed constant running repairs. She was introduced to the wardrobe mistress by a mutual friend. On her very first evening Rosenheim strode off-stage wearing buckskin breeches and cavalry boots. He was full of fire and tenderness, still under the influence of his romantic role. Fanya went down on her knees to stitch up the split seam and as she did so, she was later to tell my mother, the actor put out his hand to stroke the back of her neck. He must have been pleasantly surprised by her youth and freshness for even *ingénues* in the Yiddish theatre were performed by actresses who'd already married off their own daughters. As for Fanya, she must have been parched for the touch of such a hand, and from then on there was nothing in life she wanted more than to stand under the *chuppah* and become Mrs Rosenheim. The second Mrs Rosenheim, in fact, the actor soon confessed, but certainly, he promised, the last. When the season in London was over, he'd take her back to America and there make her his own little angel bride.

Afterwards, when the damage was done, everybody said they'd known it would end badly, but if so they were careful not to say it to the girl's face. Whenever she came round to us, the neighbours were never short of an excuse to drop in. Suddenly they ran out of sugar, or were in need of change for the gas meter, or just looked in as they were passing. The springs of the sofa sagged as one by one they settled down comfortably to stay for a cup of tea.

Fanya was excited and talkative. 'Such a cold audience last night,' she would say, 'you wouldn't believe!' Or, with evident satisfaction: 'Six curtain calls yesterday.' All of a sudden she was an expert. The future of the Yiddish theatre worried her. People would rather go to see any rubbish at the movies nowadays. And where were the playwrights, the new Sholem Aleichems? The public no longer had respect for a Jewish actor. They spat in his face. Harry – that was what she called Herschel Rosenheim – had turned down offers to play the biggest roles on Broadway, but how long could he go on making such sacrifices?

The women would surely have preferred to hear less of Rosenheim the actor and more of Rosenheim the lover. It was hard for us to believe actors were real people. Did they bleed real blood, experience real suffering, go to the lavatory? Musicians, yes. Prizefighters also. But actors? Fanya was young, foolish, she had romantic notions. Maybe it wasn't even true about Rosenheim: it could be an exaggeration. And even if it was, an ordinary working girl, what did she want with an actor? About such people one thing was sure, morals they didn't have.

My mother said: 'An orphan like you, without even a mother or a father, you have to be careful somebody doesn't take an advantage.' Everybody knew what that meant. Two minutes pleasure, nine months pain, and unspeakable ruin. 'After all, how long do you know him? Practically from yesterday! Sometimes a man pays a compliment. He makes a flirtation. Marriage,' my mother said heavily, 'is for a whole lifetime.'

Fanya was a serious girl. She thought for a while before replying, then looked into my mother's face with the solemn eyes of one who had seen her destiny. 'Sometimes you can be sure in a single minute,' she said with sombre conviction and added humbly: 'I don't know why I should be so lucky. Once Harry danced with Gloria Swanson. At a charity ball. I don't know what he can see in me.'

One Sunday morning I was standing in a crowd in Middlesex Street market absorbed in watching a small Irishman working the three-card trick. 'All you got to do is keep your eye on me hands,' he confided out of the corner of his wide rubbery mouth. 'Now watch it, sports!' He showed us the lady and dexterously shuffled the cards on a folding green baize table.

At that moment Fanya came out of Strongwater's delicatessen holding a brown paper bag. She was with a man in a curly-brimmed hat worn well back on a thatch of red hair. I could tell he was an actor by the elegant way he smoked his cigarette. Otherwise he looked no different from a tailor. Excited, I was just about to follow when the Irishman grabbed hold of me. 'There's some o' you wouldn't trust an Irish feller wid the price of a drink,' he said gloomily. 'Now look at this young laddie, a face of innocence like a holy choir boy. Put your finger on that card, lad. Now, listen! If I was to say this boy's digit is on the lovely Queen of Hearts, would any of you sports venture to believe me for ten bob?' No one ventured. Disconsolately the Irishman turned up the card. It was the Queen and I hurried away.

Fanya leaned against Rosenheim and kept turning her head with quick nervous movements as if she wanted to catch people looking at them. She was wearing a yellow sleeveless dress and her long hair gleamed like rich mahogany. Men stared at her, as they always did, but no one gave Rosenheim more than a glance. He was probably only acting the part of an ordinary person and I admired this modesty, although his lack of height disappointed me. I'd imagined him a tall, commanding figure, but without his hat he'd have been shorter than Fanya.

In Fieldgate Street I slipped over to the opposite pavement to get a good view of the actor's profile and they saw me. I gazed intensely into a watchmaker's window at a man fishing for tiny cogwheels with a magnifying glass screwed into his eye and pretended to be there accidentally. They came over.

'Well, stranger! What are you doing in this district?' Fanya said, in a modulated voice, as if we were as far afield as Oxford Street at least. I looked round and gave a simulated start of surprise. Rosenheim's hand rested on the soft inside of Fanya's upper arm and he stroked the skin musingly with his forefinger. She told him who I was. They'd obviously discussed her connection with our family because he looked at me with interest.

'I hoid a lot about your mudder and fader,' he said. The accent was just like a Chicago gangster's. 'What Fanya tells me, dey is marvellous pipple.' His pale grey eyes blinked with sincerity. 'Especially your mudder. She look after dis young goil like her own dotter.' He squeezed Fanya's plump arm and she gazed back adoringly. 'Nu, ve gotta go. Give my best to your pipple, Sonny,' he said and, as they were about to leave, remarked as an afterthought: '*Liebchen*, bring the boy vun efening. Maybe he's interested to see the backstage. Vy not?'

Frankly, I didn't expect much from the Pavilion – a Jewish theatre was not the London Palladium, after all – but it was a shock to discover that the stage door led into a building as filthy, neglected and unromantic as the corridors of our tenement. Fanya took me into the costume room. There was a treadle machine and a bench for pressing clothes. A yellowed Ministry of Labour poster on the white-washed wall was prosaically concerned with fire regulations and you could smell the toilet next door. Mrs Myers, the wardrobe mistress, was a heavy-breasted woman whose square face disappeared into the folds of her neck. But she was nice and gave me a mug of syrupy coffee. A remote drone of voices reached us from the direction of the stage, a sound that resembled the kind of argument one heard at home through the walls of a neighbouring apartment.

They were doing *Hamlet*. Mrs Myers told me the plot, although she'd never actually found time to see the play right through. It was about a Prince who had a mother, a monster.

Together with his uncle the King's brother, she poisoned his father, her own husband, then married with the murderer. From this the Prince had such aggravation, he turned against the whole world. Even to his fiancée, a beautiful girl, he behaved so badly that she drowned herself.

Mrs Myers described it all so vividly, I could hardly wait to see the drama for myself.

In semi-darkness, Fanya led me to the wings. Her hand was hot and I could feel it trembling. In a sunken well that made him look like a trapped grey mouse, an elderly man peered along his pointed nose at a copy of the play-text. Battlements rose to the rusty grinding of pulleys and were replaced by gloomy palace chambers. A man in baggy trousers picked his teeth with a matchstick held in one hand and moved a spotlight with the other. I couldn't quite follow the Shakespearian Yiddish. It wasn't in the slightest like the iambic pentameters spoken in our classroom through the pinched Gentile nostrils of Mr Parker, my schoolmaster, and it didn't sound like anything my mother said. Only when Rosenheim, gravely pacing the stage and, plucking at his chin, began the famous soliloquy, did I start to get the gist of things.

'*Tzu sein, odder nisht tzu sein,*

'*Dos is der frage,*' said Rosenheim in a slow, perplexed but remarkably resonant voice.

Fanya gazed at him with petrified eyes as if afraid he might make the wrong decision. Her lips were parted like a listening child's and she responded to Rosenheim's voice as the strings of a piano vibrate to pressure on its keyboard. As he declaimed to the half-empty auditorium, she clenched her small hands and breathed faster. Her bosom was palpitating like a small, agitated animal and I had to restrain the temptation to stroke it into calmness. Nothing that happened on the stage, not even Hamlet's grief over Ophelia's drowning, moved me so much as the madness of Fanya's love.

But soon I became terribly bored. It was more diverting to eavesdrop on the actors who stood around smoking between scenes, scratching their itching faces to avoid smearing the greasepaint and grumbling about the audience. Hamlet's mother, the famous Esther Friedenthal, nibbled a chopped liver sandwich, talking to another actress about her son in New York who had sensibly decided to study business administration.

One by one the actors stubbed out their cigarettes and went on stage to be murdered. When it was Rosenheim's turn to die, he jerked and quivered for a long time. The final curtain descended to scattered applause and the cast bowed and smiled a couple of times, exchanging supercilious glances when Rosenheim stepped forward to receive solitary homage. Patches of sweat showed on his tunic as he spread out his arms and drooped his flaming head in a crucified gesture. The sound of crunching peanut shells could be heard all over the theatre as the audience stampeded towards the exits. He stood motionless until the curtains swished together.

Fanya hurried to him. 'Harry,' she said, 'darling . . . that was so . . . marvellous! I can't tell you.' Rosenheim squeezed her hands without a word, too moved to speak, then left the stage. As he brushed past me I got a close-up of his face. It was pale, wrung-out, ecstatic. 'He really suffers,' Fanya said tearfully. 'When he plays, he gives his heart and soul.' She ran after him and disappeared into the dressing room.

There was nobody around, I advanced stealthily into the centre of the empty stage. 'Ladies and gentlemen, people of the world,' I said quietly in deep tones, gesturing towards the auditorium. Then, louder, '*Tzu sein odder nisht tzu sein*?' My voice went squeaky in the middle of a word. From pit to gallery empty rows of seats gave me their attentive silence. I felt as if at any moment a terrible eloquence would burst from my mouth and fill the whole city with resonance.

'I . . . am . . .' my voice began. 'I . . . am . . . am?' What? I would soon be fourteen. I wore glasses and had failed the scholarship. There was nothing to say.

Rosenheim's door stood slightly ajar. It was very quiet in there. A corner of the room, tilted at a crazy angle, was reflected in the dressing-table mirror and Fanya was drowning in the kisses of her red-haired Hamlet.

At home, the King, my father, was also dead, and his

usurper was in a bad mood. 'Where you been till twelve o'clock, eh? Eh?' he demanded. I pierced him with the glitter of my sword-sharp eyes.

The New York Yiddish Theatre ended its season and departed. I never saw Rosenheim again. The reason he couldn't take Fanya with him right away was because as soon as the actors returned to New York they would have to go on a tour of all the places in America where Jews lived. She begged him to take her along. After all, it was useful to have someone who was handy with the needle. But, no. Such a dog's life of travel, cheap boarding houses, draughty public halls, she should never experience, God forbid. Rosenheim wanted her to come to him like a princess. For this everything had to be made ready – a nice apartment, wall-to-wall carpets, a good air-conditioning so summer and winter would be always the same. Maybe, even, a coloured maid in a frilly apron. For his angel bride-to-be, nothing but the best. The whole of New York, America, the world, he would give to her – but it would take a little time, a little patience.

Fanya was disappointed for she only wanted Rosenhelm, not the world, but love gave her strength to wait. She brought round a postcard he sent from New York. Over the towers of Manhattan he had written in Yiddish. 'My love is bigger than the Empire State, tallest building in the whole earth, Your Harry.' From Chicago, at the back of a picture of Lake Shore Drive, were the words: 'I miss you, sweet angel, and my tears fill the lake.' The message from Pittsburgh was shorter. 'Thinking of you always.' There was a gap of some weeks, then a card from San Francisco. 'The *Examiner* writes "Rosenheim's Hamlet a triumph". Wish you were here to see.'

Next time Fanya came to tea she was wearing an old dress and her face without make-up looked as thin and hungry as when she first came to be an apprentice. My mother gazed at her keenly and led her into the bedroom. They talked in low voices, then Fanya rushed out and left, drowning in tears.

'Of course she's pregnant,' my mother muttered to Mrs

Benjamin next door. 'Anybody can see.' She leaned back in the chair, hands clasped over her own big belly.

Mrs Benjamin stared in horrified delight. 'Pregnant? From him? From the actor?'

'How else? From a wind in the stomach?'

Mrs Benjamin slapped herself on the cheek and rocked from side to side. 'Aie, aie, aie! Such a bandit, that Rosenheim. You should never trust a ginger, Rosa. In a ginger the blood boils like in a kettle. And when,' she added eagerly, 'is she expecting?'

'Tomorrow I'm taking her to see Fat Yetta.' Tears dripped from my mother's nose. She'd unsuccessfully visited Fat Yetta on a couple of occasions herself. 'Please God, it should work. That poor child is like my own daughter.'

Fat Yetta was at first reluctant to take the case, my mother told Mrs Benjamin the following day, when it was all over. She'd agreed to do so only out of pity for the plight of such a young girl. My mother got up heavily and closed the living-room door so that none of us should hear the shocking details. So, of course, we eavesdropped.

'It was terrible,' she said in an agonized whisper that penetrated the wall. 'A living child was torn from her body. Each finger nail was perfect. And the *neshumah*, the soul, was struggling to breathe. If I live to a hundred, I'll remember it all my life ...' There was a prolonged silence before she resumed speaking. 'It should be put in a coffin and sent to ... that murderer!' my mother declared in a terrible voice. She opened the door. 'Go out, children. Go out and play!'

When I came back in, Mrs Benjamin had left and the whole place was filled with the spicy aroma of boiling chicken. My mother filled a jar with soup and sealed the lid with wax paper. She told me to take it to Fanya.

It was one of those leaden Sunday afternoons in January. I carried the soup under my jacket against my breast and its warmth was the only comforting thing in a bleak walk along Brick Lane. Shreds of a poster advertising New York's brilliant Yiddish players still adhered to a board outside the Pavilion. The poster was still there months later when Fanya

Ziegelbaum moved up to Manchester where no one knew of her disgrace. Night times, passing under the railway arch, I thought how different it might have been had I been older, uncommonplace, enhanced by the glamour of strangeness.

Appelfeld intentionally does not mention the death camps b/c the absence of the horror to come is in + of itself the source of terror.

- by doing so he ~~is~~ also showing the lack of understanding for most Jews of what was to come or the denial of it
- is he also trying to universalize the terror

~~the camp~~

the irony ~~a~~ + contrast of the resort + what it becomes -- a detention camp

the trip to poland is seen almost as if it were a vacation or an expedition of the free will

- The rabbi is paralyzed
- auto-anti-semetism + (self-loathing) of Dr. Laguna, the baker + Prof. fussholt

Badenheim is portraying the blindness of denial present in Jews of that time

"The things that are most true are easily falsified." A. Appelfeld

Like Kafka he de-historicizes his story,
taking out any historical or political
Context. The historical focus must be supplied
by the reader, who have the knowledge of the
impending evil. Almost as if appelfeld telling his
story from a childs perspective

Aharon Appelfeld

BADENHEIM 1939
'Ir Nofesh'

Translated by Betsy Rosenberg

Trudy= cassandra, contemplates everything
through glass

react by blaming Austrian anti-semetism that
is caused
+
trust of leaders by Jews

sanitation department is
basically invisible, but this
is intentional b/c originally, according to
Appelfeld, no one was aware of the dept. but
the eventually evolve into a more powerful
organication

Aharon Appelfeld

AHARON APPELFELD was born in Czernovitz, now part of the Ukraine, in 1932. At the age of eight he was imprisoned in a concentration camp by the Nazis. He escaped after two years and joined the Russian army before moving to Israel in 1947. He has written eight novels, including *The Retreat* and *The Healer*, and has published six collections of short stories. He has won many literary prizes, most notably the prestigious Jerusalem Prize. He lives in Jerusalem.

BADENHEIM 1939

Spring returned to Badenheim. Bells rang in the near-by country church. The shadows of the forest drew back into the forest. The sun scattered the remaining darkness, and its light spilled out along the main street, from square to square. It was a moment of transition. Soon the holidaymakers would invade the town. Two inspectors passed from street to street, checking the flow of sewage in the drains. Over the years, the town had seen many tenants come and go but its modest beauty was still intact.

Trudy, the pharmacist's ailing wife, stood at the window. She looked about her with the feeble gaze of a chronic invalid. The beneficent sunlight touched her pallid face and she smiled. A difficult winter, a strange winter, had ended. Storms played havoc with the housetops. Rumours spread. Trudy's sleep was disturbed by hallucinations. She spoke incessantly of her married daughter, while Martin assured her that everything was all right. That was how the winter passed. Now she stood at the window, resurrected.

The low, well-kept houses looked tranquil once again. Islands of white in a green sea. This is the season when you hear nothing but the rustle of things growing and then, by chance, you catch sight of an old man holding a pair of pruning shears, with the look of a hungry raven.

'Has the post come?' asked Trudy.

'It's Monday today. The post won't arrive until afternoon.'

The carriage of Dr Pappenheim the impresario charged out of the forest and came to a halt on the main street. Dr Pappenheim alighted and waved in greeting. No one responded. The street was steeped in silence.

'Who's here?' asked Trudy.

'Dr Pappenheim has just arrived.'

Dr Pappenheim brings with him the moist breath of the big city, an air of celebration and anxiety. He'll be spending his time at the post office – sending off cables and express letters.

Apart from Dr Pappenheim's appearance in town, nothing has happened. The mild spring sunshine shone out as it does every year. People met at the café in the afternoon, and devoured pink ice-cream.

'Has the post come yet?' she asked again.

'Yes. There's nothing for us.'

'Nothing.' Her voice sounded ill.

Trudy got back into bed, feverish. Martin removed his jacket and sat down next to her: 'Don't worry. We had a letter just last week. Everything is all right.' Her hallucinations persisted: 'Why does he beat her?'

'No one beats her. Leopold is a very nice man, and he loves her. Why do you think such things?'

Trudy shut up as though she had been scolded. Martin was tired. He put his head on the pillow and fell asleep.

The first of the vacationers arrived on the following day. The pastry shop window was decorated with flowers. In the hotel garden Professor Fusshalt and his young wife were to be seen, also Dr Schutz and Frau Zauberblit – but to Trudy they looked more like convalescents in a sanatorium than people on vacation.

'Don't you know Professor Fusshalt?' asked Martin.

'They look very pale to me.'

'They're from the city,' said Martin, trying to mollify her. Now Martin knew that his wife was very ill. Medicines would be of no use. In her eyes the world was transparent, diseased and poisoned, her married daughter held captive and beaten. Martin tried in vain to convince her. She stopped listening. That night, Martin sat down to write a letter to Helena, his daughter. Spring in Badenheim is delightful, beautiful. The first vacationers are already here. But your mother misses you so.

Trudy's disease was gradually seeping into him. He, too, began to distinguish signs of pallor on people's faces. Everything at home had changed since Helena's marriage. For a year they had tried to dissuade her, but it was no use. She was in love, head over heels, as they say. A hasty marriage took place.

Dark green spring was now ascending from the gardens. Sally and Gerti, the local tarts, strolled along the boulevard dressed for the season. The townspeople had tried at one time to throw them out – a prolonged struggle that came to nought. The place had got used to them, as it had grown used to the eccentricities of Dr Pappenheim, and to the alien summer people who transplanted themselves here like an unhealthy root. The owner of the pastry shop would not let the 'ladies' set foot on his premises, thus depriving them of the most delicious cream cakes in the entire world. Boyish Dr Schutz, who liked Sally, once took some cakes out to the street. When the owner of the shop found out about it later, he made a scandal but that led nowhere either.

'And how are the young ladies?' asked Dr Pappenheim merrily.

Over the years they had lost their big city haughtiness – they had bought themselves a modest house, and dressed like the local women. There had been a period of riotous parties but the years and the courtesans of the town had pushed them aside. But for their savings, theirs would have been a sad predicament. They had nothing left but the memories which they mulled over like widows on long winter nights.

'How was it this year?'

'Everything is fine,' said Pappenheim cheerfully.

'Wasn't it a strange winter, though?'

They were fond of Pappenheim, and over the years they had become interested in his strange artistes. Here, in alien terrain, they grasped eagerly at anything whatsoever.

'Oh don't worry, don't worry – the festival is packed this year – lots of surprises.'

'Who will it be this time?'

'A child-prodigy, a *yanuka*. I discovered him this winter in Vienna.'

'*Yanuka*,' said Sally maternally.

Next day, the vacationers were all over Badenheim. The hotel bustled. Spring-sunlight and excited people filled the town, and, in the hotel garden, porters hauled the brightly coloured luggage. But Dr Pappenheim seemed to shrink in size. The festival schedule was ruined again. He ran through the streets. For years these artistes have been driving him mad, and now they want to wreck him altogether.

After leaving their luggage at the hotel, the people moved on towards the forest. Professor Fusshalt and his young wife were there. A tall man escorted Frau Zauberblit ceremoniously. 'Why don't we turn left?' said Frau Zauberblit, and the company did indeed turn to the left. Dr Schutz lagged behind as though enchanted.

'Why do they walk so slowly?' asked Trudy.

'They're on vacation, after all,' said Martin, patiently.

'Who is that man walking with Frau Zauberblit? Isn't that her brother?'

'No, my dear. Her brother is dead. He has been dead for years.'

That night the band arrived. Dr Pappenheim rejoiced as if a miracle had happened. The porters unloaded horns and drums. The musicians stood at the gate like trained birds on a stick. Dr Pappenheim offered sweets and chocolates. The driver hurried the porters on, and the musicians ate in silence. 'Why were you late?' asked Pappenheim, not without relief. 'The car was late,' they answered.

Dressed in a frock coat, the conductor stood aside, as if all this were no concern of his. He'd had a struggle with Pappenheim the year before. Pappenheim was on the verge of dismissing him, but the senior musicians sided with their conductor, and nothing came of it. The conductor had demanded a contract for the usual three-year period. The quarrel ended in a compromise.

In the past, Pappenheim had lodged them on the ground floor of the hotel, in dark, narrow rooms. There was an emphatic clause in the new contract providing for proper lodging. Now they were all anxious to see the rooms. Pappenheim walked over to the conductor and whispered in his ear: 'The rooms are ready – top floor – large well-ventilated rooms.' 'Sheets?' asked the conductor. 'Sheets as well.' Pappenheim kept his promise. They were lovely rooms. Seeing them, the musicians were inspired to change into their blue uniforms. Pappenheim stood quietly by and did not interfere. In one of the rooms a quarrel broke out – over a bed. The conductor chided them: 'Rooms like these deserve quiet. Now get everything together before you go down.'

At ten o'clock, all was ready. The musicians stood in groups of three, instruments in hand. Pappenheim was furious. He would gladly have paid them compensation and sent them packing, but he could not afford to. More than anything else, they reminded him of his failures. Thirty years gone by. Always late and unrehearsed. Their instruments produced nothing but noise. And every year, new demands.

The evening began. People swarmed over the band like hornets. The musicians blew and hammered as though trying to drive them away. Dr Pappenheim sat in the back drinking steadily.

Next day, the place was calm and quiet. Martin got up early, swept the entrance, wiped the dust off the shelves, and made out a detailed purchase order. It had been a hard night. Trudy had not stopped raving. She refused to take medicine, and finally Martin had tricked her into swallowing a sleeping mixture.

At approximately ten o'clock, an inspector from the Sanitation Department entered the pharmacy, and said that he wanted to look the place over. He asked strange questions. Ownership title. Had it come through inheritance? When and from whom was it purchased? Property value. Surprised, Martin explained that the place had been whitewashed and thoroughly disinfected. The inspector took out a folding yardstick, and measured. Then, neither thanking him nor apologizing, he went directly out into the street.

The visit made Martin angry. He believed in the authorities, and therefore he blamed himself. The back entrance was probably not in good enough repair. This short visit spoiled his morning. There was something in the wind. He went outside and stood on the lawn. A morning like any other. The milkman made his rounds bucolically, the musicians sprawled in the hotel garden sunning themselves, and Pappenheim left them alone. The conductor sat by himself shuffling a deck of cards. In the afternoon, Frau Zauberblit entered the pharmacy and announced that there is no place like Badenheim for a vacation. She was wearing a dotted poplin frock, but to Martin it seemed that her late brother was about to walk through the door.

'Isn't that strange?' he asked, not knowing what he was asking.

'Anything can happen,' she said as though she had understood the question.

Martin was angry. It was all because of Trudy.

The musicians stayed in the garden all afternoon. They looked pathetic out of uniform. For years they had been used to fighting with Pappenheim, now they fought among themselves. The conductor did not interfere. He set down his deck, and watched them. A gaunt musician took a pay receipt out of his vest pocket, and waved it at his colleagues. They showed him his mistake. From Martin's garden this looked like a shadow play, perhaps because the light was fading. One by one, long shadows unrolled across the green lawn.

At twilight, the conductor hinted that it might be advisable to go up and change into uniform. They took their time, like old soldiers worn out by long service. The conductor chatted with Pappenheim. For some reason, Pappenheim found it necessary to give a long-winded explanation of the festival programme. 'I hear Mandelbaum is on the programme too. Why, that's a spectacular achievement – how did you manage it?' 'Hard work,' said Pappenheim, and turned to go into the dining room. The guests were already eating hungrily. The waitress watched the kitchen door sharply. Her orders were late. But the cynical old waiters praised the food with an air of self-importance. Trudy's condition was no better. Martin's endless talk was futile. Everything seemed transparent and diseased to her. Helena was a prisoner on Leopold's estate, and when he comes home from the barracks at night, he beats her.

'But don't you see?' she asked.

'No, I don't see.'

'It's only my hallucinations.'

Martin was angry. Trudy frequently mentioned her parents, the little house on the banks of the Vistula. The parents died and all contact with the brothers was lost. Martin said that she was still immersed in that world, in the mountains, with the Jews. And this was, to a certain extent, the truth. She was tortured by a hidden fear, not her own, and Martin felt that her delusions were gradually penetrating into him, and that everything was on the verge of collapse.

Next day it was made known that the jurisdiction of the Department of Sanitation had been extended, and henceforth the Department would be entitled to carry out independent investigations. The modest announcement was posted on the town bulletin board. Without further ado, the clerks of the Department set about investigating all places designated on their map. The detailed investigations were carried out by means of questionnaires sent in from the district head office. One of the musicians, who bore his Polish name with a strange pride, remarked that the clerks reminded him of marionettes. His name was Leon Semitzki. Fifty years ago he had emigrated from Poland with his parents. He had a fondness for his Polish memories, and when in good spirits he would talk about his country. Dr Pappenheim liked his stories and he would sit with the musicians and listen.

The clouds vanished, and the spring sun shone warmly. A vague anxiety spread over the faces of the old musicians. They sat together and said nothing. Semitzki broke the silence all of a sudden: 'I'm homesick for Poland.' 'Why?' Pappenheim wanted to know. 'I don't know,' said Semitzki, 'I was only seven years old when I left, but it seems like only a year ago.'

'They're very poor there,' someone whispered.

'Poor, but not afraid of death.'

That night, nothing happened in Badenheim. Dr Pappenheim was melancholic. He could not get Semitzki off his mind. He too recalled those rare visits to Vienna of his grandmother from the Carpathians. She was a big woman, and brought with her the odour of millet, the smell of the forest. Pappenheim's father hated his mother-in-law. Rumours flourished. Some said that the Department was on the track of a sanitary hazard, others thought that this time it might be the Tax Department masquerading as the Sanitation Department. The musicians exchanged views. The town itself was calm, co-operative, complying with all the Department's requests. Even the proud owner of the pastry shop agreed to give information. There was nothing noticeably different, but the old musicians surveyed the town, imparting a strange unease.

At the end of April, the two reciters showed up. Dr Pappenheim wore his blue suit in their honour. They were tall and gaunt with an intensely spiritual look. Their passion was Rilke. Dr Pappenheim, who had discovered them in Vienna seven years before, at once discerned a morbid melody in their voices which enchanted him. Thereafter, he simply could not do without them. At first their recitals drew no response, but in recent years people had discovered their elusive melody – and found it intoxicating. Frau Zauberblit sighed with relief: They're here.

The reciters were twin brothers who, over the years, had become indistinguishable. But their manner of reading was not the same – as if sickness spoke with two voices; one tender and appeasing, the remains of a voice, the other clear and sharp. Frau Zauberblit declared that without the double voice, life would be meaningless. Their recitals were balm to her, and she would murmur Rilke to herself in the empty nights of spring, as though sipping pure nectar.

The musicians, who worked at dance halls in the winter and resorts in the summer, could not understand what people found in those morbid voices. In vain did Pappenheim try to explain the magic. Only Semitzki said that their voices excited his diseased cells. The conductor hated them – he called them the clowns of the modern age.

And meanwhile spring is at work. Dr Schutz pines after the schoolgirl like an adolescent. Frau Zauberblit is engrossed in conversation with Semitzki, and Professor Fusshalt's young wife changes into her bathing costume, and goes out to sunbathe on the lawn.

The twins are forever rehearsing. They can't do without the practice. 'And I was naïve enough to think that it was all spontaneous,' said Frau Zauberblit.

'Practising, practising,' said Semitzki. 'If I had practised when I was young I never would have ended up in this second rate outfit. I wasn't born here. I was born in Poland. And my parents didn't give me a musical education.' After midnight, Dr Pappenheim received a cable, worded as follows: 'Mandelbaum taken ill. Will not arrive on time.' Dr Pappenheim got up shaking and said: 'This is a catastrophe.' 'Mandelbaum,' said Frau Zauberblit. 'The entire arts' festival is at stake,' said Pappenheim. Semitzki tried to soothe them, but Pappenheim said, 'This is the last straw.' He sank into his grief like a stone. Frau Zauberblit brought out a bottle of Pappenheim's favourite French wine, but he wouldn't touch it, and all night long he moaned: 'Mandelbaum, Mandelbaum.'

And the investigations showed reality for what it was. From this point on, no one could say that the Department of Sanitation was ineffective. A feeling of strangeness, suspicion and mistrust was in the air; still, the residents went about their usual business. The vacationers had their pastimes, and the local residents had their worries. Dr Pappenheim was inconsolable over his great loss – Mandelbaum. Life was worthless since that cable had arrived. Professor Fusshalt's young wife declared that something had changed in Badenheim. The Professor did not leave the room – his definitive book was about to go to the publisher, and he was busy with the proofs. His young wife, whom he spoiled like a kitten, understood nothing about his books. Her interests were confined to cosmetics and dresses. At the hotel they called her Mitzi.

In the middle of May, a modest announcement appeared on the bulletin board, stating that all Jewish citizens must register with the Sanitation Department before the month was out.

'That's me,' said Semitzki. He seemed to be delighted.

'And me,' said Pappenheim. 'You wouldn't want to deprive me of my Jewishness, would you?'

'I would,' said Semitzki, 'But your nose is proof enough that you are no Austrian.'

The conductor, who had learned over the years to blame everything on Pappenheim, said: 'I have to get caught up in this bureaucratic mess all because of him. The clerks have gone mad, and I'm the one who suffers.'

People started avoiding Pappenheim like the plague. He seemed not to notice, and rushed back and forth between the post office and the hotel.

Trudy's condition worsened the last two weeks. She talked on and on about death. No longer out of fear – but rather as if she were coming to know it, preparing to inhabit it. The strong medications that she swallowed drew her from one sleep to the next, and Martin saw her wandering off into the other regions of her life.

People confessed to each other, as if they were talking about a chronic disease which there was no longer any reason to hide. And their reactions varied – pride and shame. Frau Zauberblit avoided talking and asking questions. She pointedly ignored them. Finally she asked Semitzki: 'Have you registered?'

'Not yet,' said Semitzki. 'I'll do it on a more festive occasion. You don't mean to say that I have the honour of addressing an Austrian citizen of Jewish origin?'

'You have indeed, sir.'

'In that case, we'll be having a family party in the near future.'

'Could you have thought otherwise?'

The sun stopped shining. The headwaiter himself served the white cherries for the cake. The lilac bushes climbed the veranda railing, and bees sucked greedily at the light blue flowers. Frau Zauberblit tied a silk scarf around her straw bonnet. 'Brought in from Waldenheim this morning – they ripened early.' 'That's simply marvellous,' said Frau Zauberblit. She adored these local voices.

'What are you thinking about?' asked Semitzki.

'I was remembering my grandfather's house – the rabbi from Kirchenhaus. He was a man of God. I spent my term

Life vs. Death =
Growth

vacations there. He used to walk along the river in the *J-Wien*
evenings. He liked growing things.' Semitzki did not stop *vs.*
drinking: 'Don't worry, children. Soon we'll be on our way. *≠ fall*
Just think – back to Poland.' *+ death*

Dr Schutz runs about in a stupor. The schoolgirl is driving
him mad: 'Dr Schutz, why not join intelligent company for
an intelligent conversation?' said Frau Zauberblit. In academic
circles, he was considered quite the prodigy – if a bit naughty.

'Have you registered?' said Semitzki.

'What?' he asked in surprise.

'Oh, you have to register, haven't you heard? According
to the regulations of the Sanitation Department – which is,
of course, a Government Department, a fine Department, a
Department whose jurisdiction has been extended these last
two months. And this most worthy Department earnestly
desires that you, Dr Schutz, should register.'

'This is no laughing matter, my dear,' said Frau Zauberblit.

'In that case,' he said, confused. He was the pampered *he*
darling of Badenheim. Everyone loved him. Dr Pappenheim *is*
lamented his wasted musical talent. The prodigal son of his *not worried*
rich old mother, who never failed to bail him out at the end of
the season.

A vague terror lurked in the eyes of the musicians. 'Don't
worry,' said Dr Pappenheim, rallying his courage, though he
was feeling melancholy. 'But aren't we guests? Must we sign
as well?' asked one of the musicians.

'It is my opinion,' said Pappenheim dramatically, 'that the
Sanitation Department wishes to boast of its distinguished
guests, and will, therefore, enter them in the Golden Book. *God's*
Now that is nice of them – don't you think?' *book of life*

'Maybe it's because of the *Ostjuden*,' said one of the
musicians. *they blame it on the Ostjuden*

Semitzki rose to his feet: 'What's the matter? You don't
like me? I'm an Eastern Jew through and through – so you
don't like me, eh?'

Badenheim's intoxicating spring was causing havoc again.
Dr Schutz was penniless, and he posted two express letters to

his mother. The schoolgirl, it seems, was costing him a
fortune. Frau Zauberblit and Semitzki sit together all day
long. He might have been the only man left in the world.
Dr Pappenheim is depressed – the intoxicating spring never
fails to make him sad. Frau Zauberblit already rebuked him:
'I'll defray the losses. Hand me the bill. If Mandelbaum
continues to give you the run around, I'll get the Krauss
chamber ensemble.' The twins wander through town looking
cryptic. People at the hotel talk about them in whispers, as if
they were sick. They eat nothing, and only drink coffee. The
headwaiter said: 'If only I could serve Rilke's death sonnets
maybe they would eat. That's probably all the food they can
digest.'

After breakfast, Frau Zauberblit, Semitzki and Pappenheim
decided unanimously to register at the Sanitation Department.
The clerk did not so much as raise an eyebrow at Frau
Zauberblit's declarations. Frau Zauberblit praised the Department for its order and beauty. No wonder it had been
promoted. Semitzki announced that his parents had come from
Poland fifty years ago, and that he was still homesick. The
clerk wrote all this down without a trace of expression.

That night Semitzki did not wear his blue uniform. The
band played. Everyone saw at a glance that Frau Zauberblit
had a sweetheart – she glowed like someone in love. The young
wife of Professor Fusshalt is going mad. Professor Fusshalt is
preoccupied with the book, and he doesn't leave his desk.
She's fed up with the people in Badenheim. What is there to
do here? Those readings again. They depress her. One of the
musicians, a cynic, tried to console her: 'Don't be angry. In
Poland, everything is beautiful, everything is interesting.'

On the following day Trudy's screams were heard in the
street. From the hotel veranda, people watched the terrible
struggle in progress. No one went down to help. Poor
Martin fell on his knees in desperation, and begged: 'Trudy,
Trudy, be calm. There is no forest here – there are no wolves.'
An alien night descended on Badenheim. The cafés were
empty, people walked the streets in silence, as though being
led along. The town seemed in the grip of some other vacation,

from another place. Dr Schutz led the tall schoolgirl about as
though he were going to tie her up. Sally and Gerti strolled,
arm in arm like schoolgirls. The moist light of spring nights
slithered on the pavement. The musicians sat on the veranda,
observing the passing flow with sharp looks.

Dr Pappenheim sat in the corner alone, reckoning sadly:
The trio has deserted me again. Nobody will forgive me. And
rightly so. Had I known, I would have planned it differently.

6

The deadline for registration was approaching. Three
investigators from the district office arrived at the Sanitation
Department. The conductor carried an interesting document
in his vest pocket – his parents' baptismal certificates. Dr
Pappenheim was taken aback, and he said: 'I would not have
believed it.' Strange, the conductor wasn't pleased.

'You're welcome to join the Jewish order, if you like. It's a
fine old order,' said Pappenheim.

'I don't believe in religion.'

'You can be a Jew without religion, if you like.'

'Who said so – the Sanitation Department?'

It poured that afternoon. They gathered in the lobby, and
were served hot wine as on autumn days. Dr Pappenheim was
deep in a chess game with Semitzki. Towards evening, Frau
Zauberblit's daughter arrived. From her father, General Von
Schmidt, she had inherited an erect carriage, blonde hair, pink
cheeks, and a deep voice. She was a student at a lyceum for
girls, far away from her mother.

General Von Schmidt is still remembered here. They came
to Badenheim the first year of their marriage, but Von Schmidt
had hated it there, and called it Pappenheim, after the
impresario. As far as he was concerned, it was no fit place for
healthy people – no horses, no tennis, no hunting – no beer!
They stopped coming after that and were gradually forgotten.
They had a daughter. Years went by, and Von Schmidt, who
had started his career as a lieutenant, rose through the ranks.
Soon after, they were divorced. After the divorce, Frau
Zauberblit, tall, slender, and suffering, appeared in Badenheim.
That was the end of the matter.

The daughter stated at once that she had brought a document, a statement surrendering the so-called 'rights of the mother'. Frau Zauberblit studied the document and asked: 'Is this what *you* wish?' 'What my father wishes, and what I wish,' she said like someone who had learnt a part. Frau Zauberblit signed. It was a hard and abrupt farewell. 'Excuse me, I'm in a hurry,' she said on her way out. The daughter's appearance shook the hotel. Frau Zauberblit sat mutely in the corner. A strange new pride seemed to show on her face.

Throughout the hotel, a secret was uniting the people. The conductor felt ill at ease for some reason, and sat down with the musicians. The twins were to perform that night. The proprietor of the hotel was arranging the small auditorium. They haven't been seen on the veranda for two days now. Cloistered. 'What do they do up there?' someone asked, and the headwaiter confirmed the fact that they had eaten nothing for two days. The people were standing by the windows, with the fading light on their faces. Pappenheim whispered, 'They're rehearsing, aren't they wonderful?'

The silence of a house of prayer filled the small auditorium that evening. The audience was early, and Pappenheim darted back and forth between the doors as if that would make the twins come down before it was time. They came down precisely at eight o'clock, and took their place by the table. Pappenheim retreated towards the door, like a guard.

For two hours, they talked about death. They spoke in a calm, modulated voice, as if they had returned from Hell and were no longer afraid. At the end of the recital, they stood up. The people bowed their heads and did not applaud. Pappenheim moved forward and took off his hat. He seemed about to fall on his knees.

Apple strudel was served in the afternoon. Frau Zauberblit had on her straw bonnet. Semitzki wore short trousers, and Pappenheim stood at the door like an unemployed actor. It seemed as if the old days were back.

At midnight, the *yanuka* arrived. The watchman refused to let him pass, because he was not on the lists. And Dr Pappenheim, who was amused, said: 'But can't you see that he's Jewish?' When she heard, Frau Zauberblit said: 'Everything is going according to plan. Isn't that wonderful?'

'You'll love him too,' Pappenheim whispered.

'The impresario is a man of his word. By the way – in what language will the young artiste sing?'

'Why – Yiddish of course – he'll sing in Yiddish.'

When Pappenheim presented him, they saw before them neither a child nor a man. He blushed, his suit was too long. 'What's your name?' asked Frau Zauberblit drawing near. 'His name is Nahum Slotzker – and speak slowly,' Pappenheim interrupted, 'he doesn't understand German.' Now they saw wrinkles around the eyes, but the face was the face of a child. The adults were confusing him.

'Where are you from – Lodz?' asked Semitzki in Polish.

The boy smiled and said: 'From Kalashin.'

It was a strange evening. Frau Zauberblit was like an amorous young girl. Semitzki paced the corridor like a retired gym instructor. The conductor shuffled cards and joked with the cook. The cook gave him freshly baked poppyseed cakes. She was of mixed parentage. Orphaned at an early age, she had been for several years the mistress of Graf Schutzheim, until his death.

'Do you think they'll let me come too?' she asked slyly.

'There's no question about it. Who will cook for us in the land of cold?'

'But I'm not wholly Jewish.'

'Well I'm not wholly anything.'

'But your parents were both Jews, weren't they?'

'Yes, my dear, Jews by birth, but they converted to Christianity.'

Next day, the patroness of the twins arrived in town. Frau Milbaum was tall and elegant, and she had an aura of majesty. Dr Pappenheim was extremely glad to see her. He was always glad to see people returning to Badenheim.

The secret surrounds them little by little, a dread born of other intimations. They tread lightly, and speak in whispers. The waiters served strawberries and cream. The frenzied shadow of summer is spread out on the broad veranda. The twins sat beside Frau Milbaum, flushed and silent. They look like children in a roomful of adults. Pappenheim has planned a full programme, and there is a strange sense of anticipation in the air. The old people die between one interrogation and the next. The town swims in alcoholic fumes. Last night at the cafe, Herr Furst fell down and died. For years he had passed through the streets in his magnificent clothes. Next door at the lottery house, another man died by the roulette table. Sometimes it seems not to be the alcohol but a freshness not from the near-by forests.

And the interrogations proceed quietly at the Sanitation Department. This is the centre, and all the strands radiate from it. The Department is now omniscient. They have maps, periodicals, a library – a person can sit and browse if he wishes. The conductor registered at the Department and came back smiling. They showed him a closetful of contracts, licences, and credentials. Strange – his father was the author of an arithmetic book in Hebrew. 'They know everything, and they're happy to show a man his past,' said the conductor.

A barrier was erected at the town gate. No entrance, no exit. But it was not a total blockade. The milkmen delivered milk in the morning and the fruit truck unloaded its crates at the hotel. Both cafés are open, and the band plays every evening. Yet it seems that another time, from another place, has broken through and is quietly entrenching itself.

The banquet given for the *yanuka*, the child prodigy, began late. The guests filed through the corridor, lamplight on their faces. There were soft woolly shadows on the carpet. The waiters served ice-cream in coffee. The tables were being laid in the hall. A few musicians played to themselves in the corner. Tongues of darkness climbed the long narrow windows.

Frau Milbaum sat on her throne, and green lights flashed from her green eyes. People avoided her look. 'Where are my twins?' she asked in an undertone. No one answered. They seemed caught in a net. The twins were talking to Sally. Sally, in a long, flowered dress, was making faces like a concert singer. The twins, who seldom conversed with women, were embarrassed, and started to laugh.

Sally told them about the first festivals. Gerti appeared and said. 'You're here.' 'Please meet two real gentlemen,' said Sally. The twins offered their long white hands. The *yanuka* sat mutely in the corner. Dr Pappenheim explained in broken Yiddish that the banquet was about to begin. Everyone was anxious to hear him sing.

The guests drank heavily. Frau Milbaum sat enthroned, and now there was venom in her green eyes. So here, too, her life was becoming involved. She thought that there was a plot against her. That morning she had registered at the Sanitation Department. The clerk did not take her titles into account, the ones bequeathed her by her first husband; and he did not so much as mention her second husband, a nobleman of the royal family. There was nothing on the form but her father's name.

Semitzki was chattering away gaily in faulty Polish. He turned good-naturedly to Frau Milbaum, and said: 'Come and join our jolly circle. You'll find it amusing, I believe.' Her look was metallic. 'I am obliged,' she said.

'A fine society – Jewish nobility,' Semitzki was relentless.

'I understand,' she said without looking.

'We would be delighted to have the lady's company,' Semitzki continued to pique her.

'Don't worry, the Duchess will get used to us,' whispered Zimbelmann the musician.

'She registered, didn't she? What's all this distance about?' added someone from the corner.

Frau Milbaum scanned them with her green eyes. 'Riffraff,' she finally spat out the word.

'She calls us riffraff,' said Zimbelmann, 'riffraff she calls us.'

The waiters served cheese wedges and Bordeaux wine. Dr Pappenheim sat with the *yanuka*. 'There's nothing to fear. These are all very nice people. You'll stand on the stage, and sing,' he said, trying to encourage the boy.

'I'm afraid.'

'Don't be afraid. They're very nice people.'

The conductor emptied one glass after another. His face was turning red. 'We're going to your native land, Semitzki. We must learn to drink.'

'They drink real alcohol there – not beer soup.'

'What will they do with a goy like me?'

'Don't worry, they'll only circumcise you,' said Zimbelmann, but felt he had gone too far. 'Don't worry. The Jews aren't barbarians for all that.'

Dr Langmann approached the duchess and said: 'I'm getting out of here tomorrow.'

'But aren't you registered at the Sanitation Department?'

'I still consider myself a free citizen of Austria. They have to send the Polish Jews to Poland. That's the country for them. I'm here by mistake. One is entitled to a mistake, now and then, isn't one? You're also here by mistake. Are we to forfeit our freedom on account of a mistake?'

Now she scrutinized Sally and Gerti as they led the twins into a corner. 'Whores,' she glowered at them. The twins were greatly amused and as gay as two boys stumbling upon a wild party.

After midnight, they set the boy on stage. He trembled. Dr Pappenheim stood over him like a father. The boy sang about the dark forest, the haunt of the wolf. It was a kind of lullaby. Seated around the stage, the musicians stared dumbly. The world was collapsing before their very eyes. Someone said, 'How wonderful!' Semitzki sobbed drunkenly. Frau Zauberblit approached him and asked: 'What happened?'

At that moment, Sally felt an oppressive fear. 'Dr Pappenheim, may we go as well? Is there room for us?'

'What a question,' he scowled at her, 'There is room in our kingdom for every Jew and for everyone who wants to be a Jew. It is a mighty kingdom.'

'I'm afraid.'

'No need to fear, my dear, we'll all be going soon.'

Gerti stood aside as though she had no right to ask questions.

The town is empty. The light no longer flowed. It seemed to

have frozen, listening intently. An alien orange shadow nibbled stealthily at the geranium leaves. Bitter damp seeped into the thatch of the creeping vines. Pappenheim worries about the musicians. He treats them to chocolate, cream cake. Such kindness makes them submissive. No more quarrels. Now the light filters through the thick drapery and illuminates the wide veranda. Dr Schutz's love is not so easy as in days gone by. The orange shadow lingers upon him and his beloved. The high-schoolgirl burrows ever more deeply into his summer coat, as though afraid of a sudden parting.

The post office is shut down. A cold light falls on the smooth marble stairs. The gate with its Gothic relief conjures up a memorial in ruins. The night before, Pappenheim stood outside the post office and laughed, 'Everything is closed.'

As Pappenheim stood laughing on the stairs of the post office, a terrible struggle was in progress at the pharmacy. Two men from out of town grabbed the poison chest. Martin fought them, snatched the jars from their hands, and shouted after them, 'I will not permit this.' These two skeletal men had arrived a few days before. Their faces were cold with desperation.

[handwritten margin note: they were trying to kill themselves]

Mandelbaum and his trio arrived like thieves in the night. Pappenheim took them downstairs, and brought tea.

'What happened?'

'We got a transfer,' said Mandelbaum.

'Did you ask for it?'

'Of course we asked for it. A young man, a junior officer, has already sent on the documents. We told him that we had to get to the festival. He laughed, and he gave us a transfer. What do you say? We're in for it.'

'That's wonderful,' said Pappenheim. 'Oh, I can't believe it. You need to rest.'

'No, dear friend. That's not why we're here. We didn't have a chance to prepare anything. We have to rehearse.'

The tin sun was fixed on the cold horizon. 'How far is it from here to Vienna?' asked someone adrift in his own limp thoughts. 'I'd say – two hundred kilometres, no more.' These words hung in the air like tired ravens. The old favourite, apple strudel, was baking down in the kitchen. The sweet smell wafted on to the veranda.

'Why don't we ask for a visa?' said a musician who had travelled in his youth.

'Say you had a visa – where would you go?' The man was struck dumb by the question. The conductor put his card down and said: 'As for me, I'm willing to go anywhere.'

Martin took the winter clothes out of storage, and the house smelled of naphthaline. The dream of Poland calmed Trudy. Martin sits down and assures her, 'In Poland, everything will be right. That's where we came from, and that's where we're bound. Those who were there have got to go back.' There's music in his voice – Trudy listens and doesn't ask questions.

A group of angry people stood by the dead phone cursing the bureaucracy that, suddenly and without warning, had cut them off from their loved ones. Order, they grumbled, order. An energetic few wrote long letters of complaint. They described all the hardships that came from being disconnected. They claimed compensation from their travel agents, from all the authorities responsible for their being here. Of course, this was all futile. All telephone lines were disconnected, the post office was shut down. Domestic servants fled as if from a fire. The town began to live in a state of siege.

'What will they do to us in Poland?' asked one of the musicians.

'What do you mean? You'll be a musician as you've always been,' answered a friend who dozed near by.

'Then why all this moving around?'

'The force of circumstance,' was the reply.

'Kill me, I don't understand. My common sense doesn't grasp it.

'In that case, kill your common sense and you'll start to understand.'

Silence enveloped the houses. The withered vines grew wild. The acacia flourished. It was autumn and spring in a strange coupling. At night there is no air to breathe. Semitzki is on the bottle. He drinks like a peasant, mixes Polish and

Yiddish. Of all his languages, the language of his childhood seems to be the only one left.

'Why are you drinking so much, dear?' asks Frau Zauberblit tenderly.

'When a man goes home he ought to be happy.'

'It's cold there, really cold.'

'Yes, but it's a pure, healthy cold, a cold with hope.'

The registrations were over. The clerks at the Sanitation Department sit around, drinking tea. They've done their duty. Now they await orders.

But surprises never cease in the streets. Several days ago, a resident of Badenheim, who had been a major in the Great War, stood near the post office, and demanded to know why it was closed. Pappenheim, who had not given up his habit of a daily visit to the closed post office, answered, perhaps incautiously, that the town was cut off.

'I don't understand,' said the major, 'Is there a plague?'

'A Jewish plague.'

'Are you trying to make fun of me?'

'No, I'm not. Try leaving.' Turning his head with the narrow, metallic gaze that was used to scanning maps and fields, the major now focussed on the short figure of Dr Pappenheim, and seemed about to reprimand him and send him away.

'Haven't you registered at the Sanitation Department?' Pappenheim continued to harass him.

For two days, he fought the Department. He cursed the Jews and he cursed the bureaucracy. He terrorized the deserted streets of town. Finally, he shot himself in the head. Dr Langmann, who never left the window, said to himself: You must admit, the Jews are an ugly people. I find them useless.

Just then, the conductor put down his cards and asked: 'Do you remember anything from home?'

'Which home?' asked Blumenthal the musician, a simple man whose life was a prolonged yawn. The conductor used to taunt him in the early days, but it was no use, he was wrapped up in his doze.

'From your Jewish home.'

'Nothing.'

'My parents converted, damn it.'

'Then forget everything and go back to Vienna.'

'My friend, I am in good standing at the Sanitation Department.'

'What do they want of us?'

'It's hard to say,' said the conductor as though faced with a difficult musical score. 'If there's truth in those rumours that we're going to Poland, then we'd better start learning. I don't know a thing.'

'At our age, we're a little rusty in the head, wouldn't you say?'

'There's no choice. We'll have to learn Polish.'

'Is that how you imagine it.'

Grey days stretched across the town. Meals were no longer being served at the hotel. People queued by the serving hatch for dinner, barley soup and dry bread. The musicians opened their bags. A whiff of dead leaves and of draughty roads blew down the long corridors.

Suddenly, the old rabbi appeared in the street. Many years ago they'd brought him to Badenheim from the east. He had served as rabbi of the local synagogue, which was in fact an old-age home, until the last members had died, leaving the place empty. The rabbi had been stricken with paralysis. It was generally believed that he passed away with the others.

The proprietor of the hotel stood at the entrance and said, 'Won't you come in, sir?' – more like a doorman than the proprietor of a hotel. Two musicians lifted the wheel-chair. The rabbi shaded his eyes, and a blue vein throbbed on his white forehead.

'Jews?' asked the rabbi.

'Jews,' said the proprietor.

'And who is your rabbi?'

'You are. You are our rabbi.'

The rabbi's face expressed some astonishment. His feeble memory tried to discover if they were playing with him.

'Perhaps you will allow us to serve you a drink?'

The rabbi frowned: 'Kosher?'

The proprietor lowered his eyes and did not answer. *the proprietor is ashamed that everyone is Jewish but that they don't keep Kosher*

'Everyone here is Jewish?' the rabbi recovered. There was a sudden gleam of cunning in his eyes.

'Everyone, I believe.'

'And what do you do?'

'Nothing,' said the proprietor of the hotel, and smiled. Semitzki rushed to his aid, 'We're planning to go back to Poland.'

'What?' said the rabbi, straining to hear.

'To go back to Poland,' repeated Semitzki.

The riddle was partially solved the next day. A kindly Christian woman had nursed him all these years, then a few days before she suddenly abandoned the house. After days of trying to manipulate the wheel-chair, the rabbi had finally succeeded.

The rabbi poses questions, and the people answer him. Many years of isolation made him forget the language, and he speaks Yiddish sprinkled with the Holy Tongue. Some musicians appeared in the doorway carrying luggage. 'Who are they?' asked the rabbi.

'Musicians.'

'Are they going to play?'

'No, they want to go home, but the roads are barricaded.'

'Let them spend the Sabbath with us.'

'What did he say?' asked the astonished musicians. *They are Jews but*

The autumnal light, the tin light governs the town these days. The proprietor stands in the kitchen like one of the *don't* servants and ladles out soup. Supplies are not delivered. *celebrate* Provisions are running low. The dining room is like a soup-*the Sabbath* kitchen. Long shadows crawl on the tables at night. There is a faltering look in the eyes of the musicians. A few days ago they were still grumbling. Now, their hopes are dashed. They comprehend: there is no going back. Pappenheim's optimism has also dissolved, the owner of the pastry shops shakes a fist at the hotel, or, more accurately, at Pappenheim, whom he threatens to murder.

'What does the rabbi say?' asked Frau Zauberblit.

'He's sleeping,' whispered the proprietor.

The musicians took no pity on the hotel and stuffed their bags with crockery and silverware. Semitzki took them to task: 'What for? No one uses fancy dishes in Poland.' 'What harm are we doing?' said one of them like an amateur thief. 'If we come back, we'll return it.'

The fleshy vines steal inside now, and spread over the veranda. This is their last burst of growth before winter. The forsaken chairs stand oafishly in place. A thick shadow nests inside the geranium pot. The flowers redden like rotten beets.

'What ever happened to the major?' asked someone.

'He killed himself.'

By the shuttered windows of the pastry shop stands Bertha Stummglanz. They brought her here last night. Her parents died some years before, and the house was transferred to the local council.

'Do you remember me?' asked Sally.

'I think I do, I think we were schoolmates.'

'No, dear. My name is Sally and this is Gerti.'

'Oh, I've made a mistake then, haven't I?' said Bertha apologetically.

'My name is Sally and this is Gerti.'

Bertha could not remember. Her memory was evidently deserting her. Her eyes wandered aimlessly.

'Why is everything closed?'

'The town is being transferred. Dr Pappenheim says that everything is going to Poland, including us.'

'Dr Pappenheim?'

'The impresario, don't you remember him?'

Strangers are brought in from the gate. Dr Pappenheim stands at the entrance of the hotel like a doorman.

'Why did you come here?' someone asked.

'They were born here, so they had to come back.'

'It's a fine place,' Dr Pappenheim interjects. 'Mandelbaum is with us, the twins are with us.'

'The twins? Who are the twins?'

'Where are you from, Jews?' asked the rabbi. An ancient grief glazed his eyes.

'This is our rabbi,' says Pappenheim proudly, 'A real one of the old school.'

The rabbi's questions never stop. The proprietor wears a skullcap, and serves him cold water.

No end to surprises. Last night, Helena came home. Her husband the lieutenant threw her off the estate. She has the face of her ailing mother. Incredulous, Trudy stroked her hands like a blind woman. Martin was drunk with joy. 'Now we can go. Together we can go anywhere.'

Every day brings more newcomers, descendants of former Badenheimers. The town's curse had pursued them all these years, and now they were caught. Dr Pappenheim received a letter from the Sanitation Department, instructing him to put his articles at its disposal. Pappenheim rejoiced – a grand tour awaits us!

Autumn turned to dust. The wind growled in the empty streets. Mandelbaum tortures the trio, polishes the music. The twins are cloistered again. An air of gravity pervades the hotel. Pappenheim walks on tiptoe, saying, 'Hush, hush, you're disturbing the sound.' The musicians quietly nibble their bread. 'Practice won't do us any good. It's too late now for what you didn't accomplish when you were young.' Pappenheim comforts them: 'In the new place, there'll be time, you'll be able to practise. Where there's a will there's a way.' He himself plans to take up research.

Dr Pappenheim makes continuing efforts to talk to the owner of the pastry shop. 'Why be angry with us? What have we done? We haven't committed a crime, after all. Tell us what our crime is. In Poland, you can open up a bigger shop. A person has to broaden his horizons.' Wasted words. The owner of the shop stands at the window, raving: 'If it weren't for this hotel, if it weren't for the corruption, they wouldn't have closed the town. It's all because of Pappenheim. He ought to be arrested.' He only stops at night.

Mandelbaum looks happier. The trio is inspiring him. He is getting new tones from his violin.

'When do we set off?' he asks Pappenheim, the way he used to ask his agent.

'Soon,' says Pappenheim like the bearer of a secret.

'We're improving, we're improving.'

It poured on Saturday night. The rabbi prayed loudly. People hugged the walls like shadows. The proprietor brought wine and candles, and the rabbi performed the Havdala service.

Immediately after the Havdala, the musicians went off to pack. The bags were big and swollen. Dr Pappenheim was surprised at the commotion, and said, 'I'm going like this – empty-handed. If they want me, they'll take me like this – empty-handed.'

The next day was bright and cold. Mandelbaum rose early and stood with the trio on the smooth steps of the hotel. The rehearsals had left their mark. His distinguished brow had turned white. Semitzki escorted Frau Zauberblit with a cumbersome elegance. Professor Fusshalt stood in his bath-robe as if he'd been shaken out of a fitful sleep: 'The proofs, what will happen to the proofs?' Zimbelmann the musician wrapped the rabbi in two velvet blankets and put him in his wheel-chair. The proprietor said: 'What must we bring?' 'Nothing, don't worry,' said Pappenheim. By the old ornamented gate, the clerk called the roll. The people answered their names as at a morning parade. A long journey stretched before them. At the familiar railway station there stood a hissing engine with many empty carriages. No one pushed. No one cried.

Dan Jacobson

THE ZULU AND THE ZEIDE

Dan Jacobson

DAN JACOBSON was born in South Africa in 1929, spent a year on a kibbutz and settled in London in his early twenties. Among his novels are *A Dance in the Sun*, *The Evidence of Love* and *The Confessions of Josef Baisz*. He has won many literary prizes including the W. Somerset Maugham Award and the J. R. Ackerley Award for his autobiography *Time and Time Again*.

THE ZULU AND THE ZEIDE

OLD man Grossman was worse than a nuisance. He was a source of constant anxiety and irritation; he was a menace to himself and to the passing motorists into whose path he would step, to the children in the streets whose games he would break up, sending them flying, to the householders who at night would approach him with clubs in their hands, fearing him a burglar; he was a butt and a jest to the African servants who would tease him on street corners.

It was impossible to keep him in the house. He would take any opportunity to slip out – a door left open meant that he was on the streets, a window unlatched was a challenge to his agility, a walk in the park was as much a game of hide-and-seek as a walk. The old man's health was good, physically; he was quite spry, and he could walk far, and he could jump and duck if he had to. And all his physical activity was put to only one purpose: to running away. It was a passion for freedom that the old man might have been said to have, could anyone have seen what joy there could have been for him in wandering aimlessly about the streets, in sitting footsore on pavements, in entering other people's homes, in stumbling behind advertisement hoardings across undeveloped building plots, in toiling up the stairs of fifteen-storey blocks of flats in which he had no business, in being brought home by large young policemen who winked at Harry Grossman, the old man's son, as they gently hauled his father out of their flying-squad cars.

'He's always been like this,' Harry would say, when people asked him about his father. And when they smiled and said: 'Always?' Harry would say, 'Always. I know what I'm talking about. He's my father, and I know what he's like. He gave my mother enough grey hairs before her time. All he knew was to run away.'

Harry's reward would come when the visitors would say: 'Well, at least you're being as dutiful to him as anyone can be.'

It was a reward that Harry always refused. 'Dutiful? What can you do? There's nothing else you can do.' Harry Grossman knew that there was nothing else he could do. Dutifulness had been his habit of life: it had had to be, having the sort of father he had, and the strain of duty had made him abrupt and begrudging: he even carried his thick, powerful shoulders curved inwards, to keep what he had to himself. He was a thick-set, bunch-faced man, with large bones, and short, jabbing gestures; he was in the prime of life, and he would point at the father from whom he had inherited his strength, and on whom the largeness of bone showed now only as so much extra leanness that the clothing had to cover, and say: 'You see him? Do you know what he once did? My poor mother saved enough money to send him from the old country to South Africa; she bought clothes for him, and a ticket, and she sent him to her brother, who was already here. He was going to make enough money to bring me out, and my mother and my brother, all of us. But on the boat from Bremen to London he met some other Jews who were going to South America, and they said to him: "Why are you going to South Africa? It's a wild country, the savages will eat you. Come to South America and you'll make a fortune." So in London he exchanges his ticket. And we don't hear from him for six months. Six months later he gets a friend to write to my mother asking her please to send him enough money to pay for his ticket back to the old country – he's dying in Argentina, the Spaniards are killing him, he says, and he must come home. So my mother borrows from her brother to bring him back again. Instead of a fortune he brought her a new debt, and that was all.'

But Harry was dutiful, how dutiful his friends had reason to see again when they would urge him to try sending the old man to a home for the aged. 'No,' Harry would reply, his features moving heavily and reluctantly to a frown, a pout, as he showed how little the suggestion appealed to him. 'I don't like the idea. Maybe one day when he needs medical attention all the time I'll feel differently about it, but not now, not now. He wouldn't like it, he'd be unhappy. We'll look after him as long as we can. It's a job. It's something you've got to do.'

More eagerly Harry would go back to a recital of the old man's past. 'He couldn't even pay for his own passage out. I had to pay the loan back. We came out together – my mother wouldn't let him go by himself again, and I had to pay off her brother who advanced the money for us. I was a boy – what was I? – sixteen, seventeen, but I paid for his passage, and my own, and my mother's and then my brother's. It took me a long time, let me tell you. And then my troubles with him weren't over.' Harry even reproached his father for his myopia; he could clearly enough remember his chagrin when shortly after their arrival in South Africa, after it had become clear that Harry would be able to make his way in the world and be a support to the whole family, the old man – who at that time had not really been so old – had suddenly, almost dramatically, grown so short-sighted that he had been almost blind without the glasses that Harry had had to buy for him. And Harry could remember too how he had then made a practice of losing the glasses or breaking them with the greatest frequency, until it had been made clear to him that he was no longer expected to do any work. 'He doesn't do that any more. When he wants to run away now he sees to it that he's wearing his glasses. That's how he's always been. Sometimes he recognizes me, at other times, when he doesn't want to, he just doesn't know who I am.'

What Harry said about his father sometimes failing to recognize him was true. Sometimes the old man would call out to his son, when he would see him at the end of a passage, 'Who are you?' Or he would come upon Harry in a room and demand of him, 'What do you want in my house?'

'Your house?' Harry would say, when he felt like teasing the old man. 'Your house?'

'Out of my house!' the old man would shout back.

'Your house? Do you call this your house?' Harry would reply, smiling at the old man's fury.

Harry was the only one in the house who talked to the old man, and then he didn't so much talk to him, as talk of him to others. Harry's wife was a dim and silent woman, crowded out by her husband and the large-boned sons like himself that she had borne him, and she would gladly have seen the old man in an old-age home. But her husband had said no, so she put up with the old man, though for herself she could see no possible better end for him than a period of residence in a home for aged Jews which she had once visited, and which had impressed her most favourably with its glass and yellow brick, the noiseless rubber tiles in its corridors, its secluded grassed grounds, and the uniforms worn by the attendants to the establishment. But she put up with the old man; she did not talk to him. The grandchildren had nothing to do with their grandfather – they were busy at school, playing rugby and cricket, they could hardly speak Yiddish, and they were embarrassed by him in front of their friends; and when the grandfather did take any notice of them it was only to call them Boers and *goyim* and *shkotzim* in sudden quavering rages which did not disturb them at all.

The house itself – a big single-storeyed place of brick, with a corrugated iron roof above and a wide stoep all round – Harry Grossman had bought years before, and in the continual rebuilding the suburb was undergoing it was beginning to look old-fashioned. But it was solid and prosperous, and withindoors curiously masculine in appearance, like the house of a widower. The furniture was of the heaviest African woods, dark, and built to last, the passages were lined with bare linoleum, and the few pictures on the walls, big brown and grey mezzotints in heavy frames, had not been looked at for years. The servants were both men, large ignored Zulus who did their work and kept up the brown gleam of the furniture.

It was from this house that old man Grossman tried to escape. He fled through the doors and the windows and out into the wide sunlit streets of the town in Africa, where the blocks of flats were encroaching upon the single-storeyed houses behind their gardens. And in these streets he wandered.

It was Johannes, one of the Zulu servants, who suggested a

way of dealing with old man Grossman. He brought to the house one afternoon Paulus, whom he described as his 'brother'. Harry Grossman knew enough to know that 'brother' in this context could mean anything from the son of one's mother to a friend from a neighbouring *kraal*, but by the speech that Johannes made on Paulus's behalf he might indeed have been the latter's brother. Johannes had to speak for Paulus, for Paulus knew no English. Paulus was a 'raw boy', as raw as a boy could possibly come. He was a muscular, moustached and bearded African, with pendulous ear-lobes showing the slits in which the tribal plugs had once hung; and on his feet he wore sandals the soles of which were cut from old motor-car tyres, the thongs from red inner tubing. He wore neither hat nor socks, but he did have a pair of khaki shorts which were too small for him, and a shirt without any buttons: buttons would in any case have been of no use for the shirt could never have closed over his chest. He swelled magnificently out of his clothing, and above there was a head carried well back, so that his beard, which had been trained to grow in two sharp points from his chin, bristled ferociously forward under his melancholy and almost mandarin-like moustache. When he smiled, as he did once or twice during Johannes's speech, he showed his white, even teeth, but for the most part he stood looking rather shyly to the side of Harry Grossman's head, with his hands behind his back and his bare knees bent a little forward, as if to show how little he was asserting himself, no matter what his 'brother' might have been saying about him.

His expression did not change when Harry said that it seemed hopeless, that Paulus was too raw, and Johannes explained what the baas had just said. He nodded agreement when Johannes explained to him that the baas said that it was a pity that he knew no English. But whenever Harry looked at him, he smiled, not ingratiatingly, but simply smiling above his beard, as though saying: 'Try me.' Then he looked grave again as Johannes expatiated on his virtues. Johannes pleaded for his 'brother'. He said that the baas knew that he, Johannes, was a good boy. Would he, then, recommend to the baas a boy who was not a good boy too? The baas could see for himself, Johannes said, that Paulus was not one of these town boys, these street loafers: he was a good boy, come straight from the *kraal*. He was not a thief or a drinker. He was strong, he was a hard worker, he was clean, and he could be as gentle as a woman. If he, Johannes, were not telling the truth about all these things, then he deserved to be chased away. If Paulus failed in any single respect, then he, Johannes, would voluntarily leave the service of the baas, because he had said untrue things to the baas. But if the baas believed him, and gave Paulus his chance, then he, Johannes, would teach Paulus all the things of the house and the garden, so that Paulus would be useful to the baas in ways other than the particular task for which he was asking the baas to hire him. And, rather daringly, Johannes said that it did not matter so much if Paulus knew no English, because the old baas, the *oubaas*, knew no English either.

It was as something in the nature of a joke – almost a joke against his father – that Harry Grossman gave Paulus his chance. For Paulus was given his chance. He was given a room in the servants' quarters in the back yard, into which he brought a tin trunk painted red and black, a roll of blankets, and a guitar with a picture of a cowboy on the back. He was given a houseboy's outfit of blue denim blouse and shorts, with red piping round the edges, into which he fitted, with his beard and physique, like a king in exile in some pantomime. He was given his food three times a day, after the white people had eaten, a bar of soap every week, cast-off clothing at odd intervals, and the sum of one pound five shillings per week, five shillings of which he took, the rest being left at his request, with the baas, as savings. He had a free afternoon once a week, and he was allowed to entertain not more than two friends at any one time in his room. And in all the particulars that Johannes had enumerated, Johannes was proved reliable. Paulus was not one of these town boys, these street loafers. He did not steal or drink, he was clean and he was honest and hard-working. And he could be gentle as a woman.

It took Paulus some time to settle down to his job; he had to conquer not only his own shyness and strangeness in the new house filled with strange people – let alone the city, which, since taking occupation of his room, he had hardly dared to enter – but also the hostility of old man Grossman, who took immediate fright at Paulus and redoubled his efforts to get away from the house upon Paulus's entry into it. As it happened, the first result of this persistence on the part of the old man was that Paulus was able to get the measure of the job, for he came to it with a willingness of spirit that the old man could not vanquish, but could only teach. Paulus had been given no instructions, he had merely been told to see that the old man did not get himself into trouble, and after a few days of bewilderment Paulus found his way. He simply went along with the old man.

At first he did so cautiously, following the old man at a distance, for he knew the other had no trust in him. But later he was able to follow the old man openly; still later he was able to walk side by side with him, and the old man did not try to escape from him. When old man Grossman went out, Paulus went too, and there was no longer any need for the doors and windows to be watched, or the police to be telephoned. The young bearded Zulu and the old bearded Jew from Lithuania walked together in the streets of the town that was strange to them both; together they looked over the fences of the large gardens and into the shining foyers of the blocks of flats; together they stood on the pavements of the main arterial roads and watched the cars and trucks rush between the tall buildings; together they walked in the small, sandy parks, and when the old man was tired Paulus saw to it that he sat on a bench and rested. They could not sit on the bench together, for only whites were allowed to sit on the benches, but Paulus would squat on the ground at the old man's feet and wait until he judged the old man had rested long enough, before moving on again. Together they stared into the windows of the suburban shops, and though neither of them could read the signs outside the shops, the advertisements on billboards, the traffic signs at the side of the road, Paulus learned to wait for the traffic lights to change from red to green before crossing a street, and together they stared at the Coca-cola girls and the advertisements for beer and the cinema posters. On a piece of cardboard which Paulus carried in the pocket of his blouse Harry had had one of his sons print the old man's name and address, and whenever Paulus was uncertain of the way home, he would approach an African or a friendly-looking white man and show him the card, and try his best to follow the instructions, or at least the gesticulations which were all of the answers of the white men that meant anything to him. But there were enough Africans to be found, usually, who were more sophisticated than himself, and though they teased him for his 'rawness' and for holding the sort of job he had, they helped him too. And neither Paulus nor old man Grossman were aware that when they crossed a street hand-in-hand, as they sometimes did when the traffic was particularly heavy, there were white men who averted their eyes from the sight of this degradation, which could come upon a white man when he was old and senile and dependent.

Paulus knew only Zulu, the old man knew only Yiddish, so there was no language in which they could talk to one another. But they talked all the same: they both explained, commented and complained to each other of the things they saw around them, and often they agreed with one another, smiling and nodding their heads and explaining again with their hands what each happened to be talking about. They both seemed to believe that they were talking about the same things, and often they undoubtedly were, when they lifted their heads sharply to see an aeroplane cross the blue sky between two buildings, or when they reached the top of a steep road and turned to look back the way they had come, and saw below them the clean impervious towers of the city thrust nakedly against the sky in brand-new piles of concrete and glass and face-brick. Then down they would go again, among the houses and the gardens where the beneficent climate encouraged both palms and oak trees to grow indiscriminately among each other – as they did in the garden of the house to which, in the evenings, Paulus and old man Grossman would eventually return.

In and about the house Paulus soon became as indispensable to the old man as he was on their expeditions out of it. Paulus dressed him and bathed him and trimmed his beard, and when the old man woke distressed in the middle of the night it would be for Paulus that he would call – '_Der schwarzer_,' he would shout (for he never learned Paulus's name), '_vo's der schwarzer_' – and Paulus would change his sheets and pyjamas and put him back to bed again. 'Baas _Zeide_', Paulus called the old man, picking up the Yiddish word for grandfather from the children of the house.

And that was something that Harry Grossman told everyone of. For Harry persisted in regarding the arrangement as a kind of joke, and the more the arrangement succeeded the more determinedly did he try to spread the joke, so that it should be a joke not only against his father but a joke against Paulus too. It had been a joke that his father should be looked after by a raw Zulu: it was going to be a joke that the Zulu was successful at it. 'Baas _Zeide_! That's what _der schwarzer_ calls him – have you ever heard the like of it? And you should see the two of them, walking about in the streets hand-in-hand like two schoolgirls. Two clever ones, _der schwarzer_ and my father going for a promenade, and between them I tell you you wouldn't be able to find out what day of the week or what time of day it is.'

And when people said, 'Still that Paulus seems a very good boy,' Harry would reply:

'Why shouldn't he be? With all his knowledge, are there so many better jobs that he'd be able to find? He keeps the old man happy – very good, very nice, but don't forget that that's what he's paid to do. What does he know any better to do, a simple kaffir from the _kraal_? He knows he's got a good job, and he'd be a fool if he threw it away. Do you think,' Harry would say, and this too would insistently be part of the joke, 'if I had nothing else to do with my time I wouldn't be able to make the old man happy?' Harry would look about his sitting-room, where the floorboards bore the weight of his

furniture, or when they sat on the stoep he would measure
with his glance the spacious garden aloof from the street
beyond the hedge. 'I've got other things to do. And I had
other things to do, plenty of them, all my life, and not only
for myself.' What these things were that he had had to do all
his life would send him back to his joke. 'No, I think the old
man has just found his level in *der schwarzer* – and I don't
think *der schwarzer* could cope with anything else.'

Harry teased the old man to his face too, about his 'black
friend', and he would ask his father what he would do if
Paulus went away; once he jokingly threatened to send the
Zulu away. But the old man didn't believe the threat, for
Paulus was in the house when the threat was made, and the old
man simply left his son and went straight to Paulus's room,
and sat there with Paulus for security. Harry did not follow
him: he would never have gone into any of his servants'
rooms least of all that of Paulus. For though he made a joke
of him to others, to Paulus himself Harry always spoke
gruffly, unjokingly, with no patience. On that day he had
merely shouted after the old man, 'Another time he won't be
there.'

Yet it was strange to see how Harry Grossman would
always be drawn to the room in which he knew his father and
Paulus to be. Night after night he came into the old man's
bedroom when Paulus was dressing or undressing the old man;
almost as often Harry stood in the steamy, untidy bathroom
when the old man was being bathed. At these times he hardly
spoke, he offered no explanation of his presence: he stood
dourly and silently in the room, in his customary powerful
and begrudging stance, with one hand clasping the wrist of
the other and both supporting his waist, and he watched
Paulus at work. The backs of Paulus's hands were smooth and
black and hairless, they were paler on the palms and at the
finger-nails, and they worked deftly about the body of the old
man, who was submissive under the ministrations of the other.
At first Paulus had sometimes smiled at Harry while he
worked, with his straightforward, even smile in which there
was no invitation to a complicity in patronage, but rather an

encouragement to Harry to draw forward. But after the first few evenings of this work that Harry had watched, Paulus no longer smiled at his master. And while he worked Paulus could not restrain himself, even under Harry's stare, from talking in a soft, continuous flow of Zulu, to encourage the old man and to exhort him to be helpful and to express his pleasure in how well the work was going. When Paulus would at last wipe the gleaming soap-flakes from his dark hands he would sometimes, when the old man was tired, stoop low and with a laugh pick up the old man and carry him easily down the passage to his bedroom. Harry would follow; he would stand in the passage and watch the burdened, bare-footed Zulu until the door of his father's room closed behind them both.

Only once did Harry wait on such an evening for Paulus to reappear from his father's room. Paulus had already come out, had passed him in the narrow passage, and had already subduedly said: 'Good night, baas,' before Harry called suddenly:

'Hey! Wait!'

'Baas,' Paulus said, turning his head. Then he came quickly to Harry. 'Baas,' he said again, puzzled and anxious to know why his baas, who so rarely spoke to him, should suddenly have called him like this, at the end of the day, when his work was over.

Harry waited again before speaking, waited long enough for Paulus to say: 'Baas?' once more, and to move a little closer, and to lift his head for a moment before letting it drop respectfully down.

'The *oubaas* was tired tonight,' Harry said. 'Where did you take him? What did you do with him?'

'Baas?' Paulus said quickly. Harry's tone was so brusque that the smile Paulus gave asked for no more than a moment's remission of the other's anger.

But Harry went on loudly: 'You heard what I said. What did you do with him that he looked so tired?'

'Baas – I – ' Paulus was flustered, and his hands beat in the air for a moment, but with care, so that he would not touch his baas. 'Please baas.' He brought both hands to his mouth, closing it forcibly. He flung his hands away. 'Johannes,' he said with relief, and he had already taken the first step down the passage to call his interpreter.

'No!' Harry called. 'You mean you don't understand what I say? I know you don't,' Harry shouted, though in fact he had forgotten until Paulus had reminded him. The sight of Paulus's startled, puzzled, and guilty face before him filled him with a lust to see this man, this nurse with the face and the figure of a warrior, look more startled, puzzled, and guilty yet; and Harry knew that it could so easily be done, it could be done simply by talking to him in the language he could not understand. 'You're a fool,' Harry said. 'You're like a child. You understand nothing, and it's just as well for you that you need nothing. You'll always be where you are, running to do what the white baas tells you to do. Look how you stand! Do you think I understood English when I came here?' Harry said, and then with contempt, using one of the few Zulu words he knew: '*Hamba*! Go! Do you think I want to see you?'

'*Au* baas!' Paulus exclaimed in distress. He could not remonstrate; he could only open his hands in a gesture to show that he knew neither the words Harry used, nor in what he had been remiss that Harry should have spoken in such angry tones to him. But Harry gestured him away, and had the satisfaction of seeing Paulus shuffle off like a school-boy.

Harry was the only person who knew that he and his father had quarrelled shortly before the accident that ended the old man's life took place; this was something that Harry was to keep secret for the rest of this life.

Late in the afternoon they quarrelled, after Harry had come back from the shop out of which he made his living. Harry came back to find his father wandering about the house, shouting for *der schwarzer*, and his wife complaining that she had already told the old man at least five times that *der schwarzer* was not in the house: it was Paulus' afternoon off.

Harry went to his father, and when his father came eagerly to him, he too told the old man, '*Der schwarzer*'s not here.' So the old man, with Harry following, turned away and continued going from room to room, peering in through the doors. '*Der schwarzer*'s not here,' Harry said. 'What do you want him for?'

Still the old man ignored him. He went down the passage towards the bedrooms. 'What do you want him for?' Harry called after him.

The old man went into every bedroom, still shouting for *der schwarzer*. Only when he was in his own bare bedroom did he look at Harry. 'Where's *der schwarzer*?' he asked.

'I've told you ten times I don't know where he is. What do you want him for?'

'I want *der schwarzer*.'

'I know you want him. But he isn't here.'

'I want *der schwarzer*.'

'Do you think I haven't heard you? He isn't here.'

'Bring him to me,' the old man said.

'I can't bring him to you. I don't know where he is.' Then Harry steadied himself against his own anger. He said quietly: 'Tell me what you want. I'll do it for you. I'm here, I can do what *der schwarzer* can do for you.'

'Where's *der schwarzer*?'

'I've told you he isn't here,' Harry shouted, the angrier for his previous moment's patience. 'Why don't you tell me what you want? What's the matter with me – can't you tell me what you want?'

'I want *der schwarzer*.'

'Please,' Harry said. He threw out his arms towards his father, but the gesture was abrupt, almost as though he were thrusting his father away from him. 'Why can't you ask it of me? You can ask me – haven't I done enough for you already? Do you want to go for a walk? – I'll take you for a walk. What do you want? Do you want – do you want – ?' Harry could not think what his father might want. 'I'll do it,' he said. 'You don't need *der schwarzer*.'

Then Harry saw that his father was weeping. The old man

was standing up and weeping, with his eyes hidden behind the thick glasses that he had to wear: his glasses and his beard made his face a mask of age, as though time had left him nothing but the frame of his body on which the clothing could hang, and this mask of his face above. But Harry knew when the old man was weeping – he had seen him crying too often before, when they had found him at the end of a street after he had wandered away, or even, years earlier, when he had lost another of the miserable jobs that seemed to be the only one he could find in a country in which his son had, later, been able to run a good business, drive a large car, own a big house.

'Father,' Harry asked, 'what have I done? Do you think I've sent *der schwarzer* away?' Harry saw his father turn away, between the narrow bed and the narrow wardrobe. 'He's coming – ' Harry said, but he could not look at his father's back, he could not look at his father's hollowed neck, on which the hairs that Paulus had clipped glistened above the pale brown discolorations of age – Harry could not look at the neck turned stiffly away from him while he had to try to promise the return of the Zulu. Harry dropped his hands and walked out of the room.

No one knew how the old man managed to get out of the house and through the front gate without having been seen. But he did manage it, and in the road he was struck down. Only a man on a bicycle struck him down, but it was enough, and he died a few days later in the hospital.

Harry's wife wept, even the grandsons wept; Paulus wept. Harry himself was stony, and his bunched, protuberant features were immovable; they seemed locked upon the bones of his face. A few days after the funeral he called Paulus and Johannes into the kitchen and said to Johannes: 'Tell him he must go. His work is finished.'

Johannes translated for Paulus, and then, after Paulus had spoken, he turned to Harry. 'He says, yes baas.' Paulus kept his eyes on the ground; he did not look up even when Harry looked directly at him, and Harry knew that this was not out of fear or shyness, but out of courtesy for his master's grief –

which was what they could not but be talking of, when they talked of his work.

'Here's his pay.' Harry thrust a few notes towards Paulus, who took them in his cupped hands, and retreated.

Harry waited for them to go, but Paulus stayed in the room, and consulted with Johannes in a low voice. Johannes turned to his master. 'He says, baas, that the baas still has his savings.'

Harry had forgotten about Paulus's savings. He told Johannes that he had forgotten, and that he did not have enough money at the moment, but would bring the money the next day. Johannes translated and Paulus nodded gratefully. Both he and Johannes were subdued by the death there had been in the house.

And Harry's dealings with Paulus were over. He took what was to have been his last look at Paulus, but this look stirred him again against the Zulu. As harshly as he told Paulus that he had to go, so now, implacably, seeing Paulus in the mockery and simplicity of his houseboy's clothing, to feed his anger to the very end Harry said: 'Ask him what he's been saving for. What's he going to do with the fortune he's made?'

Johannes spoke to Paulus and came back with a reply. 'He says, baas, that he is saving to bring his wife and children from Zululand to Johannesburg. He is saving, baas,' Johannes said, for Harry had not seemed to understand, 'to bring his family to this town also.'

The two Zulus were bewildered to know why it should have been at that moment that Harry Grossman's clenched, fist-like features should suddenly seem to have fallen from one another, nor why he should have stared with such guilt and despair at Paulus, while he cried, 'What else could I have done? I did my best,' before the first tears came.

Philip Roth

THE CONVERSION OF THE JEWS

Philip Roth

PHILIP ROTH was born in New Jersey in 1933 and educated at Bucknell University and the University of Chicago. His first book, *Goodbye, Columbus*, won the US National Book Award for Fiction in 1960. Among his other novels are *Portnoy's Complaint*, *The Breast*, *The Professor of Desire* and *The Counterlife*. His short stories have been widely reprinted in anthologies of American fiction and have appeared in Martha Foley's annual collections, *The Best American Short Stories*, and in the *O. Henry Prize Story* annuals. *Patrimony: A True Story* won the NBCC Award for Biography in 1991.

THE CONVERSION OF THE JEWS

'You're a real one for opening your mouth in the first place,' Itzie said. 'What do you open your mouth all the time for?'

'I didn't bring it up, Itz, I didn't,' Ozzie said.

'What do you care about Jesus Christ for anyway?'

'I didn't bring up Jesus Christ. He did. I didn't even know what he was talking about. Jesus is historical, he kept saying. Jesus is historical.' Ozzie mimicked the monumental voice of Rabbi Binder.

'Jesus was a person that lived like you and me,' Ozzie continued. 'That's what Binder said – '

'Yeah? . . . So what! What do I give two cents whether he lived or not. And what do you gotta open your mouth!' Itzie Lieberman favoured closed-mouthedness, especially when it came to Ozzie Freedman's questions. Mrs Freedman had to see Rabbi Binder twice before about Ozzie's questions and this Wednesday at four-thirty would be the third time. Itzie preferred to keep *his* mother in the kitchen; he settled for behind-the-back subtleties such as gestures, faces, snarls and other less delicate barnyard noises.

'He was a real person, Jesus, but he wasn't like God, and we don't believe he is God.' Slowly, Ozzie was explaining Rabbi Binder's position to Itzie, who had been absent from Hebrew School the previous afternoon.

'The Catholics,' Itzie said helpfully, 'they believe in Jesus Christ, that he's God.' Itzie Lieberman used 'the Catholics' in its broadest sense – to include the Protestants.

Ozzie received Itzie's remark with a tiny head bob, as though it were a footnote, and went on. 'His mother was Mary, and his father probably was Joseph,' Ozzie said. 'But the New Testament says his real father was God.'

'His *real* father?'

'Yeah,' Ozzie said, 'that's the big thing, his father's supposed to be God.'

'Bull.'

'That's what Rabbi Binder says, that it's impossible –'

'Sure it's impossible. That stuff's all bull. To have a baby you gotta get laid,' Itzie theologized. 'Mary hadda get laid.'

'That's what Binder says: "The only way a woman can have a baby is to have intercourse with a man."'

'He said *that*, Ozz?' For a moment it appeared that Itzie had put the theological question aside. 'He said that, intercourse?' A little curled smile shaped itself in the lower half of Itzie's face like a pink moustache. 'What you guys do, Ozz, you laugh or something?'

'I raised my hand.'

'Yeah? Whatja say?'

'That's when I asked the question.'

Itzie's face lit up. 'Whatja ask about – intercourse?'

'No, I asked the question about God, how if He could create the heaven and earth in six days, and make all the animals and the fish and the light in six days – the light especially, that's what always gets me, that He could make the light. Making fish and animals, that's pretty good –'

'That's damn good.' Itzie's appreciation was honest but unimaginative: it was as though God had just pitched a one-hitter.

'But making light . . . I mean when you think about it, it's really something,' Ozzie said. 'Anyway, I asked Binder if He could make all that in six days, and He could *pick* the six days he wanted right out of nowhere, why couldn't He let a woman have a baby without having intercourse.'

'You said intercourse, Ozz, to Binder?'

'Yeah.'

'Right in class?'

'Yeah.'

Itzie smacked the side of his head.

'I mean, no kidding around,' Ozzie said, 'that'd really be nothing. After all that other stuff, that'd practically be nothing.'

Itzie considered a moment. 'What'd Binder say?'

'He started all over again explaining how Jesus was historical and how he lived like you and me but he wasn't God. So I said I understood that. What I wanted to know was different.'

What Ozzie wanted to know was always different. The first time he had wanted to know how Rabbi Binder could call the Jews 'The Chosen People' if the Declaration of Independence claimed all men to be created equal. Rabbi Binder tried to distinguish for him between political equality and spiritual legitimacy, but what Ozzie wanted to know, he insisted vehemently, was different. That was the first time his mother had to come.

Then there was the plane crash. Fifty-eight people had been killed in a plane crash at La Guardia. In studying a casualty list in the newspaper his mother had discovered among the list of those dead eight Jewish names (his grandmother had nine but she counted Miller as a Jewish name); because of the eight she said the plane crash was 'a tragedy'. During free-discussion time on Wednesday Ozzie had brought to Rabbi Binder's attention this matter of 'some of his relations' always picking out the Jewish names. Rabbi Binder had begun to explain cultural unity and some other things when Ozzie stood up at his seat and said that what he wanted to know was different. Rabbi Binder insisted that he sit down and it was then that Ozzie shouted that he wished all fifty-eight were Jews. That was the second time his mother came.

'And he kept explaining about Jesus being historical, and so I kept asking him. No kidding, Itz, he was trying to make me look stupid.'

'So what he finally do?'

'Finally he starts screaming that I was deliberately simple-minded and a wise guy, and that my mother had to come, and this was the last time. And that I'd never get bar-mitzvahed if he could help it. Then, Itz, then he starts talking in that voice like a statue, real slow and deep, and he says that I better think over what I said about the Lord. He told me to go to his

office and think it over.' Ozzie leaned his body towards Itzie.
'Itz, I thought it over for a solid hour, and now I'm convinced
God could do it.'

Ozzie had planned to confess his latest transgression to his
mother as soon as she came home from work. But it was a
Friday night in November and already dark, and when Mrs
Freedman came through the door she tossed off her coat,
kissed Ozzie quickly on the face, and went to the kitchen
table to light the three yellow candles, two for the Sabbath and
one for Ozzie's father.

When his mother lit the candles she would move her two
arms slowly towards her, dragging them through the air, as
though persuading people whose minds were half made up.
And her eyes would get glassy with tears. Even when his
father was alive Ozzie remembered that her eyes had gotten
glassy, so it didn't have anything to do with his dying. It had
something to do with lighting the candles.

As she touched the flaming match to the unlit wick of a
Sabbath candle, the phone rang, and Ozzie, standing only a
foot from it, plucked it off the receiver and held it muffled to
his chest. When his mother lit candles Ozzie felt there should
be no noise; even breathing, if you could manage it, should be
softened. Ozzie pressed the phone to his breast and watched
his mother dragging whatever she was dragging, and he felt
his own eyes get glassy. His mother was a round, tired, grey-
haired penguin of a woman whose grey skin had begun to feel
the tug of gravity and the weight of her own history. Even
when she was dressed up she didn't look like a chosen person.
But when she lit candles she looked like something better;
like a woman who knew momentarily that God could do
anything.

After a few mysterious minutes she was finished. Ozzie
hung up the phone and walked to the kitchen table where she
was beginning to lay the two places for the four-course
Sabbath meal. He told her that she would have to see Rabbi
Binder next Wednesday at four-thirty, and then he told her
why. For the first time in their life together she hit Ozzie
across the face with her hand.

All through the chopped liver and chicken soup part of the dinner Ozzie cried; he didn't have any appetite for the rest.

On Wednesday, in the largest of the three basement classrooms of the synagogue, Rabbi Marvin Binder, a tall, handsome, broad-shouldered man of thirty with thick strong-fibred black hair, removed his watch from his pocket and saw that it was four o'clock. At the rear of the room Yakov Blotnik, the seventy-one-year-old custodian, slowly polished the large window, mumbling to himself, unaware that it was four o'clock or six o'clock, Monday or Wednesday. To most of the students Yakov Blotnik's mumbling, along with his brown curly beard, scythe nose, and two heel-trailing black cats, made of him an object of wonder, a foreigner, a relic, towards whom they were alternately fearful and disrespectful. To Ozzie the mumbling had always seemed a monotonous, curious prayer; what made it curious was that old Blotnik had been mumbling so steadily for so many years, Ozzie suspected he had memorized the prayers and forgotten all about God.

'It is now free-discussion time,' Rabbi Binder said, 'Feel free to talk about any Jewish matter at all – religion, family, politics, sports –'

There was silence. It was a gusty, clouded November afternoon and it did not seem as though there ever was or could be a thing called baseball. So nobody this week said a word about that hero from the past, Hank Greenberg – which limited free discussion considerably.

And the soul-battering Ozzie Freedman had just received from Rabbi Binder had imposed its limitation. When it was Ozzie's turn to read aloud from the Hebrew book the rabbi had asked him petulantly why he didn't read more rapidly. He was showing no progress. Ozzie said he could read faster but that if he did he was sure not to understand what he was reading. Nevertheless, at the rabbi's repeated suggestion Ozzie tried, and showed a great talent, but in the midst of a long passage he stopped short and said he didn't understand a word he was reading, and started in again at a drag-footed pace. Then came the soul-battering.

Consequently when free-discussion time rolled around none of the students felt too free. The rabbi's invitation was answered only by the mumbling of feeble old Blotnik.

'Isn't there anything at all you would like to discuss?' Rabbi Binder asked again, looking at his watch. 'No questions or comments?'

There was a small grumble from the third row. The rabbi requested that Ozzie rise and give the rest of the class the advantage of his thought.

Ozzie rose. 'I forget it now,' he said, and sat down in his place.

Rabbi Binder advanced a seat towards Ozzie and poised himself on the edge of the desk. It was Itzie's desk and the rabbi's frame only a dagger's-length away from his face snapped him to sitting attention.

'Stand up again, Oscar,' Rabbi Binder said calmly, 'and try to assemble your thoughts.'

Ozzie stood up. All his classmates turned in their seats and watched as he gave an unconvincing scratch to his forehead.

'I can't assemble any,' he announced, and plunked himself down.

'Stand up!' Rabbi Binder advanced from Itzie's desk to the one directly in front of Ozzie; when the rabbinical back was turned Itzie gave it five-fingers off the tip of his nose, causing a small titter in the room. Rabbi Binder was too absorbed in squelching Ozzie's nonsense once and for all to bother with titters. 'Stand up, Oscar. What's your question about?'

Ozzie pulled a word out of the air. It was the handiest word. 'Religion.'

'Oh, now you remember?'

'Yes.'

'What is it?'

Trapped, Ozzie blurted the first thing that came to him. 'Why can't He make anything He wants to make!'

As Rabbi Binder prepared an answer, a final answer, Itzie, ten feet behind him, raised one finger on his left hand, gestured it meaningfully towards the rabbi's back, and brought the house down.

Binder twisted quickly to see what had happened and in the midst of the commotion Ozzie shouted into the rabbi's back what he couldn't have shouted to his face. It was a loud, toneless sound that had the timbre of something stored inside for about six days.

'You don't know! You don't know anything about God!'
The rabbi spun back towards Ozzie. 'What?'
'You don't know – you don't –'
'Apologize, Oscar, apologize!' It was a threat.
'You don't –'

Rabbi Binder's hand flicked out at Ozzie's cheek. Perhaps it had only been meant to clamp the boy's mouth shut, but Ozzie ducked and the palm caught him squarely on the nose.

The blood came in a short, red spurt on to Ozzie's shirt front.

The next moment was all confusion. Ozzie screamed, 'You bastard, you bastard!' and broke for the classroom door. Rabbi Binder lurched a step backwards, as though his own blood had started flowing violently in the opposite direction, then gave a clumsy lurch forward and bolted out of the door after Ozzie. The class followed after the rabbi's huge blue-suited back, and before old Blotnik could turn from his window, the room was empty and everyone was headed full speed up the three flights leading to the roof.

If one should compare the light of day to the life of man: sunrise to birth; sunset – the dropping down over the edge – to death; then as Ozzie Freedman wiggled through the trapdoor of the synagogue roof, his feet kicking backwards bronco-style at Rabbi Binder's outstretched arms – at that moment the day was fifty years old. As a rule, fifty or fifty-five reflects accurately the age of late afternoons in November, for it is in that month, during those hours, that one's awareness of light seems no longer a matter of seeing, but of hearing: light begins clicking away. In fact, as Ozzie locked shut the trap-door in the rabbi's face, the sharp click of the bolt into the lock might momentarily have been mistaken for the sound of the heavier grey that had just throbbed through the sky.

With all his weight Ozzie kneeled on the locked door; any instant he was certain that Rabbi Binder's shoulder would fling it open, splintering the wood into shrapnel and catapulting his body into the sky. But the door did not move and below him he heard only the rumble of feet, first loud then dim, like thunder rolling away.

A question shot through his brain. 'Can this be *me*?' For a thirteen-year-old who had just labelled his religious leader a bastard, twice, it was not an improper question. Louder and louder the question came to him – 'Is it me? Is it me?' – until he discovered himself no longer kneeling, but racing crazily towards the edge of the roof, his eyes crying, his throat screaming, and his arms flying everywhichway as though not his own.

'Is it me? Is it me Me ME ME ME? It has to be me – but is it?'

It is the question a thief must ask himself the night he jimmies open his first window, and it is said to be the question with which bridegrooms quiz themselves before the altar.

In the few wild seconds it took Ozzie's body to propel him to the edge of the roof, his self-examination began to grow fuzzy. Gazing down at the street, he became confused as to the problem beneath the question: was it, is-it-me-who-called-Binder-a-bastard? or, is-it-me-prancing-around-on-the-roof? However, the scene below settled all, for there is an instant in any action when whether it is you or somebody else is academic. The thief crams the money in his pockets and scoots out the window. The bridegroom signs the hotel register for two. And the boy on the roof finds a streetful of people gaping at him, necks stretched backwards, faces up, as though he were the ceiling of the Hayden Planetarium. Suddenly you know it's you.

'Oscar! Oscar Freedman!' A voice rose from the centre of the crowd, a voice that, could it have been seen, would have looked like the writing on scroll. 'Oscar Freedman, get down from there. Immediately!' Rabbi Binder was pointing one arm stiffly up at him; and at the end of that arm, one finger aimed menacingly. It was the attitude of a dictator, but one – the eyes confessed all – whose personal valet had spit neatly in his face.

Ozzie didn't answer. Only for a blink's length did he look towards Rabbi Binder. Instead his eyes began to fit together the world beneath him, to sort out people from places, friends from enemies, participants from spectators. In little jagged starlike clusters, his friends stood around Rabbi Binder, who was still pointing. The topmost point on a star compounded not of angels but of five adolescent boys was Itzie. What a world it was, with those stars below, Rabbi Binder below . . . Ozzie, who a moment earlier hadn't been able to control his own body, started to feel the meaning of the word control: he felt Peace and he felt Power.

'Oscar Freedman, I'll give you three to come down.'

Few dictators give their subjects three to do anything; but, as always, Rabbi Binder only looked dictatorial.

'Are you ready, Oscar?'

Ozzie nodded his head yes, although he had no intention in the world – the lower one or the celestial one he'd just entered – of coming down even if Rabbi Binder should give him a million.

'All right then,' said Rabbi Binder. He ran a hand through his black Samson hair as though it were the gesture prescribed for uttering the first digit. Then, with his other hand cutting a circle out of the small piece of sky around him, he spoke.
'One!'

There was no thunder. On the contrary, at that moment, as though 'one' was the cue for which he had been waiting, the world's least thunderous person appeared on the synagogue steps. He did not so much come out the synagogue door as lean out, onto the darkening air. He clutched at the doorknob with one hand and looked up at the roof.

'Oy!'

Yakov Blotnik's old mind hobbled slowly, as if on crutches, and though he couldn't decide precisely what the boy was doing on the roof, he knew it wasn't good – that is, it wasn't-good-for-the-Jews. For Yakov Blotnik life had fractionated itself simply: things were either good-for-the-Jews or no-good-for-the-Jews.

He smacked his free hand to his in-sucked cheek, gently. 'Oy, Gut!' And then quickly as he was able, he jacked down his head and surveyed the street. There was Rabbi Binder (like a man at an auction with only three dollars in his pocket, he had just delivered a shaky 'Two!'); there were the students, and that was all. So far it wasn't-so-bad-for-the-Jews. But the boy had to come down immediately, before anybody saw. The problem: how to get the boy off the roof?

Anybody who has ever had a cat on the roof knows how to get him down. You call the fire department. Or first you call the operator and you ask her for the fire department. And the next thing there is great jamming of brakes and clanging of bells and shouting of instructions. And then the cat is off the roof. You do the same thing to get a boy off the roof.

That is, you do the same thing if you are Yakov Blotnik and you once had a cat on the roof.

When the engines, all four of them, arrived, Rabbi Binder had four times given Ozzie the count of three. The big hook-and-ladder swung around the corner and one of the firemen leaped from it, plunging headlong towards the yellow fire hydrant in front of the synagogue. With a huge wrench he began to unscrew the top nozzle. Rabbi Binder raced over to him and pulled at his shoulder.

'There's no fire . . .'

The fireman mumbled back over his shoulder and, heatedly, continued working at the nozzle.

'But there's no fire, there's no fire . . .' Binder shouted. When the fireman mumbled again, the rabbi grasped his face with both his hands and pointed it up at the roof.

To Ozzie it looked as though Rabbi Binder was trying to tug the fireman's head out of his body, like a cork from a bottle. He had to giggle at the picture they made: it was a family portrait – rabbi in black skullcap, fireman in red fire hat, and the little yellow hydrant squatting beside like a kid brother, bareheaded. From the edge of the roof Ozzie waved at the portrait, a one-handed, flapping, mocking wave; in doing it his right foot slipped from under him. Rabbi Binder covered his eyes with his hands.

Firemen work fast. Before Ozzie had even regained his balance, a big, round, yellowed net was being held on the synagogue lawn. The firemen who held it looked up at Ozzie with stern, feelingless faces.

One of the firemen turned his head towards Rabbi Binder. 'What, is the kid nuts or something?'

Rabbi Binder unpeeled his hands from his eyes, slowly, painfully, as if they were tape. Then he checked: nothing on the sidewalk, no dents in the net.

'Is he gonna jump, or what?' the fireman shouted.

In a voice not at all like a statue, Rabbi Binder finally answered. 'Yes, yes, I think so ... He's been threatening to ...'

Threatening to? Why, the reason he was on the roof, Ozzie remembered, was to get away; he hadn't even thought about jumping. He had just run to get away, and the truth was that he hadn't really headed for the roof as much as he'd been chased there.

'What's his name, the kid?'

'Freedman,' Rabbi Binder answered. 'Oscar Freedman.'

The fireman looked up at Ozzie. 'What is it with you, Oscar? You gonna jump, or what?'

Ozzie did not answer. Frankly, the question had just arisen.

'Look, Oscar, if you're gonna jump, jump – and if you're not gonna jump, don't jump. But don't waste our time, willya?'

Ozzie looked at the fireman and then at Rabbi Binder. He wanted to see Rabbi Binder cover his eyes one more time.

'I'm going to jump.'

And then he scampered around the edge of the roof to the corner, where there was no net below, and he flapped his arms at his sides, swishing the air and smacking his palms to his trousers on the down-beat. He began screaming like some kind of engine, 'Wheeeee ... wheeeeee,' and leaning way out over the edge with the upper half of his body. The firemen whipped around to cover the ground with the net. Rabbi Binder mumbled a few words to somebody and covered his eyes. Everything happened quickly, jerkily, as in a silent movie. The crowd, which had arrived with the fire engines, gave out a long, Fourth-of-July fireworks oooh-aahhh. In the excitement no one had paid the crowd much heed, except, of course, Yakov Blotnik, who swung from the doorknob counting heads. 'Fier und tsvantsik ... finf und tsvantsik ... Oy, Gut!' It wasn't like this with the cat.

Rabbi Binder peeked through his fingers, checked the sidewalk and net. Empty. But there was Ozzie racing to the other corner. The firemen raced with him but were unable to keep up. Whenever Ozzie wanted to he might jump and splatter himself upon the sidewalk, and by the time the firemen scooted to the spot all they could do with their net would be to cover the mess.

'Wheeeee ... wheeeee ...'

'Hey, Oscar,' the winded fireman yelled. 'What the hell is this, a game or something?'

'Wheeeee ... wheeeee ...'

'Hey, Oscar –'

But he was off now to the other corner, flapping his wings fiercely. Rabbi Binder couldn't take it any longer – the fire engines from nowhere, the screaming suicidal boy, the net. He fell to his knees, exhausted, and with his hands curled together in front of his chest like a little dome, he pleaded, 'Oscar, stop it, Oscar. Don't jump, Oscar. Please come down ... Please don't jump.'

And further back in the crowd a single voice, a single young voice, shouted a lone word to the boy on the roof.

'Jump!'

It was Itzie. Ozzie momentarily stopped flapping.

'Go ahead, Ozz – jump!' Itzie broke off his point of the star and courageously, with the inspiration not of a wise-guy but of a disciple, stood alone. 'Jump, Ozz, jump!'

Still on his knees, his hands still curled, Rabbi Binder twisted his body back. He looked at Itzie, then, agonizingly, back to Ozzie.

'OSCAR, DON'T JUMP! PLEASE, DON'T JUMP... please please...'

'Jump!' This time it wasn't Itzie but another point of the star. By the time Mrs Freedman arrived to keep her four-thirty appointment with Rabbi Binder, the whole little upside-down heaven was shouting and pleading for Ozzie to jump, and Rabbi Binder no longer was pleading with him not to jump, but was crying into the dome of his hands.

Understandably Mrs Freedman couldn't figure out what her son was doing on the roof. So she asked.

'Ozzie, my Ozzie, what are you doing? My Ozzie, what is it?'

Ozzie stopped wheeeeeing and slowed his arms down to a cruising flap, the kind birds use in soft winds, but he did not answer. He stood against the low, clouded, darkening sky – light clicked down swiftly now, as on a small gear – flapping softly and gazing down at the small bundle of a woman who was his mother.

'What are you doing, Ozzie?' She turned towards the kneeling Rabbi Binder and rushed so close that only a paper-thickness of dusk lay between her stomach and his shoulders.

'What is my baby doing?'

Rabbi Binder gaped up at her but he too was mute. All that moved was the dome of his hands; it shook back and forth like a weak pulse.

'Rabbi, get him down! He'll kill himself. Get him down, my only baby...'

'I can't,' Rabbi Binder said, 'I can't...' and he turned his handsome head towards the crowd of boys behind him. 'It's them. Listen to them.'

And for the first time Mrs Freedman saw the crowd of boys, and she heard what they were yelling.

'He's doing it for them. He won't listen to me. It's them.' Rabbi Binder spoke like one in a trance.

'For them?'

'Yes.'

'Why for them?'

'They want him to . . .'

Mrs Freedman raised her two arms upward as though she were conducting the sky. 'For them he's doing it!' And then in a gesture older than pyramids, older than prophets and floods, her arms came slapping down to her sides. 'A martyr I have. Look!' She tilted her head to the roof. Ozzie was still flapping softly. 'My martyr.'

'Oscar, come down, *please*,' Rabbi Binder groaned.

In a startlingly even voice Mrs Freedman called to the boy on the roof. 'Ozzie, come down. Ozzie, don't be a martyr, my baby.'

As though it were a litany, Rabbi Binder repeated her words. 'Don't be a martyr, my baby. Don't be a martyr.'

'Gawhead, Ozz – *be* a Martin!' It was Itzie. 'Be a Martin, be a Martin,' and all the voices joined in singing for Martindom, whatever *it* was. 'Be a Martin, be a Martin . . .'

Somehow when you're on a roof the darker it gets the less you can hear. All Ozzie knew was that two groups wanted two new things: his friends were spirited and musical about what they wanted; his mother and the rabbi were even-toned, chanting, about what they didn't want. The rabbi's voice was without tears now and so was his mother's.

The big net stared up at Ozzie like a sightless eye. The big, clouded sky pushed down. From beneath it looked like a grey corrugated board. Suddenly, looking up into that unsympathetic sky, Ozzie realized all the strangeness of what these people, his friends, were asking: they wanted him to jump, to kill himself; they were singing about it now – it made them that happy. And there was an even greater strangeness: Rabbi Binder was on his knees, trembling. If there was a question to be asked now it was not 'Is it me?' but rather 'Is it us? . . . Is it us?'

Being on the roof, it turned out, was a serious thing. If he jumped would the singing become dancing? Would it? What would jumping stop? Yearningly, Ozzie wished he could rip open the sky, plunge his hands through, and pull out the sun;

Light equals understanding

and on the sun, like a coin, would be stamped JUMP or DON'T JUMP.

Ozzie's knees rocked and sagged a little under him as though they were setting him for a dive. His arms tightened, stiffened, froze, from shoulders to fingernails. He felt as if each part of his body were going to vote as to whether he should kill himself or not – and each part as though it were independent of *him*.

The light took an unexpected click down and the new darkness, like a gag, hushed the friends singing for this and the mother and rabbi chanting for that.

Ozzie stopped counting votes, and in a curiously high voice, like one who wasn't prepared for speech, he spoke.

ref. to 4 Sons

'Mamma?'

'Yes, Oscar.'

'Mamma, get down on your knees, like Rabbi Binder.'

'Oscar –'

'Get down on your knees,' he said, 'or I'll jump.'

Ozzie heard a whimper, then a quick rustling, and when he looked down where his mother had stood he saw the top of a head and beneath that a circle of dress. She was kneeling beside Rabbi Binder.

He spoke again. 'Everybody kneel.' There was the sound of everybody kneeling.

Ozzie looked around. With one hand he pointed towards the synagogue entrance. 'Make *him* kneel.'

There was a noise, not of kneeling, but of body-and-cloth stretching. Ozzie could hear Rabbi Binder saying in a gruff whisper, '. . . or he'll *kill* himself,' and when next he looked there was Yakov Blotnik off the doorknob and for the first time in his life upon his knees in the Gentile posture of prayer.

As for the firemen – it is not as difficult as one might imagine to hold a net taut while you are kneeling.

Ozzie looked around again; and then he called to Rabbi Binder.

'Rabbi?'

'Yes, Oscar.'

'Rabbi Binder, do you believe in God?'

'Yes.'

'Do you believe God can do Anything?' Ozzie leaned his head out into the darkness. 'Anything?'

'Oscar, I think –'

'Tell me you believe God can do Anything.'

There was a second's hesitation. Then: 'God can do Anything.'

'Tell me you believe God can make a child without intercourse.'

'He can.'

'Tell me!'

'God,' Rabbi Binder admitted, 'can make a child without intercourse.'

'Mamma, you tell me.'

'God can make a child without intercourse,' his mother said.

'Make *him* tell me.' There was no doubt who *him* was.

In a few moments Ozzie heard an old comical voice say something to the increasing darkness about God.

Next, Ozzie made everybody say it. And then he made them all say they believed in Jesus Christ – first one at a time, then all together.

When the catechizing was through it was the beginning of evening. From the street it sounded as if the boy on the roof might have sighed.

'Ozzie?' A woman's voice dared to speak. 'You'll come down now?'

There was no answer, but the woman waited, and when a voice finally did speak it was thin and crying, and exhausted as that of an old man who has just finished pulling the bells.

'Mamma, don't you see – you shouldn't hit me. He shouldn't hit me. You shouldn't hit me about God, Mamma. You should never hit anybody about God –'

'Ozzie, please come down now.'

'Promise me, promise me you'll never hit anybody about God.'

He had asked only his mother, but for some reason everyone kneeling in the street promised he would never hit anybody about God.

Once again there was silence.

'I can come down now, Mamma,' the boy on the roof finally said. He turned his head both ways as though checking the traffic lights. 'Now I can come down . . .'

And he did, right into the centre of the yellow net that glowed in the evening's edge like an overgrown halo.

the sun? again we returns to the light motif

Saul Bellow

THE OLD SYSTEM

Saul Bellow

SAUL BELLOW, born in Canada in 1915 and brought up in Chicago, was awarded the Nobel Prize for Literature in 1977, the most prestigious of a series of literary prizes beginning with the National Book Award for Fiction in 1954. His novels include *The Adventures of Augie March*, *Seize the Day*, *Herzog* and *Humboldt's Gift*. Among his collections of short stories are *Mosby's Memoirs* and *Him with His Foot in His Mouth and Other Stories*. He has written three short plays. In 1984 he was made a Commandeur de la Légion d'Honneur.

THE OLD SYSTEM

It was a thoughtful day for Dr Braun. Winter. Saturday. The short end of December. He was alone in his apartment and woke late, lying in bed until noon, in the room kept very dark, working with a thought – a feeling: Now you see it, now you don't. Now a content, now a vacancy. Now an important individual, a force, a necessary existence; suddenly nothing. A frame without a picture, a mirror with missing glass. The feeling of necessary existence might be the aggressive, instinctive vitality we share with a dog or an ape. The difference being in the power of the mind or spirit to declare *I am*. Plus the inevitable inference *I am not*. Dr Braun was no more pleased with being than with its opposite. For him an age of equilibrium seemed to be coming in. How nice! Anyway, he had no project for putting the world in rational order, and for no special reason he got up. Washed his wrinkled but not elderly face with freezing tap water, which changed the nighttime white to a more agreeable color. He brushed his teeth. Standing upright, scrubbing the teeth as if he were looking after an idol. He then ran the big old-fashioned tub to sponge himself, backing into the thick stream of the Roman faucet, soaping beneath with the same cake of soap he would apply later to his beard. Under the swell of his belly, the tip of his parts, somewhere between his heels. His heels needed scrubbing. He dried himself with yesterday's shirt, an economy. It was going to the laundry anyway. Yes, with the self-respecting expression human beings inherit from ancestors for whom bathing was a solemnity. A sadness.

But every civilized man today cultivated an unhealthy self-detachment. Had learned from art the art of amusing self-observation and objectivity. Which, since there had to be something amusing to watch, required art in one's conduct. Existence for the sake of such practices did not seem worth while. Mankind was in a confusing, uncomfortable, disagreeable stage in the evolution of its consciousness. Dr Braun

(Samuel) did not like it. It made him sad to feel that the thought, art, belief of great traditions should be so mis-employed. Elevation? Beauty? Torn into shreds, into ribbons for girls' costumes, or trailed like the tail of a kite at Happenings. Plato and the Buddha raided by looters. The tombs of Pharaohs broken into by desert rabble. And so on, thought Dr Braun as he passed into his neat kitchen. He was well pleased by the blue-and-white Dutch dishes, cups hanging, saucers standing in slots.

He opened a fresh can of coffee, much enjoyed the fragrance from the punctured can. Only an instant, but not to be missed. Next he sliced bread for the toaster, got out the butter, chewed an orange; and he was admiring long icicles on the huge red, circular roof tank of the laundry across the alley, the clear sky, when he discovered that a sentiment was approaching. It was said of him, occasionally, that he did not love anyone. This was not true. He did not love anyone steadily. But unsteadily he loved, he guessed, at an average rate.

The sentiment, as he drank his coffee, was for two cousins in upstate New York, the Mohawk Valley. They were dead. Isaac Braun and his sister Tina. Tina was first to go. Two years later, Isaac died. Braun now discovered that he and Cousin Isaac had loved each other. For whatever use or meaning this fact might have within the peculiar system of light, movement, contact, and perishing in which he tried to find stability. Toward Tina, Dr Braun's feelings were less clear. More passionate once, but at present more detached.

Isaac's wife, after he died, had told Braun, 'He was proud of you. He said, "Sammy has been written up in *Time*, in all the papers, for his research. But he never says a word about his scientific reputation!"'

'I see. Well, computers do the work, actually.'

'But you have to know what to put into these computers.'

This was more or less the case. But Braun had not continued the conversation. He did not care much for being *first* in his field. People were boastful in America. Matthew Arnold, a not entirely appetizing figure himself, had correctly observed this in the U.S. Dr Braun thought this native American boastfulness had aggravated a certain weakness in Jewish immigrants. But a proportionate reaction of self-effacement was not praiseworthy. Dr Braun did not want to be interested in this question at all. However, his cousin Isaac's opinions had some value for him.

In Schenectady there were two more Brauns of the same family, living. Did Dr Braun, drinking his coffee this afternoon, love them, too? They did not elicit such feelings. Then did he love Isaac more because Isaac was dead? There one might have something.

But in childhood, Isaac had shown him great kindness. The others, not very much.

Now Braun remembered certain things. A sycamore tree beside the Mohawk River. Then the river couldn't have been so foul. Its color, anyhow, was green, and it was powerful and dark, an easy, level force – crimped, green, blackish, glassy. A huge tree like a complicated event, with much splitting and thick chalky extensions. It must have dominated an acre, brown and white. And well away from the leaves, on a dead branch, sat a gray-and-blue fish hawk. Isaac and his little cousin Braun passed in the wagon, the old coarse-tailed horse, walking, the steady head, with blinders, working onward. Braun, seven years old, wore a gray shirt with large bone buttons and had a short summer haircut. Isaac was dressed in work clothes, for in those days the Brauns were in the secondhand business – furniture, carpets, stoves, beds. His senior by fifteen years, Isaac had a mature business face. Born to be a man, in the direct Old Testament sense, as that bird on the sycamore was born to fish in water. Isaac, when he had come to America, was still a child. Nevertheless his old-country Jewish dignity was very firm and strong. He had the outlook of ancient generations on the New World. Tents and kine and wives and maidservants and manservants. Isaac was handsome, Braun thought – dark face, black eyes, vigorous hair, and a long scar on the cheek. Because, he told his scientific cousin, his mother had given him milk from a tubercular cow in the old country. While his father was serving in the Russo-Japanese War. Far away. In the Yiddish metaphor, on the lid of hell. As though hell were a caldron, a covered pot. How those old-time Jews despised the *goy* wars, their vainglory and obstinate *Dummheit*. Conscription, mustering, marching, shooting, leaving the corpses everywhere. Buried, unburied. Army against army. Gog and Magog. The czar, that weak, whiskered arbitrary and woman-ridden man, decreed that Uncle Braun would be swept away to Sakhalin. So by irrational decree, as in *The Arabian Nights*, Uncle Braun, with his greatcoat and short humiliated legs, little beard, and great eyes, left wife and child to eat maggoty pork. And when the war was lost Uncle Braun escaped through Manchuria. Came to Vancouver on a Swedish ship. Labored on the railroad. He did not look so strong, as Braun remembered him in Schenectady. His chest was deep and his arms long, but the legs like felt, too yielding, as if the escape from Sakhalin and trudging in Manchuria had been too much. However, in the Mohawk Valley, monarch of used stoves and fumigated mattresses – dear Uncle Braun! He had a small, pointed beard, like George V, like Nick of Russia. Like Lenin, for that matter. But large, patient eyes in his wizened face, filling all of the space reserved for eyes.

A vision of mankind Braun was having as he sat over his coffee Saturday afternoon. Beginning with those Jews of 1920.

Braun as a young child was protected by the special affection of his cousin Isaac, who stroked his head and took him on the wagon, later the truck, into the countryside. When Braun's mother had gone into labor with him, it was Isaac whom Aunt Rose sent running for the doctor. He found the doctor in the saloon. Faltering, drunken Jones, who practiced among Jewish immigrants before those immigrants had educated their own doctors. He had Isaac crank the Model T. And they drove. Arriving, Jones tied Mother Braun's hands to the bedposts, a custom of the times.

Having worked as a science student in laboratories and kennels, Dr Braun had himself delivered cats and dogs. Man, he knew, entered life like these other creatures, in a transparent bag or caul. Lying in a bag filled with transparent fluid, a purplish water. A color to mystify the most rational philosopher. What is this creature that struggles for birth in its membrane and clear fluid? Any puppy in its sac, in the blind terror of its emergence, any mouse breaking into the external world from this shining, innocent-seeming blue-tinged transparency!

Dr Braun was born in a small wooden house. They washed him and covered him with mosquito netting. He lay at the foot of his mother's bed. Tough Cousin Isaac dearly loved Braun's mother. He had great pity for her. In intervals of his dealing, of being a Jewish businessman, there fell these moving reflections of those who were dear to him.

Aunt Rose was Dr Braun's godmother, held him at his circumcision. Bearded, nearsighted old Krieger, fingers stained with chicken slaughter, cut away the foreskin.

Aunt Rose, Braun felt, was the original dura mater – the primal hard mother. She was not a big woman. She had a large bust, wide hips, and old-fashioned thighs of those corrupted shapes that belong to history. Which hampered her walk. Together with poor feet, broken by the excessive female weight she carried. In old boots approaching the knee. Her face was red, her hair powerful, black. She had a straight sharp nose. To cut mercy like a cotton thread. In the light of her eyes Braun recognized the joy she took in her hardness. Hardness of reckoning, hardness of tactics, hardness of dealing and of speech. She was building a kingdom with the labor of Uncle Braun and the strength of her obedient sons. They had their shop, they had real estate. They had a hideous synagogue of such red brick as seemed to grow in upstate New York by the will of the demon spirit charged with the ugliness of America in that epoch, which saw to it that a particular comic ugliness should influence the soul of man. In Schenectady, in Troy, in Gloversville, Mechanicville, as far west as Buffalo. There was a sour paper mustiness in this synagogue. Uncle Braun not only had money, he also had some learning and he was respected. But it was a quarrelsome congregation. Every question was disputed. There was rivalry, there were rages; slaps were given, families stopped speaking. Pariahs, thought Braun, with the dignity of princes among themselves.

Silent, with silent eyes crossing and recrossing the red water tank bound by twisted cables, from which ragged ice hung down and white vapor rose, Dr Braun extracted a moment four decades gone in which Cousin Isaac had said, with one of those archaic looks he had, that the Brauns were descended from the tribe of Naphtali.

'How do we know?'

'People – families – *know*.'

Braun was reluctant, even at the age of ten, to believe such things. But Isaac, with the authority of a senior, almost an uncle, said, 'You'd better not forget it.'

As a rule, he was gay with young Braun. Laughing against the tension of the scar that forced his mouth to one side. His eyes black, soft, and flaming. Off his breath, a bitter fragrance that translated itself to Braun as masculine earnestness and gloom. All the sons in the family had the same sort of laugh. They sat on the open porch, Sundays, laughing, while Uncle Braun read aloud the Yiddish matrimonial advertisements. 'Attractive widow, 35, dark-favored, owning her own dry-goods business in Hudson, excellent cook, Orthodox, well bred, refined. Plays the piano. Two intelligent, well-behaved children, eight and six.'

All but Tina, the obese sister, took part in this satirical Sunday pleasure. Behind the screen door, she stood in the kitchen. Below, the yard, where crude flowers grew – zinnias, plantain lilies, trumpet vine on the chicken shed.

Now the country cottage appeared to Braun, in the Adirondacks. A stream. So beautiful! Trees, full of great strength. Wild strawberries, but you must be careful about the poison ivy. In the drainage ditches, polliwogs. Braun slept in the attic with Cousin Mutt. Mutt danced in his undershirt in the morning, naked beneath, and sang an obscene song:

> 'I stuck my nose up a nanny goat's ass
> And the smell was enough to blind me.'

He was leaping on bare feet, and his thing bounded from thigh to thigh. Going into saloons to collect empty bottles, he had learned this. A ditty from the stokehold. Origin, Liverpool or Tyneside. Art of the laboring class in the machine age.

An old mill. A pasture with clover flowers. Braun, seven years old, tried to make a clover wreath, pinching out a hole in the stems for other stems to pass through. He meant the wreath for fat Tina. To put it on her thick savory head, her smoky black harsh hair. Then in the pasture, little Braun overturned a rotten stump with his foot. Hornets pursued and bit him. He screamed. He had painful crimson lumps all over his body. Aunt Rose put him to bed and Tina came huge into the attic to console him. An angry fat face, black eyes, and the dilated nose breathing at him. Little Braun, stung and burning. She lifted her dress and petticoat to cool him with her body. The belly and thighs swelled before him. Braun felt too small and frail for this ecstasy. By the bedside was a chair, and she sat. Under the dizzy heat of the shingled roof, she rested her legs upon him, spread them wider, wider. He saw the barbarous and coaly hair. He saw the red within. She parted the folds with her fingers. Parting, her dark nostrils opened, the eyes looked white in her head. She motioned that he should press his child's genital against her fat-flattened thighs. Which, with agonies of incapacity and pleasure, he did. All was silent. Summer silence. Her sexual odor. The flies and gnats stimulated by delicious heat or the fragrance. He heard a mass of flies tear themselves from the window-pane. A sound of detached adhesive. Tina did not kiss, did not embrace. Her face was menacing. She was defying. She was drawing him – taking him somewhere with her. But she promised nothing, told him nothing.

When he recovered from his bites, playing once more in the yard, Braun saw Isaac with his fiancée, Clara Sternberg, walking among the trees, embracing very sweetly. Braun tried to go with them, but Cousin Isaac sent him away. When he still followed, Cousin Isaac turned him roughly toward the cottage. Little Braun then tried to kill his cousin. He wanted with all his heart to club Isaac with a piece of wood. He was still struck by the incomparable happiness, the luxury of that pure murderousness. Rushing toward Isaac, who took him by the back of the neck, twisted his head, held him under the pump. He then decreed that little Braun must go home, to Albany. He was far too wild. Must be taught a lesson. Cousin Tina said in private, 'Good for *you*, Sam. I hate him, too.' She took Braun with her dimpled, inept hand and walked down the road with him in the Adirondack dust. Her gingham-fitted bulk. Her shoulders curved, banked, like the earth of the hill-cut road. And her feet turned outward by the terrifying weight and deformity of her legs.

Later she dieted. Became for a while thinner, more civilized. Everyone was more civilized. Little Braun became a docile, bookish child. Did very well at school.

All clear? Quite clear to the adult Braun, considering his fate no more than the fate of others. Before his tranquil look, the facts arranged themselves – rose, took a new arrangement. Remained awhile in the settled state and then changed again. We were getting somewhere.

Uncle Braun died angry with Aunt Rose. He turned his face to the wall with his last breath to rebuke her hardness. All the men, his sons, burst out weeping. The tears of the women were different. Later, too, their passion took other forms. They bargained for more property. And Aunt Rose defied Uncle Braun's will. She collected rents in the slums of Albany and Schenectady from properties he had left to his sons. She dressed herself in the old fashion, calling on nigger tenants or the Jewish rabble of tailors and cobblers. To her the old Jewish words for these trades – *Schneider*, *Schuster* – were terms of contempt. Rents belonging mainly to Isaac she banked in her own name. Riding ancient streetcars in the factory slums. She did not need to buy widow's clothes. She had always worn suits, they had always been black. Her hat was three-cornered, like the town crier's. She let the black braid hang behind, as though she were in her own kitchen. She had trouble with bladder and arteries, but ailments did not keep her at home and she had no use for doctoring and drugs. She blamed Uncle Braun's death on Bromo-Seltzer, which, she said, had enlarged his heart.

Isaac did not marry Clara Sternberg. Though he was a manufacturer, her father turned out on inquiry to have started as a cutter and have married a housemaid. Aunt Rose would not tolerate such a connection. She took long trips to make genealogical investigations. And she vetoed all the young women, her judgements severe without limit. 'A false dog.' 'Candied poison.' 'An open ditch. A sewer. A born whore!'

The woman Isaac eventually married was pleasant, mild, round, respectable, the daughter of a Jewish farmer.

Aunt Rose said, 'Ignorant. A common man.'

'He's honest, a hard worker on the land,' said Isaac. 'He recites the Psalms even when he's driving. He keeps them under his wagon seat.'

'I don't believe it. A son of Ham like that. A cattle dealer. He stinks of manure.' And she said to the bride in Yiddish, 'Be so good as to wash thy father before bringing him to the synagogue. Get a bucket and scalding water, and 20 Mule Team Borax and ammonia, and a horse brush. The filth is ingrained. Be sure to scrub his hands.'

The rigid madness of the orthodox. Their haughty, spinning, crazy spirit.

Tina did not bring her young man from New York to be examined by Aunt Rose. Anyway, he was neither young, nor handsome, nor rich. Aunt Rose said he was a minor hoodlum, a slugger. She had gone to Coney Island to inspect his family – a father who sold pretzels and chestnuts from a cart, a mother who cooked for banquets. And the groom himself – so thick, so bald, so grim, she said, his hands so common and his back and chest like fur, a fell. He was a beast, she told young Sammy Braun. Braun was a student then at Rensselaer Polytechnic and came to see his aunt in her old kitchen – the great black-and-nickel stove, the round table on its oak pedestal, the dark-blue-and-white check of the oilcloth, a still life of peaches and cherries salvaged from the secondhand shop. And Aunt Rose, more feminine with her corset off and a gaudy wrapper over her thick Victorian undervests, camisoles, bloomers. Her silk stockings were gartered below the knee and the wide upper portions, fashioned for thighs, drooped down flimsy, nearly to her slippers.

Tina was then handsome, if not pretty. In high school she took off eighty pounds. Then she went to New York City without getting her diploma. What did *she* care for such things! said Rose. And how did she get to Coney Island by herself? Because she was perverse. Her instinct was for freaks. And there she met this beast. This hired killer, this second Lepke of Murder, Inc. Upstate, the old woman read the melodramas of the Yiddish press, which she embroidered with her own ideas of wickedness.

But when Tina brought her husband to Schenectady, installing him in her father's secondhand shop, he turned out to be a big innocent man. If he had ever had guile, he lost it with his hair. His baldness was total, like a purge. He had a sentimental, dependent look. Tina protected him. Here Dr Braun had sexual thoughts, about himself as a child and about her childish bridegroom. And scowling, smoldering Tina, her angry tenderness in the Adirondacks, and how she was beneath, how hard she breathed in the attic, and the violent strength and obstinacy of her crinkled, sooty hair.

Nobody could sway Tina. That, thought Braun, was probably the secret of it. She had consulted her own will, kept her own counsel for so long, that she could accept no outer guidance. Anyone who listened to others seemed to her weak.

When Aunt Rose lay dead, Tina took from her hand the ring Isaac had given her many years ago. Braun did not remember the entire history of that ring, only that Isaac had loaned money to an immigrant who disappeared, leaving this jewel, which was assumed to be worthless but turned out to be valuable. Braun could not recall whether it was ruby or emerald; nor the setting. But it was the one feminine adornment Aunt Rose wore. And it was supposed to go to Isaac's wife, Sylvia, who wanted it badly. Tina took it from the corpse and put it on her own finger.

'Tina, give that ring to me. Give it here,' said Isaac.

'No. It was hers. Now it's mine.'

'It was not Mama's. You know that. Give it back.'

She outfaced him over the body of Aunt Rose. She knew he would not quarrel at the deathbed. Sylvia was enraged. She did what she could. That is, she whispered, 'Make her!' But it was no use. He knew he could not recover it. Besides, there were too many other property disputes. His rents in Aunt Rose's savings bank.

But only Isaac became a millionaire. The others simply hoarded, old immigrant style. He never sat waiting for his legacy. By the time Aunt Rose died, Isaac was already worth a great deal of money. He had put up an ugly apartment building in Albany. To him, an achievement. He was out with his men at dawn. Having prayed aloud while his wife, in curlers, pretty but puffy with sleepiness, sleepy but obedient, was in the kitchen fixing breakfast. Isaac's ortho-doxy only increased with his wealth. He soon became an old-fashioned Jewish paterfamilias. With his family he spoke a Yiddish unusually thick in old Slavic and Hebrew expressions. Instead of 'important people, leading citizens', he said '*Anshe ha-ir*', Men of the City. He, too, kept the Psalms near. As active, worldly Jews for centuries had done. One copy lay in the glove compartment of his Cadillac. To which his great gloomy sister referred with a twist of the face – she had become obese again, wider and taller, since those Adirondack days. She said, 'He reads the Tehillim aloud in his air-conditioned Caddy when there's a long freight train at the crossing. That crook! He'd pick God's pocket!'

One could not help thinking what fertility of metaphor there was in all of these Brauns. Dr Braun himself was no exception. And what the explanation might be, despite twenty-five years of specialization in the chemistry of heredity, he couldn't say. How a protein molecule might carry such propensities of ingenuity, and creative malice and negative power. Originating in an invisible ferment. Capable of printing a talent or a vice upon a billion hearts. No wonder Isaac Braun cried out to his God when he sat sealed in his great black car and the freights rumbled in the polluted shimmering of this once-beautiful valley

> Answer me when I call, O God of my
> righteousness.

'But what do you think?' said Tina. 'Does he remember his brothers when there is a deal going? Does he give his only sister a chance to come in?'

Not that there was any great need. Cousin Mutt, after he was wounded at Iwo Jima, returned to the appliance business. Cousin Aaron was a C.P.A. Tina's husband, bald Fenster, branched into housewares in his secondhand shop. Tina was back of that, of course. No one was poor. What irritated Tina was that Isaac would not carry the family into real estate, where the tax advantages were greatest. The big depreciation allowances, which she understood as legally sanctioned graft. She had her money in savings accounts at a disgraceful two and a half percent, taxed at the full rate. She did not trust the stock market.

Isaac had tried, in fact, to include the Brauns when he built the shopping center at Robbstown. At a risky moment, they abandoned him. A desperate moment, when the law had to be broken. At a family meeting, each of the Brauns had agreed to put up $25,000, the entire amount to be given under the table to Ilkington. Old Ilkington headed the board of directors of the Robbstown Country Club. Surrounded by factories, the club was moving farther into the country. Isaac had learned this from the old caddiemaster when he gave him a lift, one morning of fog. Mutt Braun had caddied at Robbstown in the early twenties, had carried Ilkington's clubs. Isaac knew Ilkington, too, and had a private talk with him. The old *goy*, now seventy, retiring to the British West Indies, had said to Isaac, 'Off the record. One hundred thousand. And I don't want to bother about Internal Revenue.' He was a long, austere man with a marbled face. Cornell 1910 or so. Cold but plain. And, in Isaac's opinion, fair. Developed as a shopping center, properly planned, the Robbstown golf course was worth half a million apiece to the Brauns. The city in the postwar boom was spreading fast. Isaac had a friend on the zoning board who would clear everything for five grand. As for the contracting, he offered to do it all on his own. Tina insisted that a separate corporation be formed by the Brauns to make sure the building profits were shared equally. To this Isaac agreed. As head of the family, he took the burden upon himself. He would have to organize it all. Only Aaron the C.P.A. could help him, setting up the books. The meeting, in Aaron's office, lasted from noon to three p.m. All the difficult problems were examined. Four players, specialists in the harsh music of money, studying a score. In the end, they agreed to perform.

But when the time came, ten a.m. on a Friday, Aaron balked. He would not do it. And Tina and Mutt also reneged. Isaac told Dr Braun the story. As arranged, he came to Aaron's office carrying the $25,000 for Ilkington in an old briefcase. Aaron, now forty, smooth, shrewd, and dark, had the habit of writing tiny neat numbers on his memo pad as he spoke to you. Dark fingers quickly consulting the latest tax publications. He dropped his voice very low to the secretary on the intercom. He wore white-on-white shirts and silk-brocade ties, signed 'Countess Mara'. Of them all, he looked most like Uncle Braun. But without the beard, without the kingly pariah derby, without the gold thread in his brown eye. In many externals, thought scientific Braun, Aaron and Uncle Braun were drawn from the same genetic pool. Chemically, he was the younger brother of his father. The differences within were due possibly to heredity. Or perhaps to the influence of business America.

'Well?' said Isaac, standing in the carpeted office. The grandiose desk was superbly clean.

'How do you know Ilkington can be trusted?'

'I think he can.'

'*You* think. He could take the money and say he never heard of you in all his life.'

'Yes, he might. But we talked that over. We have to gamble.'

Probably on his instructions, Aaron's secretary buzzed him. He bent over the instrument and out of the corner of his mouth he spoke to her very deliberately and low.

'Well, Aaron,' said Isaac. 'You want me to guarantee your investment? Well? Speak up.'

Aaron had long ago subdued his thin tones and spoke in the gruff style of a man always sure of himself. But the sharp breaks, mastered twenty-five years ago, were still there. He stood up with both fists on the glass of his desk, trying to control his voice.

He said through clenched teeth, 'I haven't slept!'

'Where is the money?'

'I don't have that kind of cash.'

'No?'

'You know damn well. I'm licensed. I'm a certified accountant. I'm in no position . . .'

'And what about Tina – Mutt?'

'I don't know anything about them.'

'Talked them out of it, didn't you? I have to meet Ilkington at noon. Sharp. Why didn't you tell me sooner?'

Aaron said nothing.

Isaac dialed Tina's number and let the phone ring. Certain that she was there, gigantically listening to the steely, beady drilling of the telephone. He let it ring, he said, about five minutes. He made no effort to call Mutt. Mutt would do as Tina did.

'I have an hour to raise this dough.'

'In my bracket,' Aaron said, 'the twenty-five would cost me more than fifty.'

'You could have told me this yesterday. Knowing what it means to me.'

'You'll turn over a hundred thousand to a man you don't know? Without a receipt? Blind? Don't do it.'

But Isaac had decided. In our generation, Dr Braun thought, a sort of playboy capitalist has emerged. He gaily takes a flier in rebuilt office machinery for Brazil, motels in East Africa, high-fidelity components in Thailand. A hundred thousand means little. He jets down with a click to see the scene. The governor of a province is waiting in his Thunderbird to take the guests on jungle expressways built by graft and peons to a surf-and-champagne weekend where the executive, youthful at fifty, closes the deal. But Cousin Isaac had put his stake together penny by penny, old style, starting with rags and bottles as a boy; then fire-salvaged goods; then used cars; then learning the building trades. Earth moving, foundations, concrete, sewage, wiring, roofing, heating systems. He got his money the hard way. And now he went to the bank and borrowed $75,000, at full interest. Without security, he gave it to Ilkington in Ilkington's parlor. Furnished in old *goy* taste and disseminating an old *goy* odor of tiresome, silly, respectable things. Of which Ilkington was clearly so proud. The applewood, the cherry, the wing tables and cabinets, the upholstery with a flavor of dry paste, the pork-pale colors of gentility. Ilkington did not touch Isaac's briefcase. He did not intend, evidently, to count the bills, nor even to look. He offered Isaac a martini. Isaac, not a drinker, drank the clear gin. At noon. Like something distilled in outer space. Having no color. He sat there sturdily, but felt lost – lost to his people, his family, lost to God, lost in the void of America. Ilkington drank a shaker of cocktails, gentlemanly, stony, like a high slab of something generically human, but with few human traits familiar to Isaac. At the door he did not say he would keep his word. He simply shook hands with Isaac, saw him to the car. Isaac drove home and sat in the den of his bungalow. Two whole days. Then on Monday, Ilkington phoned to say that the Robbstown directors had decided to accept his offer for the property. A pause. Then Ilkington added that no written instrument could replace trust and decency between gentlemen.

Isaac took possession of the country club and filled it with a shopping center. All such places are ugly. Dr Braun could not say why this one struck him as especially brutal in its ugliness. Perhaps because he remembered the Robbstown Club. Restricted, of course. But Jews could look at it from the road. And the elms had been lovely – a century or older. The light, delicate. And the Coolidge-era sedans turning in, with small curtains at the rear window, and holders for artificial flowers. Hudsons, Auburns, Bearcats. Only machinery. Nothing to feel nostalgic about.

Still, Braun was startled to see what Isaac had done. Perhaps in an unconscious assertion of triumph – in the vividness of victory. The green acres reserved, it was true, for mild idleness, for hitting a little ball with a stick, were now paralyzed by parking for 500 cars. Supermarket, pizza joint, chop suey, Laundromat, Robert Hall clothes, a dime store.

And this was only the beginning. Isaac became a millionaire. He filled the Mohawk Valley with housing developments. And he began to speak of 'my people', meaning those who lived in the buildings he had raised. He was stingy with land, he built too densely, it was true, but he built with benevolence. At six in the morning, he was out with his crews. He lived very simply. Walked humbly with his God, as the rabbi said. A Madison Avenue rabbi, by this time. The little synagogue was wiped out. It was as dead as the Dutch painters who would have appreciated its dimness and its shaggy old peddlers. Now there was a temple like a World's Fair pavilion. Isaac was president, having beaten out the father of a famous hoodlum, once executioner for the Mob in the Northeast. The worldly rabbi with his trained voice and tailored suits, like a Christian minister except for the play of Jewish cleverness in his face, hinted to the old-fashioned part of the congregation that he had to pour it on for the sake of the young people. America. Extraordinary times. If you wanted the young women to bless Sabbath candles, you had to start their rabbi at $20,000, and add a house and a Jaguar.

Cousin Isaac, meantime, grew more old-fashioned. His car was ten years old. But he was a strong sort of man. Self-assured, a dark head scarcely thinning at the top. Upstate women said he gave out the positive male energy they were beginning to miss in men. He had it. It was in the manner with which he picked up a fork at the table, the way he poured from a bottle. Of course, the world had done for him exactly what he had demanded. That meant he had made the right demand and in the right place. It meant his reading of life was metaphysically true. Or that the Old Testament, the Talmud, and Polish Ashkenazi orthodoxy were irresistible.

But that wouldn't altogether do, thought Dr Braun. There

was more there than piety. He recalled his cousin's white teeth and scar-twisted smile when he was joking. 'I fought on many fronts,' Cousin Isaac said, meaning women's bellies. He often had a sound American way of putting things. Had known the back stairs in Schenectady that led to the sheets, the gripping arms and spreading thighs of workingwomen. The Model T was parked below. Earlier, the horse waited in harness. He got great pleasure from masculine reminiscences. Recalling Dvorah the greenhorn, on her knees, hiding her head in pillows while her buttocks soared, a burst of kinky hair from the walls of whiteness, and her feeble voice crying, '*Nein*.' But she did not mean it.

Cousin Mutt had no such anecdotes. Shot in the head at Iwo Jima, he came back from a year in the hospital to sell Zenith, Motorola, and Westinghouse appliances. He married a respectable girl and went on quietly amid a bewildering expansion and transformation of his birthplace. A computer center taking over the bush-league park where a scout had him spotted before the war as material for the majors. On most important matters, Mutt went to Tina. She told him what to do. And Isaac looked out for him, whenever possible buying appliances through Mutt for his housing developments. But Mutt took his problems to Tina. For instance, his wife and her sister played the horses. Every chance they got, they drove to Saratoga, to the trotting races. Probably no great harm in this. The two sisters with gay lipstick and charming dresses. And laughing continually with their pretty jutting teeth. And putting down the top of the convertible.

Tina took a mild view of this. Why shouldn't they go to the track? Her fierceness was concentrated, all of it, on Braun the millionaire.

'That whoremaster!' she said.

'Oh, no. Not in years and years,' said Mutt.

'Come, Mutt. I know whom he's been balling. I keep an eye on the orthodox. Believe me, I do. And now the governor has put him on a commission. Which is it?'

'Pollution.'

'Water pollution, that's right. Rockefeller's buddy.'

'Well, you shouldn't, Tina. He's our brother.'

'He feels for *you*.'

'Yes, he does.'

'A multimillionaire – lets you go on drudging in a little business? He's heartless. A heartless man.'

'It's not true.'

'What? He never had a tear in his eye unless the wind was blowing,' said Tina.

Hyperbole was Tina's greatest weakness. They were all like that. The mother had bred it in them.

Otherwise, she was simply a gloomy, obese woman, sternly combed, the hair tugged back from her forehead, tight, so that the hairline was a fighting barrier. She had a totalitarian air. And not only toward others. Toward herself, also. Absorbed in the dictatorship of her huge person. In a white dress, and with the ring on her finger she had seized from her dead mother. By a *putsch* in the bedroom.

In her generation – Dr Braun had given up his afternoon to the hopeless pleasure of thinking affectionately about his dead – in her generation, Tina was also old-fashioned for all her modern slang. People of her sort, and not only the women, cultivated charm. But Tina willed consistently to appeal for nothing, to have no charm. Absolutely none. She never tried to please. Her aim must have been majesty. Based on what? She had no great thoughts. She built on her own nature. On a primordial idea, hugely blown up. Somewhat as her flesh in its dress of white silk, as last seen by Cousin Braun some years ago, was blown up. Some sub-suboffice of the personality, behind a little door of the brain where the restless spirit never left its work, had ordered this tremendous female form, all of it, to become manifest, with dark hair on the forearms, conspicuous nostrils in the white face, and black eyes staring. The eyes had an affronted expression; sometimes a look of sulphur; a clever look – they had all the looks, even the look of kindness that came from Uncle Braun. The old man's sweetness. Those who try to interpret humankind through its eyes are in for much strangeness – perplexity.

The quarrel between Tina and Isaac lasted for years. She

accused him of shaking off the family when the main chance came. He had refused to cut them in. He said that they had all deserted him at the zero hour. Eventually, the brothers made it up. Not Tina. She wanted nothing to do with Isaac. In the first phase of enmity she saw to it that he should know exactly what she thought of him. Brothers, aunts, and old friends reported what she was saying about him. He was a crook. Mama had lent him money; he would not repay; that was why she had collected those rents. Also, Isaac had been a silent partner of Zaikas, the Greek, the racketeer from Troy. She said that Zaikas had covered for Isaac, who was implicated in the state-hospital scandal. Zaikas took the fall, but Isaac had to put $50,000 in Zaikas's box at the bank. The Stuyvesant Bank, that was. Tina said she even knew the box number. Isaac said little to these slanders, and after a time they stopped.

And it was when they stopped that Isaac actually began to feel the anger of his sister. He felt it as head of the family, the oldest living Braun. After he had not seen his sister for two or three years, he began to remind himself of Uncle Braun's affection for Tina. The only daughter. The youngest. Our baby sister. Thoughts of the old days touched his heart. Having gotten what he wanted, Tina said to Mutt, he could redo the past in sentimental colors. Isaac would remember that in 1920 Aunt Rose wanted fresh milk, and the Brauns kept a cow in the pasture by the river. What a beautiful place. And how delicious it was to crank the Model T and drive at dusk to milk the cow beside the green water. Driving, they sang songs. Tina, then ten years old, must have weighed two hundred pounds, but the shape of her mouth was very sweet, womanly – perhaps the pressure of the fat, hastening her maturity. Somehow she was more feminine in childhood than later. It was true that at nine or ten she sat on a kitten in the rocker, unaware, and smothered it. Aunt Rose found it dead when her daughter stood up. 'You huge thing,' she said to her daughter, 'you animal.' But even this Isaac recollected with amused sadness. And since he belonged to no societies, never played cards, never spent an evening drinking, never went to Florida, never went to Europe, never went to see the

State of Israel, he had plenty of time for reminiscences.
Respectable elms about his house sighed with him for the past.
The squirrels were orthodox. They dug and saved. Mrs Isaac
Braun wore no cosmetics. Except a touch of lipstick when
going out in public. No mink coats. A comfortable Hudson
seal, yes. With a large fur button on the belly. To keep her,
as he liked her, warm. Fair, pale, round, with a steady innocent
look, and hair worn short and symmetrical. Light brown,
with kinks of gold. One gray eye, perhaps, expressed or came
near expressing slyness. It must have been purely involuntary.
At least there was not the slightest sign of conscious criticism
or opposition. Isaac was master. Cooking, baking, laundry,
all housekeeping, had to meet his standard. If he didn't like
the smell of the cleaning woman, she was sent away. It was an
ample plain old-fashioned respectable domestic life on an
eastern European model completely destroyed in 1939 by
Hitler and Stalin. Those two saw to the eradication of the old
conditions, made sure that certain modern concepts became
social realities. Maybe the slightest troubling ambiguity in
one of Cousin Sylvia's eyes was the effect of a suppressed
historical comment. As a woman, Dr Braun considered,
she had more than a glimmering of this modern transformation. Her husband was a multimillionaire. Where was the
life this might have bought? The houses, servants, clothes,
and cars? On the farm she had operated machines. As his
wife, she was obliged to forget how to drive. She was a docile,
darling woman, and she was in the kitchen baking spongecake
and chopping liver, as Isaac's mother had done. Or should
have done. Without the flaming face, the stern meeting
brows, the rigorous nose and the club of powerful braid
lying on her spine. Without Aunt Rose's curses.

In America, the abuses of the Old World were righted. It
was appointed to be the land of historical redress. However,
Dr Braun reflected, new uproars filled the soul. Material
details were of the greatest importance. But still the largest
strokes were made by the spirit. Had to be! People who said
this were right.

Cousin Isaac's thoughts: a web of computations, of

frontages, elevations, drainage, mortgages, turn-around money. And since, in addition, he had been a strong, raunchy young man, and this had never entirely left him (it remained only as witty comment), his piety really did appear to be put on. Superadded. The psalm-saying at building sites. *When I consider the heavens, the work of Thy fingers ... what is Man that Thou art mindful of him?* But he evidently meant it all. He took off whole afternoons before high holidays. While his fair-faced wife, flushed with baking, noted with the slightly Biblical air he expected of her, that he was bathing, changing upstairs. He had visited the graves of his parents. Announcing, 'I've been to the cemetery.'

'Oh,' she said with sympathy, the one beautiful eye full of candor. The other fluttering with a minute quantity of slyness.

The parents, stifled in the clay. Two crates, side by side. Grass of burning green sweeping over them, and Isaac repeating a prayer to the God of Mercy. And in Hebrew with a Baltic accent at which modern Israelis scoffed. September trees, yellow after an icy night or two, now that the sky was blue and warm, gave light instead of shadow. Isaac was concerned about his parents. Down there, how were they? The wet, the cold, above all the worms worried him. In frost, his heart shrank for Aunt Rose and Uncle Braun, though as a builder he knew they were beneath the frost line. But a human power, his love, affected his practical judgement. It flew off. Perhaps as a builder and housing expert (on two of the governor's commissions, not one) he especially felt his dead to be unsheltered. But Tina – they were her dead, too – felt he was still exploiting Papa and Mama and that he would have exploited her, too, if she had let him.

For several years, at the same season, there was a scene between them. The pious thing before the Day of Atonement was to visit the dead and to forgive the living – forgive and ask forgiveness. Accordingly, Isaac went annually to the old home. Parked his Cadillac. Rang the bell, his heart beating hard. He waited at the foot of the long enclosed staircase. The small brick building, already old in 1915 when Uncle Braun had bought it, passed to Tina, who tried to make it

modern. Her ideas came out of *House Beautiful*. The paper with
which she covered the slanted walls of the staircase was
unsuitable. It did not matter. Tina, above, opened the door,
saw the masculine figure and scarred face of her brother and
said, 'What do you want?'

'Tina! For God's sake, I've come to make peace.'

'What peace! You swindled us out of a fortune.'

'The others don't agree. Now, Tina, we are brother and
sister. Remember Father and Mother. Remember . . .'

She cried down at him, 'You son of a bitch, I *do* remember!
Now get the hell out of here.'

Banging the door, she dialed her brother Aaron, lighting
one of her long cigarettes. 'He's been here again,' she said.
'What shit! He's not going to practice his goddamn
religion on me.'

She said she hated his orthodox cringe. She could take him
straight. In a deal. Or a swindle. But she couldn't bear his
sentiment.

As for herself, she might smell like a woman, but she acted
like a man. And in her dress, while swooning music came from
the radio, she smoked her cigarette after he was gone,
thundering inside with great flashes of feeling. For which,
otherwise, there was no occasion. She might curse him,
thought Dr Braun, but she owed him much. Aunt Rose, who
had been such a harsh poet of money, had left her daughter
needs – such needs! Quiet middle-age domestic decency (husband, daughter, furnishings) did nothing for needs like hers.

So when Isaac Braun told his wife that he had visited the
family graves, she knew that he had gone again to see Tina.
The thing had been repeated. Isaac, with a voice and gesture
that belonged to history and had no place or parallel in upstate
industrial New York State, appealed to his sister in the eyes
of God, and in the name of souls departed, to end her anger.
But she cried from the top of the stairs, 'Never! You son of
a bitch, never!' and he went away.

He went home for consolation, and walked to the temple
later with an injured heart. A leader of the congregation,
weighted with grief. Striking breast with fist in old-fashioned

penitence. The new way was the way of understatement.
Anglo-Saxon restraint. The rabbi, with his Madison Avenue
public-relations airs, did not go for these European Judaic,
operatic fist-clenchings. Tears. He made the cantor tone it
down. But Isaac Braun, covered by his father's prayer shawl
with its black stripes and shedding fringes, ground his teeth
and wept near the ark.

These annual visits to Tina continued until she became
sick. When she went into the hospital, Isaac phoned Dr
Braun and asked him to find out how things really stood.

'But I'm not a medical doctor.'

'You're a scientist. You'll understand it better.'

Anyone might have understood. She was dying of cancer
of the liver. Cobalt radiation was tried. Chemotherapy. Both
made her very sick. Dr Braun told Isaac, 'There is no hope.'

'I know.'

'Have you seen her?'

'No. I hear from Mutt.'

Isaac sent word through Mutt that he wanted to come to
her bedside.

Tina refused to see him.

And Mutt, with his dark sloping face, unhandsome but
gentle, dog-eyed, softly urged her, 'You should, Tina.'

But Tina said, 'No. Why should I? A Jewish deathbed
scene, that's what he wants. No.'

'Come, Tina.'

'No,' she said, even firmer. Then she added, 'I hate him.'
As though explaining that Mutt should not expect her to give
up the support of this feeling. And a little later she added, in a
lower voice, as though speaking generally, 'I can't help him.'

But Isaac phoned Mutt daily, saying, 'I have to see my
sister.'

'I can't get her to do it.'

'You've got to explain it to her. She doesn't know what's
right.'

Isaac even telephoned Fenster, though, as everyone was
aware, he had a low opinion of Fenster's intelligence. And
Fenster answered, 'She says you did us all dirt.'

'I? She got scared and backed out. I had to go it alone.'

'You shook us off.'

Quite simple-mindedly, with the directness of the Biblical fool (this was how Isaac saw him, and Fenster knew it), he said, 'You wanted it all for yourself, Isaac.'

That they should let him, ungrudgingly, enjoy his great wealth, Isaac told Dr Braun, was too much to expect. Of human beings. And he was very rich. He did not say how much money he had. This was a mystery in the family. The old people said, 'He himself doesn't know.'

Isaac confessed to Dr Braun, 'I never understood her.' He was much moved, even then, a year later.

Cousin Tina had discovered that one need not be bound by the old rules. That, Isaac's painful longing to see his sister's face being denied, everything was put into a different sphere of advanced understanding, painful but truer than the old. From her bed she appeared to be directing this research.

'You ought to let him come,' said Mutt.

'Because I'm dying?'

Mutt, plain and dark, stared at her, his black eyes momentarily vacant as he chose an answer. 'People recover,' he said.

But she said, with peculiar indifference to the fact, 'Not this time.' She had already become gaunt in the face and high in the belly. Her ankles were swelling. She had seen this in others and understood the signs.

'He calls every day,' said Mutt.

She had had her nails done. A dark-red, almost maroon color. One of those odd twists of need or desire. The ring she had taken from her mother was now loose on the finger. And, reclining on the raised bed, as if she had found a moment of ease, she folded her arms and said, pressing the lace of the bed jacket with her finger tips, "Then give Isaac my message, Mutt. I'll see him, yes, but it'll cost him money.'

'Money?'

'If he pays me twenty thousand dollars.'

'Tina, that's not right.'

'Why not! For my daughter. She'll need it.'

'No, she doesn't need that kind of dough.' He knew what Aunt Rose had left. 'There's plenty and you know it.'

'If he's got to come, that's the price of admission,' she said. 'Only a fraction of what he did us out of.'

Mutt said simply, 'He never did me out of anything.' Curiously, the shrewdness of the Brauns was in his face, but he never practiced it. This was not because he had been wounded in the Pacific. He had always been like that. He sent Tina's message to Isaac on a piece of business stationery, BRAUN APPLIANCES, 42 CLINTON. Like a contract bid. No word of comment, not even a signature.

For 20 grand cash Tina says yes otherwise no.

In Dr Braun's opinion, his Cousin Tina had seized upon the force of death to create a situation of opera. Which at the same time was a situation of parody. As he stated it to himself, there was a feedback of mockery. Death the horrid bridegroom, waiting with a consummation life had never offered. Life, accordingly, she devalued, filling up the clear light remaining (which should be reserved for beauty, miracle, nobility) with obese monstrosity, rancor, failure, self-torture.

Isaac, on the day he received Tina's terms, was scheduled to go out on the river with the governor's commission on pollution. A boat was sent by the Fish and Game Department to take the five members out on the Hudson. They would go south as far as Germantown. Where the river, with mountains on the west, seems a mile wide. And back again to Albany. Isaac would have canceled this inspection, he had so much thinking to do, was so full of things. 'Overthronged' was the odd term Braun chose for it, which seemed to render Isaac's state best. But Isaac could not get out of this official excursion. His wife made him take his Panama hat and wear a light suit. He bent over the side of the boat, hands clasped tight on the dark-red, brass-jointed rail. He breathed through his teeth. At the back of his legs, in his neck, his pulses beating; and in the head an arterial swell through which he was aware, one-sidedly, of the air streaming, and gorgeous water. Two young professors from Rensselaer lectured on the geology

and wildlife of the upper Hudson and on the industrial and
community problems of the region. The towns were dumping
raw sewage into the Mohawk and the Hudson. You could
watch the flow from giant pipes. Cloacae, said the professor
with his red beard and ruined teeth. Much dark metal in his
mouth, pewter ridges instead of bone. And a pipe with which
he pointed to the turds yellowing the river. The cities,
spilling their filth. How dispose of it? Methods were discussed
– treatment plants. Atomic power. And finally he presented
an ingenious engineering project for sending all waste into
the interior of the earth, far under the crust, thousands of
feet into deeper strata. But even if pollution were stopped
today, it would take fifty years to restore the river. The fish
had persisted but at last abandoned their old spawning
grounds. Only a savage scavenger eel dominated the water.
The river great and blue in spite of the dung pools and the
twisting of the eels.

One member of the governor's commission had a face
remotely familiar, long and high, the mouth like a latch, cheeks
hollow, the bone warped in the nose, and hair fading. Gentle.
A thin person. His thoughts on Tina, Isaac had missed his
name. But looking at the printed pages prepared by the staff,
he saw that it was Ilkington Junior. This quiet, likable man
examining him with such meaning from the white bulkhead,
long trousers curling in the breeze as he held the metal rail
behind him.

Evidently he knew about the $100,000.

'I think I was acquainted with your father,' Isaac said, his
voice very low.

'You were, indeed,' said Ilkington. He was frail for his
height; his skin was pulled tight, glistening on the temples,
and a reddish blood lichen spread on his cheekbones. Capil-
laries. 'The old man is well.'

'Well. I'm glad.'

'Yes. He's well. Very feeble. He had a bad time, you know.'

'I never heard.'

'Oh, yes, he invested in hotel construction in Nassau and
lost his money.'

'All of it?' said Isaac.

'All his legitimate money.'

'I'm very sorry.'

'Lucky he had a little something to fall back on.'

'He did?'

'He certainly did.'

'Yes, I see. That *was* lucky.'

'It'll last him.'

Isaac was glad to know and appreciated the kindness of Ilkington's son in telling him. Also the man knew what the Robbstown Country Club had been worth to him, but did not grudge him, behaved with courtesy. For which Isaac, filled with thankfulness, would have liked to show gratitude. But what you showed, among these people, you showed with silence. Of which, it seemed to Isaac, he was now beginning to appreciate the wisdom. The native, different wisdom of Gentiles, who had much to say but refrained. What was this Ilkington Junior? He looked into the pages again and found a paragraph of biography. Insurance executive. Various government commissions. Probably Isaac could have discussed Tina with such a man. Yes, in heaven. On earth they would never discuss a thing. Silent impressions would have to do. Incommunicable diversities, kindly but silent contact. The more they had in their heads, the less people seemed to know how to tell it.

'When you write to your father, remember me to him.'

Communities along the river, said the professor, would not pay for any sort of sewage-treatment plants. The Federal Government would have to arrange it. Only fair, Isaac considered, since Internal Revenue took away to Washington billions in taxes and left small change for the locals. So they pumped the excrements into the waterways. Isaac, building along the Mohawk, had always taken this for granted. Building squalid settlements of which he was so proud ... Had been proud.

He stepped onto the dock when the boat tied up. The State Game Commissioner had taken an eel from the water to show the inspection party. It was writhing toward the river in swift, powerful loops, tearing its skin on the planks, its crest of fin standing. *Treph!* And slimy black, the perishing mouth open.

The breeze had dropped and the wide water stank. Isaac drove home, turning on the air conditioner of his Cadillac. His wife said, 'What was it like?'

He had no answer to give.

'What are you doing about Tina?'

Again, he said nothing.

But knowing Isaac, seeing how agitated he was, she predicted that he would go down to New York City for advice. She told this later to Dr Braun, and he saw no reason to doubt it. Clever wives can foretell. A fortunate husband will be forgiven his predictability.

Isaac had a rabbi in Williamsburg. He was orthodox enough for that. And he did not fly. He took a compartment on the Twentieth Century when it left Albany just before daybreak. With just enough light through the dripping gray to see the river. But not the west shore. A tanker covered by smoke and cloud divided the bituminous water. Presently the mountains emerged.

They wanted to take the crack train out of service. The carpets were filthy, the toilets stank. Slovenly waiters in the dining car. Isaac took toast and coffee, rejecting the odors of ham and bacon by expelling breath. Eating with his hat on. Racially distinct, as Dr Braun well knew. A blood group characteristically eastern Mediterranean. The very fingerprints belonging to a distinctive family of patterns. The nose, the eyes long and full, the skin dark, slashed near the mouth by a Russian doctor in the old days. And looking out as they rushed past Rhinecliff, Isaac saw, with the familiarity of hundreds of journeys, the grand water, the thick trees – illuminated space. In the compartment, in captive leisure, shut up with the foul upholstery, the rattling door. The old arsenal, Bannerman's Island, the playful castle, yellow-green willows around it, and the water sparkling, as green as he remembered it in 1910 – one of the forty million foreigners coming to America. The steel rails, as they were then, the twisting currents and the mountain round at the top, the wall of rock curving steeply into the expanding river.

From Grand Central, carrying a briefcase with all he needed in it, Isaac took the subway to his appointment. He waited in the anteroom, where the rabbi's bearded followers went in and out in long coats. Dressed in business clothes, Isaac, however, seemed no less archaic than the rest. A bare floor. Wooden seats, white stippled walls. But the windows were smeared, as though the outside did not matter. Of these people, many were survivors of the German holocaust. The rabbi himself had been through it as a boy. After the war, he had lived in Holland and Belgium and studied sciences in France. At Montpellier. Biochemistry. But he had been called – summoned – to these spiritual duties in New York; Isaac was not certain how this happened. And now he wore the full beard. In his office, sitting at a little table with a green blotting pad, and a pen and note paper. The conversation was in the *jargón* – in Yiddish.

'Rabbi, my name is Isaac Braun.'

'From Albany. Yes, I remember.'

'I am the eldest of four – my sister, the youngest, the *muzinka*, is dying.'

'Are you sure of this?'

'Of cancer of the liver, and with a lot of pain.'

'Then she is. Yes, she is dying.' From the very white, full face, the rabbi's beard grew straight and thick in rich bristles. He was a strong, youthful man, his stout body buttoned straining in the shiny black cloth.

'A certain thing happened soon after the war. An opportunity to buy a valuable piece of land for building. I invited my brothers and my sister to invest with me, Rabbi. But on the day . . .'

The rabbi listened, his white face lifted toward a corner of the ceiling, but fully attentive, his hands pressed to the ribs, above the waist.

'I understand. You tried to reach them that day. And you felt abandoned.'

'They deserted me, Rabbi, yes.'

'But that was also your good luck. They turned their faces from you, and this made you rich. You didn't have to share.'

Isaac admitted this but added, 'If it hadn't been one deal, it would have been another.'

'You were destined to be rich?'

'I was sure to be. And there were so many opportunities.'

'Your sister, poor thing, is very harsh. She is wrong. She has no ground for complaint against you.'

'I am glad to hear that,' said Isaac. 'Glad', however, was only a word, for he was suffering.

'She is not a poor woman, your sister?'

'No, she inherited property. And her husband does pretty well. Though I suppose the long sickness costs.'

'Yes, a wasting disease. But the living can only will to live. I am speaking of Jews. They wanted to annihilate us. To give our consent would have been to turn from God. But about your problem: Have you thought of your brother Aaron? He advised the others not to take the risk.'

'I know.'

'It was to his interest that she should be angry with you, and not with him.'

'I realize that.'

'He is guilty. He is sinning against you. Your other brother is a good man.'

'Mutt? Yes, I know. He is decent. He barely survived the war. He was shot in the head.'

'But is he still himself?'

'Yes, I believe so.'

'Sometimes it takes something like that. A bullet through the head.' The rabbi paused and turned his round face, the black quill beard bent on the folds of shiny cloth. And then, as Isaac told him how he went to Tina before the high holidays, he looked impatient, moving his head forward, but his eyes turning sideward. 'Yes. Yes.' He was certain that Isaac had done the right things. 'Yes. You have the money. She grudged you. Unreasonable. But that's how it seems to her. You are a man. She is only a woman. You are a rich man.'

'But, Rabbi,' said Isaac, 'now she is on her deathbed, and I have asked to see her.'

'Yes? Well?'

'She wants money for it.'

'Ah? Does she? Money?'

'Twenty thousand dollars. So that I can be let into the room.'

The burly rabbi was motionless, white fingers on the armrests of the wooden chair. 'She knows she is dying, I suppose?' he said.

'Yes.'

'Yes. Our Jews love deathbed jokes. I know many. Well. America had not changed everything, has it? People assume that God has a sense of humor. Such jokes made by the dying in anguish show a strong and brave soul, but skeptical. What sort of woman is your sister?'

'Stout. Large.'

'I see. A fat woman. A chunk of flesh with two eyes, as they used to say. Staring at the lucky ones. Like an animal in a cage, perhaps. Separated. By sensual greed and despair. A fat child like that – people sometimes behave as though they were alone when such a child is present. So those little monster souls have a strange fate. They see people as people are when no one is looking. A gloomy vision of mankind.'

Isaac respected the rabbi. Revered him, thought Dr Braun. But perhaps he was not old-fashioned enough for him, notwithstanding the hat and beard and gaberdine. He had the old tones, the manner, the burly poise, the universal calm judgement of the Jewish moral genius. Enough to satisfy anyone. But there was also something foreign about him. That is, contemporary. Now and then there was a sign from the science student, the biochemist from the south of France, from Montpellier. He would probably have spoken English with a French accent, whereas Cousin Isaac spoke like anyone else from upstate. In Yiddish they had the same dialect – White Russian. The Minsk region. The Pripet Marshes, thought Dr Braun. And then returned to the fish hawk on the brown and chalky sycamore beside the Mohawk. Yes. Perhaps.

Among these recent birds, finches, thrushes, there was Cousin
Isaac with more scale than feather in his wings. A more
antique type. The ruddy brown eye, the tough muscles of the
jaw working under the skin. Even the scar was precious to
Dr Braun. He knew the man. Or rather, he had the longing
of having known. For these people were dead. A useless love.

'You can afford the money?' the rabbi asked. And when
Isaac hesitated, he said, 'I don't ask you for the figure of
your fortune. It is not my concern. But could you give her
the twenty thousand?'

And Isaac, looking greatly tried, said, 'If I had to.'

'It wouldn't make a great difference in your fortune?'

'No.'

'In that case, why shouldn't you pay?'

'You think I should?'

'It's not for me to tell you to give away so much money.
But you gave – you gambled – you trusted the man, the *goy*.'

'Ilkington? That was a business risk. But Tina? So you
believe I should pay?'

'Give in. I would say, judging the sister by the brother,
there is no other way.'

Then Isaac thanked him for his time and his opinion. He
went out into the broad daylight of the street, which smelled
of muck. The tedious mortar of tenements, settled out of line.
the buildings swaybacked, with grime on grime, as if built of
castoff shoes, not brick. The contractor observing. The
ferment of sugar and roasting coffee was strong, but the
summer air moved quickly in the damp under the huge
machine-trampled bridge. Looking about for the subway
entrance, Isaac saw instead a yellow cab with a yellow light
on the crest. He first told the driver, 'Grand Central,' but
changed his mind at the first corner and said, 'Take me to the
West Side Air Terminal.' There was no fast train to Albany
before late afternoon. He could not wait on Forty-second
Street. Not today. He must have known all along that he
would have to pay the money. He had come to get strength
by consulting the rabbi. Old laws and wisdom on his side.
But Tina from the deathbed had made too strong a move. If he

refused to come across, no one could blame him. But he would feel greatly damaged. How would he live with himself? Because he made these sums easily now. Buying and selling a few city lots. Had the price been $50,000, Tina would have been saying that he would never see her again. But $20,000 – the figure was a shrewd choice. And orthodoxy had no remedy. It was entirely up to him.

Having decided to capitulate, he felt a kind of deadly recklessness. He had never been in the air before. But perhaps it was high time to fly. Everyone had lived enough. And anyway, as the cab crept through the summer lunch-time crowds on Twenty-third Street, there seemed plenty of humankind already.

On the airport bus, he opened his father's copy of the Psalms. The black Hebrew letters only gaped at him like open mouths with tongues hanging down, pointing upward, flaming but dumb. He tried – forcing. It did no good. The tunnel, the swamps, the auto skeletons, machine entrails, dumps, gulls, sketchy Newark trembling in fiery summer, held his attention minutely. As though he were not Isaac Braun but a man who took pictures. Then in the jet running with concentrated fury to take off – the power to pull away from the magnetic earth; and more: When he saw the ground tilt backward, the machine rising from the runway, he said to himself in clear internal words, '*Shema Yisrael*,' Hear, O Israel, God alone is God! On the right, New York leaned gigantically seaward, and the plane with a jolt of retracted wheels turned toward the river. The Hudson green within green, and rough with tide and wind. Isaac released the breath he had been holding, but sat belted tight. Above the marvelous bridges, over clouds, sailing in atmosphere, you know better than ever that you are no angel.

The flight was short. From Albany airport, Isaac phoned his bank. He told Spinwall, with whom he did business there, that he needed $20,000 in cash. 'No problem,' said Spinwall. 'We have it.'

Isaac explained to Dr Braun. 'I have passbooks for my savings accounts in my safe-deposit box.'

Probably in individual accounts of $10,000, protected by federal deposit insurance. He must have had bundles of these.

He went through the round entrance of the vault, the mammoth delicate door, circular, like the approaching moon seen by space navigators. A taxi waited as he drew the money and took him, the dollars in his briefcase, to the hospital. Then at the hospital, the hopeless flesh and melancholy festering and drug odors, the splashy flowers and wrinkled garments. In the large cage elevator that could take in whole beds, Pulmotors, and laboratory machines, his eyes were fixed on the silent, beautiful Negro woman dreaming at the control as they moved slowly from lobby to mezzanine, from mezzanine to first. The two were alone, and since there was no going faster, he found himself observing her strong, handsome legs, her bust, the gold wire and glitter of her glasses, and the sensual bulge in her throat, just under the chin. In spite of himself, struck by these as he slowly rose to his sister's deathbed,

At the elevator, as the gate opened, was his brother Mutt.

'Isaac!'

'How is she?'

'Very bad.'

'Well, I'm here. With the money.'

Confused, Mutt did not know how to face him. He seemed frightened. Tina's power over Mutt had always been great. Though he was three or four years her senior. Isaac somewhat understood what moved him and said, 'That's all right, Mutt, if I have to pay. I'm ready. On her terms.'

'She may not even know.'

'Take it. Say I'm here. I want to see my sister, Mutt.'

Unable to look at Isaac, Mutt received the briefcase and went in to Tina. Isaac moved away from her door without glancing through the slot. Because he could not stand still, he moved down the corridor, hands clasped behind his back. Past the rank of empty wheelchairs. Repelled by these things made for weakness. He hated such objects, hated the stink of hospitals. He was sixty years old. He knew the route he, too, must go, and soon. But only knew, did not yet feel it. Death still was at a distance. As for handing over the money, about which Mutt was ashamed, taking part unwillingly in something unjust, grotesque – yes, it was farfetched, like things women imagined they wanted in pregnancy, hungry for peaches, or beer, or eating plaster from the walls. But as for himself, as soon as he handed over the money, he felt no more concern for it. It was nothing. He was glad to be rid of it. He could hardly understand this about himself. Once the money was given, the torment stopped. Nothing at all. The thing was done to punish, to characterize him, to convict him of something, to put him in a category. But the effect was just the opposite. What category? Where was it? If she thought it made him suffer, it did not. If she thought she understood his soul better than anyone – his poor dying sister; no, she did not.

And Dr Braun, feeling with them this work of wit and despair, this last attempt to exchange significance, rose, stood, looking at the shafts of ice, the tatters of vapor in winter blue.

Then Tina's private nurse opened the door and beckoned to Isaac. He hurried in and stopped with a suffocated look. Her upper body was wasted and yellow. Her belly was huge with the growth, and her legs, her ankles were swollen. Her distorted feet had freed themselves from the cover. The soles like clay. The skin was tight on her skull. The hair was white. An intravenous tube was taped to her arm, and other tubes from her body into excretory jars beneath the bed. Mutt had laid the briefcase before her. It had not been unstrapped. Fleshless, hair coarse, and the meaning of her black eyes impossible to understand, she was looking at Isaac.

'Tina!'

'I wondered,' she said.

'It's all there.'

But she swept the briefcase from her and in a choked voice said, 'No. Take it.' He went to kiss her. Her free arm was lifted and tried to embrace him. She was too feeble, too drugged. He felt the bones of his obese sister. Death. The end. The grave. They were weeping. And Mutt, turning away at the foot of the bed, his mouth twisted open and the tears running from his eyes. Tina's tears were much thicker and slower.

The ring she had taken from Aunt Rose was tied to Tina's wasted finger with dental floss. She held out her hand to the nurse. It was all prearranged. The nurse cut the thread. Tina said to Isaac, 'Not the money. I don't want it. You take Mama's ring.'

And Dr Braun, bitterly moved, tried to grasp what emotions were. What good were they! What were they for! And no one wanted them now. Perhaps the cold eye was better. On life, on death. But, again, the cold of the eye would be proportional to the degree of heat within. But once humankind had grasped its own idea, that it was human and human through such passions, it began to exploit, to play, to disturb for the sake of exciting disturbance, to make an uproar, a crude circus of feelings. So the Brauns wept for Tina's death. Isaac held his mother's ring in his hand. Dr Braun, too, had tears in his eyes. Oh, these Jews – these Jews! Their feelings, their hearts! Dr Braun often wanted nothing more than to stop all this. For what came of it? One after another you gave over your dying. One by one they went. You went. Childhood, family, friendship, love were stifled in the grave. And these tears! When you wept them from the heart, you felt you justified something, understood something. But what did you understand? Again, *nothing*! It was only an intimation of understanding. A promise that mankind might – *might*, mind you – eventually, through its gift which might – *might* again! – be a divine gift, comprehend why it lived. Why life, why death.

And again, why these particular forms – these Isaacs and these Tinas? When Dr Braun closed his eyes, he saw, red on black, something like molecular processes – the only true heraldry of being. As later, in the close black darkness when the short day ended, he went to the dark kitchen window to have a look at stars. These things cast outward by a great begetting spasm billions of years ago.

Cynthia Ozick

THE PAGAN RABBI

Cynthia Ozick

CYNTHIA OZICK was born in New York and graduated from New York University. She holds a master's degree from Ohio State University and has been a university teacher of English and a fiction workshop instructor. Her first novel, *Trust*, appeared in 1966. Her other books include *Bloodshed*, *Levitation*, *The Cannibal Galaxy* and *The Pagan Rabbi and Other Stories*, one of several collections of short stories. Her essays, stories and translations have appeared in numerous periodicals and anthologies.

THE PAGAN RABBI

> Rabbi Jacob said: 'He who is walking alone and studying,
> but then breaks off to remark, "How lovely is that tree!"
> or "How beautiful is that fallowfield!"? – Scripture regards
> such a one as having hurt his own being.' From *The
> Ethics of the Fathers*

WHEN I heard that Isaac Kornfeld, a man of piety and brains,
had hanged himself in the public park, I put a token in the
subway stile and journeyed out to see the tree.

We had been classmates in the rabbinical seminary. Our
fathers were both rabbis. They were also friends, but only in a
loose way of speaking: in actuality our fathers were enemies.
They vied with one another in demonstrations of charitable-
ness, in the captious glitter of their scholiae, in the number of
their adherents. Of the two, Isaac's father was the milder.
I was afraid of my father; he had a certain disease of the
larynx, and if he even uttered something so trivial as 'Bring
the tea' to my mother, it came out splintered, clamorous,
and vindictive.

Neither man was philosophical in the slightest. It was the
one thing they agreed on. 'Philosophy is an abomination,'
Isaac's father used to say. 'The Greeks were philosophers,
but they remained children playing with their dolls. Even
Socrates, a monotheist, nevertheless sent money down to the
temple to pay for incense to their doll.'

'Idolatry is the abomination,' Isaac argued, 'not philosophy.'

'The latter is the corridor to the former,' his father said.

My own father claimed that if not for philosophy I would
never have been brought to the atheism which finally led me
to withdraw, in my second year, from the seminary. The
trouble was not philosophy – I had none of Isaac's talent: his
teachers later said of him that his imagination was so remarkable he could concoct holiness out of the fine line of a serif.
On the day of his funeral the president of his college was

criticized for having commented that although a suicide Isaac Kornfeld was *ipso facto* consecrated. It should be noted that Isaac hanged himself several weeks short of his thirty-sixth birthday; he was then at the peak of his renown; and the president, of course, did not know the whole story. He judged by Isaac's reputation, which was at no time more impressive than just before his death.

I judged by the same, and marvelled that all that holy genius and intellectual surprise should in the end be raised no higher than the next-to-lowest limb of a delicate young oak, with burly roots like the toes of a gryphon exposed in the wet ground.

The tree was almost alone in a long rough meadow, which sloped down to a bay filled with sickly clams and a bad smell. The place was called Trilham's Inlet, and I knew what the smell meant: that cold brown water covered half the city's turds.

On the day I came to see the tree the air was bleary with fog. The weather was well into autumn and, though it was Sunday, the walks were empty. There was something historical about the park just then, with its rusting grasses and deserted monuments. In front of a soldier's cenotaph a plastic wreath left behind months before by some civic parade stood propped against a stone frieze of identical marchers in the costume of an old war. A banner across the wreath's belly explained that the purpose of war is peace. At the margins of the park they were building a gigantic highway. I felt I was making my way across a battlefield silenced by the victory of the peace machines. The bulldozers had bitten far into the park, and the rolled carcasses of the sacrificed trees were already cut up into logs. There were dozens of felled maples, elms, and oaks. Their moist inner wheels breathed out a fragrance of barns, countryside, decay.

In the bottommost meadow fringing the water I recognized the tree which had caused Isaac to sin against his own life. It looked curiously like a photograph – not only like that newspaper photograph I carried warmly in my pocket, which showed the field and its markers – the drinking-fountain a few

yards off, the ruined brick wall of an old estate behind. The
caption-writer had particularly remarked on the 'rope'. But
the rope was no longer there; the widow had claimed it. It was
his own prayer-shawl that Isaac, a short man, had thrown
over the comely neck of the next-to-lowest limb. A Jew is
buried in his prayer-shawl; the police had handed it over to
Sheindel. I observed that the bark was rubbed at that spot.
The tree lay back against the sky like a licked postage-stamp.
Rain began to beat it flatter yet. A stench of sewage came up
like a veil in the nostril. It seemed to me I was a man in a
photograph standing next to a grey blur of tree. I would
stand through eternity beside Isaac's guilt if I did not run,
so I ran that night to Sheindel herself.

I loved her at once. I am speaking now of the first time I
saw her, though I don't exclude the last. The last – the last
together with Isaac – was soon after my divorce; at one stroke
I left my wife and my cousin's fur business to the small
upstate city in which both had repined. Suddenly Isaac and
Sheindel and two babies appeared in the lobby of my hotel –
they were passing through: Isaac had a lecture engagement in
Canada. We sat under scarlet neon and Isaac told how my
father could now not speak at all.

'He keeps his vow,' I said.

'No, no, he's a sick man,' Isaac said. 'An obstruction in the
throat.'

'I'm the obstruction. You know what he said when I left
the seminary. He meant it, never mind how many years it is.
He's never addressed a word to me since.'

'We were reading together. He blamed the reading, who
can blame *him*? Fathers like ours don't know how to love.
They live too much indoors.'

It was an odd remark, though I was too much preoccupied
with my own resentments to notice. 'It wasn't what we read,'
I objected. 'Torah tells that an illustrious man doesn't have
an illustrious son. Otherwise he wouldn't be humble like
other people. This much scholarly stuffing I retain. Well, so
my father always believed he was more illustrious than
anybody, especially more than your father. *There*fore,' I

delivered in Talmudic cadence, 'what chance did I have? A nincompoop and no *sitz fleish*. Now you, you could answer questions that weren't even invented yet. Then you invented them.'

'Torah isn't a spade,' Isaac said. 'A man should have a livelihood. You had yours.'

'The pelt of a dead animal isn't a living either, it's an indecency.'

All the while Sheindel was sitting perfectly still; the babies, female infants in long stockings, were asleep in her arms. She wore a dark thick woollen hat – it was July – that covered every part of her hair. But I had once seen it in all its streaming black shine.

'And Jane?' Isaac asked finally.

'Speaking of dead animals. Tell my father – he won't answer a letter, he won't come to the telephone – that in the matter of the marriage he was right, but for the wrong reason. If you share a bed with a Puritan you'll come into it cold and you'll go out of it cold. Listen, Isaac, my father calls me an atheist, but between the conjugal sheets every Jew is a believer in miracles, even the lapsed.'

He said nothing then. He knew I envied him his Sheindel and his luck. Unlike our fathers, Isaac had never condemned me for my marriage, which his father regarded as his private triumph over my father, and which my father, in his public defeat, took as an occasion for declaring me as one dead. He rent his clothing and sat on a stool for eight days, while Isaac's father came to watch him mourn, secretly satisfied, though aloud he grieved for all apostates. Isaac did not like my wife. He called her a tall yellow straw. After we were married he never said a word against her, but he kept away.

I went with my wife to his wedding. We took the early train down especially, but when we arrived the feast was well under way, and the guests far into the dancing.

'Look, look, they don't dance together,' Jane said.

'Who?'

'The men and the women. The bride and the groom.'

'Count the babies,' I advised. 'The Jews are also Puritans, but only in public.'

The bride was enclosed all by herself on a straight chair in the centre of a spinning ring of young men. The floor heaved under their whirl. They stamped, the chandeliers shuddered, the guests cried out, the young men with linked arms spiralled and their skullcaps came flying off like centrifugal balloons. Isaac, a mist of black suit, a stamping foot, was lost in the planet's wake of black suits and emphatic feet. The dancing young men shouted bridal songs, the floor leaned like a plate, the whole room teetered.

Isaac had told me something of Sheindel. Before now I had never seen her. Her birth was in a concentration camp, and they were about to throw her against the electrified fence when an army mobbed the gate; the current vanished from the terrible wires, and she had nothing to show for it afterwards but a mark on her cheek like an asterisk, cut by a barb. The asterisk pointed to certain dry footnotes: she had no mother to show, she had no father to show, but she had, extraordinarily, God to show – she was known to be, for her age and sex, astonishingly learned. She was only seventeen.

'What pretty hair she has,' Jane said.

Now Sheindel was dancing with Isaac's mother. All the ladies made a fence, and the bride, twirling with her mother-in-law, lost a shoe and fell against the long laughing row. The ladies lifted their glistering breasts in their lacy dresses and laughed; the young men, stamping two by two, went on shouting their wedding songs. Sheindel danced without her shoe, and the black river of her hair followed her.

'After today she'll have to hide it all,' I explained.

Jane asked why.

'So as not to be a temptation to men,' I told her, and covertly looked for my father. There he was, in a shadow, apart. My eyes discovered his eyes. He turned his back and gripped his throat.

'It's a very anthropological experience,' Jane said.

'A wedding is a wedding,' I answered her, 'among us even more so.'

'Is that your father over there, that little scowly man?'

To Jane all Jews were little. 'My father the man of the cloth. Yes.'

'A wedding is not a wedding,' said Jane: we had had only a licence and a judge with bad breath.

'Everybody marries for the same reason.'

'No,' said my wife. 'Some for love and some for spite.'

'And everybody for bed.'

'Some for spite,' she insisted.

'I was never cut out for a man of the cloth,' I said. 'My poor father doesn't see that.'

'He doesn't speak to you.'

'A technicality. He's losing his voice.'

'Well, he's not like you. He doesn't do it for spite,' Jane said.

'You don't know him,' I said.

He lost it altogether the very week Isaac published his first remarkable collection of responsa. Isaac's father crowed like a passionate rooster, and packed his wife and himself off to the Holy Land to boast on the holy soil. Isaac was a little relieved; he had just been made Professor of Mishnaic History, and his father's whims and pretences and foolish rivalries were an embarrassment. It is easy to honour a father from afar, but bitter to honour one who is dead. A surgeon cut out my father's voice, and he died without a word.

Isaac and I no longer met. Our ways were too disparate. Isaac was famous, if not in the world, certainly in the kingdom of jurists and scholars. By this time I had acquired a partnership in a small book store in a basement. My partner sold me his share, and I put up a new sign: 'The Book Cellar'; for reasons more obscure than filial (all the same I wished my father could have seen it) I established a department devoted especially to not-quite-rare theological works, chiefly in Hebrew and Aramaic, though I carried some Latin and Greek. When Isaac's second volume reached my shelves (I had now expanded to street level), I wrote him to congratulate him, and after that we corresponded, not with any regularity. He took to ordering all his books from me, and we exchanged awkward little jokes. 'I'm still in the jacket business,' I told him, 'but now I feel I'm where I belong. Last time I went too fur.' 'Sheindel is well, and Naomi and Esther have a sister,' he wrote. And later: 'Naomi, Esther, and Miriam have a sister,' And still later: 'Naomi, Esther, Miriam, and Ophra have a sister.' It went on until there were seven girls. 'There's nothing in Torah that prevents an illustrious man from having illustrious daughters,' I wrote him when he said he had given up hope of another rabbi in the family. 'But where do you find seven illustrious husbands?' he asked. Every order brought another quip, and we bantered back and forth in this way for some years.

I noticed that he read everything. Long ago he had in-flamed my taste, but I could never keep up. No sooner did I catch his joy in Saadia Gaon, than he had already sprung ahead to Yehudah Halevi. One day he was weeping with Dostoyevski and the next leaping in the air over Thomas Mann. He introduced me to Hegel and Nietzsche while our fathers wailed. His mature reading was no more peaceable than those frenzies in his youth, when I would come upon him in an abandoned classroom at dusk, his stocking feet on the window sill, the light already washed from the lowest city clouds, wearing the look of a man half-sotted with print.

But when the widow asked me – covering a certain excess of alertness or irritation – whether to my knowledge Isaac had lately been ordering any books on horticulture, I was aston-ished.

'He bought so much,' I demurred.

'Yes, yes, yes,' she said. 'How could you remember?'

She poured the tea and then, with a discreetness of gesture, lifted my dripping raincoat from the chair where I had thrown it and took it out of the room. It was a crowded apartment, not very neat, far from slovenly, cluttered with dolls and tiny dishes and an array of tricycles. The dining table was as large as a desert. An old-fashioned crocheted lace runner divided it into two nations, and on the end of this, in the neutral zone, so to speak, Sheindel had placed my cup. There was no physical relic of Isaac: not even a book.

She returned. 'My girls are all asleep, we can talk. What an ordeal for you, weather like this and going out so far to that place.'

It was impossible to tell whether she was angry or not. I had rushed in on her like the rainfall itself, scattering drops, my shoes stuck all over with leaves.

'I comprehend exactly why you went out there. The impulse of a detective,' she said. Her voice contained an irony that surprised me. It was brilliantly and unmistakably accented, and because of this jaggedly precise. It was as if every word emitted a quick white thread of great purity, like hard silk, which she was then obliged to bite cleanly off. 'You went to find something? An atmosphere? The sadness itself?'

'There was nothing to see,' I said, and thought I was lunatic to have put myself in her way.

'Did you dig in the ground? He might have buried a note for goodbye.'

'Was there a note?' I asked, startled.

'He left nothing behind for ordinary humanity like yourself.'

I saw she was playing with me. 'Rebbetzin Kornfeld,' I said, standing up, 'forgive me. My coat, please, and I'll go.'

'Sit,' she commanded. 'Isaac read less lately, did you notice that?'

I gave her a civil smile. 'All the same he was buying more and more.'

'Think,' she said. 'I depend on you. You're just the one who might know. I had forgotten this. God sent you perhaps.'

'Rebbetzin Kornfeld, I'm only a bookseller.'

'God in his judgement sent me a bookseller. For such a long time Isaac never read at home. Think! Agronomy?'

'I don't remember anything like that. What would a Professor of Mishnaic History want with agronomy?'

'If he had a new book under his arm he would take it straight to the seminary and hide it in his office.'

'I mailed to his office. If you like I can look up some of the titles –'

'You were in the park and you saw nothing?'

'Nothing.' Then I was ashamed. 'I saw the tree.'

'And what is that? A tree is nothing.'

'Rebbetzin Kornfeld,' I pleaded, 'It's a stupidity that I came here. I don't know myself why I came, I beg your pardon, I had no idea –'

'You came to learn why Isaac took his life. Botany? Or even, please listen, even mycology? He never asked you to send something on mushrooms? Or having to do with herbs? Manure? Flowers? A certain kind of agricultural poetry? A book about gardening? Forestry? Vegetables? Cereal growing?'

'Nothing, nothing like that,' I said excitedly. 'Rebbetzin Kornfeld, your husband was a rabbi!'

'I know what my husband was. Something to do with vines? Arbors? Rice? Think, think, think! Anything to do with land – meadows – goats – a farm, hay – anything at all, anything rustic or lunar –'

'Lunar! My God! Was he a teacher or a nurseryman? Goats! Was he a furrier? Sheindel, are you crazy? *I* was the furrier! What do you want from the dead?'

Without a word she replenished my cup, though it was more than half full, and sat down opposite me, on the other side of the lace boundary-line. She leaned her face into her palms, but I saw her eyes. She kept them wide.

'Rebbetzin Kornfeld,' I said, collecting myself, 'with a tragedy like this –'

'You imagine I blame the books. I don't blame the books, whatever they were. If he had been faithful to his books he would have lived.'

'He lived,' I cried, 'in books, what else?'

'No,' said the widow.

'A scholar. A rabbi. A remarkable Jew!'

At this she spilled a furious laugh. 'Tell me, I have always been very interested and shy to inquire. Tell me about your wife.'

I intervened: 'I haven't had a wife in years.'

'What are they like, those people?'

'They're exactly like us, if you can think what we would be if we were like them.'

'We are not like them. Their bodies are more to them than ours are to us. Our books are holy, to them their bodies are holy.'

'Jane's was so holy she hardly ever let me get near it,' I muttered to myself.

'Isaac used to run in the park, but he lost his breath too quickly. Instead he read in a book about runners with hats made of leaves.'

'Sheindel, Sheindel, what did you expect of him? He was a student, he sat and he thought, he was a Jew.'

She thrust her hands flat. 'He was not.'

I could not reply. I looked at her merely. She was thinner now than in her early young-womanhood, and her face had an in-between cast, poignant still at the mouth and jaw, beginning to grow coarse on either side of the nose.

'I think he was never a Jew,' she said.

I wondered whether Isaac's suicide had unbalanced her.

'I'll tell you a story,' she resumed. 'A story about stories. These were the bedtime stories Isaac told Naomi and Esther: about mice that danced and children who laughed. When Miriam came he invented a speaking cloud. With Ophra it was a turtle that married a blade of withered grass. By Leah's time the stones had tears for their leglessness. Rebecca cried because of a tree that turned into a girl and never grew colours again in the autumn. Shiphrah, the littlest, believes that a pig has a soul.'

'My own father used to drill me every night in sacred recitation. It was a terrible childhood.'

'He insisted on picnics. Each time we went farther and farther into the country. It was a madness. Isaac never troubled to learn to drive a car, and there was always a clumsiness of baskets to carry and a clutter of buses and trains and seven exhausted wild girls. And he would look for special places – we couldn't settle just here or there, there had to be a brook or such-and-such a slope or else a little grove. And then, though he said it was all for the children's pleasure, he would leave them and go off alone and never come back until sunset when everything was spilled and the air freezing and the babies crying.'

'I was a grown man before I had the chance to go on a picnic,' I admitted.

'I'm speaking of the beginning,' said the widow. 'Like you, wasn't I fooled? I was fooled, I was charmed. Going home with our baskets of berries and flowers we were a romantic huddle. Isaac's stories on those nights were full of dark invention. May God preserve me, I even begged him to write them down. Then suddenly he joined a club, and Sunday mornings he was up and away before dawn.'

'A club? So early? What library opens at that hour?' I said, stunned that a man like Isaac should ally himself with anything so doubtful.

'Ah, you don't follow, you don't follow. It was a hiking club, they met under the moon. I thought it was a pity, the whole week Isaac was so inward, he needed air for the mind. He used to come home too fatigued to stand. He said he went for the landscape. I was like you, I took what I heard, I heard it all and never followed. He resigned from the hikers finally, and I believed all that strangeness was finished. He told me it was absurd to walk at such a pace, he was a teacher and not an athlete. Then he began to write.'

'But he always wrote,' I objected.

'Not this way. What he wrote was only fairy tales. He kept at it and for a while he neglected everything else. It was the strangeness in another form. The stories surprised me, they were so poor and dull. They were a little like the ideas he used to scare the girls with, but choked all over with notes, appendices, prefaces. It struck me then he didn't seem to understand he was only doing fairy tales. Yet they were really very ordinary – full of sprites, nymphs, gods, everything ordinary and old.'

'Will you let me see them?'

'Burned, all burned.'

'Isaac burned them?'

'You don't think I did! I see what you think.'

It was true that I was marvelling at her hatred. I supposed she was one of those born to dread imagination. I was overtaken by a coldness for her, though the sight of her small hands with their tremulous staves of fingers turning and turning in front of her face like a gate on a hinge reminded me of where she was born and who she was. She was an orphan and had been saved by magic and had a terror of it. The coldness fled. 'Why should you be bothered by little stories?' I inquired. 'It wasn't the stories that killed him.'

'No, no, not the stories,' she said. 'Stupid corrupt things. I was glad when he gave them up. He piled them in the bathtub and lit them with a match. Then he put a notebook in his coat pocket and said he would walk in the park. Week after week he tried all the parks in the city. I didn't dream what he could be after. One day he took the subway and rode to the end of the line, and this was the right park at last. He went every day after class. An hour going, an hour back. Two, three in the morning he came home. "Is it exercise?" I said. I thought he might be running again. He used to shiver with the chill of night and the dew. "No, I sit quite still," he said. "Is it more stories you do out there?" "No, I only jot down what I think." "A man should meditate in his own house, not by night near bad water," I said. Six, seven in the morning he came home. I asked him if he meant to find his grave in that place.'

She broke off with a cough, half artifice and half resignation, so loud that it made her crane toward the bedrooms to see if she had awakened a child. 'I don't sleep any more,' she told me. 'Look around you. Look, look everywhere, look on the windowsills. Do you see any plants, any common houseplants? I went down one evening and gave them to the garbage collector. I couldn't sleep in the same space with plants. They are like little trees. Am I deranged? Take Isaac's notebook and bring it back when you can.'

I obeyed. In my own room, a sparse place, with no ornaments but a few pretty stalks in pots, I did not delay and seized the notebook. It was a tiny affair, three inches by five, with ruled pages that opened on a coiled wire. I read searchingly, hoping for something not easily evident. Sheindel by her melancholy innuendo had made me believe that in these few sheets Isaac had revealed the reason for his suicide. But it was all a disappointment. There was not a word of any importance. After a while I concluded that, whatever her motives, Sheindel was playing with me again. She meant to punish me for asking the unaskable. My inquisitiveness offended her; she had given me Isaac's notebook not to enlighten but to rebuke. The handwriting was recognizable yet oddly formed, shaky and even senile, like that of a man outdoors and deskless who scribbles in his palm or on his lifted knee or leaning on a bit of bark; and there was no doubt that the wrinkled leaves, with their ragged corners, had been in and out of someone's pocket. So I did not mistrust Sheindel's mad anecdote; this much was true: a park, Isaac, a notebook, all at once, but signifying no more than that a professor with a literary turn of mind had gone for a walk. There was even a green stain straight across one of the quotations, as if the pad had slipped grassward and been trod on.

I have forgotten to mention that the notebook, though scantily filled, was in three languages. The Greek I could not read at all, but it had the shape of verse. The Hebrew was simply a miscellany, drawn mostly from Leviticus and Deuteronomy. Among these I found the following extracts, transcribed not quite verbatim:

> Ye shall utterly destroy all the places of the gods, upon the high mountains, and upon the hills, and under every green tree.

> And the soul that turneth after familiar spirits to go a-whoring after them, I will cut him off from among his people.

These, of course, were ordinary unadorned notes, such as any classroom lecturer might commonly make to remind himself of the text, with a phrase cut out here and there for the sake of speeding his hand. Or I thought it possible that Isaac might at that time have been preparing a paper on the

Talmudic commentaries for these passages. Whatever the case, the remaining quotations, chiefly from English poetry, interested me only slightly more. They were the elegiac favourites of a closeted Romantic. I was repelled by Isaac's Nature: it wore a capital letter, and smelled like my own Book Cellar. It was plain to me that he had lately grown painfully academic: he could not see a weed's tassel without finding a classical reference for it. He had put down a snatch of Byron, a smudge of Keats (like his Scriptural copyings, these too were quick and fragmented), a pair of truncated lines from Tennyson, and this unmarked and clumsy quatrain:

> And yet all is not taken. Still one Dryad
>   Flits through the wood, one Oread skims the hill;
> White in the whispering stream still gleams a Naiad;
>   The beauty of the earth is haunted still.

All of this was so cloying and mooning and ridiculous, and so pedantic besides, that I felt ashamed for him. And yet there was almost nothing else, nothing to redeem him and nothing personal, only a sentence or two in his rigid self-controlled scholar's style, not unlike the starched little jokes of our correspondence. 'I am writing at dusk sitting on a stone in Trilham's Inlet Park, within sight of Trilham's Inlet, a bay to the north of the city, and within two yards of a slender tree, *Quercus velutina*, the age of which, should one desire to measure it, can be ascertained by (God forbid) cutting the bole and counting the rings. The man writing is thirty-five years old and aging too rapidly, which may be ascertained by counting the rings under his poor myopic eyes.' Below this, deliberate and readily more legible than the rest, appeared three curious words:

> Great Pan lives.

That was all. In a day or so I returned the notebook to Sheindel. I told myself that she had seven orphans to worry over, and repressed my anger at having been cheated.

She was waiting for me. 'I am so sorry, there was a letter in the notebook, it had fallen out. I found it on the carpet after you left.'

'Thank you, no,' I said. 'I've read enough out of Isaac's pockets.'

'Then why did you come to see me to begin with?'

'I came,' I said, 'just to see you.'

'You came for Isaac.' But she was more mocking than distraught. 'I gave you everything you needed to see what happened and still you don't follow. Here.' She held out a large law-sized paper. 'Read the letter.'

'I've read his notebook. If everything I need to fathom Isaac is in the notebook I don't need the letter.'

'It's a letter he wrote to explain himself,' she persisted.

'You told me Isaac left you no notes.'

'It was not written to me.'

I sat down on one of the dining room chairs and Sheindel put the page before me on the table. It lay face up on the lace divider. I did not look at it.

'It's a love letter,' Sheindel whispered. 'When they cut him down they found the notebook in one pocket and the letter in the other.'

I did not know what to say.

'The police gave me everything,' Sheindel said. 'Everything to keep.'

'A love letter?' I repeated.

'That is what such letters are commonly called.'

'And the police – they gave it to you, and that was the first you realized what' – I floundered after the inconceivable – 'what could be occupying him?'

'What could be occupying him,' she mimicked. 'Yes. Not until they took the letter and the notebook out of his pocket.'

'My God. His habit of life, his mind . . . I can't imagine it. You never guessed?'

'No.'

'These trips to the park –'

'He had become aberrant in many ways. I have described them to you.'

'But the park! Going off like that, alone – you didn't think he might be meeting a woman?'

'It was not a woman.'

Disgust like a powder clotted my nose. 'Sheindel, you're crazy.'

'I'm crazy, is that it? Read his confession! Read it! How long can I be the only one to know this thing? Do you want my brain to melt? Be my confidant,' she entreated so unexpectedly that I held my breath.

'You've said nothing to anyone?'

'Would they have recited such eulogies if I had? Read the letter!'

'I have no interest in the abnormal,' I said coldly.

She raised her eyes and watched me for the smallest space. Without any change in the posture of her suppliant head her laughter began; I have never since heard sounds like those – almost mouselike in density for fear of waking her sleeping daughters, but so rational in intent that it was like listening to astonished sanity rendered into a cackling fugue. She kept it up for a minute and then calmed herself. 'Please sit where you are. Please pay attention. I will read the letter to you myself.'

She plucked the page from the table with an orderly gesture. I saw that this letter had been scrupulously prepared; it was closely written. Her tone was cleansed by scorn.

'"My ancestors were led out of Egypt by the hand of God,"' she read.

'Is this how a love letter starts out?'

She moved on resolutely. ' "We were guilty of so-called abominations well-described elsewhere. Other peoples have been nourished on their mythologies. For aeons we have been weaned from all traces of the same."'

I felt myself becoming impatient. The fact was I had returned with a single idea: I meant to marry Isaac's widow when enough time had passed to make it seemly. It was my intention to court her with great subtlety at first, so that I would not appear to be presuming on her sorrow. But she was possessed. 'Sheindel, why do you want to inflict this treatise on me? Give it to the seminary, contribute it to a symposium of professors.'

'I would sooner die.'

At this I began to attend in earnest.

'"I will leave aside the wholly plausible position of so-called animism within the concept of the One God. I will omit a historical illumination of its continuous but covert expression even within the Fence of the Law. Creature, I leave these aside – "'

'What?' I yelped.

'"Creature,"' she repeated, spreading her nostrils. '"What is human history? What is our philosophy? What is our religion? None of these teaches us poor human ones that we are alone in the universe, and even without them we would know that we are not. At a very young age I understood that a foolish man would not believe in a fish had he not had one enter his experience. Innumerable forms exist and have come to our eyes, and to the still deeper eye of the lens of our instruments; from this minute perception of what already is, it is easy to conclude that further forms are possible, that all forms are probable. God created the world not for Himself alone, or I would not now possess this consciousness with which I am enabled to address thee, Loveliness."'

'Thee,' I echoed, and swallowed a sad bewilderment.

'You must let me go on,' Sheindel said, and grimly went on. '"It is false history, false philosophy, and false religion which declare to us human ones that we live among Things. The arts of physics and chemistry begin to teach us differently, but their way of compassion is new, and finds few to carry fidelity to its logical and beautiful end. The molecules dance inside all forms, and within the molecules dance the atoms, and within the atoms dance still profounder sources of divine vitality. There is nothing that is Dead. There is no Non-life. Holy life subsists even in the stone, even in the bones of dead dogs and dead men. Hence in God's fecundating Creation there is no possibility of Idolatry, and therefore no possibility of committing this so-called abomination."'

'My God, my God,' I wailed. 'Enough, Sheindel, it's more than enough, no more – '

'There is more,' she said.

'I don't want to hear it.'

'He stains his character for you? A spot, do you think?

You will hear.' She took up in a voice which all at once reminded me of my father's: it was unforgiving. '"Creature, I rehearse these matters though all our language is as breath to thee; as baubles for the juggler. Where we struggle to understand from day to day, and contemplate the grave for its riddle, the other breeds are born fulfilled in wisdom. Animal races conduct themselves without self-investigations; instinct is a higher and not a lower thing. Alas that we human ones – but for certain pitifully primitive approximations in those few reflexes and involuntary actions left to our bodies – are born bare of instinct! All that we unfortunates must resort to through science, art, philosophy, religion, all our imaginings and tormented strivings, all our meditations and vain questionings, all! – are expressed naturally and rightly in the beasts, the plants, the rivers, the stones. The reason is simple, it is our tragedy: our soul is included in us, it inhabits us, we contain it, when we seek our soul we must seek in ourselves. To *see* the soul, to confront it – that is divine wisdom. Yet how can we see into our dark selves? With the other races of being it is differently ordered. The soul of the plant does not reside in the chlorophyll, it may roam if it wishes, it may choose whatever form or shape it pleases. Hence the other breeds, being largely free of their soul and able to witness it, can live in peace. To see one's soul is to know all, to know all is to own the peace our philosophies futilely envisage. Earth displays two categories of soul: the free and the indwelling. We human ones are cursed with the indwelling – "'

'Stop!' I cried.

'I will not,' said the widow.

'Please, you told me he burned his fairy tales.'

'Did I lie to you? Will you say I lied?'

'Then for Isaac's sake why didn't you? If this isn't a fairy tale what do you want me to think it could be?'

'Think what you like.'

'Sheindel,' I said, 'I beg you, don't destroy a dead man's honour. Don't look at this thing again, tear it to pieces, don't continue with it.'

'I don't destroy his honour. He had none.'

'Please! Listen to yourself! My God, who was the man? Rabbi Isaac Kornfeld! Talk of honour! Wasn't he a teacher? Wasn't he a scholar?'

'He was a pagan.'

Her eyes returned without hesitation to their task. She commenced: '"All these truths I learned only gradually, against my will and desire. Our teacher Moses did not speak of them; much may be said under this head. It was not out of ignorance that Moses failed to teach about those souls that are free. If I have learned what Moses knew, is this not because we are both men? He was a man, but God addressed him; it was God's will that our ancestors should no longer be slaves. Yet our ancestors, being stiffnecked, would not have abandoned their slavery in Egypt had they been taught of the free souls. They would have said: 'Let us stay, our bodies will remain enslaved in Egypt, but our souls will wander at their pleasure in Zion. If the cactus-plant stays rooted while its soul roams, why not also a man?' And if Moses had replied that only the world of Nature has the gift of the free soul, while man is chained to his, and that a man, to free his soul, must also free the body that is its vessel, they would have scoffed. 'How is it that men, and men alone, are different from the world of Nature? If this is so, then the condition of men is evil and unjust, and if this condition of ours is evil and unjust in general, what does it matter whether we are slaves in Egypt or citizens in Zion?' And they would not have done God's will and abandoned their slavery. Therefore Moses never spoke to them of the free souls, lest the people not do God's will and go out from Egypt."'

In an instant a sensation broke in me – it was entirely obscure, there was nothing I could compare it with, and yet I was certain I recognized it. And then I did. It hurtled me into childhood – it was the crisis of insight one experiences when one has just read out, for the first time, that conglomeration of figurines which makes a word. In that moment I penetrated beyond Isaac's alphabet into his language. I saw that he was on the side of possibility: he was both sane and inspired.

His intention was not to accumulate mystery but to dispel it.

'All that part is brilliant,' I burst out.

Sheindel meanwhile had gone to the sideboard to take a sip of cold tea that was standing there. 'In a minute,' she said, and pursued her thirst. 'I have heard of drawings surpassing Rembrandt daubed by madmen who when released from the fit couldn't hold the chalk. What follows is beautiful, I warn you.'

'The man was a genius.'

'Yes.'

'Go on,' I urged.

She produced for me her clownish jeering smile. She read:

"'Sometimes in the desert journey on the way they would come to a watering-place, and some quick spry boy would happen to glimpse the soul of the spring (which the wild Greeks afterwards called naiad), but not knowing of the existence of the free souls he would suppose only that the moon had cast a momentary beam across the water. Love-liness, with the same innocence of accident I discovered thee. Loveliness, Loveliness.'"

She stopped.

'Is that all?'

'There is more.'

'Read it.'

'The rest is the love letter.'

'Is it hard for you?' But I asked with more eagerness than pity.

'I was that man's wife, he scaled the Fence of the Law. For this God preserved me from the electric fence. Read it for yourself.'

Incontinently I snatched the crowded page.

"'Loveliness, in thee the joy, substantiation, and supernal succour of my theorem. How many hours through how many years I walked over the cilia-forests of our enormous aspirat-ing vegetable-star, this light rootless seed that crawls in its single furrow, this shaggy mazy unimplanted cabbage-head of our earth! – never, all that time, all those days of unfulfil-

ment, a white space like a desert thirst, never, never to grasp.
I thought myself abandoned to the intrigue of my folly. At
dawn, on a hillock, what seemed the very shape and seizing
of the mound's nature – what was it? Only the haze of the
sunball growing great through hoarfrost. The oread slipped
from me, leaving her illusion; or was never there at all; or was
there but for an instant, and ran away. What sly ones the free
souls are! They have a comedy we human ones cannot dream:
the laughing drunkard feels in himself the shadow of the
shadow of the shadow of their wit, and only because he has
made himself a vessel, as the two banks and the bed of a rivulet
are the naiad's vessel. A naiad I may indeed have viewed whole:
all seven of my daughters were once wading in a stream in a com-
pact but beautiful park, of which I had much hope. The youngest
being not yet two, and fretful, the older ones were told to keep
her always by the hand, but they did not obey. I, having
passed some way into the woods behind, all at once heard a
scream and noise of splashes, and caught sight of a tiny body
flying down into the water. Running back through the trees I
could see the others bunched together, afraid, as the baby
dived helplessly, all these little girls frozen in a garland –
when suddenly one of them (it was too quick a movement for
me to recognize which) darted to the struggler, who was now
underwater, and pulled her up, and put an arm around her to
soothe her. The arm was blue – blue. As blue as a lake. And
fiercely, from my spot on the bank, panting, I began to count
the little girls. I counted eight, thought myself not mad but
delivered, again counted, counted seven, knew I had counted
well before, knew I counted well even now. A blue-armed
girl had come to wade among them. Which is to say the shape
of a girl. I questioned my daughters: each in her fright
believed one of the others had gone to pluck up the tiresome
baby. None wore a dress with blue sleeves.'''

'Proofs,' said the widow. 'Isaac was meticulous, he used to
account for all his proofs always.'

'How?' My hand in tremor rustled Isaac's letter; the paper
bleated as though whipped.

'By eventually finding a principle to cover them,' she

finished maliciously. 'Well, don't rest even for me, you don't oblige me. You have a long story to go, long enough to make a fever.'

'Tea,' I said hoarsely.

She brought me her own cup from the sideboard, and I believed as I drank that I swallowed some of her mockery and gall.

'Sheindel, for a woman so pious you're a great sceptic.' And now the tremor had command of my throat.

'An atheist's statement,' she rejoined. 'The more piety, the more scepticism. A religious man comprehends this. Superfluity, excess of custom, and superstition would climb like a choking vine on the Fence of the Law if scepticism did not continually hack them away to make freedom for purity.'

I then thought her fully worthy of Isaac. Whether I was worthy of her I evaded putting to myself; instead I gargled some tea and returned to the letter.

'"It pains me to confess,"' I read, '"how after that I moved from clarity to doubt and back again. I had no trust in my conclusions because all my experiences were evanescent. Everything certain I attributed to some other cause less certain. Every voice out of the moss I blamed on rabbits and squirrels. Every motion among leaves I called a bird, though there positively was no bird. My first sight of the Little People struck me as no more than a shudder of literary delusion, and I determined they could only be an instantaneous crop of mushrooms. But one night, a little after ten o'clock at the crux of summer – the sky still showed strings of light – I was wandering in this place, this place where they will find my corpse –"'

'Not for my sake,' said Sheindel when I hesitated.

'It's terrible,' I croaked, 'terrible.'

'Withered like a shell,' she said, as though speaking of the cosmos; and I understood from her manner that she had a fanatic's acquaintance with this letter, and knew it nearly by heart. She appeared to be thinking the words faster than I could bring them out, and for some reason I was constrained to hurry the pace of my reading.

'" – where they will find my corpse withered like the shell of an insect,"' I rushed on. '"The smell of putrefaction lifted clearly from the bay. I began to speculate about my own body after I was dead – whether the soul would be set free immediately after the departure of life; or whether only gradually, as decomposition proceeded and more and more of the indwelling soul was released to freedom. But when I considered how a man's body is no better than a clay pot, a fact which none of our sages has ever contradicted, it seemed to me then that an indwelling soul by its own nature would be obliged to cling to its bit of pottery until the last crumb and grain had vanished into earth. I walked through the ditches of that black meadow grieving and swollen with self-pity. It came to me that while my poor bones went on decaying at their ease, my soul would have to linger inside them, waiting, despairing, longing to join the free ones. I cursed it for its gravity-despoiled, slow, interminably languishing purse of flesh; better to be encased in vapour, in wind, in a hair of a coconut! Who knows how long it takes the body of a man to shrink into gravel, and the gravel into sand, and the sand into vitamin? A hundred years? Two hundred, three hundred? A thousand perhaps! Is it not true that bones nearly intact are constantly being dug up by the palaeontologists two million years after burial?" – Sheindel,' I interrupted, 'this is death, not love. Where's the love letter to be afraid of here? I don't find it.'

'Continue,' she ordered. And then: 'You see I'm not afraid.'

'Not of love?'

'No. But you recite much too slowly. Your mouth is shaking. Are you afraid of death?'

I did not reply.

'Continue,' she said again. 'Go rapidly. The next sentence begins with an extraordinary thought.'

'"An extraordinary thought emerged in me. It was luminous, profound, and practical. More than that, it had innumerable precedents; the mythologies had documented it a dozen dozen times over. I recalled all those mortals reputed to have coupled with gods (a collective word, showing much common sense, signifying what our philosophies more abstrusely call Shekhina), and all that poignant miscegenation represented by centaurs, satyrs, mermaids, fauns, and so forth, not to speak of that even more famous mingling in Genesis, whereby the sons of God took the daughters of men for brides, producing giants and possibly also those abortions leviathan and behemoth of which we read in Job, along with unicorns and other chimeras and monsters abundant in Scripture, hence far from fanciful. There existed also the example of the succubus Lilith, who was often known to couple in the medieval ghetto even with pre-pubescent boys. By all these evidences I was emboldened in my confidence that I was surely not the first man to conceive such a desire in the history of our earth. Creature, the thought that took hold of me was this: if only I could couple with one of the free souls, the strength of the connection would likely wrest my own soul from my body – seize it, as if by a tongs, draw it out, so to say, to its own freedom. The intensity and force of my desire to capture one of these beings now became prodigious. I avoided my wife –"'

Here the widow heard me falter.

'Please,' she commanded, and I saw creeping in her face the completed turn of a sneer.

'" – lest I be depleted of potency at that moment (which might occur in any interval, even, I assumed, in my own bedroom) when I should encounter one of the free souls. I was borne back again and again to the fetid viscosities of the Inlet, borne there as if on the rising stink of my own enduring and tedious putrefaction, the idea of which I could no longer shake off – I envisaged my soul as trapped in my last granule, and that last granule itself perhaps petrified, never to dissolve, and my soul condemned to minister to it throughout eternity! It seemed to me my soul must be released at once or be lost to sweet air forever. In a gleamless dark, struggling with this singular panic, I stumbled from ditch to ditch, strained like a blind dog for the support of solid verticality; and smacked my palm against bark. I looked up and in the black could not fathom the size of the tree – my head lolled forward, my brow met the trunk with all its gravings. I busied my fingers in the interstices of the bark's cuneiform. Then with forehead flat on the tree, I embraced it with both arms to measure it. My hands united on the other side. It was a young narrow weed, I did not know of what family. I reached to the lowest branch and plucked a leaf and made my tongue travel meditatively along its periphery to assess its shape: oak. The taste was sticky and exaltingly bitter. A jubilation lightly carpeted my groin. I then placed one hand (the other I kept around the tree's waist, as it were) in the bifurcation (disgustingly termed crotch) of that lowest limb and the elegant and devoutly firm torso, and caressed that miraculous juncture with a certain languor, which gradually changed to vigour. I was all at once savagely alert and deeply daring: I chose that single tree together with the ground near it for an enemy which in two senses would not yield: it would neither give nor give in. 'Come, come,' I called aloud to Nature. A wind blew out a braid of excremental malodour into the heated air. 'Come,' I called, 'couple with me, as thou didst with Cadmus, Rhoecus, Tithonus, Endymion, and that king Numa Pompilius to whom thou didst give secrets. As Lilith comes without a sign, so come thou. As the sons of God came to copulate with women, so now let a daughter of Shekhina the Emanation reveal herself to me. Nymph, come now, come now.'

'"Without warning I was flung to the ground. My face smashed into earth, and a flaky clump of dirt lodged in my open mouth. For the rest, I was on my knees, pressing down on my hands, with the fingernails clutching dirt. A superb ache lined my haunch. I began to weep because I was certain I had been ravished by some sinewy animal. I vomited the earth I had swallowed and believed I was defiled, as it is written: 'Neither shalt thou lie with any beast.' I lay sunk in the grass, afraid to lift my head to see if the animal still lurked. Through some curious means I had been fully positioned and aroused and exquisitely sated, all in half a second, in a fashion impossible to explain, in which, though I performed as with my own wife, I felt as if a preternatural rapine had been committed upon me. I continued prone, listening for the animal's breathing. Meanwhile, though every tissue of my flesh was gratified in its inmost awareness, a marvellous voluptuousness did not leave my body; sensual exultations of a wholly supreme and paradisal order, unlike anything our poets have ever defined, both flared and were intensely satisfied in the same moment. This salubrious and delightful perceptiveness excited my being for some time: a conjoining not dissimilar (in metaphor only; in actuality it cannot be described) from the magical contradiction of the tree and its issuance-of-branch at the point of bifurcation. In me were linked, *in the same instant*, appetite and fulfilment, delicacy and power, mastery and submissiveness, and other paradoxes of entirely remarkable emotional import.

'"Then I heard what I took to be the animal treading through the grass quite near my head, all cunningly: it withheld its breathing, then snored it out in a cautious and wisplike whirr that resembled a light wind through rushes. With a huge energy (my muscular force seemed to have increased) I leaped up in fear of my life; I had nothing to use for a weapon but – oh, laughable! – the pen I had been writing with in a little notebook I always carried about with me in those days (and still keep on my person as a self-shaming souvenir of my insipidness, my bookishness, my pitiable conjecture and wishfulness in a time when, not yet knowing thee, I knew nothing). What I saw was not an animal but a girl no older than my oldest daughter, who was then fourteen. Her skin was as perfect as an eggplant's and nearly of that colour. In height she was half as tall as I was. The second and third fingers of her hands – this I noticed at once – were peculiarly fused, one slotted into the other, like the ligula of a leaf. She was entirely bald and had no ears but rather a type of gill or envelope, one only, on the left side. Her toes displayed the same oddity I had observed in her fingers. She was neither naked nor clothed – that is to say, even though a part of her body, from hip to just below the breasts (each of which appeared to be a kind of velvety colourless pear, suspended from a very short, almost invisible stem), was luxuriantly covered with a flossy or spore-like material, this was a natural efflorescence in the manner of, with us, hair. All her sexual portion was wholly visible, as in any field flower. Aside from these express deviations, she was commandingly human in aspect, if unmistakably flowerlike. She was, in fact, the reverse of our hackneyed euphuism, as when we say a young girl blooms like a flower – she, on the contrary, seemed a flower transfigured into the shape of the most stupendously lovely child I had ever seen. Under the smallest push of wind she bent at her superlative waist; this, I recognized, and not the exhalations of some lecherous beast, was the breathlike sound that had alarmed me at her approach: these motions of hers made the blades of grass collide. (She herself, having no lungs, did not 'breathe'.) She stood bobbing joyfully before me, with a face as tender as a morning-glory, strangely phosphorescent: she shed her own light, in effect, and I had no difficulty in confronting her beauty.

'"Moreover, by experiment I soon learned that she was not only capable of language, but that she delighted in playing with it. This she literally could do – if I had distinguished her hands before anything else, it was because she had held them out to catch my first cry of awe. She either caught my words like balls or let them roll, or caught them and then darted off to throw them into the Inlet. I discovered that whenever I spoke I more or less pelted her; but she liked this, and told me ordinary human speech only tickled and amused, whereas laughter, being highly plosive, was something of an assault. I then took care to pretend much solemnity, though I was lightheaded with rapture. Her own 'voice' I apprehended rather than heard – which she, unable to imagine how we human ones are prisoned in sensory perception, found hard to conceive. Her sentences came to me not as a series of differentiated frequencies but (impossible to develop this idea in language) as a diffused cloud of field fragrances; yet to say that I assimilated her thought through the olfactory nerve would be a pedestrian distortion. All the same it was clear that whatever she said reached me in a shimmer of pellucid perfumes, and I understood her meaning with an immediacy of glee and with none of the ambiguities and suspiciousness of motive that surround our human communication.

"'Through this medium she explained that she was a dryad and that her name was Iripomonoéià (as nearly as I can render it in our narrowly limited orthography, and in this dunce's alphabet of ours which is notoriously impervious to odoriferous categories). She told me what I had already seized: that she had given me her love in response to my call.

"" 'Wilt thou come to any man who calls?' I asked.

"" 'All men call, whether realizing it or not. I and my sisters sometimes come to those who do not realize. Almost never, unless for sport, do we come to that man who calls knowingly – he wishes only to inhabit us out of perversity or boastfulness or to indulge a dreamed-of disgust.'

"" 'Scripture does not forbid sodomy with the plants,' I exclaimed, but she did not comprehend any of this and lowered her hands so that my words would fly past her uncaught. 'I too called thee knowingly, not for perversity but for love of Nature.'

"" 'I have caught men's words before as they talked of Nature, you are not the first. It is not Nature they love so much as Death they fear. So Coryĺyĺyb my cousin received it in a season not long ago coupling in a harbour with one of your kind, one called Spinoza, one that had catarrh of the lung. I am of Nature and immortal and so I cannot pity your deaths. But return tomorrow and say Iripomonoéià.' Then she chased my last word to where she had kicked it, behind the tree. She did not come back. I ran to the tree and circled it diligently but she was lost for that night.

"'Loveliness, all the foregoing, telling of my life and meditations until now, I have never before recounted to thee or any other. The rest is beyond mean telling: those rejoicings from midnight to dawn, when the greater phosphorescence of the whole shouting sky frightened thee home! How in a trance of happiness we coupled in the ditches, in the long grasses, behind a fountain, under a broken wall, once recklessly on the very pavement, with a bench for roof and trellis! How I was taught by natural arts to influence certain chemistries engendering explicit marvels, blisses, and transports no man has slaked himself with since Father Adam pressed out the forbidden chlorophyll of Eden! Loveliness, Loveliness, none like thee. No brow so sleek, no elbow-crook so fine, no eye so green, no waist so pliant, no limbs so pleasant and acute. None like immortal Iripomonoéià.

'"Creature, the moon filled and starved twice, and there was still no end to the glorious archaic newness of Iripomonoéià.

'"Then last night. Last night! I will record all with simplicity.

'"We entered a shallow ditch. In a sweet-smelling voice of extraordinary redolence – so intense in its sweetness that even the barbaric stinks and wind-lifted farts of the Inlet were overpowered by it – Iripomonoéià inquired of me how I felt without my soul. I replied that I did not know this was my condition. 'Oh yes, your body is now an empty packet, that is why it is so light. Spring.' I sprang in air and rose effortlessly. 'You have spoiled yourself, spoiled yourself with confusions,' she complained, 'now by morning your body will be crumpled and withered and ugly, like a leaf in its sere hour, and never again after tonight will this place see you.' 'Nymph!' I roared, amazed by levitation. 'Oh, oh, that damaged,' she cried, 'you hit my eye with that noise,' and she wafted a deeper aroma, a leeklike mist, one that stung the mucous membranes. A white bruise disfigured her petally lid. I was repentant and sighed terribly for her injury. 'Beauty marred is for our kind what physical hurt is for yours,' she reproved me. 'Where you have pain, we have ugliness. Where you profane yourselves by immorality, we are profaned by ugliness. Your soul has taken leave of you and spoils our pretty game.' 'Nymph!' I whispered, 'heart, treasure, if my soul is separated how is it I am unaware?'

'"'Poor man,' she answered, 'you have only to look and you will see the thing.' Her speech had now turned as acrid as an herb, and all that place reeked bitterly. 'You know I am a spirit. You know I must flash and dart. All my sisters flash and dart. Of all races we are the quickest. Our very religion is all-of-a-sudden. No one can hinder us, no one may delay us. But yesterday you undertook to detain me in your embrace, you stretched your kisses into years, you called me your treasure and your heart endlessly, your soul in its slow greed kept me close and captive, all the while knowing well how a spirit cannot stay and will not be fixed. I made to leap from you, but your obstinate soul held on until it was snatched straight from your frame and escaped with me. I saw it hurled out onto the pavement, the blue beginning of day was already seeping down, so I ran away and could say nothing until this moment.'

""'My soul is free? Free entirely? And can be seen?'

""'Free. If I could pity any living thing under the sky I would pity you for the sight of your soul. I do not like it, it conjures against me.'

""'My soul loves thee,' I urged in all my triumph, 'it is freed from the thousand-year grave!' I jumped out of the ditch like a frog, my legs had no weight; but the dryad sulked in the ground, stroking her ugly violated eye. 'Iripomonoéià, my soul will follow thee with thankfulness into eternity.'

""'I would sooner be followed by the dirty fog. I do not like that soul of yours. It conjures against me. It denies me, it denies every spirit and all my sisters and every nereid of the harbour, it denies all our multiplicity, and all gods diversiform, it spites even Lord Pan, it is an enemy, and you, poor man, do not know your own soul. Go, look at it, there it is on the road.'

"'I scudded back and forth under the moon.

""'Nothing, only a dusty old man trudging up there.'

""'A quite ugly old man?'

""'Yes, that is all. My soul is not there.'

""'With a matted beard and great fierce eyebrows?'

""'Yes, yes, one like that is walking on the road. He is half bent over under the burden of a dusty old bag. The bag is stuffed with books – I can see their ravelled bindings sticking out.'

""'And he reads as he goes?'

""'Yes, he reads as he goes.'

"'"What is it he reads?'

"'"Some huge and terrifying volume, heavy as a stone.' I peered forward in the moonlight. 'A Tractate. A Tractate of the Mishnah. Its leaves are so worn they break as he turns them, but he does not turn them often because there is much matter on a single page. He is so sad! Such antique weariness broods in his face! His throat is striped from the whip. His cheeks are folded like ancient flags, he reads the Law and breathes the dust.'

"'"And are there flowers on either side of the road?'

"'"Incredible flowers! Of every colour! And noble shrubs like mounds of green moss! And the cricket crackling in the field. He passes indifferent through the beauty of the field. His nostrils sniff his book as if flowers lay on the clotted page, but the flowers lick his feet. His feet are bandaged, his notched toenails gore the path. His prayer-shawl droops on his studious back. He reads the Law and breathes the dust and doesn't see the flowers and won't heed the cricket spitting in the field.'

"'"That,' said the dryad, 'is your soul.' And was gone with all her odours.

"'"My body sailed up to the road in a single hop. I alighted near the shape of the old man and demanded whether he were indeed the soul of Rabbi Isaac Kornfeld. He trembled but confessed. I asked if he intended to go with his books through the whole future without change, always with his Tractate in his hand, and he answered that he could do nothing else.

"'"Nothing else! You, who I thought yearned for the earth! You, an immortal, free, and caring only to be bound to the Law!'

"'"He held a dry arm fearfully before his face, and with the other arm hitched up his merciless bag on his shoulder. 'Sir,' he said, still quavering, 'didn't you wish to see me with your own eyes?'

"'"I know your figure!' I shrieked. 'Haven't I seen that figure a hundred times before? On a hundred roads? It is not mine! I will not have it be mine!'

"'"If you had not contrived to be rid of me, I would have stayed with you till the end. The dryad, who does not exist, lies. It was not I who clung to her but you, my body. Sir, all that has no real existence lies. In your grave beside you I would have sung you David's songs, I would have moaned Solomon's voice to your last grain of bone. But you expelled me, your ribs exile me from their fate, and I will walk here alone always, in my garden' – he scratched on his page – 'with my precious birds' – he scratched at the letters – 'and my darling trees' – he scratched at the tall side-column of commentary.

"'"He was so impudent in his bravery – for I was all fleshliness and he all floppy wraith – that I seized him by the collar and shook him up and down, while the books on his back made a vast rubbing one on the other, and bits of shredding leather flew out like a rain.

"'"The sound of the Law,' he said, 'is more beautiful than the crickets. The smell of the Law is more radiant than the moss. The taste of the Law exceeds clear water.'

"'"At this nervy provocation – he more than any other knew my despair – I grabbed his prayer-shawl by its tassels and whirled around him once or twice until I had unwrapped it from him altogether, and wound it on my own neck and in one bound came to the tree.

"'"Nymph!' I called to it. 'Spirit and saint! Iripomonoéià, come! None like thee, no brow so sleek, no elbow-crook so fine, no eye so green, no waist so pliant, no limbs so pleasant and acute. For pity of me, come, come.'

"'"But she does not come.

"'"Loveliness, come.'

"'"She does not come.

"'"Creature, see how I am coiled in the snail of this shawl as if in a leaf. I crouch to write my words. Let soul call thee lie, but body . . .

"'" . . . body . . .

"'" . . . fingers twist, knuckles dark as wood, tongue dries like grass, deeper now into silk . . .

'"' . . . silk of pod of shawl, knees wilt, knuckles wither, neck . . ."'

Here the letter suddenly ended.

'You see? A pagan!' said Sheindel, and kept her spiteful smile. It was thick with audacity.

'You don't pity him,' I said, watching the contempt that glittered in her teeth.

'Even now you don't see? You can't follow?'

'Pity him,' I said.

'He who takes his own life does an abomination.'

For a long moment I considered her, 'You don't pity him? You don't pity him at all?'

'Let the world pity me.'

'Goodbye,' I said to the widow.

'You won't come back?'

I gave what amounted to a little bow of regret.

'I told you you came just for Isaac! But Isaac' – I was in terror of her cough, which was unmistakably laughter – 'Isaac disappoints. "A scholar. A rabbi. A remarkable Jew!" Ha! he disappoints you?'

'He was always an astonishing man.'

'But not what you thought,' she insisted. 'An illusion.'

'Only the pitiless are illusory. Go back to that park, Rebbetzin,' I advised her.

'And what would you like me to do there? Dance around a tree and call Greek names to the weeds?'

'Your husband's soul is in that park. Consult it.' But her low derisive cough accompanied me home: whereupon I remembered her earlier words and dropped three green houseplants down the toilet; after a journey of some miles through conduits they straightway entered Trilham's Inlet, where they decayed amid the civic excrement.

Amos Oz

SETTING THE WORLD TO RIGHTS

Translated by Nicholas de Lange

Amos Oz

AMOS OZ, born in Jerusalem in 1939, is a widely translated writer and a former member of a kibbutz. His books include *Elsewhere, Perhaps*, *In the Land of Israel*, *Black Box* and *To Know a Woman*. He has been Visiting Professor at St Cross College, Oxford, and at Boston University. He is an Officer of L'Ordre des Arts et des Lettres.

SETTING THE WORLD TO RIGHTS

All his life he lived on hatred.

He was a solitary man, who hoarded gloom. At night a thick smell filled his bachelor room on the edge of the kibbutz. His sunken, severe eyes saw shapes in the dark. The hater and his hatred fed on one another. So it has ever been. A solitary, huddled man, if he does not shed tears or play the violin, if he does not fasten his claws in other people, experiences, over the years, a constantly mounting pressure, until he faces a choice between lunacy and suicide. And those who live around him breathe a sigh of relief.

Good people are afraid of hatred, and even tend not to believe in it. If it appears before their eyes, they generally call it dedication, or some such name.

And so we of the kibbutz thought of him as a man who lived by his faith, and who because of his faith dealt severely with the world and with all of us. He was not considered one of the leaders of the kibbutz. His dedication never earned him a position of authority or respect, in a committee or council, for example. And so it came about that in the course of time we invested him with a halo of self-sufficient reticence.

This halo preserved him from gossip. What can one say, he is not like everyone else, he says little and does much. Admittedly, a solitary man. It can't be helped. But the kibbutz depends for its existence on men like him. And if he sometimes says harsh things about us, we are forced to admit to ourselves that our everyday lives do not always conform to the ideals which we profess, and consequently we deserve his rebukes.

He works with machines.

At six o'clock every morning he is awakened by his alarm clock. He struggles into his greasy overalls and goes down to the dining hall. Here he munches a thick slice of brown bread smothered in jam, and washes it down with coffee. Then, from quarter past six to nine o'clock, he dirties himself with grease in a tin shed which roasts in the summer heat like an oven, while in winter the rain beats upon it a dull, monotonous tattoo. At nine he returns to the hall, and washes his rough hands with paraffin, with coarse soap and with ordinary soap, to get rid of the black grease. But the black never goes away, it merely turns grey.

Over breakfast he casts his eye over the outer pages of the morning paper, looking for news on which hatred can flourish: crime, corruption, degeneracy, betrayal of the ideals for which the State was founded.

After breakfast he returns to his shed. This is his battle field against cog-wheels, fanbelts, carburettors and radiators, sparking plugs and batteries. We see in him a skilled craftsman and, in our usual undemonstrative way, we admire his workmanship. He wrestles with implements and components as if they had a will of their own, a treacherous, rebellious will which it is his task to subjugate and set on the right path. Only on rare occasions does he hurl some part away and hiss: 'It's no good. Dead. We'll have to get a new one.' On such rare occasions he resembles a military commander who has suffered a setback which he resolves to bear with dignity but with clenched teeth.

In most cases, however, he manages to mend, to repair, to set to rights. His sunken eyes fasten on a rebellious oil-pump, and there is suppressed rage coupled with infinite patience in his look. A schoolmasterly patience, we once remarked to ourselves.

The two phrases most commonly heard on his lips are 'we'll see' and 'so that's it'. At times he grinds between his teeth the word 'really'.

He is a heavily-built man. So heavily built that it sometimes seems as if the lines of his face and body are sagging gradually downwards, as though he suffers more than most men from the law of gravity. The furrows in his face are vertical, so are the hopeless wrinkles round his mouth, his broad shoulders are hunched, his hands dangle when he walks, even his grey hair always falls down over his forehead.

At half past twelve he leaves the shed and walks up to the dining hall. He always piles his plate high with meat, potatoes and an indiscriminate assortment of vegetables. While he vigorously masticates this meal his eyes once more run over the newspaper, finding change and decay in all around.

At quarter past one he returns to the shed and works until close on four o'clock. These are the hardest hours. In summer the shed roasts and in winter the wind's icy claws penetrate through the broken windows. He sighs deeply, almost aloud, but staunchly carries on with his work. He spreads a black piece of sacking on the concrete floor under the machine, and prostrates himself on it so to peer into the motor from beneath. In twenty-seven years he has never entered a single day's illness in the kibbutz work register.

When his working day is over he returns once more to the hall. He gorges himself again, as he did first thing in the morning, on brown bread and jam. He washes it down with warm milk. Then he goes to his room. Here he showers, shaves, lies down on his bachelor's bed and leafs through the newspaper until he dozes off. He has still not reached the middle pages.

The evening twilight wakes him from his nap as if it had bitten him. At this time he is always seized by a great dread, despair, a premonition. As if this twilight was final. Once and for all. He hurriedly puts on his trousers, makes himself a cup of coffee, and settles himself in the armchair to tackle the middle pages of the paper. As he reads the leading article, the commentary and analysis columns, the personal opinions, summaries of the speeches by the leaders of the Movement and the Party, he experiences a pain which is almost physical. His face wears an expression of ascetic, mortified severity, far from all charity or compassion. Damn them. What are they doing to us. Why do they ruin everything worthwhile. There is a grim judicial look in his eye. His lips tremble. Occasionally there flashes in his eyes a momentary sparkle of hatred, that hatred which others interpret as dedication. He follows the articles with his pencil. Makes notes. Not in words, but with signs alone. Question mark. Question mark, exclamation

mark. Vertical stroke. Double exclamation marks. And
sometimes even a furious crossing out in the body of the
article.

The twilight fades and darkness comes on. He must turn on
the light. The electric light tires his eyes and dulls the alertness without which lucid thought is impossible. He is
terrified of this yellow light, as if it were trying to bribe him,
to subvert his judgement. Clear reasoning becomes cloudy,
and after half an hour or an hour apparitions begin to arrive.
He can no longer pursue the claim of sharp, analytical
argument. He no longer has the power to bring the current
events of which the paper speaks before the high tribunal of
the teaching of the great visionaries, the fathers of the
Movement. And he is tired of judging. The electric light hurts
his eyes. He stares vacantly. Apparitions come to him. And
with them comes pain. His face loses its grim, judicial
expression, which can, albeit with great difficulty, be described
as attractive or even spiritual, and without it he is suddenly
an ugly, an almost unbearably ugly man. The kibbutz
children call him 'wicked Haman' behind his back, and point
their fingers at him.

But the time between the onset of twilight and the arrival of
the darkness is the best time of all.

He has the time, before he must turn the electric light on and
submit to tiredness and haziness, to put things in their proper
order. He studies the newspaper with pure, ice-cold hatred.
He drafts the charge-sheet with penetrating acuteness, section
after section. How the State has betrayed her visionaries'
vision, how she has played the whore and defiled herself. A
whole nation is giving itself up to debauchery and abandoning
every vision. The Jewish State was meant to begin a new
chapter in the history of the Jews, and instead it is coming
to look like a kind of farewell party, an orgy to celebrate the
happy ending of the terrible history of the Jews. But the
terrible history is still at its height. The knives are even now
being sharpened.

For generations upon generations the Jews were a deep

and serious people. Now they have become a degenerate
Levantine rabble, rushing to gratify themselves and satisfy
their lusts with every kind of novel excitement. Until one day
the enemy will come and gather in his spoil like driftwood,
and we shall wake up to find that all our hopes have turned to
dust. Peoples do not perish through military defeat or
economic collapse. They do not understand this. Even those
who call themselves the leaders, the heirs of the fathers of
the Movement, do not understand it. No, peoples fall into
decay, and only then does the enemy come and enter the gate;
he conquers everything at the height of the feast, when the
defenders are besotted and enfeebled. Disaster will strike
like lightning out of a clear sky. At the height of the great
banquet. It is not war that will destroy the land, but corruption. Already the stench lies heavy on the air, night is
falling, everything is becoming hazy in this yellow electric
light. Perhaps I ought to write a letter to the editor. But who
am I.

A good pair of spectacles might perhaps have relieved his
suffering. But this simple solution does not occur to him.
Wearily and painfully he squints at the yellow light bulb and
sees apparitions. He sees the crowds of voluptuous painted
women thronging the city streets as though they were born
only to give and receive pleasure. He sees the young men,
dressed like Americans in the pictures, wearing elegant ties
fastened with silver clips. They wear dark glasses and a
purposeful air. He sees the boys and girls, grandchildren of
the Maccabees, heirs of the guardians and defenders and
dreamers, and here they are wrecking the public telephones or
singing dirty songs in the streets at night. He sees the
outrageously low-cut dress of his younger sister, Esther. He
sees her shapely form boarding the Italian airplane: parting at
the airport. They are only going away for a few years, she
and her husband Gideon, until he is promoted to a respectable
office job which will allow him to live permanently in his own
town instead of roaming around foreign capitals like an
errand boy. Then the feel of his sister's body in their parting
embrace. He sees the plane: the hubbub of people arriving,

leaving, seeing off, meeting, the stewards loving everyone indiscriminately, and me in the middle of this airport carnival like an evil spirit: why are they all leaving, why all this commotion, what's the matter, surely at times like this we should all be overcome with wonderment. Then the sound of tyres on the grey asphalt, like lecherous whispers in the middle of the night: two o'clock in the morning, in a stream of quiet, powerful, brightly-coloured cars in which new, free Jews sit two by two, male and female. Where are they going, all these crowds of people, at two o'clock in the morning. Who will get up for work tomorrow. And who needs these new buildings, concrete and glass, curved shapes like a woman's hips. All the contagious effluvia of America in this land of dreams. Even the Hebrew policeman in the night smiles a kind of stylized, courteous smile at me as if he too shares in the universal friendliness. And the universal sobriety. The whispering seduction. The cold humour which is lechery, which is seething debauchery, which is abomination itself. We tried to realize a dream, and it has all turned into a Hollywood. The Land of Israel is a whore. The man who hates his country is called a traitor, but the man who hates the treacherous whore is truly loyal to the dream that has been betrayed. If the pain in your eyes is driving you to distraction, you can always go out into the darkness and take a little walk outside the kibbutz, then make a good supper on a huge salad with cream and salt fish, three slices of bread and cream cheese, and two glasses of tea. Should you find yourself next to someone suitable, you can sit and chat. Not about party strategy, calculations of political profit and loss, but about setting the world to rights.

After supper he does not leave the hall, but takes a seat at the table where the evening newspaper is being read. This is the copy which the treasurer has brought back with him from town. It is surrounded by a ring of veteran comrades. Those who are standing read standing, over the heads of those who are seated. And some of those who are seated read upside-down. Gradually a discussion begins, an argument develops.

It begins with explanations, interpretations, comparisons between what is happening now and what happened in the old days. Then the heat rises, because the discussion turns to what ought to happen, and what we should be doing. There are moderates and there are extremists, and there are those who always seek the golden mean between the two.

Most of them are unable to see where things are leading. Or perhaps they consciously deceive themselves. He is obliged to open their eyes, because these are the last of the faithful. He sets to work explaining to them how the rot has attacked the roots. How this crazy country is gorging itself on its own flesh unawares. Admittedly, the structure is still growing and spreading. Apparently settlements are being added, new roads are being built. But any biologist will testify that even a corpse will go on growing hair and nails until it is decomposed. The whole structure is already doomed to destruction, from corruption and into corruption. The cancer will feed on the whore until she dies. Drunken shouts, parochial boasts, empty words cannot conceal the treachery. The people has betrayed its leaders, the leaders have betrayed the people, and both alike have betrayed the vision. The kibbutz might have been the last bastion of the Third Commonwealth, but even it has been betrayed, its leaders and people have gone together to the whore.

All his listeners discern a great deal of exaggeration in this, but the older veterans know that it contains an element of holy anger, and perhaps even truth, and it is as well for some of the younger men to take these words at their face value and perhaps receive a jolt.

But the younger men, three or four in number, merely grin. They find it strange that a man can be a brilliant mechanic and at the same time such an utter fool.

Since the disputants are working men, not layabouts, they generally stop towards ten o'clock and say:

'We'll talk about this some other time. We'll argue it all out then.'

Then they all go to their rooms, and only the night-watchmen are left awake, and even they do not go out and lurk in the dark along the perimeter fence, but linger in the dining-hall, taking tiny sips of their tea to kill time and flirting with the night-nurses, who ought to be at the nursery, not here. Nothing is as it should be.

He goes back to his room. He crosses the lawn and finds a sprinkler left on and a leaking hosepipe. He must conquer his hatred. Reaching his room he turns on the light. Again it hurts his eyes. Despite the tiredness he takes an old tome down from the rough wooden bookcase and settles himself to read the words of the founders. Others still sustain themselves on what they have read in their youth and do not realize that forgetfulness is gradually eating away at their faith.

Whereas he persistently returns every evening to what he was taught many years ago in the Zionist Youth Movement in Lithuania. He devotes himself heart and soul to the cruel beauty of the words of the vision. True, most of the fathers of the Movement did not write polished Hebrew, but their thinking was polished, and nothing of their analytical vigour has been lost. And there are some pages which only now, in these unsavoury times, suddenly take on the full depth of their meaning.

After a few pages tiredness gets the better of him: he is no longer young, he spends long hours each day in arduous physical work, and every evening he wrestles with all his might with theories and ideas. Obviously he would have liked to go on reading with all his might and main, only his body is tired.

During the night the thick smell always begins to fill the room. Even in summer, when all the windows are wide open, there is no refuge from it. The sounds of the night come in and swoop at him as soon as he turns out the light and tries to go to sleep. Even a man with a clear view of the world is helpless in the face of these wild sounds.

He tries to hear in the sounds an echo of his thoughts, either by a play on the words 'wind' and 'spirit' or by translating the howling of the jackals into the wailing of foxes, which is a common image for national calamity, and also for lunacy and death. But the night-sounds here in our kibbutz between the mountains and the winding valleys are stronger than any image, they sweep everything away, they swoop down on you in the night, and words are lost.

He was a solitary man, who hoarded gloom. The hater and his hatred fed on one another. So it has ever been. Many years ago he had a wife: a refugee, odd, very thin, acid, a survivor of one of the ghetto risings. She had come here to tell him how both his brothers had died heroically, firing at the Germans until their ammunition ran out. She went on talking. When she stopped, night had fallen. So she stayed the night. And the next night. She was several years older than he.

After their marriage she tried to make him leave the kibbutz. Her plan was to live on help from her relations, on German reparation money, to set herself up properly and live well: the kibbutz was a good enough place, but not for her. She had suffered enough for the Jewish people: let others suffer now for a change, she wanted to live a little, at long last.

She was thin and acid. Her body satisfied and yet did not satisfy his hunger. After a few months they parted. She went her way, he remained. Her relations gave her a little, the reparation money made up the rest, and she opened a fashion salon which was every bit as good as the salon she had had in Warsaw before.

Since she had not remarried, he continued to visit her on his rare trips to town. He went to beg for her body. Sometimes she granted it, with a sigh, telling him to be quick and not mess about, chiding herself for her good nature which was always landing her in trouble. He would start arguing with her about the point of it all. He hated her, of course, with all his heart. But this was a daytime hatred, which was entirely different from the nocturnal hatred to which the night sounds outside responded.

The night is alive. His sunken, severe eyes see shapes in the dark. The room is not clean. Dust here and there. Under the bed a forgotten pair of socks. The sound of the crickets comes in waves. Distant lowing of cattle. A shriek. A tractor growling in a far-off field. Dogs barking as though demented. Laughter of couples crossing the lawn, sinking into the darkness of the wadi. Damn them. And jackals in the vineyard. A hot wind blows from the desert and ruffles the trees, warning them of the fire and the axe for which they are growing: there is nothing new in the world.

He tries turning on the radio to silence these tormenting sounds. What is there on the radio? A sensual tune, a lascivious song, a sickeningly warm, moist voice. He switches off and curses the singer, and meanwhile all the night sounds return. Sleep hits him suddenly, like a *coup de grâce*.

In his sleep, voluptuous women, with hips and laughs and hair.

Then a scream may sound in the night. The watchmen say: 'Poor devil. What can be done.'

A few days before New Year he went to Tel Aviv in connection with his work, to inspect and possibly order a new kind of American piston.

As usual, he went to see his ex-wife. She made him coffee. They argued a little about the news and the point of it all. He asked for her body. She refused and he begged a little. In vain: it transpired that she was about to remarry. No, not for love. What a crazy idea: who would marry for love, at her age and with her experience? No. Her man was also from Warsaw, he had also lost his former family, he too had been miraculously saved and he too dealt in ladies' clothes. Together they could go far.

He left his ex-wife without saying good-bye.

He stepped hesitantly out into the city. Gradually his stride became more confident and even furious. He went to his sister's flat, forgetting that she and her husband were in Europe, and would remain there for another year or two at least, until Gideon got his promotion.

The tenants received him politely. They thought he had

come to check up on the state of the furniture. They promised
they were taking good care of the flat. They invited him in,
to have a drink and to ascertain with his own eyes that
everything was in good order. But he stood in the doorway,
cursed them and left. He walked the streets of Tel Aviv until
nightfall, and saw that everything was lost. At dusk the
fluorescent street-lights came on and hurt his eyes. He turned
into the dark side streets. Towards midnight he came on the
agricultural machinery showrooms where he had intended to
inspect and possibly order the new piston he had read about
in the prospectus. The street was in darkness and the showroom was closed and deserted. A wave of hatred rose in his
chest until he could hear his own breathing. The bastards had
shut up shop and gone off to chase women. How wonderful
were the early fathers of the Labour Movement, who foresaw
it all and even warned us in advance. We made light of their
writings. Even a corpse goes on growing hair and nails
until it finally rots.

At the end of the same street he picked up a whore,
followed her to a cheap hotel, and gave her the money he had
intended to spend in the showroom. He stayed with her till
morning and hated her and himself profoundly. Next day he
returned to the kibbutz and worked on his machines; he read
the special New Year number of the newspaper from cover to
cover and waited for darkness to fall. When it was dark he
went out to the orchard and hanged himself from a tree.
We found him after the festival, and praised his devotion to
his work and his dedication to the ideals to which we hold fast.

The burial of a man who has devoted himself to setting
the world to rights is no different from that of any other man,
and we have nothing more to add. He was a solitary man. May
he rest in peace.

Bernard Malamud

MAN IN THE DRAWER

Bernard Malamud

BERNARD MALAMUD (1914–86) was, together with Saul Bellow and Philip Roth, a leading figure in the brilliant movement of American-Jewish writing that profoundly influenced American literature after the Second World War. His first novel, *The Natural*, appeared in 1952. His other books include *The Assistant*, *The Magic Barrel*, *The Fixer* and *Rembrandt's Hat*, a collection of short stories. He won the US National Book Award and the Pulitzer Prize for Literature.

MAN IN THE DRAWER

A SOFT shalom I thought I heard, but considering the Slavic cast of the driver's face, it seemed unlikely. He had been eyeing me in his rear-view mirror since I had stepped into the taxi and, to tell the truth, I had momentary apprehensions. I'm forty-seven and have recently lost weight but not, I confess, nervousness. It's my American clothes, I thought at first. One is a recognizable stranger. Unless he had been tailing me to begin with, but how could that be if it was a passing cab I had hailed myself?

He had picked me up in his noisy Volga of ancient vintage on the Lenin Hills, where I had been wandering all afternoon in and around Moscow University. Finally I'd had enough of sightseeing, and when I saw the cab, hallooed and waved both arms. The driver, cruising in a hurry, had stopped, you might say, on a kopek, as though I were someone he was dying to give a ride to; maybe somebody he had mistaken for a friend. Considering my recent experiences in Kiev, a friend was someone I wouldn't mind being mistaken for.

From the moment we met, our eyes were caught in a developing recognition although we were complete strangers. I knew nobody in Moscow except an Intourist girl or two. In the mottled mirror his face seemed mildly distorted – badly reflected; but not the eyes, small, canny, curious – they probed, tugged, doubted, seemed to beg to know: give him a word and he'd be grateful, though why and for what cause he didn't say. Then, as if the whole thing wearied him insufferably, he pretended no further interest.

Serves him right, I thought, but it wouldn't hurt if he paid a little attention to the road now and then or we'll never get where we're going, wherever that is. I realized I hadn't said because I wasn't sure myself – anywhere but back to the Metropole just yet. It was one of those days I couldn't stand a hotel room.

'Shalom!' he said finally out loud.

'Shalom to you.' So it was what I had heard, who would have thought so? We both relaxed, looking at opposite sides of the street.

The taxi driver sat in his shirt sleeves on a cool June day, not more than 55° Fahrenheit. He was a man in his thirties who looked as if what he ate didn't fully feed him – in afterthought a discontented type, his face on the tired side; not bad-looking – now that I'd studied him a little, even though the head seemed pressed a bit flat by somebody's heavy hand although protected by a mat of healthy hair. His face, as I said, veered to Slavic: round; broad cheekbones, small firm chin; but he sported also a longish nose and a distinctive larynx on a slender hairy neck; a mixed type, it appeared. At any rate, the shalom had seemed to alter his appearance, even of the probing eyes. He was dissatisfied for certain this fine June day – his job, fate, appearance – what? And a sort of indigenous sadness hung on him, coming God knows from where; nor did he seem to mind if who he was was immediately visible; not everybody could do that or wanted to. This one showed himself. Not too prosperous, I would say, yet no underground man. He sat firm in his seat, all of him driving, a touch frantically. I have an experienced eye for such details.

'Israeli?' he asked in a whisper.

'Amerikansky.' I know no Russian, just a few polite words.

He dug into his shirt pocket for a thin pack of cigarettes and swung his arm over the seat, the Volga swerving to avoid a truck making a turn.

'Take care!'

I was thrown sideways – no apologies. Extracting a Bulgarian cigarette I wasn't eager to smoke – too strong – I handed him his pack. I was considering offering my prosperous American cigarettes in return but didn't want to affront him.

'Feliks Levitansky,' he said. 'How do you do? I am the taxi driver.' His accent was strong, verging on fruity, but redeemed by fluency of tongue.

'Ah, you speak English? I sort of thought so.'

'My profession is translator – English, French.' He shrugged sideways.

'Howard Harvitz is my name. I'm here for a short vacation, about three weeks. My wife died not so long ago, and I'm traveling partly to relieve my mind.'

My voice caught, but then I went on to say that if I could manage to dig up some material for a magazine article or two, so much the better.

In sympathy Levitansky raised both hands from the wheel.

'Watch out, for God's sake!'

'Horovitz?' he asked.

I spelled it for him. 'Frankly, it was Harris after I entered college but I changed it back recently. My father had it legally changed after I graduated from high school. He was a doctor, a practical sort.'

'You don't look to me Jewish.'

'If so why did you say shalom?'

'Sometimes you say.' After a minute he asked, 'For which reason?'

'For which reason what?'

'Why you changed back your name?'

'I had a crisis in my life.'

'Existential? Economic?'

'To tell the truth I changed it back after my wife died.'

'What is the significance?'

'The significance is I am closer to my true self.'

The driver popped a match with his thumbnail and lit his cigarette.

'I am marginal Jew,' he said, 'although my father – Avrahm Isaakovich Levitansky – was Jewish. Because my mother was Gentile woman I was given choice, but she insisted me to register for internal passport with notation of Jewish nationality in respect for my father. I did so.'

'You don't say?'

'My father died in my childhood. I was rised – raised? – to respect Jewish people and religion but I went my own way. I am atheist. This is almost inevitable.'

'You mean Soviet life?'

Levitansky smoked without replying as I grew embarrassed by my question. I looked around to see if I knew where we were. In afterthought he asked, 'to which destination?'

I said, still on the former subject, that I had been not much of a Jew myself. 'My mother and father were totally assimilated.'

'By their choice?'

'Of course by their choice.'

'Do you wish,' he then asked, 'to visit Central Synagogue on Arkhipova Street? Very interesting experience.'

'Not just now,' I said, 'but take me to the Chekhov Museum on Sadovaya Kudrinskaya.'

At that the driver, sighing, seemed to take heart.

Rose, I said to myself.

I blew my nose. After her death I had planned to visit the Soviet Union but couldn't get myself to move. I'm a slow man after a blow, though I confess I've never been one for making his mind up in a hurry about important things. Eight months later, when I was more or less packing, I felt that some of the relief I was looking for derived, in addition to what was still on my mind, from the necessity of making an unexpected serious personal decision. Out of loneliness I had begun to see my former wife, Lillian, in the spring; and before long, since she had remained unmarried and still attractive, to my surprise there was some hesitant talk of remarriage; these things slip from one sentence to another before you know it. If we did get married we could turn the Russian trip into a sort of honeymoon – I won't say second because we hadn't had much of a first. In the end, since our lives had been so frankly complicated – hard on each other – I found it impossible to make up my mind, though Lillian, I give her credit, seemed to be willing to take the chance. My feelings were so difficult to define to myself I decided to decide nothing for sure. Lillian, who is a forthright type with a mind like a lawyer's, asked me if I was cooling off to the idea, and I told her that since the death of my wife I had been examining my life and needed more time to see where I stood. 'Still?' she said, meaning the self-searching, and implying, I thought, forever. All I could answer was 'Still,' and then in anger, 'Forever.' I warned myself afterward: Beware of any more complicated entanglements.

Well, that almost killed it. It wasn't a particularly happy evening, though it had its moments. I had once been very much in love with Lillian. I figured then that a change of scene for me, maybe a month abroad, might be helpful. I had for a long time wanted to visit the U.S.S.R., and taking the time to be alone and, I hoped, at ease to think things through, might give the trip additional value.

So I was surprised, once my visa was granted – though not too surprised – that my anticipation was by now blunted and I was experiencing some uneasiness. I blamed it on a dread of traveling that sometimes hits me before long trips, that I have to make my peace with before I can move. Will I get there? Will the plane be hijacked? Maybe a war breaks out and I'm surrounded by artillery. To be frank, though I've resisted the idea, I consider myself an anxious man, which, when I try to explain it to myself, means being this minute halfway into the next. I sit still in a hurry, worry uselessly about the future, and carry the burden of an over-ripe conscience.

I realized that what troubled me mostly about going into Soviet Russia were those stories in the papers of some tourist or casual traveler in this or that Soviet city, who is, without warning, grabbed by the secret police on charges of 'spying', 'illegal economic activity', 'hooliganism', or whatnot. This poor guy, like somebody from Sudbury, Mass., is held incommunicado until he confesses, and is then sentenced to a prison camp in the wilds of Siberia. After I got my visa I sometimes had fantasies of a stranger shoving a fat envelope of papers into my hand, and then arresting me as I was stupidly reading them – of course for spying. What would I do in that case? I think I would pitch the envelope into the street, shouting, 'Don't pull that one on me, I can't read Russian,' and walk away with whatever dignity I had, hoping that would freeze them in their tracks. A man in danger, if he's walking away from it, seems indifferent, innocent. At least to himself; then in my mind I hear the sound of footsteps coming after me, and since my reveries tend to the rational, two husky KGB men grab me, shove my arms up my back and make the arrest. Not for littering the streets, as I hope might be the case, but for 'attempting to dispose of certain incriminating documents', a fact it's hard to deny.

I see H. Harvitz yelling, squirming, kicking right and left, till his mouth is shut by somebody's stinking palm and he is dragged by superior force – not to mention a blackjack whack on the skull – into the inevitable black Zis I've read about and see on movie screens.

The cold war is a frightening business, though I suppose for some more than others. I've sometimes wished spying had reached such a pitch of perfection that both the U.S.S.R. and the U.S.A. knew everything there is to know about the other, and having sensibly exchanged this information by trading computers that keep facts up to date, let each other alone thereafter. That ruins the spying business; there's that much more sanity in the world, and for a man like me the thought of a trip to the Soviet Union is pure pleasure.

Right away at the Kiev airport I had a sort of fright, after flying in from Paris on a mid-June afternoon. A customs official confiscated from my suitcase five copies of *Visible Secrets*, a poetry anthology for high school students I had edited some years ago, which I had brought along to give away to Russians I met who might be interested in American poetry. I was asked to sign a document the official had carefully written out in Cyrillic, except that *Visible Secrets* was printed in English, 'secrets' underlined. The uniformed customs officer, a heavy-set man with a layer of limp hair on a smallish head, red stars on his shoulders, said that the paper I was required to sign stated I understood it was not permitted to bring five copies of a foreign book into the Soviet Union; but I would get my property back anyway at the Moscow airport when I left the country. I worried that I oughtn't to sign but was urged to by my lady Intourist guide, a bleached blonde with wobbly heels whose looks and good humor kept

me more or less calm, though my clothes were frankly steam-
ing. She said it was a matter of no great consequence and
advised me to write my signature quickly because it was
delaying our departure to the Dniepro Hotel.

At that point I asked what would happen if I willingly
parted with the books, no longer claimed them as my
property. The Intouristka inquired of the customs man, who
answered calmly, earnestly, and at great length.

'He says,' she said, 'that the Soviet Union will not take
away from a foreign visitor his legal property.'

Since I had only four days in the city and time was going
fast, faster than usual, I reluctantly signed the paper plus
four carbons – one for each book – or five mysterious
government departments? – and was given a copy, which I
filed in my billfold.

Despite this incident – it had its comic quality – my stay in
Kiev, in spite of the loneliness I usually experience my first
few days in a strange city, went quickly and interestingly. In
the mornings I was driven around in a private car on guided
tours of the hilly, broad-avenued, green-leaved city, whose
colors were reminiscent of a subdued Rome. But in the afternoons I wandered around alone. I would start by taking a
bus or streetcar, riding a few kilometers, then getting off to
walk in this or that neighborhood. Once I strayed into a
peasants' market where collective farmers and country folk
in beards and boots out of a nineteenth-century Russian novel
sold their produce to city people. I thought I must write
about this to Rose – I meant of course Lillian. Another time,
in a deserted street when I happened to think of the customs
receipt in my billfold, I turned in my tracks to see if I were
being followed. I wasn't but enjoyed the adventure.

An experience I enjoyed less was getting lost one late
afternoon several kilometers above a boathouse on the
Dnieper. I was walking along the riverbank liking the boats
and island beaches, and before I knew it, had come a good
distance from the hotel and was eager to get back because I
was hungry. I didn't feel like retracing my route on foot –
much too much tourism in three days – so I thought of a cab,

and since none was around, maybe an autobus that might be
going in the general direction I had come from. I tried
approaching a few passers-by whom I addressed in English
or pidgin-German, and occasionally trying 'Pardonnez-moi';
but the effect was apparently to embarrass them. One young
woman ran a few awkward steps from me before she began to
walk again. I stepped into an oculist's shop to ask advice of a
professional-looking lady in her fifties, wearing pince-nez,
a hairnet and white smock. When I addressed her in English,
after five seconds of amazement her face froze and she turned
her back on me. Hastily thumbing through my guidebook to
the phonetic expressions in Russian, I asked, 'Gdye hotel?'
adding 'Dniepro?' To that she gave me an overwrought
'Nyet.' 'Taxi?' I asked. 'Nyet,' again, this time clapping a
hand to her heaving bosom. I figured we'd both had enough
and left. Though frustrated, irritated, I spoke to two men
passing by, one of whom, the minute he heard my first few
words, walked on quickly, his eyes aimed straight ahead, the
other indicating by gestures he was deaf and dumb. On
impulse I tried him in halting Yiddish that my grandfather
had taught me when I was a child, and was then directed, in
an undertone in the same language, to a nearby bus stop.

As I was unlocking the door to my room, thinking this
was a story I would be telling friends all winter, my phone
was ringing. It was a woman's voice. I understood 'Gospodin
Garvitz' and one or two other words as she spoke at length
in musical Russian. Her voice had the lilt of a singer's. Though
I couldn't get the gist of her remarks, I had this sudden vivid
reverie, you might call it, of me walking with a pretty Russian
girl in a white birchwood near Yasnaya Polyana and coming
out of the trees, sincerely talking, into a meadow that sloped
to the water; then rowing her around, both of us quiet, in a
small lovely lake. It was a peaceful business. I even had
thoughts: Wouldn't it be something if I got myself engaged
to a Russian girl? That was the general picture, but when the
caller was done talking, whatever I had to say I said in
English and she slowly hung up.

After breakfast the next morning, she, or somebody who

sounded like her – I was aware of a contralto quality – called again.

'If you understood English,' I said, 'or maybe a little German or French – even Yiddish if you happen to know it – we'd get along fine. But not in Russian, I'm sorry to say. Nyet Russki. I'd be glad to meet you for lunch or whatever you like; so if you get the drift of my remarks why don't you say da? Then dial the English interpreter on extension 37. She could explain to me what's what and we can meet at your convenience.'

I had the impression she was listening with both ears, but after a while the phone hung silent in my hand. I wondered where she had got my name, and was someone testing me to find out whether I did or didn't speak Russian. I honestly did not.

Afterward I wrote a short letter to Lillian, telling her I would be leaving for Moscow via Aeroflot, tomorrow at four p.m., and I intended to stay there for two weeks, with a break of maybe three or four days in Leningrad, at the Astoria Hotel. I wrote down the exact dates and later airmailed the letter in a street box some distance from the hotel, whatever good that did. I hoped Lillian would get it in time to reach me by return mail before I left the Soviet Union. To tell the truth I was uneasy all day.

But by the next morning my mood had shifted, and as I was standing at the railing in a park above the Dnieper, looking at the buildings going up across the river in what had once been steppeland, I experienced a curious sense of relief. The vast construction I beheld – it was as though two or three scattered small cities were rising out of the earth – astonished me. This sort of thing was going on all over Russia – halfway around the world – and when I considered what it meant in terms of sheer labor, capital goods, plain morale, I was then and there convinced that the Soviet Union would never willingly provoke a war, nuclear or otherwise, with the United States. Neither would America, in its right mind, with the Soviet Union.

For the first time since I had come to Russia I felt secure

and safe, and I enjoyed there, at the breezy railing above the Dnieper, a rare few minutes of euphoria.

Why is it that the most interesting architecture is from Tsarist times? I asked myself, and if I'm not mistaken Levitansky quivered, no doubt coincidental. Unless I had spoken aloud to myself, which I sometimes do; I decided I hadn't. We were on our way to the museum, hitting a fast eighty kilometers, which translated to fifty miles an hour was not too bad because traffic was sparse.

'What do you think of my country, the Union of Soviet Socialist Republics?' the driver inquired, turning his head a half circle to see where I was.

'I would appreciate it if you kept your eyes on the road.'

'Don't be nervous, I drive now for years.'

'I don't like needless risks.'

Then I answered I was impressed by much I had seen. Obviously it was a great country.

Levitansky's round face appeared in the mirror smiling pleasantly, his teeth eroded. The smile seemed to have appeared from within the mouth. Now that he had revealed his half-Jewish antecedents I had the impression he looked more Jewish than Slavic, and possibly more dissatisfied than I had previously thought. That I got from the eyes.

'Also our system – Communism?'

I answered carefully, not wanting to give offense, 'I'll be honest with you. I've seen some unusual things – even inspiring – but my personal taste is for a lot more individual freedom than people seem to have here. America has its serious faults, God knows, but at least we're privileged to criticize, if you know what I mean. My father used to say, "You can't beat the Bill of Rights." It's an open society, which means freedom of choice, at least in theory.'

'Communism is altogether better political system.' Levitansky replied calmly, 'although it is not in present stage totally realized. In present stage' – he swallowed, reflected, did not finish the thought. Instead he said, 'Our revolution was magnificent and holy event. I love early Soviet history, excitement of Communist idealism, and magnificent victory over bourgeois and imperialist forces. Overnight was lifted up – uplifted – the whole suffering masses. It was born a new life of possibilities for all in society. Pasternak called this "splendid surgery". Evgeny Zamyatin – maybe you know his books? – spoke thus: "The revolution consumes the earth with fire, but then is born a new life." Many of our poets said similar things.'

I didn't argue, each to his revolution.

'You told before,' said Levitansky, glancing at me again in the mirror, 'that you wish to write articles about your visit. Political or not political?'

'I don't write on politics although interested in it. What I have in mind is something on the literary museums of Moscow for an American travel magazine. That's the sort of thing I do. I'm a free-lance writer.' I laughed a little apologetically. It's strange how stresses shift when you're in another country.

Levitansky politely joined in the laugh, stopping in midcourse. 'I wish to be certain, what is free-lance writer?'

'Well, an editor might propose an article and I either accept the idea or I don't, or I can write about something that happens to interest me and take my chances I will sell it. Sometimes I don't, and that's so much down the drain financially. What I like about it is I am my own boss. I also edit a bit. I've done anthologies of poetry and essays, both for high school kids.'

'We have here free-lance. I am a writer also,' Levitansky said solemnly.

'You don't say? You mean as translator?'

'Translation is my profession but I am also original writer.'

'Then you do three things to earn a living – write, translate, and drive this cab?'

'The taxi is not my true work.'

'Are you translating anything in particular now?'

The driver cleared his throat. 'In present time I have no translation project.'

'What sort of thing do you write?'

'I write stories.'

'Is that so? What kind, if I might ask?'

'I will tell you what kind – little ones – short stories, imagined from life.'

'Have you published any?'

He seemed about to turn around to look me in the eye but reached instead into his shirt pocket. I offered my American pack. He shook out a cigarette and lit it, exhaling smoke slowly.

'A few pieces although not recently. To tell the truth' – he sighed – 'I write presently for the drawer. You know this expression? Like Isaac Babel, "I am master of the genre of silence."'

'I've heard it,' I said, not knowing what else to say.

'The mice should read and criticize,' Levitansky said bitterly. 'This what they don't eat they make their drops – droppings – on. It is perfect criticism.'

'I'm sorry about that.'

'We arrive now to Chekhov Museum.'

I leaned forward to pay him and made the impulsive mistake of adding a one-rouble tip. His face flared. 'I am Soviet citizen.' He forcibly returned the rouble.

'Call it a thoughtless error,' I apologized. 'No harm meant.'

'Hiroshima! Nagasaki!' he taunted as the Volga took off in a burst of smoke. 'Aggressor against the suffering poor people of Vietnam!'

'That's none of my doing,' I called after him.

An hour and a half later, after I had signed the guest book and was leaving the museum, I saw a man standing, smoking, under a linden tree across the street. Nearby was a parked taxi. We stared at each other – I wasn't certain at first who it was, but Levitansky nodded amiably to me, calling, 'Welcome! Welcome!' He waved an arm, smiling open-mouthed. He had combed his thick hair and was wearing a loose dark suit coat over a tieless white shirt, and yards of baggy pants. His socks, striped red-white-and-blue, you could see under his sandals.

I am forgiven, I thought. 'Welcome to you,' I said, crossing the street.

'How did you enjoy Chekhov Museum?'

'I did indeed. I've made a lot of notes. You know what they have there? They have one of his black fedoras, also his pince-nez that you see in pictures of him. Awfully moving.'

Levitansky wiped an eye – to my surprise. He seemed not quite the same man, at any rate modified. It's funny, you hear a few personal facts from a stranger and he changes as he speaks. The taxi driver is now a writer, even if part-time. Anyway, that's my dominant impression.

'Excuse me my former anger,' Levitansky explained. 'Now is not for me the best of times. "It was the best of times, it was the worst of times,"' he quoted, smiling sadly.

'So long as you pardon my unintentional blunder. Are you perhaps free to drive me to the Metropole or are you here by coincidence?'

I looked around to see if anyone was coming out of the museum.

'If you wish to engage me I will drive you, but at first I wish to show you something – how do you say? – of interest.'

He reached through the open front window of the taxi and brought forth a flat package wrapped in brown paper tied with red string.

'Stories which I wrote.'

'I don't read Russian,' I said.

'My wife has translated of them, four. She is not by her profession a translator, although her English is advanced and sensitive. She had been for two years in England for Soviet Purchasing Commission. We became acquainted in university. I prefer not to translate my own stories because I do not translate so well Russian into English, although I do it beautifully the opposite. Also I will not force myself – it is like self-imitation. Perhaps the stories appear a little awkward in English – also my wife admits this – but you can read and form opinion.'

Though he offered the package hesitantly, he offered it as if it were a bouquet of spring flowers. Can it be some sort of trick? I asked myself. Are they testing me because I signed that damned document in the Kiev airport, five copies no less?

Levitansky seemed to know my thought. 'It is purely stories.'

He bit the string in two, and laying the package on the fender of the Volga, unpeeled the wrapping. There were four stories, clipped separately, typed on long sheets of thin blue paper. I took one Levitansky handed me and scanned the top page – it seemed a story – then I flipped through the other pages and handed the manuscript back. 'I'm not much of a critic of stories.'

'I don't seek critic. I seek for reader of literary experience and taste. If you have redacted books of poems and also essays, you will be able to judge literary quality of my stories. Please, I request that you will read them.'

After a long minute I heard myself say, 'Well, I might at that.' I didn't recognize the voice and wasn't sure why I had said what I had. You could say I spoke apart from myself, with reluctance that either he wasn't aware of or chose to ignore.

'If you respect – if you approve my stories, perhaps you will be able to arrange for publication in Paris or either London?' His larynx wobbled.

I stared at the man. 'I don't happen to be going to Paris, and I'll be in London only between planes to the U.S.A.'

'In this event, perhaps you will show to your publisher, and he will publish my work in America?' Levitansky was now visibly uneasy.

'In America?' I said, raising my voice in disbelief.

For the first time he gazed around cautiously before replying.

'If you will be so kind to show them to publisher of your books – he is reliable publisher? – perhaps he will wish to put out volume of my stories? I will make contract whatever he will like. Money, if I could get, is not an ideal.'

'Whatever volume are you talking about?'

He said that from thirty stories he had written he had chosen eighteen, of which these four were a sample. 'Unfortunately more are not now translated. My wife is biochemist assistant and works long hours in laboratory. I am sure your publisher will enjoy to read these. It will depend on your opinion.'

Either this man has a fantastic imagination or he's out of his right mind. 'I wouldn't want to get myself involved in smuggling a Russian manuscript out of Russia.'

'I have informed you that my manuscript is of made-up stories.'

'That may be but it's still a chancy enterprise. I'd be taking chances I have no desire to take, to be frank.'

'At least if you will read,' he sighed.

I took the stories again and thumbed slowly through each. What I was looking for I couldn't say: maybe a booby trap? Should I or shouldn't I? I thought. Why should I?

He handed me the wrapping paper and I rolled up the stories in it. The quicker I read them, the quicker I've read them. I got into the cab.

'As I said, I'm at the Metropole. Come by tonight about nine o'clock and I'll give you my opinion for what it's worth. But I'm afraid I'll have to limit it to that, Mr Levitansky, without further obligation or expectations, or it's no deal. My room number is 538.'

'Tonight? – so soon?' he said, scratching both palms. 'You must read with care so you will realize the art.'

'Tomorrow night, then, same time. I'd rather not have them in my room longer than that.'

Levitansky agreed. Whistling softly through his eroded teeth, he drove me carefully to the Metropole.

That night, sipping vodka from a drinking glass, I read Levitansky's stories. They were simply and strongly written – I had almost expected it – and not badly translated; in fact the translation read much better than I had been led to think although there were of course some gaffes – odd constructions, ill-fitting stiff words, some indicated by question marks, and taken, I suppose, from a thesaurus. And the stories, short tales dealing – somewhat to my surprise – mostly with Moscow Jews, were good, artistically done, really moving. The situations they revealed weren't exactly news to me: I'm a careful reader of *The Times*. But the stories weren't written to complain. What they had to say was achieved as form, no telling the dancer from the dance. I poured myself another glass of the potato potion – I was beginning to feel high, occasionally wondering why I was putting so much away – relaxing, I guess. I then reread the stories with admiration for Levitansky. I had the feeling he was no ordinary man. I felt excited, then depressed, as if I had been let in on a secret I didn't want to know.

It's a hard life here for a fiction writer, I thought.

Afterward, having the stories around made me uneasy. In one of them a Russian writer burns his stories in the kitchen sink. Obviously nobody had burned these. I thought to myself, If I'm caught with them in my possession, considering what they indicate about conditions here, there's no question I'll be up to my hips in trouble. I wish I had insisted that Levitansky come back for them tonight.

There was a solid rap on the door. I felt I had risen a good few inches out of my chair. It was, after a while, Levitansky.

'Out of the question,' I said, thrusting the stories at him. 'Absolutely out of the question!'

The next night we sat facing each other over glasses of cognac in the writer's small, book-crowded study. He was dignified, at first haughty, wounded, hardly masking his impatience. I wasn't myself exactly comfortable.

I had come out of courtesy and other considerations, I guess; principally a dissatisfaction I couldn't exactly define, except it tied up with the kind of man I am or want to be, the self that sometimes gets me involved in matters I don't like to get involved in – always a dangerous business.

Levitansky, the taxi driver rattling around in his Volga–Pegasus, amateur trying to palm off a half-ass MS., had faded in my mind, and I saw him now as a serious Soviet writer with publishing problems. There are others. What can I do for him? I thought. Why should I?

'I didn't express what I really felt last night,' I apologized. 'You caught me by surprise, I'm sorry to say.'

Levitansky was scratching each hand with the blunt fingers of the other. 'How did you acquire my address?'

I reached into my pocket for a wad of folded brown wrapping paper. 'It's on this – Novo Ostapovskaya Street, 488, Flat 59. I took a cab.'

'I had forgotten this.'

Maybe, I thought.

Still, I had practically had to put my foot in the door to get in. Levitansky's wife had answered my uncertain knock, her eyes worried, an expression I took to be the one she lived with. The eyes, astonished to behold a stranger, became outright hostile once I had inquired in English for her husband. I felt, as in Kiev, that my native tongue had become my enemy.

'Have you not the wrong apartment?'

'I hope not. Not if Gospodin Levitansky lives here. I came to see him about his – ah – manuscript.'

Her startled eyes darkened as her face paled. Ten seconds later I was in the flat, the door locked behind me.

'Levitansky!' she summoned him. It had a reluctant quality: Come but don't come.

He appeared in apparently the same shirt, pants, tricolor socks. There was at first pretend-boredom in a tense, tired face. He could not, however, conceal excitement, his lit eyes roving, returning, roving.

'Oh ho,' Levitansky said, whatever it meant.

My God, I thought, has he been expecting me?

'I came to talk to you for a few minutes, if you don't mind,' I said. 'I want to say what I really think of the stories you kindly let me read.'

He curtly spoke in Russian to his wife and she snapped an answer back. 'I wish to introduce my wife, Irina Filipovna Levitansky, biochemist. She is patient although not a saint.'

She smiled tentatively, an attractive woman about twenty-eight, a little on the hefty side, in house slippers and plain dress. The edge of her slip hung below her skirt.

There was a touch of British in her accent. 'I am pleased to be acquainted.' If so one hardly noticed. She stepped into black pumps and slipped a bracelet on her wrist, a lit cigarette dangling from the corner of her mouth. Her legs and arms were shapely, her brown hair cut short. I had the impression of tight thin lips in a pale face.

'I will go to Kovalevsky, next door,' she said.

'Not on my account, I hope? All I have to say – '

'Our neighbors in the next flat,' Levitansky grimaced. 'Also thin walls.' He knocked a knuckle on a hollow, wall.

I indicated my dismay.

'Please, not long,' Irina said, 'because I am afraid.'

Surely not of me? Agent Howard Harvitz, C.I.A. – a comical thought.

Their small square living room wasn't unattractive but Levitansky signaled the study inside. He offered sweet cognac in whiskey tumblers, then sat facing me at the edge of his chair, repressed energy all but visible. I had the momentary sense his chair was about to move, fly off.

If it does he goes alone.

'What I came to say,' I told him, 'is that I like your stories and am sorry I didn't say so last night. I like the primary, close-to-the-bone quality of the writing. The stories impress me as strong if simply wrought; I appreciate your feeling for people and at the same time the objectivity with which you render them. It's sort of Chekhovian in quality, but more compressed, sinewy, direct, if you know what I mean. For instance, that story about the old father coming to see his son who ducks out on him. I can't comment on your style, having only read the stories in translation.'

'Chekhovian,' Levitansky admitted, smiling through his worn teeth, 'is fine compliment. Mayakovsky, our early Soviet poet, described him "the strong and gay artist of the word". I wish it was possible for Levitansky to be so gay in life and art.' He seemed to be staring at the drawn shade in the room, though maybe no place in particular, then said, perhaps heartening himself, 'In Russian is magnificent my style – precise, economy, including wit. The style is difficult to translate in English because is less rich language.'

'I've heard that said. In fairness I should add I have some reservations about the stories, yet who hasn't on any given piece of creative work?'

'I have myself reservations.'

The admission made, I skipped the criticism. I had been wondering about a picture on his bookcase and then asked who it was. 'It's a face I've seen before. The eyes are poetic, you might say.'

'So is the voice. This is picture of Boris Pasternak as young man. On the wall yonder is Mayakovsky. He was also remarkable poet, wild, joyful, neurasthenic, a lover of the revolution. He spoke: "This is *my* revolution." To him was it "a holy washerwoman who cleaned off all the filth from the earth". Unfortunately he was later disillusioned and shot himself.'

'I read that.'

'He wrote: "I wish to be understood by my country – but if no, I will fly through Russia like a slanting rainstorm."'

'Have you by chance read *Dr Zhivago*?'

'I have read,' the writer sighed, and then began to declaim in Russian – I guessed some lines from a poem.

'It is to Marina Tsvetayeva, Soviet poetess, good friend of Pasternak.' Levitansky fiddled with the pack of cigarettes on the table. 'The end of her life was unfortunate.'

'Is there no picture of Osip Mandelstam?' I hesitated as I spoke the name.

He reacted as though he had just met me. 'You know Mandelstam?'

'Just a few poems in an anthology.'

'Our best poet – he is holy – gone with so many others. My wife does not let me hang his photograph.'

'I guess why I really came,' I said after a minute, 'is I wanted to express my sympathy and respect.'

Levitansky popped a match with his thumbnail. His hand

trembled, so he shook the flame out without lighting the cigarette.

Embarrassed for him, I pretended to be looking elsewhere. 'It's a small room. Does your son sleep here?'

'Don't confuse my story of writer, which you have read, with life of author. My wife and I are married eight years though without children.'

'Might I ask whether the experience you describe in that same story – the interview with the editor – was true?'

'Not true although truth,' the writer said impatiently. 'I write from imagination. I am not interested to repeat contents of diaries or total memory.'

'On that I go along.'

'Also, which is not in story, I have submitted to Soviet journals sketches and tales many many times but only few have been published, although not my best. Some people, but also few, know my work through samizdat, which is passing from one to another the manuscript.'

'Did you submit any of the Jewish stories?'

'Please, stories are stories, they have not nationality.'

'I mean by that those about Jews.'

'Some I have submitted but they were not accepted.'

Brave man, I thought. 'After reading the four you gave me, I wondered how it is you write so well about Jews? You call yourself a marginal one – I believe that was your word – yet you write with authority about them. Not that one can't, I suppose, but it's surprising when one does.'

'Imagination makes authority. When I write about Jews comes out stories, so I write about Jews. I write on subjects that make for me stories. Is not important that I am half-Jew. What is important is observation, feeling, also the art. In the past I have observed my Jewish father. Also I study sometimes Jews in the synagogue. I sit there on the bench for strangers. The gabbai watches me with dark eyes and I watch him. But whatever I write, whether is about Jews, Galicians, or Georgians, must be work of invention or for me it does not live.'

'I'm not much of a synagogue-goer myself,' I told him,

'but I like to drop in once in a while to be refreshed by the language and images of a time and place where God was. That's funny because I have no religious education to speak of.'

'I am atheist.'

'I understand what you mean by imagination – that praying-shawl story. But am I right' – I lowered my voice – 'that you are saying also something about the condition of Jews in this country?'

'I do not make propaganda,' Levitansky said sternly. 'I am not Israeli spokesman. I am Soviet artist.'

'I didn't mean you weren't but there's a strong sympathy for Jews, and, after all, ideas are born in life.'

'My purpose belongs to me.'

'One senses an awareness of injustice.'

'Whatever is the injustice, the product must be art.'

'Well, I respect your philosophy.'

'Please do not respect so much,' the writer said irritably. 'We have in my country a quotation: "It is impossible to make out of apology a fur coat." The idea is similar. I appreciate your respect but need now practical assistance.'

Expecting words of the sort I started to say something non-committal.

'Listen at first to me,' Levitansky said, slapping the table with his palm. 'I am in desperate condition – situation. I have written for years but little is published. In the past, one – two editors who were friendly told me, private, that my stories are excellent but I violate social realism. This what you call objectivity they called it excessive naturalism and sentiment. It is hard to listen to such nonsense. They advise me swim but not to use my legs. They have warned me; also they have made excuses for me which I do not like them. Even they said I am crazy although I explained them I submit my stories *because* Soviet Union is great country. A great country does not fear what artist writes. A great country breathes into its lungs work of writers, painters, musicians, and becomes more great, more healthy. That I told to them but they replied I am not sufficient realist. This is the reason I am not invited to be member of Writers Union. Without this is impossible to be published.' He smiled sourly. 'They have warned me to stop submitting to journals my work, so I have stopped.'

'I'm sorry about that,' I said. 'I don't myself believe any good comes from exiling the poets.'

'I cannot continue longer any more in this fashion,' Levitansky said, laying his hand on his heart. 'I feel I am locked in drawer with my poor stories. Now I must get out or I suffocate. It becomes for me each day more difficult to write. I need help. It is not easy to request a stranger for such important personal favor. My wife advised me not. She is angry, also frightened, but it is impossible to go on in this way. I am convinced I am important Soviet writer. I must have audience. I wish to see my books to be read by Soviet people. I wish to have in minds different than my own and my wife acknowledgment of my art. I wish them to know my work is related to Russian writers of the past as well as modern. I am in tradition of Chekhov, Gorky, Isaac Babel. I know if book of my stories will be published, it will make for me fine reputation. This is reason why you must help me – it is necessary for my interior liberty.'

His confession came in an agitated burst. I use the word advisedly because that's partly what upset me. I have never cared for confessions such as are meant to involve unwilling people in others' personal problems. Russians are past masters of the art – you can see it in their novels.

'I appreciate the honor of your request,' I said, 'but all I am is a passing tourist. That's a pretty tenuous relationship between us.'

'I do not ask tourist – I ask human being – man,' Levitansky said passionately. 'Also you are free-lance writer. You know now what I am and what is on my heart. You sit in my house. Who else can I ask? I would prefer to publish in Europe my stories, maybe with Mondadori or Einaudi in Italy, but if this is impossible to you I will publish in America. Someday will my work be read in my own country, maybe after I am dead. This is terrible irony but my generation lives on such ironies. Since I am not now ambitious to die it will be great relief to me to know that at least in one language is alive my art. Mandelstam wrote: "I will be enclosed in some alien speech." Better so than nothing.'

'You say I know who you are but do you know who *I* am?' I asked him. 'I'm a plain person, not very imaginative though I don't write a bad article. My whole life, for some reason, has been without much real adventure, except I was divorced once and remarried happily to a woman whose death I am still mourning. Now I'm here more or less on a vacation, not to jeopardize myself by taking serious chances of an unknown sort. What's more – and this is the main thing I came to tell you – I wouldn't at all be surprised if I am already under suspicion and would do you more harm than good.'

I told Levitansky about the airport incident in Kiev. 'I signed a document I couldn't even read, which was a foolish thing to do.'

'In Kiev this happened?'

'That's right.'

He laughed dismally. 'It would not happen to you if you entered through Moscow. In the Ukraine – what is your word? – they are rubes, country people.'

'That might be – nevertheless I signed the paper.'

'Do you have copy?'

'Not with me. In my desk drawer in the hotel.'

'I am certain this is receipt for your books which officials will return to you when you depart from Soviet Union.'

'That's what I'd be afraid of.'

'Why afraid?' he asked. 'Are you afraid to receive back umbrella which you have lost?'

'I'd be afraid one thing might lead to another – more questions, other searches. It would be stupid to have your manuscript in my suitcase, in Russian, no less, that I can't even read. Suppose they accuse me of being some kind of courier transferring stolen documents?'

The thought raised me to my feet. I then realized the tension in the room was thick as steam, mostly mine.

Levitansky rose, embittered. 'There is no question of spying. I do not think I have presented myself as traitor to my country.'

'I didn't say anything of the sort. All I'm saying is I don't want to get into trouble with the Soviet authorities. Nobody can blame me for that. In other words the enterprise isn't for me.'

'I have made inquirings,' Levitansky insisted. 'You will have nothing to fear for tourist who has been a few weeks in U.S.S.R. under guidance of Intourist and does not speak Russian. My wife said to me your baggage will not be further inspected. They sometimes do so to political people, also to bourgeois journalists who have made bad impression. I would deliver to you the manuscript in the last instance. It is typed on less than one hundred fifty sheets thin paper and will make small package, weightless. If it should look to you like trouble you can leave it in dustbin. My name will not be anywhere and if they find it and track – trace to me the stories, I will answer I have thrown them out myself. They won't believe this but what other can I say? It will make no difference anyway. If I stop my writing I may as well be dead. No harm will come to you.'

'I'd rather not if you don't mind.'

With what I guess was a curse of despair, Levitansky reached for the portrait on his bookcase and flung it against the wall. Pasternak struck Mayakovsky, splattering him with glass, shattering himself, and both pictures crashed to the floor.

'Free-lance writer,' he shouted, 'go to hell to America! Tell to Negroes about Bill of Rights! Tell them they are free although you keep them slaves! Talk to sacrificed Vietnamese people that you respect them!'

Irina Filipovna entered the room on the run. 'Feliks,' she entreated, 'Kovalevsky hears every word!'

'Please,' she begged me, 'please go away. Leave poor Levitansky alone. I beg you from my miserable heart.'

I left in a hurry. The next day I left for Leningrad.

Three days later, not exactly at my best after a tense visit to

Leningrad, I was sitting loosely in a beat-up taxi with a cheerful Intouristka, a half hour after my arrival at the Moscow airport. We were driving to the Ukraine Hotel, where I was assigned for my remaining days in the Soviet Union. I would have preferred the Metropole again because it is so conveniently located and I was used to it, but on second thought, better some place where a certain party wouldn't know I lived. The Volga we were riding in seemed somehow familiar, but if so it was safely in the hands of a small stranger with a large wool cap, a man wearing sunglasses who paid me no particular attention.

I had had a rather special several minutes in Leningrad on my first day. On a white summer's evening, shortly after I had unpacked in my room at the Astoria, I discovered the Winter Palace and Hermitage after a walk along Nevsky Prospekt. Chancing on Palace Square, vast, deserted at the moment, I felt an unexpected intense emotion in thinking of the revolutionary events that had occurred on this spot. My God, I thought, why should I feel myself part of Russian history? It's a contagious business, what happens to men. On the Palace Bridge I gazed at the ice-blue Neva, in the distance the golden steeple of the cathedral built by Peter the Great, gleaming under masses of wind-driven clouds in patches of green sky. It's the Soviet Union but it's still Russia.

The next day I woke up anxious. In the street I was approached twice by strangers speaking English; I think my suede shoes attracted them. The first, tight-eyed and badly dressed, wanted to sell me black-market roubles. 'Nyet,' I said, tipping my straw hat and hurrying on. The second, a tall, bearded boy of about nineteen, with a left-sided tuft longer than right, wearing a home-knitted green pullover, offered to buy jazz records, 'youth clothes', and American cigarettes. 'Sorry, nothing for sale.' I escaped him too, except that green sweater followed me for a kilometer along one of the canals. I broke into a run. When I looked back he had disappeared. I slept badly – it stayed light too long past midnight; and in the morning inquired about the possibility of an immediate flight to Helsinki. I was informed I couldn't book one for a week. Calming myself, I decided to return to Moscow a day before I had planned to, mostly to see what they had in the Dostoevsky Museum.

I had been thinking a good deal about Levitansky. How much of a writer was he really? I had read four of eighteen stories he wanted to publish. Suppose he had showed me the best and the others were mediocre or thereabouts? Was it worth taking a chance for that kind of book? I thought, the best thing for my peace of mind is to forget the guy. Before checking out of the Astoria I received a chatty letter from Lillian, forwarded from Moscow, apparently not in response to my recent one to her but written earlier. Should I marry her? Did I dare? The phone rang piercingly, but when I picked up the receiver no one answered. On the plane to Moscow I had visions of a crash; there must be many in the Soviet Union nobody ever reads of.

In my room on the twelfth floor of the Ukraine I relaxed in a green plastic-covered armchair. There was also a single low bed and a utilitarian pinewood desk, an apple-green telephone plunked on it for instant use. I'll be home in a week, I thought. Now I'd better shave and see if anything is left in the way of a concert or opera ticket for tonight. I'm in a mood for music.

The electric plug in the bathroom didn't work, so I put away my shaver and was lathering up when I jumped to a single explosive knock on the door. I opened it cautiously and there stood Levitansky with a brown paper packet in his hand.

Is this son-of-a-bitch out to compromise me?

'How did you happen to find out where I was only twenty minutes after I got here, Mr Levitansky?'

'How I found you?' the writer shrugged. He seemed deathly tired, the face longer, leaner, resembling a hungry fox on his last unsteady legs but still in business.

'My brother-in-law was chauffeur for you from the airport. He heard the girl inquire your name. We have spoke of you. Dmitri – this is my wife's brother – informed me you have registered at the Ukraine. I inquired downstairs your room number and it was granted to me.'

'However it happened,' I said firmly, 'I want you to know I haven't changed my mind. I don't want to get more involved. I thought it all through while I was in Leningrad and that's my final decision.'

'I may come in?'

'Please, but for obvious reasons I'd appreciate a short visit.'

Levitansky sat, somewhat shriveled, thin knees pressed together, in the armchair, his parcel awkwardly on his lap. If he was happy he had found me it did nothing for his expression.

I finished shaving, put on a fresh white shirt, and sat down on the bed. 'Sorry I have nothing to offer in the way of an aperitif but I could call downstairs?'

Levitansky twiddled his fingers no. He was dressed without change down to his socks. Did his wife wash out the same pair every night or were all his socks red-white-and-blue?

'To speak frankly,' I said, 'I have to protest this constant tension you've whipped up in and around me. Nobody in his right mind can expect a complete stranger visiting the Soviet Union to pull his chestnuts out of the fire. It's your country that's hindering you as a writer, not me or the United States of America, and since you live here what can you do but live with it?'

'I love my country,' Levitansky said.

'Nobody denies that. So do I love mine, though love for country – let's face it – is a mixed bag of marbles. Nationality isn't soul, as I'm sure you agree. But what I'm also saying is there are things about his country one might not like that he has to make his peace with. I'm assuming you're not thinking of counter-revolution. So if you're up against a wall you can't climb or dig under or outflank, at least stop banging your head against it, not to mention mine. Do what you can. It's amazing, for instance, what can be said in a fairy tale.'

'I have written already my fairy tales,' Levitansky said moodily. 'Now is the time for truth without disguises. I will make my peace to this point where it interferes with work of my imagination – my interior liberty; and then I must stop to make my peace. My brother-in-law has also told to me, "You must write acceptable stories, others can do it, so why cannot you?" And I have answered to him, "They must be acceptable to *me*!"'

'In that case, aren't you up against the impossible? If you permit me to say it, are those Jews in your stories, if they can't have their matzos and prayer books, any freer in their religious lives than you are as a writer? That's what you're really saying when you write about them. What I mean is, one has to face up to the nature of his society.'

'I have faced up. Do you face up to yours?' he asked with a flash of scorn.

'Not as well as I might. My own problem is not that I can't express myself but that I don't. In my own mind Vietnam is a horrifying and demoralizing mistake, yet I've never really opposed it except to sign a couple of petitions and vote for congressmen who say they're against the war. My first wife used to criticize me. She said I wrote the wrong things and was involved in everything but useful action. My second wife knew this but made me think she didn't. In a curious way I'm just waking up to the fact that the United States Government has for years been mucking up my soul.'

From the heat of my body I could tell I was blushing.

Levitansky's large larynx moved up like a flag on a pole, then sank wordlessly.

He tried again, saying, 'The Soviet Union preservates for us the great victories of our revolution. Because of this I have remained for years at peace with the State. Communism is still to me inspirational ideal although this historical period is spoiled by leaders with impoverished view of humanity. They have pissed on revolution.'

'Stalin?'

'Him especially but also others. Even so I have obeyed Party directives, and when I could not longer obey I wrote for drawer. I said to myself, "Levitansky, history changes every minute and also Communism will change." I believed if the State restricts two, three generations of artists, what is this against development of true socialist society – maybe best society of world history? So what does it mean if some of us are sacrificed to Party purpose? The aesthetic mode is not in necessity greater than politics – than needs of revolution. And what if are suppressed two generations of artists? Therefore will be so much less bad books, poor painting, bad music. Then in fifty years more will be secure the State and all Soviet artists will say whatever they wish. This is what I thought, or tried to think, but do not longer think so. I do not believe more in partiinost, which is guided thought, an expression which is to me ridiculous. I do not believe in bolshevization of literature. I do not think revolution is fulfilled in country of unpublished novelists, poets, playwriters, who hide in drawers whole libraries of literature that will never be printed, or if so, it will be printed after they stink in their graves. I think now the State will never be secure – never! It is not in the nature of politics, or human condition, to be finished with revolution. Evgeny Zamyatin told: "There is no final revolution. Revolutions are infinite!"'

'I guess that's along my own line of thinking,' I said, hoping for reasons of personal safety to forestall Levitansky's ultimate confession – one he, with brooding eyes, was already relentlessly making – lest in the end it imprison me in his will and history.

'I have learned from writing my stories,' the writer was saying, 'that imagination is enemy of the State. I have learned from my writing that I am not free man. This is my conclusion. I ask for your help, not to harm my country, which still has magnificent socialistic possibilities, but to help me escape its worst errors. I do not wish to defame Russia. My purpose in my work is to show its true heart. So have done our writers from Pushkin to Pasternak and also, in his way, Solzhenitsyn. If you believe in democratic humanism you must help artist to be free. Is not true?'

I got up, I think to shake myself free of that question. 'What exactly is my responsibility to you, Levitansky?' I tried to contain the exasperation I felt.

'We are members of mankind. If I am drowning you must assist to save me.'

'In unknown waters if I can't swim?'

'If not, throw to me rope.'

'I'm a visitor here. I've told you I may be suspect. For all I know you yourself might be a Soviet agent out to get me, or the room may be bugged and then where are we? Mr Levitansky, please, I don't want to hear or argue any more. I'll just plead personal inability and ask you to leave.'

'Bugged?'

'Some sort of listening device planted in this room.'

Levitansky slowly turned gray. He sat a moment in motionless meditation, then rose wearily from the chair.

'I withdraw now request for your assistance. I accept your word that you are not capable. I do not wish to make criticism of you. All I wish to say, Gospodin Garvitz, is it requires more to change a man's character than to change his name.'

Levitansky left the room, leaving in his wake faint fumes of cognac. He had also passed gas.

'Come back!' I called, not too loudly, but if he heard through the door he didn't answer. Good riddance, I thought. Not that I don't sympathize with him but look what he's done to *my* interior liberty. Who has to come thousands of miles to Russia to get caught up in this kind of mess? It's a helluva way to spend a vacation.

The writer had gone but not his sneaky manuscript. It was lying on my bed.

'It's his baby, not mine.' Angered, I knotted my tie and slipped on my coat, then via the English-language number, called a cab. But I had forgotten his address. A half hour later I was still in the taxi, riding anxiously back and forth along Novo Ostapovskaya Street until I spotted the apartment house I thought it might be. It wasn't, it was another like it. I paid the driver and walked on till once again I thought I had the house. After going up the stairs I was sure it was. When I knocked on Levitansky's door, the writer, looking older, more distant – as if he'd been away on a trip and had just returned; or maybe simply interrupted at his work, his thoughts still in his words on the page on the table, his pen in hand – stared blankly at me. Very blankly.

'Levitansky, my heart breaks for you, I swear, but I can't

take the chance. I believe in you but am not, at this time of my life, considering my condition and recent experiences, in much of a mood to embark on a dangerous adventure. Please accept deepest regrets.'

I thrust the manuscript into his hand and rushed down the stairs. Hurrying out of the building, I was, to my horror, unable to avoid Irina Levitansky coming in. Her eyes lit in fright as she recognized me an instant before I hit her full force and sent her sprawling along the walk.

'Oh, my God, what have I done? I beg your pardon!' I helped the dazed, hurt woman to her feet, brushing off her soiled skirt, and futilely, her pink blouse, split and torn on her lacerated arm and shoulder. I stopped dead when I felt myself experiencing erotic sensations.

Irina Filipovna held a handkerchief to her bloody nostril and wept a little. We sat on a stone bench, a girl of ten and her little brother watching us. Irina said something to them in Russian and they moved off.

'I was frightened of you also as you are of us,' she said. 'I trust you now because Levitansky does. But I will not urge you to take the manuscript. The responsibility is for you to decide.'

'It's not a responsibility I want,' I said unhappily.

She said as though to herself. 'Maybe I will leave Levitansky. He is wretched so much it is no longer a marriage. He drinks. Also he does not earn a living. My brother Dmitri allows him to drive the taxi two, three hours of the day, to my brother's disadvantage. Except for a rouble or two from this, I support him. Levitansky does not longer receive translation commissions. Also a neighbor in the house – I am sure Kovalevsky – has denounced him to the police for delinquency and parasitism. There will be a hearing. Levitansky says he will burn his manuscripts.'

'Good God, I've just returned the package of stories!'

'He will not,' she said. 'But even if he burns he will write more. If they take him away in prison he will write on toilet paper. When he comes out, he will write on newspaper margins. He sits this minute at his table. He is a magnificent writer. I cannot ask him not to write, but now I must decide if this is the condition I wish for myself for the rest of my life.'

Irina sat in silence, an attractive woman with shapely legs and feet, in a soiled skirt and torn blouse. I left her on the stone bench, her handkerchief squeezed in her fist.

That night – 2 July, I was leaving the Soviet Union on the fifth – I experienced massive self-doubt. If I'm a coward why has it taken so long to find out? Where does anxiety end and cowardice begin? Feelings get mixed, sure enough, but not all cowards are anxious men, and not all anxious men are cowards. Many 'sensitive' (Rose's word), tense, even frightened human beings did in fear what had to be done, the fear calling up energy when it's time to fight or jump off a rooftop into a river. There comes a time in a man's life when to get where he has to go – if there are no doors or windows – he walks through a wall.

On the other hand, suppose one is courageous in a foolish cause – you concentrate on courage and not enough on horse sense? To get to the point of the problem endlessly on my mind, how do I finally decide it's a sensible and worthwhile thing to smuggle out Levitansky's manuscript, given my reasonable doubts of the ultimate worth of the operation? Granted, as I now grant, he's a trustworthy guy and his wife is that and more; still, does it pay a man like me to run the risk?

If six thousand Soviet writers can't do very much to squeeze out another inch of freedom as artists, who am I to fight their battle – H. Harvitz, knight-of-the-free-lance from Manhattan? How far do you go, granted all men, including Communists, are created free and equal and justice is for all? How far do you go for art, if you're for Yeats, Matisse, and Ludwig van Beethoven? Not to mention Gogol, Tolstoy, and Dostoevsky. So far as to get yourself intentionally involved: the HH MS. Smuggling Service? Will the President and State Department send up three loud cheers for my contribution to the cause of artistic social justice? And suppose it amounts to no more than a gaffe in the end? – What will I prove if I sneak out Levitansky's manuscript and all it turns out to be is just another passable book of stories?

That's how I argued with myself on more than one occasion, but in the end I argued myself into solid indecision.

What it boils down to, I'd say, is he expects me to help him because I'm an American. That's quite a nerve.

Two nights later – odd not to have the Fourth of July on 4 July (I was listening for firecrackers) – a quiet light-lemon summer's evening in Moscow, after two monotonously uneasy days, though I was still writing museum notes, for relief I took myself off to the Bolshoi to hear *Tosca*. It was sung in Russian by a busty lady and handsome tenor, but the Italian plot was unchanged, and in the end, Scarpia, who had promised 'death' by fake bullets, gave in sneaky exchange a fusillade of hot lead; another artist bit the dust and Floria Tosca learned the hard way that love wasn't what she had thought.

Next to me sat another full-breasted woman, this one a lovely Russian of maybe thirty in a white dress that fitted a well-formed mature figure, her blond hair piled in a birdlike mass on her splendid head. Lillian could look like that, though not Rose. This woman – alone, it turned out – spoke flawless English in a mezzo-soprano with a slight accent.

During the first intermission she asked in friendly fashion, managing to seem detached but interested: 'Are you American? Or perhaps Swedish?'

'Not Swedish. American is correct. How did you happen to guess?'

'I noticed, if it does not bother you that I say it,' she remarked with a charming laugh, 'a certain self-satisfaction.'

'You got the wrong party,' I said.

When she opened her purse a fragrance of springtime burst forth – fresh flowers; the warmth of her body rose to my nostrils. I was moved by memories of the hungers of youth – dreams, longing.

During intermission she touched my arm and said in a low voice, 'May I ask a favor? Do you depart from the Soviet Union?'

'In fact tomorrow.'

'How fortunate for me. Would it offer too much difficulty to mail wherever you are going an airmail letter addressed to my husband, who is presently in Paris? Our airmail service takes two weeks to arrive in the West. I shall be grateful.'

I glanced at the envelope addressed half in French, half in Cyrillic, and said I wouldn't mind. But during the next act sweat grew active on my flesh and at the end of the opera, after Tosca's shriek of suicide, I handed the letter back to the not wholly surprised lady, saying I was sorry. Nodding to her, I left the theater. I had the feeling I had heard her voice before. I hurried back to the hotel, determined not to leave my room for any reason other than breakfast, then out and into the wide blue sky.

I later fell asleep over a book and a bottle of sweetish warm beer a waiter had brought up, pretending to myself I was relaxed though I was as usual concerned beforehand with worried thoughts of the departure and flight home; and when I awoke, three minutes on my wristwatch later, it seemed to me I had made the acquaintance of a spate of new nightmares. I was momentarily panicked by the idea that someone had planted a letter on me, and I searched through the pockets of my two suits. Nyet. Then I recalled that in one of my dreams a drawer in a table I was sitting at had slowly come open and Feliks Levitansky, a dwarf who lived in it along with a few friendly mice, managed to scale the wooden wall on the comb he used as a ladder, and to hop from the drawer ledge to the top of the table. He leered into my face, shook his Lilliputian fist, and shouted in high-pitched but (to me) understandable Russian, 'Atombombnik! You massacred innocent Japanese people! Amerikansky bastards!'

'That's unfair,' I cried out, 'I was no more than a kid in college.'

That's a sad dream, I thought.

Afterwards this occurred to me: Suppose what happened to Levitansky happens to me. Suppose America gets caught up in a war with China in some semi-reluctant stupid way, and to make fast hash of it – despite my frantic loud protestations: mostly I wave my arms and shout obscenities till my face turns green – we spatter them, before they can get going, with a few dozen H-bombs, boiling up a thick atomic soup of about two hundred million Orientals – blood, gristle, marrow, and lots of floating Chinese eyeballs. We win the war because the Soviets hadn't been able to make up their minds who to shoot their missiles at first. And suppose after this unheard-of slaughter, about ten million Americans, in self-revulsion, head for the borders to flee the country. To stop the loss of wealth, the refugees are intercepted by the army in tanks and turned back. Harvitz hides in his room with shades drawn, writing in a fury of protest a long epic poem condemning the mass butchery by America. What nation, Asiatic or other, is next? Nobody in the States wants to publish the poem because it might start riots and another flight of refugees to Canada and Mexico; then one day there's a knock on the door, and it isn't the F.B.I. but a bearded Levitansky, in better times a Soviet tourist, a modern, not medieval Communist. He kindly offers to sneak the manuscript of the poem out for publication in the Soviet Union.

Why? Harvitz suspiciously asks.

Why not? To give the book its liberty.

I awoke after a restless night. I had been instructed by Intourist to be in the lobby with my baggage two hours before flight time at eleven a.m. I was shaved and dressed by six, and at seven had breakfast – I was very hungry – of yogurt, sausage, and scrambled eggs in the twelfth-floor buffet. I then went out to hunt for a taxi. They were hard to come by at this hour but I finally located one near the American Embassy, not far from the hotel. Speaking my usual mixture of primitive German and French, I persuaded the driver by first suggesting, then slipping him an acceptable two roubles, to take me to Levitansky's house and wait a few minutes till I came out. Going hastily up the stairs, I knocked on his door, apologizing when he opened it, to the half-pajamaed, iron-faced writer, for awaking him this early in the day. Without peace of mind or certainty of purpose I asked him whether he still wanted me to smuggle out his manuscript of stories. I got for my trouble the door slammed in my face.

A half hour later I had everything packed and was locking the suitcase. A knock on the door – half a rap, you might call it. For the suitcase, I thought. I was momentarily frightened by the sight of a small man in a thick cap wearing a long trench coat. He winked, and against the will I winked back. I had recognized Levitansky's brother-in-law Dmitri, the taxi driver. He slid in, unbuttoned his coat, and brought forth the wrapped manuscript. Holding a finger to his lips, he handed it to me before I could say I was no longer interested.

'Levitansky changed his mind?'

'Not changed mind. Was afraid your voice to be heard by Kovalevsky.'

'I'm sorry, I should have thought of that.'

'Levitansky say not write to him,' the brother-in-law whispered. 'When is published book please send to him copy of *Das Kapital*. He will understand message.'

I reluctantly agreed.

The brother-in-law, a short shapeless figure with sad Jewish eyes, winked again, shook hands with a steamy palm, and slipped out of my room.

I unlocked my suitcase and laid the manuscript on top of my shirts. Then I unpacked half the contents and slipped the manuscript into a folder containing my notes on literary museums and a few letters from Lillian. I then and there decided that if I got back to the States, the next time I saw her I would ask her to marry me. The phone was ringing as I left the room.

On my way to the airport, alone in a taxi – no Intourist girl accompanied me – I felt, on and off, nauseated. If it's not the sausage and yogurt it must just be ordinary fear. Still, if Levitansky has the courage to send these stories out the least I can do is give him a hand. When one thinks of it it's little enough he does for human freedom in the course of his life. At the airport if I can dig up a bromo or its Russian equivalent I know I'll feel better.

The driver was observing me in the mirror, a stern man with the head of a scholar, impassively smoking.

'Le jour fait beau,' I said.

He pointed with an upraised finger to a sign in English at one side of the road to the airport:

'Long live peace in the world!'

Peace with freedom. I smiled at the thought of somebody, not Howard Harvitz, painting that in red on the Soviet sign.

We drove on, I foreseeing my exit from the Soviet Union. I had made discreet inquiries from time to time and an Intourist girl in Leningrad had told me I had first to show my papers at the passport-control desk, turn in my roubles – a serious offense to walk off with any – and then check luggage; no inspection, she swore. And that was that. Unless, of course, the official at the passport desk found my name on a list and said I had to go to the customs office for a package. In that case – if nobody said so I wouldn't remind him – I would go get the books. I figured I wouldn't open the package, just tear off a bit of the wrapping, if they were wrapped, as though to make sure they were the books I expected, and then saunter away with the package under my arm. If they asked me to sign another five copies of a document in Russian I would write at the bottom: 'It is understood that I can't speak or read Russian' and sign my name to that.

I had heard that a KGB man was stationed at the ramp as one boarded a plane. He asked for your passport, checked the picture, threw you a stare through dark lenses, and if there was no serious lack of resemblance, tore out your expired visa, pocketed it, and let you embark.

In ten minutes you were aloft, seat belts fastened in three languages, watching the plane banking west. Maybe if I looked hard I might see in the distance Feliks Levitansky on the roof waving his red-white-and-blue socks on a bamboo pole. Then the plane leveled off, and we were above the clouds, flying westward. And that's what I would be doing for five or six hours unless the pilot received radio instructions to turn back; or maybe land in Czechoslovakia or East Germany, where two big-hatted detectives boarded the plane. By an act of imagination and will I made it some other passenger they were arresting. I got the plane into the air again and we flew on without incident until we touched down in London.

As the taxi approached the Moscow airport, fingering my ticket and gripping my suitcase handle, I wished for courage equal to Levitansky's when they discovered he was the author of a book of stories I had managed to sneak out and get published, and his trial and suffering began.

Levitansky's first story of the four in English was about an old father, a pensioner, who was not feeling well and wanted his son, with whom he had had continuous strong disagreements, and whom he hadn't seen in eight months, to know. He decided to pay him a short visit. Since the son had moved from his flat to a larger one and had not forwarded his address, the father went to call on him at work. The son was an official of some sort with an office in a new State building. The father had never been there although he knew where it was because a neighbor on a walk with him had pointed it out.

The pensioner sat in a chair in his son's large outer office, waiting for him to be free for a few minutes. 'Yuri,' he thought he would say, 'all I want to tell you is that I'm not up to my usual self. My breath is short and I have pains in my chest. In fact, I'm not well. After all, we're father and son and you ought to know the state of my health, seeing it's not so good and your mother is dead.'

The son's assistant secretary, a modern girl in a short tight skirt, said he was attending an important administrative conference.

'A conference is a conference,' the father said. He wouldn't want to interfere with it and didn't mind waiting although he was still having nauseating twinges of pain.

The father waited patiently in the chair for several hours; and though he had a few times risen and urgently spoken to the assistant secretary, he was, by the end of the day, still unable to see his son. The girl, putting on her pink hat, advised the old man that the official had already left the building. He hadn't been able to see his father because he had unexpectedly been called away on an important State matter.

'Go home and he will telephone you in the morning.'

'I have no telephone,' said the old pensioner impatiently. 'He knows that.'

The assistant secretary; the private secretary, an older woman from the inside office; and later the caretaker of the building, all tried to persuade the father to go home, but he wouldn't leave.

The private secretary said her husband was expecting her and she could stay no longer. After a while the assistant secretary with the pink hat also left. The caretaker, a man with wet eyes and a ragged mustache, tried to persuade the old man to leave. 'What sort of foolishness is it to wait all night in a pitch-dark building? You'll frighten yourself out of your wits, not to speak of other discomforts you're bound to suffer.'

'No,' said the sick father, 'I will wait. When my son comes in tomorrow morning I'll tell him something he hasn't learned yet. I'll tell him what he does to me his children will do to him.'

The caretaker departed. The old man was left alone waiting for his son to appear in the morning.

'I'll report him to the Party,' he muttered.

The second story was about another old man, a widower of sixty-eight, who hoped to have matzos for Passover. Last year he had got his quota. They had been baked at the State bakery and sold in State stores; but this year the State bakeries were not permitted to bake them. The officials said the machines had broken down but who believed them.

The old man went to the rabbi, an older man with a tormented beard, and asked him where he could get matzos. He was frightened that he mightn't have them this year.

'So am I,' confessed the old rabbi. He said he had been told to tell his congregants to buy flour and bake them at home. The State stores would sell them the flour.

'What good is that for me?' asked the widower. He reminded the rabbi that he had no home to speak of, a single

small room with a one-burner electric stove. His wife had
died two years ago. His only living child, a married daughter,
was with her husband in Birobijan. His other relatives – the
few who were left after the German invasion – two female
cousins his age – lived in Odessa; and he himself, even if he
could find an oven, did not know how to bake matzos. And
if he couldn't what should he do?

The rabbi then promised he would try to get the widower a
kilo or two of matzos, and the old man, rejoicing, blessed
him.

He waited anxiously a month but the rabbi never mentioned
the matzos. Maybe he had forgotten. After all he was an old
man burdened with worries and the widower did not want to
press him. However, Passover was coming on wings, so he
must do something. A week before the Holy Days he hurried
to the rabbi's flat and spoke to him there.

'Rabbi,' he begged, 'you promised me a kilo or two of
matzos. What has happened to them?'

'I know I promised,' said the rabbi, 'but I'm no longer
sure to whom. It's easy to promise.' He dabbed at his face
with a damp handkerchief. 'I was warned one could be
arrested on charges of profiteering in the production and sale
of matzos. I was told it could happen even if I were to give
them away for nothing. It's a new crime they've invented.
Still, take them anyway. If they arrest me, I'm an old man,
and how long can an old man live in Lubyanka? Not so long,
thank God. Here, I'll give you a small pack but you must tell
no one where you got the matzos.'

'May the Lord eternally bless you, rabbi. As for dying in
prison, rather let it happen to our enemies.'

The rabbi went to his closet and got out a small pack of
matzos, already wrapped and tied with knotted twine. When
the widower offered in a whisper to pay him, at least the cost
of the flour, the rabbi wouldn't hear of it. 'God provides,'
he said, 'although at times with difficulty.' He said there was
hardly enough for all who wanted matzos, so he must take
what he got and be thankful.

'I will eat less,' said the old man. 'I will count mouthfuls.

I will save the last matzo to look at and kiss if there isn't enough to last me. God will understand.'

Overjoyed to have even a few matzos, he rode home on the trolley car and there met another Jew, a man with a withered hand. They conversed in Yiddish in low tones. The stranger had glanced at the almost square package, then at the widower, and had hoarsely whispered, 'Matzos?' The widower, tears starting in his eyes, nodded. 'With God's grace.' 'Where did you get them?' 'God provides.' 'So if He provides let Him provide me,' the stranger brooded. 'I'm not so lucky. I was hoping for a package from relatives in Cleveland, America. They wrote they would send me a large pack of the finest matzos but when I inquire of the authorities they say no matzos have arrived. You know when they will get here?' he muttered. 'After Passover by a month or two, and what good will they be then?'

The widower nodded sadly. The stranger wiped his eyes with his good hand and after a short while left the trolley amid a number of people getting off. He had not bothered to say goodbye, and neither had the widower, nor to remind him of his own good fortune. When the time came for the old man to leave the trolley he glanced down between his feet where he had placed the package of matzos but nothing was there. His feet were there. The old man felt harrowed, as though someone had ripped a nail down his spine. He searched frantically throughout that car, going a long way past his stop, querying every passenger, the woman conductor, the motorman, but no one had seen his matzos.

Then it occurred to him that the stranger with the withered hand had stolen them.

The widower in his misery asked himself, would a Jew have robbed another of his precious matzos? It didn't seem possible. Still, who knows, he thought, what one will do to get matzos if he has none.

As for me I haven't even a matzo to look at now. If I could steal any, whether from Jew or Russian, I would steal them. He thought he would even steal them from the old rabbi.

The widower went home without his matzos and had none for Passover.

The third story, a tale called 'Tallith', concerned a youth of seventeen, beardless but for some stray hairs on his chin, who had come from Kirov to the steps of the synagogue on Arkhipova Street in Moscow. He had brought with him a capacious prayer shawl, a white garment of luminous beauty which he offered for sale to a cluster of Jews of various sorts and sizes – curious, apprehensive, greedy at the sight of the shawl – for fifteen roubles. Most of them avoided the youth, particularly the older Jews, despite the fact that some of the more devout among them were worried about their prayer shawls, eroded on their shoulders after years of daily use, which they could not replace. 'It's the informers among us who have put him up to this,' they whispered among themselves, 'so they will have someone to inform on.'

Still, in spite of the warnings of their elders, several of the younger men examined the tallith and admired it. 'Where did you get such a fine prayer shawl?' the youth was asked. 'It was my father's who recently died,' he said. 'It was given to him by a rich Jew he had once befriended.' 'Then why don't you keep it for yourself, you're a Jew, aren't you?' 'Yes,' said the youth, not the least embarrassed, 'but I am going to Bratsk as a komsomol volunteer and I need a few roubles to get married. Besides I'm a confirmed atheist.'

One young man with fat unshaven cheeks, who admired the deeply white shawl, its white glowing in whiteness, with its long silk fringes, whispered to the youth he might consider buying it for five roubles. But he was overheard by the gabbai, the lay leader of the congregation, who raised his cane and shouted at the whisperer, 'Hooligan, if you buy that shawl, beware it doesn't become your shroud.' The Jew with the unshaven cheeks retreated.

'Don't strike him,' cried the frightened rabbi, who had come out of the synagogue and saw the gabbai, with his cane upraised. He urged the congregants to begin prayers at once. To the youth he said, 'Please go away from here, we are burdened with enough troubles as it is. It is forbidden for anyone to sell religious articles. Do you want us to be accused of criminal economic activity? Do you want the doors of the shul to be closed forever? So do us and yourself a mitzvah and go away.'

The congregants moved inside. The youth was left standing alone on the steps; but then the gabbai came out of the door, a man with a deformed spine and a wad of cotton stuck in his leaking ear.

'Look here,' he said. 'I know you stole it. Still, after all is said and done, a tallith is a tallith and God asks no questions of His worshippers. I offer eight roubles for it, take it or leave it. Talk fast before the services end and the others come out.'

'Make it ten and it's yours,' said the youth.

The gabbai gazed at him shrewdly. 'Eight is all I have but wait here and I'll borrow two roubles from my brother-in-law.'

The youth waited patiently. Dusk was thickening. In a few minutes a black car drove up, stopped in front of the synagogue, and two policemen got out. The youth realized at once that the gabbai had informed on him. Not knowing what else to do he hastily draped the prayer shawl over his head and began loudly to pray. He prayed a passionate kaddish. The police hesitated to approach him while he was praying, and they stood at the bottom of the steps waiting for him to be done. The congregants came out and could not believe their ears. No one imagined the youth could pray so fervently. What moved them was the tone, the wail and passion of a man truly praying. Perhaps his father had indeed recently died. All listened attentively, and many wished he would pray forever, for they knew that when he stopped he would be seized and thrown into prison.

It has grown dark. A moon hovers behind murky clouds over the synagogue steeple. The youth's voice is heard in prayer. The congregants are huddled in the dark street, listening. Both police agents are still there, although they cannot be seen. Neither can the youth. All that can be seen is the white shawl luminously praying.

*

The last of the four stories translated by Irina Filipovna was about a writer of mixed parentage, a Russian father and Jewish mother, who had secretly been writing stories for years. He had from a young age wanted to write but had at first not had the courage to – it seemed like such a merciless undertaking – so he had gone into translation instead; and then when he had, one day, started to write seriously and exultantly, after a while he found to his surprise that many of his stories, about half, were about Jews.

For a half-Jew that's a reasonable proportion, he thought. The others were about Russians who sometimes resembled members of his father's family. 'It's good to have such different sources for ideas,' he told his wife. 'This way I can cover a varied range of experiences in life.'

After several years of work he had submitted a selection of his stories to a trusted friend of university days, Viktor Zverkov, an editor of the Progress Publishing House; and the writer appeared at his office one morning after receiving a hastily scribbled cryptic note from his friend, to discuss his work with him. Zverkov, a troubled man to begin with – he told everyone his wife did not respect him – jumped up from his chair and turned the key in the door, his ear pressed a minute at the crack. He then went quickly to his desk and withdrew the manuscript from a drawer he first had to unlock with a key he kept in his pocket. He was a heavy-set man with a flushed complexion, stained teeth, and a hoarse voice; and he handled the writer's manuscript with unease, as though it might leap up and wound him in the face.

'Please, Tolya,' he whispered breathily, bringing his head close to the writer's, 'you must take these dreadful stories away at once.'

'What's the matter with you? Why are you shaking so?'

'Don't pretend to be so naïve. You know why I am disturbed. I am frankly amazed that you are submitting such unorthodox material for publication. My opinion as an editor is that they are of doubtful literary merit – I won't say devoid of it, Tolya, I want to be honest – but as stories they are a frightful affront to our society. I can't understand why you should take it on yourself to write about Jews. What do you know about them? Your culture is not the least Jewish, it's Soviet Russian. The whole business smacks of hypocrisy and you may be accused of anti-Semitism.'

He got up to shut the window and peered into a closet before sitting down.

'Are you out of your mind, Viktor? My stories are in no sense anti-Semitic. One would have to read them standing on his head to make that judgement.'

'There can be only one logical interpretation,' the editor argued. 'According to my most lenient analysis, which is favorable to you as a person of let's call it decent intent, the stories fly in the face of socialist realism and reveal a dangerous inclination – perhaps even a stronger word should be used – to anti-Soviet sentiment. Maybe you're not entirely aware of this – I know how a story can pull a writer by the nose. As an editor I have to be sensitive to such things. I know, Tolya, from our conversations that you are a sincere believer in our socialism; I won't accuse you of being defamatory to the Soviet system, but others may. In fact, I know they will. If one of the editors of *Oktyabr* were to read your stories, believe me, your career would explode in a mess. You seem not to have a normal awareness of what self-preservation is, and what's appallingly worse, you're not above entangling innocent bystanders in your fate. If these stories were mine, I assure you I would never have brought them to you. I urge you to destroy them at once, before they destroy you.'

He drank thirstily from a glass of water on his desk.

'That's the last thing I would do,' answered the writer in anger. 'These stories, if not in tone or subject matter, are written in the spirit of our early Soviet writers – the joyous spirits of the years just after the revolution.'

'I think you know what happened to many of those "joyous spirits".'

The writer for a moment stared at him. 'Well, then, what of the stories that are not about the experience of Jews? Some are pieces about homely aspects of Russian life; for instance the one about the pensioner father and his invisible son. What I hoped is that you might personally recommend one or two such stories to *Novy Mir* or *Yunost*. They are innocuous sketches and well written.'

'Not the one of the two prostitutes,' said the editor. 'That contains hidden social criticism and is adversely naturalistic.'

'A prostitute lives a social life.'

'That may be but I can't recommend it for publication. I must advise you, Tolya, if you expect to receive further commissions for translations from us, you must immediately rid yourself of this whole manuscript so as to avoid the possibility of serious consequences both to yourself and family, and to this publishing house that has employed you so faithfully and generously in the past.'

'Since you didn't write the stories yourself, you needn't be afraid, Viktor Alexandrovich,' the writer said coldly.

'I am not a coward, if that's what you're hinting, Anatoly Borisovich, but if a wild locomotive is running loose on the rails, I know which way to jump.'

The writer hastily gathered up his manuscript, stuffed the papers into his leather case, and returned home by bus. His wife was still away at work. He took out the stories, and after reading through one, burned it, page by page, in the kitchen sink.

His nine-year-old son, returning from school, said, 'Papa, what are you burning in the sink? That's no place for a fire.'

'I am burning my integrity,' said the writer. Then he said, 'My talent. My heritage.'

Muriel Spark

THE GENTILE JEWESSES

Muriel Spark

MURIEL SPARK was born in Edinburgh of part-Jewish origin on both sides of her family and is a novelist, poet, playwright and biographer. Her novels include *Memento Mori*, *The Prime of Miss Jean Brodie*, *The Abbess of Crewe* and *A Far Cry from Kensington*. Her collected short stories were published in 1987. She was elected to L'Ordre des Arts et des Lettres in 1988.

THE GENTILE JEWESSES

ONE day a madman came into my little grandmother's shop at Watford. I say my little grandmother but 'little' refers only to her height and to the dimensions of her world by the square foot – the small shop full of varieties, her parlour behind it, and behind that the stone kitchen and the two bedrooms over her head.

'I shall murder you,' said the madman, standing with legs straddled in the door frame, holding up his dark big hands as one about to pounce and strangle. His eyes stared from a face covered with tangled eyebrows and beard.

The street was empty. My grandmother was alone in the house. For some years, from frequent hearing of the story, I believed I was standing by her side at the time, but my grandmother said no, this was long before I was born. The scene is as clear as a memory to me. The madman – truly escaped from the asylum in a great park near by – lifted his hairy hands, cupped as for strangling. Behind him was the street, empty save for sunshine.

He said, 'I'm going to murder you.'

She folded her hands over her white apron which lay over the black apron and looked straight at him.

'Then you'll get hung,' she said.

He turned and shuffled away.

She should have said 'hanged' and I remember at one telling of the story remarking so to my grandmother. She replied that 'hung' had been good enough for the madman. I could not impress her with words, but I was so impressed by the tale that very often afterwards I said 'hung' instead of 'hanged'.

I seem to see the happening so plainly in my memory it is difficult to believe I know it only by hearsay; but indeed it happened before I was born. My grandfather was a young man then, fifteen years younger than his wife and dispossessed by his family for having married her. He was gone to arrange about seedlings when the madman had appeared.

My grandmother had married him for pure love, she had chased him and hunted him down and married him, he was so beautiful and useless. She never cared at all that she had to work and keep him all his life. She was astonishingly ugly, one was compelled to look at her. In my actual memory, late in their marriage, he would bring her a rose from the garden from time to time, and put cushions under her head and feet when she reclined on the sofa in the parlour between the hours of two and three in the afternoon. He could not scrub the counter in her shop for he did not know how to do it, but he knew about dogs and birds and gardens, and had photography for a pastime.

He said to my grandmother, 'Stand by the dahlias and I will take your likeness.'

I wished she had known how to take his likeness because he was golden-haired even in my day, with delicate features and glittering whiskers. She had a broad pug nose, she was sallow skinned with bright black eyes staring straight at the world and her dull black hair pulled back tight into a knot. She looked like a white negress; she did not try to beautify herself except by washing her face in rain water.

She had come from Stepney. Her mother was a Gentile and her father was a Jew. She said her father was a Quack by profession and she was proud of this, because she felt all curing was done by the kindly manner of the practitioner in handing out bottles of medicine rather than by the contents. I always forced my elders to enact their stories. I said, 'Show me how he did it.'

Willingly she leaned forward in her chair and handed me an invisible bottle of medicine. She said, 'There you are, my dear, and you won't come to grief, and don't forget to keep your bowels regular.' She said, 'My father's medicine was only beetroot juice but he took pains with his manners, and he took pains with the labels, and the bottles were threepence a gross. My father cured many an ache and pain, it was his gracious manner.'

This, too, entered my memory and I believed I had seen the glamorous Quack Doctor who was dead before I was born. I thought of him when I saw my grandfather, with his gracious manner, administering a tiny dose of medicine out of a blue bottle to one of his small coloured birds. He opened its beak with his finger and tipped in a drop. All the little garden was full of kennels, glass and sheds containing birds and flower-pots. His photographs were not quite real to look at. One day he called me Canary and made me stand by the brick wall for my likeness. The photograph made the garden look tremendous. Perhaps he was reproducing in his photographs the grander garden of his youth from which he was expelled avengingly upon his marriage to my grandmother long before I was born.

After his death, when my grandmother came to live with us I said to her one day,

'Are you a Gentile, Grandmother, or are you a Jewess?' I was wondering how she would be buried, according to what religion, when her time came to die.

'I am a Gentile Jewess,' she said.

All during the time she kept the shop of all sorts in Watford she had not liked the Jewish part of her origins to be known, because it was bad for business. She would have been amazed at any suggestion that this attitude was a weak one or a wrong one. To her, whatever course was sensible and good for business was good in the sight of the Almighty. She believed heartily in the Almighty. I never heard her refer to God by any other title except to say, God bless you. She was a member of the Mothers' Union of the Church of England. She attended all the social functions of the Methodists, Baptists and Quakers. This was bright and agreeable as well as being good for business. She never went to church on Sundays, only for special services such as on Remembrance Day. The only time she acted against her conscience was when she attended a spiritualist meeting; this was from sheer curiosity, not business. There, a bench fell over on to her foot and she limped for a month; it was a judgement of the Almighty.

I inquired closely about spiritualism. 'They call up the dead

from their repose,' she said. 'It vexes the Almighty when the
dead are stirred before they are ready.'

Then she told me what happened to spiritualists after a
number of years had passed over their heads. 'They run up
the garden path, look back over their shoulders, give a
shudder, and run back again. I dare say they see spirits.'

I took my grandmother's hand and led her out to the
garden to make her show me what spiritualists did. She ran
up the path splendidly with her skirts held up in her hands,
looked round with sudden bright eyes, shuddered horribly,
then, with skirts held higher so that her white petticoat frills
flickered round her black stockings, she ran gasping back
towards me.

My grandfather came out to see the fun with his sandy
eyebrows raised high among the freckles. 'Stop your larks,
Adelaide,' he said to my grandmother.

So my grandmother did it again, with a curdling cry, 'Ah-
ah-ah.'

Rummaging in the shop, having climbed up on two empty
fizz-pop crates, I found on an upper shelf some old bundles
of candles wrapped in interesting-looking literature. I
smoothed out the papers and read, 'Votes for Women! Why
do you Oppress Women?' Another lot of candles was wrapped
in a larger bill on which was printed an old-fashioned but
military-looking young woman waving the Union Jack and
saying, 'I'm off to join the Suffragettes.' I asked my grandmother where the papers came from, for she never threw
anything away and must have had them for another purpose
before wrapping up the candles before I was born. My grandfather answered for her, so far forgetting his refinement as
to say, 'Mrs Spank-arse's lark.'

'Mrs Pankhurst, he means. I'm surprised at you, Tom, in
front of the child.'

My grandfather was smiling away at his own joke. And so
all in one afternoon I learned a new word, and the story of
my grandmother's participation in the Women's Marches
down Watford High Street, dressed in her best clothes, and
I learned also my grandfather's opinion about these happen-

ings. I saw, before my very eyes, my grandmother and her banner, marching in the sunshiny street with her friends, her white petticoat twinkling at her ankles as she walked. In a few years' time it was difficult for me to believe I had not stood and witnessed the march of the Watford Suffragettes moving up the High Street, with my grandmother swiftly in the van before I was born. I recalled how her shiny black straw hat gleamed in the sun.

Some Jews came to Watford and opened a bicycle shop not far from my grandmother's. She would have nothing to do with them. They were Polish immigrants. She called them Pollacks. When I asked what this meant she said, 'foreigners.' One day the mama-foreigner came to the door of her shop as I was passing and held out a bunch of grapes. She said, 'Eat.' I ran, amazed, to my grandmother who said, 'I told you that foreigners are funny.'

Amongst ourselves she boasted of her Jewish blood because it had made her so clever. I knew she was so clever that it was unnecessary for her to be beautiful. She boasted that her ancestors on her father's side crossed over the Red Sea; the Almighty stretched forth his hands and parted the waves, and they crossed over from Egypt on to dry land. Miriam, the sister of Moses, banged her timbrel and led all the women across the Red Sea, singing a song to the Almighty. I thought of the Salvation Army girls who quite recently had marched up Watford High Street in the sunshine banging their tambourines. My grandmother had called me to the shop door to watch, and when they and their noise were dwindled away she turned from the door and clapped her hands above her head, half in the spontaneous spirit of the thing, half in mimicry. She clapped her hands. 'Alleluia!' cried my grandmother. 'Alleluia!'

'Stop your larks, Adelaide, my dear.'

Was I present at the Red Sea crossing? No, it had happened before I was born. My head was full of stories, of Greeks and Trojans, Picts and Romans, Jacobites and Redcoats, but these were definitely outside of my lifetime. It was different where my grandmother was concerned. I see her in the vanguard, leading the women in their dance of triumph, clanging the tambourine for joy and crying Alleluia with Mrs Pankhurst and Miriam the sister of Moses. The hands of the Almighty hold back the walls of the sea. My grandmother's white lace-edged petticoat flashes beneath her black skirt an inch above her boots, as it did when she demonstrated up and down the garden path what happens to spiritualists. What part of the scene I saw and what happened before I was born can be distinguished by my reason, but my reason cannot obliterate the scene or diminish it.

Great-aunts Sally and Nancy, my grandfather's sisters, had been frigidly reconciled to him at some date before I was born. I was sent to visit them every summer. They lived quietly now, a widow and a spinster of small means. They occupied themselves with altar-flowers and the vicar. I was a Gentile Jewess like my grandmother, for my father was a Jew, and these great-aunts could not make it out that I did not look like a Jew as did my grandmother. They remarked on this in my presence as if I could not understand that they were discussing my looks. I said that I did look like a Jew and desperately pointed to my small feet. 'All Jews have very little feet,' I claimed. They took this for fact, being inexperienced in Jews, and admitted to each other that I possessed this Jewish characteristic.

Nancy's face was long and thin and Sally's was round. There seemed to be a lot of pincushions on tiny tables. They gave me aniseed cake and tea every summer while the clock ticked loudly in time to their silence. I looked at the yellowish-green plush upholstery which caught streaks of the sunny afternoon outside, I looked until I had absorbed its colour and texture in a total trance during the great-aunts' silences. Once when I got back to my grandmother's and looked in the glass it seemed my eyes had changed from blue to yellow-green plush.

On one of these afternoons they mentioned my father's being an engineer. I said all Jews were engineers. They were fascinated by this fact which at the time I thought was possibly true with the exception of an occasional Quack.

Then Sally looked up and said, 'But the Lingens are not engineers.'

The Lingens were not Jews either, they were Gentiles of German origin, but it came to the same thing in those parts. The Lingens were not classified as foreigners by my grandmother because they did not speak in broken English, being all of a London-born generation.

The Lingen girls were the main friends of my mother's youth. There was Lottie who sang well and Flora who played the piano and Susanna who was strange. I remember a long evening in their house when Lottie and my mother sang a duet to Flora's piano playing, while Susanna loitered darkly at the door of the drawing-room with a smile I had never seen on any face before. I could not keep my eyes off Susanna, and got into trouble for staring.

When my mother and Lottie were seventeen they hired a cab one day and went to an inn, some miles away in the country, where they drank gin. They supplied the driver with gin as well, and, forgetting that the jaunt was supposed to be a secret one, returned two hours later standing up in the cab, chanting 'Horrid little Watford. Dirty little Watford. We'll soon say good-bye to nasty little Watford.' They did not consider themselves to be village girls and were eager to be sent away to relatives elsewhere. This was soon accomplished; Lottie went to London for a space and my mother to Edinburgh. My mother told me the story of the wild return of carriage and horses up the High Street and my grandmother confirmed it, adding that the occurrence was bad for business. I can hear the clopping of hooves, and see the girls standing wobbly in the cab dressed in their spotted muslins, although I never actually saw anything but milk-carts, motor cars and buses, and girls with short skirts in the High Street, apart from such links with antiquity as fat old Benskin of Benskins' Breweries taking his morning stroll along the bright pavement, bowing as he passed to my grandmother.

'I am a Gentile Jewess.'

She was buried as a Jewess since she died in my father's house, and notices were put in the Jewish press. Simultaneously my great-aunts announced in the Watford papers that she fell asleep in Jesus.

My mother never fails to bow three times to the new moon wherever she might be at the time of first catching sight of it. I have seen her standing on a busy pavement with numerous cold rational Presbyterian eyes upon her, turning over her money, bowing regardless and chanting, 'New moon, new moon, be good to me.' In my memory this image is fused with her lighting of the Sabbath candles on a Friday night, chanting a Hebrew prayer which I have since been told came out in a very strange sort of Hebrew. Still, it was her tribute and solemn observance. She said that the Israelites of the Bible and herself were one and the same because of the Jewish part of her blood, and I did not doubt this thrilling fact. I thought of her as the second Gentile Jewess after my grandmother, and myself as the third.

My mother carries everywhere in her handbag a small locket containing a picture of Christ crowned with thorns. She keeps on one table a rather fine Buddha on a lotus leaf and on another a horrible replica of the Venus de Milo. One way and another all the gods are served in my mother's household although she holds only one belief and that is in the Almighty. My father, when questioned as to what he believes, will say, 'I believe in the Blessed Almighty who made heaven and earth,' and will say no more, returning to his racing papers which contain problems proper to innocent men. To them, it was no great shock when I turned Catholic, since with Roman Catholics too, it all boils down to the Almighty in the end.